BY THE AWARD-WINNING AUTHOR OF <u>CARRY THE WIND</u>
AND <u>BUFFALO PALACE</u>

TERRY C. JOHNSTON

WOLF MOUNTAIN MOON

THE BATTLE OF THE BUTTE, 1877

Tongue River Cantonment, 1876–1877.
(Courtesy National Archives)

Artillery at Tongue River Cantonment,
December 29, 1876.
(Courtesy National Archives)

ISBN 0-553-29977-8

US $6.50 / $8.99 CAN

50650

First Lt. Frank D. Baldwin.
(Courtesy Library of Congress)

S

John "Liver-Eating" Johnston.
(Courtesy Denver Public
Library, Western History
Section)

Luther S. "Yellowstone" Kelly.
(Courtesy Denver Public Library,
Western History Section)

*Colonel Nelson A. Miles and officers of the Fifth Infantry,
December 29, 1876. From left: Lt. O.F. Long, Surgeon H.R.
Tilton, Lt. J.W. Pope, Col. N.A. Miles, Lt. F.D. Baldwin, Lt. C.E.
Hargous, and Lt. H.K. Bailey.*
(Courtesy Montana Historical Society)

Wooden Leg's drawing of his rescue of Big Crow.
(Courtesy Little Bighorn Battlefield National Monument)

Fifth Infantry soldiers at Tongue River Cantonment in winter dress.
(Courtesy Little Bighorn Battlefield National Monument)

BOOKS BY TERRY C. JOHNSTON

Carry the Wind
BorderLords
One-Eyed Dream

Cry of the Hawk
Winter Rain
Dream Catcher

SONS OF THE PLAINS NOVELS

Long Winter Gone
Seize the Sky
Whisper of the Wolf

THE PLAINSMEN NOVELS

Sioux Dawn
Red Cloud's Revenge   NEED
The Stalkers
Black Sun
Devil's Backbone
Shadow Riders
Dying Thunder
Blood Song
Reap the Whirlwind
A Cold Day in Hell
Trumpet on the Land
Wolf Mountain Moon

WOLF MOUNTAIN MOON

The Fort Peck Expedition,
the Fight at Ash Creek, and the
Battle of the Butte—January 8, 1877

Terry C. Johnston

BANTAM BOOKS

NEW YORK   TORONTO   LONDON   SYDNEY   AUCKLAND

WOLF MOUNTAIN MOON
A Bantam Book / February 1997

ISBN 0-553-29977-8

Published simultaneously in the United States and Canada

Bantam Books are published by Bantam Books, a division of Bantam
Doubleday Dell Publishing Group, Inc. Its trademark, consisting of
the words "Bantam Books" and the portrayal of a rooster, is
Registered in U.S. Patent and Trademark Office and in other
countries. Marca Registrada. Bantam Books, 1540 Broadway, New
York, New York 10036.

for all his enthusiastic assistance
helping me write
the past four Plainsmen novels,
the dedication of this novel to
the widely respected National Park Service historian
and published Indian Wars authority
Jerome A. Greene
is long overdue

Cast of Characters

Seamus Donegan   *Samantha Donegan*

Military

Brigadier General George C. Crook—Department of the Platte

Colonel William B. Hazen—commanding Sixth U.S. Infantry, Fort Buford, M.T.

Colonel Nelson A. Miles—commanding Fifth U.S. Infantry, Tongue River Cantonment, M.T.

Colonel Ranald S. Mackenzie—commanding Fourth U.S. Cavalry

Lieutenant Colonel Elwell S. Otis—Twenty-second U.S. Infantry

Lieutenant Colonel Joseph Whistler—Fifth U.S. Infantry

Major Alfred L. Hough—Seventeenth U.S. Infantry, commanding at Glendive Cantonment

Major Henry R. Tilton—Surgeon, Fifth U.S. Infantry

Major Edwin F. Townsend—Commanding Officer, Fort Laramie, W.T.

Captain Charles J. Dickey—E Company, Twenty-second Infantry

Captain Ezra P. Ewers—E Company, Fifth U.S. Infantry

Captain—Randall—Quartermaster, Fifth U.S. Infantry, Tongue River Cantonment, M.T.

Captain Wyllys Lyman—I Company, Fifth U.S. Infantry

Captain James S. Casey—A Company, Fifth U.S. Infantry

Captain Andrew S. Bennett—B Company, Fifth U.S. Infantry

Captain Edmond Butler—C Company, Fifth U.S. Infantry

Captain Simon Snyder—F Company, Fifth U.S. Infantry

Captain Edwin Pollock—Ninth U.S. Infantry, commander of Reno Cantonment

First Lieutenant Frank D. Baldwin—Fifth U.S. Infantry

First Lieutenant Cornelius C. Cusick—F Company, Twenty-second Infantry

First Lieutenant Mason Carter—K Company, Fifth U.S. Infantry

First Lieutenant George W. Baird—regimental adjutant, Fifth U.S. Infantry

First Lieutenant Robert McDonald—D Company, Fifth U.S. Infantry

Second Lieutenant Russell H. Day—Sixth U.S. Infantry, commanding garrison at Fort Peck

Second Lieutenant David Q. Rousseau—G Company, Fifth U.S. Infantry

Second Lieutenant William H. Wheeler—Eleventh U.S. Infantry

Second Lieutenant Frank S. Hinkle—H Company, Fifth U.S. Infantry

Second Lieutenant Charles E. Hargous—Fifth U.S. Infantry, commanding mounted infantry to Wolf Mountain

Second Lieutenant Hobart K. Bailey—Fifth U.S. Infantry, aide-de-camp to Miles

Second Lieutenant James Worden Pope—E Company, Fifth U.S. Infantry, commanding Rodman gun

Second Lieutenant Edward W. Casey—Twenty-second U.S. Infantry, assisting Pope's artillery detail: in charge of Napoleon gun

Second Lieutenant Oscar F. Long—Fifth U.S. Infantry, acting engineering officer

Second Lieutenant William H. C. Bowen—Fifth U.S. Infantry, in charge of supply wagons

Second Lieutenant James H. Whitten—I Company, Fifth U.S. Infantry, in charge of pack animals

Trumpeter Edwin M. Brown

Private Thomas Kelly—I Company, Fifth U.S. Infantry
Private Richard Bellows—E Company, Fifth U.S. Infantry
Private Philip Kennedy—C Company, Fifth U.S. Infantry
Private Patton G. Whited—C Company, Fifth U.S. Infantry
Assistant Surgeon Louis S. Tesson

Civilians

Thomas J. Mitchell—agent at Fort Peck
Elizabeth Burt
Martha Luhn
Nettie Capron

Army Scouts

Johnny Bruguier / "Big Leggings"
Luther S. (Sage) "Yellowstone" Kelly

Robert Jackson	William Jackson
Victor Smith	John Johnston
George Johnson	James Parker
William Cross	Jim Woods
Tom Leforge	Joe Culbertson
Edward Lambert	George Boyd

Left Hand—Yanktonai scout for Baldwin on Fort Peck expedition
Buffalo Horn—Bannock scout for Miles on Wolf Mountain Campaign

Lakota

Sitting Bull	Gall
Three Bears	Little Big Man
Pretty Bear	Foolish Thunder
White Bull	Bull Eagle
Small Bear	Touch-the-Clouds
Roman Nose	Spotted Elk
Red Horse	Tall Bull
Packs the Drum / "Sitting Bull the Good"	
Yellow Eagle	Foolish Bear
Important Man	Long Dog

Black Moon
Crow
Iron Dog
Four Horns
Drag
White Horse
Fat Hide / Fat on the Beef
Lame Red Skirt / Red Cloth
Bad Leg
Long Feather
Jumping Bull
Crazy Horse
He Dog
Long Hair

Little Knife
Spotted Blackbird
Yellow Liver
Red Horn
Hollow Horns
Red Horses
The Yearling
Lone Horn
No Neck
Rising Sun
Black Shawl
Runs-the-Bear
Hump

Cheyenne

"Tse-tsehese-staeste"
"Those Who Are Hearted Alike"

White Bull
Black Moccasin (Limber Lance)
Black Hawk
Big Crow
Sits in the Night
Little Wolf
Young Two Moon
Left-Handed Wolf
Big Horse
Gypsum
High Wolf
Coal Bear
Medicine Bear

Wooden Leg
Yellow Weasel
Yellow Hair
Crow Split Nose
Morning Star
Old Bear
Beaver Claws
Beaver Dam
Crow Necklace
Brave Wolf
Box Elder
Long Jaw

Cheyenne Party Captured by Miles's Scouts

Old Wool Woman / Sweet Taste Woman
Crooked Nose Woman
Twin Woman
Red Hood

Fingers Woman
Crane Woman
Black Horse

Crow

Half Yellow Face   Old Bear

Assiniboine

White Dog

Casualties:

* Private William H. Batty—C Company, Fifth U.S. Infantry

* Corporal Augustus Rothman—A Company, Fifth U.S. Infantry

* / † Private Bernard McCann—F Company, Twenty-second U.S. Infantry

† Sergeant Hiram Spangenberg—F Company, Twenty-second U.S. Infantry

† Corporal Thomas Roehm—F Company, Fifth U.S. Infantry

† Private Henry Rodenburgh—A Company, Fifth U.S. Infantry

† Private George Danha—H Company, Fifth U.S. Infantry

† Private William H. Daily—D Company, Fifth U.S. Infantry

† Private —— McHugh—H Company, Fifth U.S. Infantry

† Private —— Simond—D Company, Fifth U.S. Infantry

* —killed in action
† partial listing of wounded in action

During the Indian Wars, the [Regular Army] soldier, isolated from his own people and faced by a skilled enemy, lived under conditions that would have broken the spirit of most groups. Badly armed and clothed, underfed and plopped into holes on the prairie, the soldier made do and "re-upped," left the army after a single hitch, or deserted. It is most remarkable that they did not all desert.

—Neil Baird Thompson
Crazy Horse Called Them
Walk-a-Heaps

The Sioux campaigns of 1876 were marked with few engagements, but those that did take place were conspicuous for the desperateness with which they were fought and the severe losses sustained. Nearly four hundred and fifty officers and men of the army were killed and wounded during the year. . . . The enemy's loss is now known to have been severe at the Rosebud, Little Big Horn, Slim Buttes and Bates Creek. But the far-reaching results of the campaigns extended beyond the consideration of how many were killed and wounded. They led to the disintegration of many of the hostile bands of savages, who gladly sought safety upon the reservations and who have not since attempted any warlike demonstrations.

—George F. Price
Across the Continent with
the Fifth Cavalry

Desperate, hungry, and weary of fighting, the rapidly weakening Indian coalition rallied one last time at Wolf Mountains, when the soldiers threatened the sanctity of their homes. But for the Sioux and Cheyennes, offensive warfare was over. Sitting Bull and Crazy Horse never again united. Instead, the disintegration of the massive Indian resistance was finally at hand. As Miles averred, "We . . . had taught the destroyers of Custer that there was one small command that could whip them as long as they dared face it."

—Jerome Greene
Yellowstone Command

It is the opinion of some who had had years of experience in Indian fighting, that there has rarely, if ever, been a fight before in which the Sioux and Cheyennes showed such determination and persistency, where they were finally defeated.

> —Captain Edmond Butler
> "Army and Navy Journal"
> March 31, 1877

If a Crazy Horse camp could be struck, where would the people be safe?

> —Mari Sandoz
> *Crazy Horse—Strange Man of the Oglala*

Foreword

While Seamus Donegan pushes north by west away from Crook and Mackenzie's camp on the Belle Fourche River, you and I are going to have to step back in time a few weeks so that we can catch up with all that's been happening in the Yellowstone country, where Miles's Fifth Infantry are scrambling about trying to find out where Sitting Bull scampered off to after the fight at Cedar Creek.

To write with continuity the final half of *A Cold Day in Hell*, our previous volume, I was faced with a dilemma. I could chop up the action in the Mackenzie / Fourth Cavalry / Morning Star story line by yanking the reader back and forth from the Bighorn country to the northern plains patrolled by the Fifth Infantry . . . or I could charge straight ahead with one story line instead of dealing with two simultaneously. I chose this second option.

Since this present novel deals with the tale of Nelson A. Miles's efforts in the rugged country north of the Yellowstone, we are free now to drop back a few weeks in time before the conclusion of *A Cold Day in Hell* so that we might learn how the colonel's men were faring in their hunt for Sitting Bull's Hunkpapa at the same moment Crook and Mackenzie were crushing the last of Northern Cheyenne resistance.

This means that after we get Seamus riding off to the north into Crazy Horse country, we're going to leave him for a few days as we leap on north to catch up with all the action we've missed while we've been busy with the Fourth Cavalry and their Battle of the Red Fork.

And because we are going back on the calendar, we won't be starting out right away with the newspaper headlines as we normally do. Once we bring all our characters closer to mid-December, when the Irishman reaches the Tongue River Cantonment, those news reports will continue.

At the beginning of some chapters and some scenes you're going to read the very same news stories devoured by the officers' wives and those civilians employed at army posts or those living in adjacent frontier settlements, taken from the front page of the daily newspapers just as Samantha Donegan herself would read them—newspapers that arrived as much as a week or more late, due to the wilderness distances to be traveled by freight carriers.

Copied verbatim from the headlines and graphic accounts of the day, these reports and stories were the only news available for those people who had a most personal interest in the frontier army's last great campaign—those families who had tearfully watched a loved one march off to war that winter of the Great Sioux War of 1876.

My hope is that you will be struck with the immediacy of each day's front page as you finish reading that day's news—just as Samantha Donegan would have read the sometimes reassuring, ofttimes terrifying, news from her relative safety at Fort Laramie. But unlike her and the rest of those left behind at the posts and frontier settlements, you will be thrust back into the footsteps of those cold, frightened infantrymen and the harried villages of hungry people the army is searching for here in the maw of that most terrible winter.

An army knowing it is now only a matter of time until they succeed in what was begun many months before in the trampled, bloody snow along the Powder River.

The Lakota and Cheyenne realizing at last that their culture, an ancient way of life, is taking its last breath.

To be no more.

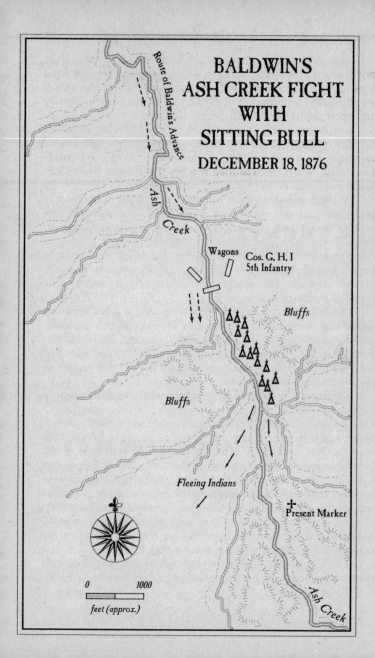

BALDWIN'S
ASH CREEK FIGHT
WITH
SITTING BULL
DECEMBER 18, 1876

Route of Baldwin's Advance

Ash Creek

Wagons

Cos. G, H, I
5th Infantry

Bluffs

Bluffs

Fleeing Indians

Present Marker

Ash Creek

0   1000

feet (approx.)

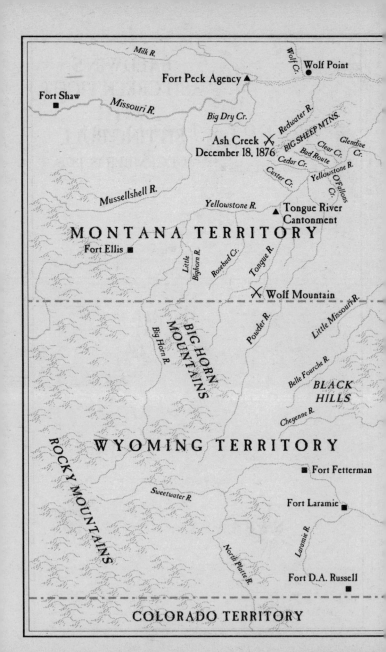

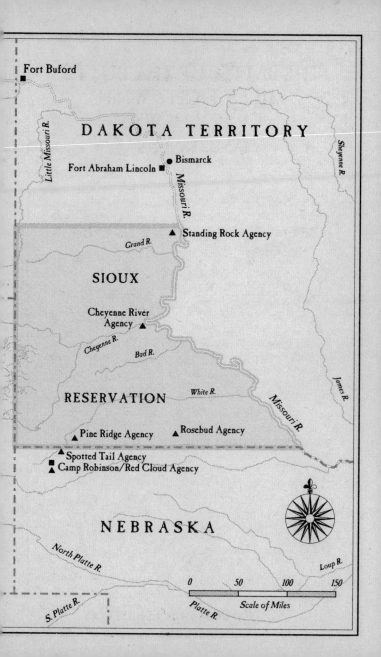

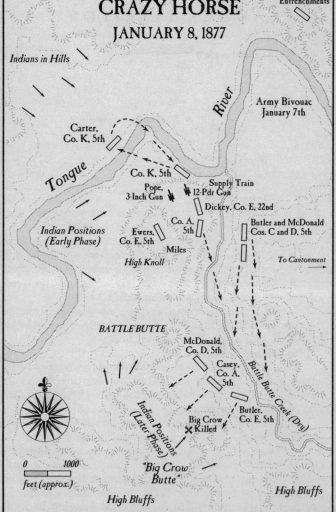

THE BATTLE OF THE BUTTE
MILES' FIGHT WITH CRAZY HORSE
JANUARY 8, 1877

Cusick,
Co. F, 22nd
Entrenchments

Indians in Hills

River

Army Bivouac
January 7th

Carter,
Co. K, 5th

Tongue

Co. K, 5th

Pope,
3-Inch Gun

Supply Train

12-Pdr Gun

Dickey, Co. E, 22nd

Co. A,
5th

Butler and McDonald
Cos. C and D, 5th

*Indian Positions
(Early Phase)*

Ewers,
Co. E, 5th

Miles

To Cantonment

High Knoll

BATTLE BUTTE

McDonald,
Co. D, 5th

Casey,
Co. A,
5th

Butler,
Co. E, 5th

Battle Butte Creek (Dry)

*Indian Positions
(Later Phase)*

Big Crow
✗ Killed

"Big Crow
Butte"

High Bluffs

High Bluffs

0   1000

feet (approx.)

PROLOGUE

Mid-December 1876

He watched the three of them until they dropped out of sight beyond that last far rise to the south.

Then he watched that snowy sliver of empty ground a little while longer, just to be sure those three horsemen might not reappear there where the icy gray blanket of earth pressed against the lowering slate-gray sky. Hoping the riders might . . . but knowing they wouldn't.

Seamus Donegan took a deep breath—so deep, the sub-freezing air shocked his chest. Then he gently nudged the roan to the left and pointed their noses north.

To the Yellowstone.

Right through the heart of the country where the Cheyenne survivors of Mackenzie's attack on Morning Star's village were fleeing. Dead center through the land where Crazy Horse was said to be wintering.

As if it had been lying in wait for those three Indian scouts to sign talk their hurried farewells in the bitter cold—as if it had been patient only long enough until he could turn his face back to the north—the wind came up, leaping out of hiding suddenly that midday. The Irishman glanced back over his shoulder at the southern rim of that monochrome sky, unable to make out where the sun was hanging in its low travels. Nothing but a slate of clouds for as far as the eye could see. Gray above, and gray-white below.

He glanced one last time at the top of that ridge where he'd last seen the faraway figures of Three Bears and the other two scouts, knowing they were long gone now. Only a foolish man would tarry in these parts. This was enemy country if ever there was one. Here between Sitting Bull's Yellowstone and Crazy Horse's Powder. No matter that Three Bears and his scouts were all three Lakota: truth was, they had just led the soldiers north against the winter roamers.

Already the great hoop was cracking. Agency Indian against free Indian. Good Injun against hostile.

Tugging the wide wool scarf farther up his raw cheeks and nose, Seamus dabbed at the tears pooling in his eyes. It was a wind strong enough that the roan beneath him kept quartering around, bitter enough to make Donegan tuck his own head down to the side, turtling it as far as he could within the big upturned flap of the collar on his wool mackinaw. Thank the merciful saints for the wolf-hide cap Richard Closter had handed him that morning before Donegan had ridden away in the dark behind those three sullen, silent Indian scouts. With a scrap of old wool scarf from last winter's campaign to the Powder with Crook and Reynolds just long enough to pull over the top of his head and down over his ears, Donegan clamped it in place with the wolf-hide cap he tied beneath his chin with a pair of thongs.

Around his neck twisted and tossed the drawstring on his wide-brimmed prairie hat, which the wind tugged this way and that, shoving and fluttering with each gust. The wool muffler and wolf hide were both much better for this weather and this wind, he thought as he raised a horsehide gauntlet mitten and snugged the furry cap down to the bridge of his nose. Then he blinked more tears away as he steered the horse off the ridge, down another ravine that come next spring would be a creek. For now the bare willow and alder stood out like skeletal claws against the deep, drifted snow pocked in those places hidden back from the short-season's southerly sunlight.

In the dim glow of their tiny fire that first night away from the army column, he and the sullen Three Bears had talked with their hands about the task that lay before them—what would eventually face the lone white man once the four of them had reached the mouth of the Little Powder and the White River Agency Sioux would turn back.

Tell me if I am a fool to go on down the Powder.

For a long time the old warrior stared into the low flames and glowing bed of crimson coals, his face shining like polished copper. *We believe the Crazy Horse people are upstream.* And he had pointed south.

So it would be safe enough for me to follow the Powder down to the Elk River?*

With a wag of his head Three Bears finally looked up into Donegan's face. *The chances are good the Hunkpatila have already started downstream . . . moving north to reach Sitting Bull, Gall, and the fighting Hunkpapa.*

Seamus pointed. *To the north?*

Three Bears nodded.

Then I should not go down the Powder.

It is not wise.

At that fire of theirs in the shadow of Inyan Kara† the Lakota instructed him to cross the Powder after they had parted company, to ascend the divide that would lead him over to Mizpah Creek, take him beyond that to Pumpkin Creek and eventually to the Tongue itself.

For three and a half days they pushed their ponies through the cold and the snow from dawn till dusk. But the White River Agency scouts would not travel after sundown. Nor could Seamus get them started before light. Which meant the four of them sat out the long winter nights around a tiny fire built back against the overhang of some washed-out bluff, or far up from the mouth of a deep ravine so the glow of the low flames would not reflect their reddish hue so readily against the low clouds and snowy landscape.

Those nights Donegan found he would doze in fits, remembering how it was to hold Samantha. How he had cradled his baby boy and paced that tiny room above the Fort Laramie parade. Other times he had nightmares of the terrible cold that never warmed during that long day in hell along the Red Fork Valley. Recalling the sounds of war, the inhuman cries of

* The Yellowstone River.

† Devil's Tower

man and horse, the flitting shadows of a half-naked enemy: women, children, old ones fleeing into the hills. What Mackenzie's Fourth had started . . . winter would surely end.

The destruction of the Northern Cheyenne.

Only those strong enough would make it, he knew. Where they were headed now in the trackless wilderness, no man could know for certain. But a safe bet would be that the Cheyenne were once more limping for the safety of the Crazy Horse people. Starving, bleeding, freezing—stripped of everything but their pride.

At least he had a small fire, Seamus consoled himself as he shivered through his lonely watch each night, arms tucked around his legs, chin resting on his knees while the others tried sleeping. And at least he had his heavy winter clothing, along with two thick blankets and that old wolf-hide hat of Uncle Dick's. He had the clumsy buffalo hides wrapped around his boots while many of the fleeing survivors had no moccasins. He had warm wool gloves he kept stuffed inside the stiff horsehide cavalry gauntlets. He had so much, and Morning Star's Cheyenne had so little. . . . How was it they always managed to survive?

Was it their hatred for him and his kind that kept them warm? Was it that fury smoldering down inside each one of them that allowed the Cheyenne to survive?

He wasn't sure just how much the temperatures had moderated since leaving Crook's command, but he was sure that during the last three days it had finally climbed above zero . . . before plummeting again as the sun fell each night.

That's what he reminded himself now as he turned and glanced to the south one last time. Just keep the sun behind my left shoulder like they told me, he thought that afternoon. Don't take the first creek flowing south. And he was not to turn off at the second either, Three Bears had reminded him more than once before they had parted.

Instead, he was to wait until reaching the third—that would be the Tongue River.

So he was alone again.

As spooky as they were, the Lakota didn't like traveling at night. But tonight Seamus figured he would do just that, to make up some ground and time, at least until he and the horse grew too weary, or it became too dark to pick out good footing from something slick and icy.

A day and a half, Three Bears had explained. *If a man is careful and watches over his animal—a day and a half to the Tongue River.*

If he pushed on tonight, and pushed hard come daylight, he might well reach the Tongue sometime around sundown tomorrow.

How far from there?

To the Elk River? The war chief had blinked rapidly, staring off into the cloudy night, calculating, remembering, sizing things up. *Maybe another three days. Four perhaps.*

I'll make it in three, Seamus had been promising himself. All told, that made it another day and a half cross-country to the Tongue, then something on the order of sixty or so miles down to the Yellowstone, where he would run onto the army's cantonment, deliver his dispatches, fill himself with hot food more than once, and maybe even sleep for the better part of twenty-four hours beside a sheet-iron stove before he resaddled the freshly grained roan and pointed their noses south.

Each time he dwelled on it, Seamus was struck again with just how far south a journey he would be facing once he started for home. Not just to return all the way to the upper reaches of the Powder, or to the Crazy Woman Crossing, even farther to Fort Fetterman on the North Platte . . . but much, much farther still to reach Fort Laramie, a final ninety twisting miles beyond.

The wind seemed all the colder now as the sun continued to sink behind him. The country around Donegan seemed all the more desolate and foreboding, scarred by erosion, cut by coulee and ravine and mud slide—all of it buried now in a mantle of white beneath the leaden dome of never-ending sky. Colder still because he was beginning to realize he would not be home for Christmas, his son's first. And chances were damned good he wouldn't make it back to Samantha to celebrate the arrival of a new year either.

At least the two of them were safe. At least they were warm and had decent food for their bellies. Small comforts like those went a long way to cause him to straighten his back, to stiffen his resolve. He would push as hard as it was prudent to push. Then, tonight, when he finally dropped from the saddle, Seamus decided he would build himself a warming fire—something big enough to keep him from freezing. After all, he doubted there would be any warriors out and moving in this horrid cold, across this desolate stretch of country after sundown . . . not even Morning Star's Cheyenne, or the Hunkpatila of Crazy Horse.

Chances were, they'd be keeping an eye on Crook's column. They'd have no suspicion of a lone horseman slipping through this unforgiving winter wilderness on his lonesome.

Yet he told himself it could not be a fire big enough that it would warm him too much. He realized he must stay cold enough that deep sleep was impossible. A man who slept too deep in these temperatures never awoke again. Instead, Donegan realized he must stay just cold enough that it was impossible to sleep for long at a stretch: he must arouse himself early enough to move out before false dawn. Mounting up and pushing on beneath the light of the waxing moon, on through the day, past the next sundown until he knew they both could go no farther without some rest. How he would depend on this strong, wide-hipped roan gelding across the next few days.

They watered together, and they ate together twice a day—as the horse grazed on some ground blown clear by the incessant wind, or a patch of grass where Seamus had kicked aside most of the snow, and he tore at the stringy jerked meat—how it made his mouth water to watch the whitetail, the mule deer, the elk cross his path . . . knowing he didn't dare take a shot in Indian country.

Best just not to think about his belly, or the cold. Or to let his mind slip too far south to Fort Laramie.

Tomorrow morning he vowed he would have them up and away again after that bright winter moon had slipped from the sky, riding into the darkness for those two hours or so before the sun ever began to make its brief appearance far to the east, climbing into the thick blanket of clouds that hovered over this endless aching land as far as the eye could see.

For now he pointed them toward the Mizpah in the fading light of that shrinking day. A lone horseman hurrying across a great white landscape like a hard-shelled dung beetle trudging across some cottonwood fluff. The yawning expanse around him swallowing all sound, he found it so eerily quiet the horse's muted hoof falls were near all he heard, save for the wind tumbling across the icy crust of the snow. That, and the thoughts tumbling through his head.

So quiet was it out here that he could dwell on Sam and the boy. Out here where the mind had far too much time to think, and the heart had far too much time to ache.

He was a man being paid well to do a dangerous job, Seamus reminded himself, and yanked the wolf-hide hat down against the stiffening wind. No doubt that he had made sure his little family was taken care of with army scrip . . . whether or not he returned to them from this lonely journey. This was simply a job too good for a husband, a father, a family man to pass up.

Just the sort of man the army might look for when it needed a fool to set off on a fool's errand.

Fool or not . . . Seamus loved Sam and their boy more than he loved life itself.

Chapter 1

26 October–3 November 1876

Sitting Bull had given him the slip again.

There wasn't much that could gall Nelson A. Miles the way that did.

After he had managed to stay right behind the warrior bands he'd flushed and fought at Cedar Creek,* nearly all the Sioux leaders had given up their flight—some even turning themselves over to the soldier chief as hostages in good faith that their followers would return to their reservations. The arrival of supply wagons on Thursday, 26 October, ultimately convinced chiefs like Pretty Bear and Lame Red Skirt, Bull Eagle and Small Bear, even White Bull and Foolish Thunder, to give up rather than cause their people to suffer the continued harassment of the Bear Coat's "walk-a-heaps."

But not Sitting Bull.

The irascible Hunkpapa had managed once again to elude his white nemesis when he splintered off from the other Lakota leaders, taking no more than thirty lodges with him across Bad Route Creek to sneak away, slipping down the north bank of the Yellowstone while the soldiers were in hot

* *A Cold Day in Hell*, vol. 11, The Plainsmen Series.

pursuit of the greater part of that village continuing to flee south from Miles's Fifth Infantry.

At first, however, despite the walk-a-heaps' harassment, the bands remained committed to their traditional philosophy of fighting and fleeing, which enabled them to hunt buffalo and live their lives in the manner of their grandfathers. The best Miles could manage was to get them to say they would talk a bit.

Which suited the colonel just fine . . . for the moment. In the meantime he had ordered his train of empty wagons on east those twenty-four miles to the Glendive Cantonment for supplies.

By the time that supply train returned, carrying enough rations to permit the Fifth Infantry to continue its chase another twenty days, Miles's hunch had paid off in a big way: those wagons had indeed proved to be the straw that broke the will of the Northern Sioux to resist.

When they came to the army's camp to talk terms of surrender, Lame Red Skirt and the other Miniconjou chiefs repeated their assertions that their people lacked clothing for a long winter's march; besides, their horses were far too poor to make the journey—yet they vowed their intention of going in to the agencies.

"Look upon my wagons," Miles explained to the headmen through his interpreters. "With my supplies I can follow you wherever you attempt to go."

The dark eyes of those Lakota seated in council with Miles regarded the wagons filled to the gunwales with boxes and barrels and kegs of supplies. They could see for themselves that the soldiers were dressed warmly around their fires, their bellies full while the fragrance of frying pork perfumed the winter air . . . at the same time their people cried out in hunger, suffered with the cold as the season advanced and the creekbanks began to rime with ice.

Miles had them just where he wanted them. But now that they were ready to surrender, he damn well couldn't take the massive village back to Tongue River Cantonment with him. There simply wasn't enough to supply his troops and all these Sioux in hopes of lasting out the coming winter, until the river ice broke up and the first steamer arrived from down the Missouri.

Nor could he dare take the time needed to escort this bunch of Sioux all the way over to the Cheyenne River Agency, a decision that would take his men right out of any chance of catching up to Sitting Bull.

The Bear Coat ended up proposing that the chiefs give him their solemn promise to turn themselves in to their agents at Cheyenne River. In addition, Miles declared that five of their number must volunteer to stay behind with him, those men to be delivered to an army prison in St. Paul, Minnesota, as a means of guaranteeing the eventual surrender of their people at their agency.

Lame Red Skirt and the other Miniconjou chiefs repeated their assertions that their people lacked clothing for a long winter's march and their horses were far too poor to make the journey.

Fuming with indignation, Miles stormed to his feet before the chiefs seated on their robes, which were spread over a thin layer of crusted snow. Clearly impatient to be after the big prize, he slapped one of his thick gauntlets against the side of his leg and said, "This is my final offer: I will see that your people have rations to make the trek to your reservation. And I will allow your bands thirty-five days to make the trip. In addition, I agree to give your people five additional days to stay right where they are now so your men can hunt buffalo for meat and hides."

For a long time the chiefs huddled, talking among themselves. Finally Lame Red Skirt stood, dour-faced.

"I will go with the Bear Coat, to show the goodwill of my people."

One by one the other leaders rose in turn from their robes to be counted among those who would fight no more. The older White Bull, a Miniconjou and father of Small Bear. Foolish Thunder, Black Eagle, and Sun Rise, all three Sans Arc. Then, too, Bull Eagle and Small Bear vowed they would be responsible for getting their people to the reservation in the days Bear Coat had allowed them. In that timely journey, more of the headmen vowed they would not fail the soldier chief: Tall Bull, Yellow Eagle, Two Elk, Foolish Bear, Spotted Elk, and Poor Bear.

As each leader stood to make his surrender, Nelson Miles felt his heart leap anew. Better than twenty-five hundred Miniconjou, Sans Arc, and Hunkpapa—accounting for more than three hundred lodges—had surrendered without the Fifth Infantry firing another shot.

Maybe now he had a chance to get his hands on the old, elusive Sitting Bull himself.

Maybe tonight Miles would sleep better than he had in a long, long time. Perhaps even a far better sleep than he had experienced since he had come to these northern plains last summer to find both Crook and Terry unable or unwilling to get the job done.* At the least Miles could boast that the rigors of campaigning and the chase after his archnemesis had caused him to shed a few pounds since leaving Fort Leavenworth, Kansas.

What he felt ready to accomplish here in the north would perhaps be even more important than what he had accomplished on the southern plains.† Miles was looking in the eye of what might well be the greatest test of his military career. Simply put: the commander who defeated Sitting Bull or Crazy Horse, the man who corralled and herded the great war chiefs back to the reservations—why, that man would have his general's stars handed to him on a silver platter. And there might even be a special place in Washington City carved out for him too.

Although he knew it would never be easy for foot soldiers to catch the elusive warrior villages, Miles remained steadfast in his belief that his Fighting Fifth could whip the Sioux horsemen every time the enemy was engaged.

After writing his wife of his success securing the chiefs' surrender, as well as carefully phrasing some correspondence with Mary's uncle, General William Tecumseh Sherman, Miles penned a dispatch to General Alfred H. Terry in St. Paul:

> I consider this the beginning of the end. [The Indians] are very suspicious, and of course [are] afraid that some terrible punishment will be inflicted upon them [should they go in to their agencies]. . . . While we have fought and routed these people, and driven them away from their ancient homes, I cannot

---

* *Trumpet on the Land*, vol. 10, The Plainsmen Series.
† *Dying Thunder*, vol. 7, The Plainsmen Series.

but feel regret that they are compelled to submit to starvation, for I fear they will be reduced to that condition as were the southern tribes in 1874.

"What now of Sitting Bull, General?" asked Captain Wyllys Lyman as the wind came up, blowing right out of the north, picking up bluster as it roared across the breadth of Montana Territory.

After a moment of reflection that dark Thursday night while icy points of snow lanced down from a lowering sky, Nelson A. Miles sighed. "Yes. Sitting Bull. He's still out there waiting for me, isn't he?"

Captain Edmond Butler inquired, "Will we go after him now?"

Miles watched the first snowflakes whirl to the cold ground. "We'll march the command back to Tongue River, recoup, then set out again—yes. By all means," he replied gravely. "Although that old Hunkpapa is still out there, roaming free for now . . . I have nonetheless accomplished one thing I set out to do. I have succeeded in dividing the Sioux against themselves. We've damn well whittled away at their forces wherever we can find and engage them."

"That's more than either of the other two columns have accomplished in all their marching through this country!" declared Andrew S. Bennett.

"We won't dare name names here, Captain," Miles cautioned flatly, waving off that comment pointed at both Terry and Crook. "From the reports of their disgraceful failures of late, I judge that the nation sooner or later will understand the difference between doing *something* and doing nothing."

Kneeling at the edge of the fire, civilian Luther S. Kelly filled his tin with coffee steaming into the sharp autumn air, then stood to ask, "Will we fight on into the winter, General?"

"You have my assurance of that, Mr. Kelly!" Miles said enthusiastically as he turned to regard his chief of scouts. "Along with my guarantee of a job for as long as Sitting Bull and Crazy Horse are free. Those two may try to hide from me this winter—but we will find them. While they and their criminals take shelter and recoup in their camps, my soldiers will not retire from the chase. On the contrary: I will endeavor to keep the tribes divided, and take them in detail. Never more will the hostiles band together."

"As you wrote General Terry, sir," said adjutant Hobart Bailey, "this is surely the beginning of the end for the Sioux."

Miles nodded, turning back to his chief of scouts. "Make no mistake about it, Mr. Kelly—there's no other outfit, not one other column, that you will find venturing out until spring. No one else to do what needs doing now as the cold descends around us."

Kelly took the coffee tin from his lips. "Then I take it you won't be giving Sitting Bull any rest."

For a moment Miles stared into the winter clouds blotting out the starry night sky. "Gentlemen, there's no one else who dares tackle what lays before us this winter. It's up to us, and us alone, to finish this matter with the Sioux. Once and for all."

Until the Sioux had all become agency farmers on their reservation plots, Colonel Nelson A. Miles would be the sort of man with the dogged determination to track the warrior bands and wear them down piecemeal.

Luther S. "Yellowstone" Kelly, the Fifth Infantry's chief of scouts, was beginning to realize just how dogged Miles could be.

"My endeavor has been to convince the Sioux, first, of our superior power, and second, that we will deal fairly and justly with them," the colonel explained that Tuesday, the last day of October, after his headquarters group had reached their post at the mouth of the Tongue on the Yellowstone River.

Kelly observed, "But Sitting Bull is another matter altogether, isn't he?"

Miles nodded. "Precisely." He looked down at those few lines inked on the map to the north and east of his Tongue River Cantonment. "Sitting Bull leads the worst set of rascals I have ever seen together."

Ezra P. Ewers said, "You're doing well to break up their confederation, Colonel."

"We've only begun, Captain," Miles replied. "I will waste no time in laying plans to strike these outlaws . . . and strike them hard."

On the following day seven of his companies returned to

the cantonment. And on 3 November the last three companies came in. That same day all of the remaining Fifth arrived upriver from Fort Leavenworth, including the regimental band and some additional headquarters staff. The entire party had steamed up the Missouri aboard the *General Meade* until they had reached Fort Buford at the mouth of the Yellowstone back on 22 October. Under the command of First Lieutenant Frank D. Baldwin they had marched the rest of the way to the Tongue River on foot. Baldwin, who had served as Miles's battalion adjutant during August's fruitless maneuverings under General Terry, had himself been on detached service at Leavenworth. As soon as he arrived at Tongue River, the lieutenant began to grump about missing out on the regiment's fight with the Sioux at Cedar Creek.*

"Mr. Baldwin here proved himself more than capable during our campaign against the southern hostiles two years ago," Miles explained to Kelly.

"The general flatters me," the bearded Baldwin said in that quiet, unassuming manner of his.

"Balderdash!" Miles cried, turning to look at Kelly again. With emphatic jabs with the stem of his clay pipe, he said, "If it weren't for Baldwin's gutsy charge into Gray Beard's Cheyenne camp with his men in wagons—I don't think we would have routed them the way we did."†

"General, you give me too much credit."

"Hush, Lieutenant," Miles replied with a grin. "I want Mr. Kelly to know just who he's dealing with here. Indeed, with my officers, I feel I have some of the finest Indian fighters a commander could put in the field. Mr. Baldwin, had you not made the charge you did without regard for your own safety—why, I don't think we would have rescued those two little girls# alive, snatching them from the clutches of their captors."

"Mr. Kelly," Baldwin said, turning to the scout with a smile of admiration and some hopes of steering the conversation away from himself, "is it really true what I hear of how you introduced yourself to the general here?"

* *A Cold Day in Hell*, vol. 11, The Plainsmen Series.
† *Dying Thunder*, vol. 7, The Plainsmen Series.
# Adelaide and Julia German (*Dying Thunder*, vol. 7).

Miles snorted, "With that goddamn bear's paw?"

"So," the lieutenant said, "the tale is true."

"It was only a cinnamon bear," Kelly replied with a shrug.

"Now, don't you go belittling what you've done!" the colonel chided, turning to Baldwin. "See how you two are cut of the same mold?" Miles laid one hand on Kelly's shoulder, the other on Baldwin's. "This chief of scouts of mine—I like him because he's a straight-talking, no-nonsense sort. And the lieutenant here—I admire him because he came up the hard way."

Baldwin said, "Just like you did, General."

"Without the starch, and pull, and politics of the academy," Miles added gruffly. "The way others have greased their way up the ladder!"

"We're going to find your general's star out there," Baldwin declared emphatically. "Out there, maybe even this winter. Why, I'll bet that old reprobate Sitting Bull himself is the star you've been waiting for."

"If not for Crook and Mackenzie—that star might already be on my shoulder," Miles grumped, turning back to his desk and taking the pipe from his teeth. "Their column will be on its way north from Fetterman shortly to find and defeat Crazy Horse, if they aren't on the march already."

"But in a matter of days we'll be shadowing Sitting Bull ourselves!" Baldwin said enthusiastically. "The Fighting Fifth will round up the last of the great hostile bands!"

Already the post was alive with preparations for that renewed campaign a restless, discontented Miles was determined to pursue. But on this campaign the Fifth Infantry would be marching north. This time they would be facing a Montana winter.

Kelly hoped Miles and his officers sure as hell knew what they were doing.

Chapter 2

4–17 November 1876

—※◎◎※—

> I congratulate you and all concerned on the prospect
> of closing this Sioux war. . . . Genl Miles has dis-
> played his usual earnestness & energy and I hope he
> will crown his success by capturing or killing Sitting
> Bull and his remnant of outlaws.
> —General William T. Sherman,
> telegram to General Philip H. Sheridan

I f army command thought they had their war all but won,
they would soon learn just how overoptimistic they could
be.

Dismissing their earlier plans to remove all the Sioux hostiles to Indian Territory as impractical, Sherman and Sheridan
were now at work planning to corral the defeated warrior
bands on a tiny tract of land between Standing Rock Agency
and Fort Randall along the west bank of the Missouri River.
There they believed the army could keep an eye on the dismounted and disarmed Sioux as they were turned into Chris-
tian farmers.

But first the army had to catch the winter roamers.

During the two days following his arrival at Tongue River

Cantonment, Frank Baldwin, Miles's newly appointed adjutant for the campaign, joined the other officers readying their command to take to the field. Miles purchased a small herd of cattle from a private contractor upriver—enough beef to supply ten thousand rations for his troops on the coming march. Two civilian wranglers were hired to watch over the herd. In the meantime a supply train of Bozeman vegetables arrived from the mouth of the Bighorn, escorted by elements of Lieutenant Colonel Elwell S. Otis's Twenty-second Infantry.

Otis himself was on his way downriver, replaced back on the twenty-eighth of October by Major Alfred L. Hough as commander of the Glendive Cantonment, charged with protecting the wagon trains that supplied Tongue River. An old war veteran himself, Hough was galled to find the horrid conditions his men suffered at their outpost as the season turned cold. The paltry number of crude huts Otis expected to protect the soldiers from the coming winter were woefully inadequate. With no cots nor mattresses at Glendive, the Seventeenth were forced to sleep on a corduroy of poles and sagebrush to keep their bodies off the cold ground. In those last few days of October, Hough's men immediately began to construct more dugouts while others labored to lay in more firewood once they learned from army command that they would not be abandoning the upper river for the approaching winter.

Miles wanted the Seventeenth to remain active and alert, guarding the country along the Yellowstone east of the Tongue while he himself went in search of Sitting Bull.

On the fourth of November the quartermaster at Tongue River issued the Fifth Infantry some of that special clothing Miles had ordered sent upriver so that his regiment could conduct their continued campaign.

"I am satisfied that if the Indians can live here on the northern plains in the winter," Miles told his officer corps, "white men can also—if properly equipped with all the advantages we can give our troops, which are certainly superior to those obtainable by the Indians."

Baldwin and many of the others agreed. They and their men had suffered during the winter campaign against the Southern Cheyenne, Kiowa, and Comanche during the Buffalo Wars. Still, as cold as the weather had been in the panhandle of Texas, it in no way prepared the Fifth Infantry for what they were about to be asked to endure on the plains of Montana Territory.

Even Sherman himself had written to Miles, "Winter on the Yellowstone is another matter from winter on the Red River."

While General Terry did not actually expect Miles to conduct a campaign under the frigid conditions known to batter the northern prairie, the colonel had never been the sort to sit on his hands. North of the Yellowstone, where Miles planned to pursue the hostiles of Sitting Bull, the capricious weather could one day be pleasant and sunny, whereas the next could find a man fighting a blizzard as temperatures plummeted far enough to freeze the mercury at the bottom of a surgeon's thermometer. And then there was the much-feared factor of windchill. An ambient temperature of ten degrees below zero—which was the daily high documented time and again by the written record of the Fifth Infantry over the next month—would with any sort of wind behind it have the brutal effect of anywhere between fifty-eight to sixty-eight below.

As the Fifth had already learned about being stationed in Montana Territory, the wind is a constant companion.

Already the colonel had requested the Quartermaster Corps to ship him arctic clothing from the closest supply depot, as well as asking that buffalo coats and leggings be constructed for his men. But that equipment, along with the Sibley tents he had begged for, had yet to arrive. Miles remained undeterred—his regiment would march in the best they could muster for the moment: layers of army wool draped them from head to toe, as well as some burlap feed sacks the men wrapped around their feet to do what they could to prevent frostbite.

At dawn on Sunday, 5 November, the Fifth Infantry began muscling the ropes lashed to their crude ferries, cordelling those ungainly craft across the Yellowstone to the north bank. Back and forth the ferries plied the frothy current, every trip burdened with two of the campaign's thirty-eight supply wagons all loaded with a month's rations, each wagon to be pulled by a six-mule hitch. Already the river's surface was beginning to slake with ice and the wind was blustering down the valley.

It was destined to be an early, and long, winter on the northern plains.

Plowing through three additional inches of new snow the following morning, the entire command eventually marched away from the north bank to begin their search for Sitting Bull. While two companies of Hough's Twenty-second Infantry stayed behind to garrison the post, Miles rode at the head of 15 officers and more than 430 foot soldiers. Joining the infantry were 10 civilians and 2 Indian scouts. With them came the twelve-pound Napoleon gun and three-inch Rodman ordnance rifle, both of which had proved so successful in putting the Sioux village to flight at Cedar Creek. In addition to his wagon train—which carried 250 rounds of rifle ammunition for each man—Miles brought along two ambulances, an assortment of pack mules, and that small beef herd.

After reaching Sunday Creek the scouts led the command roughly north across a rugged piece of country, where many times the men were required to construct crude bridges or corduroy the sides of ravines for their wagons. After making no more than nine grueling miles, the Fifth went into camp late that first afternoon as the sun began to set.

"It's election day, General," Baldwin cheered the morning of the seventh as Miles stomped up to the fire in the gray light of dawn.

"Let's hope the folks back east get us a president who won't let the army shrink any more than Congress has done to us already."

The sun came out, eventually warming the air and turning the snow to slush beneath every hoof, wagon wheel, and waterlogged boot. Through a countryside dotted with greasewood and cactus the men trudged and shivered, forced to cross and recross Sunday Creek more than a dozen times in less than five hours. At twilight many of the weary men gathered around hasty fires, wolfed down their rations, and curled into their two blankets with a bunkie.

Setting off before dawn beneath a bright moon, they made nineteen miles that eighth day of November, following the tributaries of Sunday Creek as the command climbed the barren divide that would eventually drop them into the drainage of the alkali-laced Little Dry Creek. Here they began to see more in the way of buffalo and antelope along their route.

Frank Baldwin spotted the long-haired civilian scout appear on the hilltop ahead, loping back to rejoin Miles at the head of the column.

"The Jackson brothers agree with me, General."

"How's that, Kelly?"

"This country east of the Musselshell and south of the Missouri just happens to be some of the prime feeding grounds for buffalo at this season of the year."

"Oh?" Miles replied. "Have these buffalo migrated up from the south?"

"Out of the north, General," Kelly explained. "They find shelter in the lee of the Bear's Paw Mountains and the valley of the Milk River. For many a generation traders and half-breeds have been coming down from the Canadian side to hunt and make robes, or trade them for some Red River rum."

Miles shivered as the wind gusted. "A little rum right now would sure as hell warm the inner man in me, gentlemen!"

Without finding much in the way of timber, the men at sunset hunkered around their smoldering buffalo-chip fires to boil coffee and warm frozen hands and feet.

Under a clear and starry sky the following morning, the Fifth moved out behind Miles, his staff, and the scouts, who all rode some two to three miles ahead of the column, watching from the high ground for any sign of warriors. Early that afternoon of the ninth they reached a branch of Big Dry Creek, where they made camp after putting another twenty miles behind them.

On Friday afternoon just past two P.M., as the command was going into camp among the cottonwoods along the Big Dry, Yellowstone Kelly and William "Billy" Cross arrived to report that they had discovered a fresh Indian trail ahead. It was clear the village was on its way north to the Missouri.

The following morning the men awoke to a keen north wind whistling down the valley, driving an icy snow at their backs as they moved out for the day. It wasn't long before they crossed the lodgepole trail Kelly had discovered the day before. An hour later they came across some butchered buffalo carcasses. But by late morning the drifting, blowing snow had completely masked all sign of the enemy. On down the creek bottom the soldiers pressed despite the dropping temperatures. At times the wagons broke through the thickening ice as they rumbled along the dry bed of the Big Dry, no more than some twenty feet wide. Courageously managing to plod some fourteen miles in the teeth of that storm, the Fifth settled in for the night at the site of a camp used by the northbound Sioux only days before. The surgeon reported that the temperature stood at ten below, continuing to drop.

"Kelly's scouts tell me we're following Iron Dog's village," Miles explained to a hastily convened officers' meeting that night after sundown.

"How many's the lodge, General?" Baldwin asked, using Miles's brevet, or honorary, rank.

"Could be a hundred and twenty," the colonel replied. "Seems they're planning to cross the Missouri, aiming to reach Fort Peck for supplies."

"Maybe we can catch them before they do," Baldwin said, feeling optimistic despite the weather and trail conditions.

"If we don't get to them by the time they reach Fort Peck," Miles assured his officers, "then, by damned, we'll get them eventually."

Knowing his commander wasn't the sort to give up a chase, Baldwin rubbed his mittens together in anticipation. "Maybe when this bunch has joined back up with Sitting Bull."

But unlike the Sioux traveling on horseback and on foot through the falling temperatures and deepening snow, Miles found it tough going for his wagons the following day. Struggling to squeeze their way through nearly impassable ravines, climbing up and down nearly perpendicular bluffs, the column put no more than a dozen miles behind them that Sunday of driving wind and four more inches of snow. In the shelter of a cottonwood grove the surgeon's thermometer read twelve below that night of the twelfth.

So cold was it with the howling wind the morning of the thirteenth that the colonel kept his men in camp to recoup both them and the stock. After sending a courier to Fort Buford to inform Colonel William B. Hazen of his movements and asking for any word on the Hunkpapa bands, Miles had his trusted Baldwin lead a battalion comprising E and H companies to comb the snowy countryside for any sign of the enemy. Frank returned empty-handed after covering more than thirteen miles of the valley. Just before sundown the

temperature climbed all the way to sixteen degrees before it
began to plummet once more.

On the following day the men struggled valiantly to make
twenty-three miles, what with their wagons continually breaking through the ice caked along the bottom of the Big Dry, or
bogging down in the slushy quicksand of the creek bottom.
That night the soldiers made their bivouac in country beginning to change from barren coulees and ravines to gently rolling hillsides covered with waist-high autumn-cured grasses
tracked with thickly timbered water courses—a clear indication they were drawing close to the Missouri River. All day
they marched in sight of growing herds of buffalo, as well as
hundreds upon hundreds of antelope that dashed and cavorted on both sides of the column.

At midmorning on the fifteenth, some of Kelly's scouts
came loping back to the head of the column with word that
Indians had been spotted across the river ahead. After deploying his command into a protective square around his wagons and beef herd, Miles moved out once more, soon
discovering that the enemy causing all the alarm was only
agency Indians across the Missouri.

A real disappointment to Baldwin, who had yearned to
have himself and his men a good fight of it after enduring the
last ten days of arduous march and horrid temperatures.

In less than a month the lieutenant would have his wish
come true.

Johnny Bruguier did not know who those soldiers
camped across the river were, but soldiers were soldiers. And
white men were white men.

For the better part of two days he did his best to lay low,
and when he did have to move about the Fort Peck Agency, he
did so wrapped in a blanket or with a buffalo robe pulled over
his head.

Wouldn't be smart for him to take any chances—after all,
some of those white men making camp across the Missouri
just might be some of the soldiers who had attacked Sitting
Bull's camp on Cedar Creek a matter of weeks ago in the
Moon When Leaves Fall.

For most of the last month the half-breed had clung tight
as a buffalo tick to Sitting Bull and his thirty lodges. Here was

the greatest of Lakota chiefs, the man who had single-handedly put together the largest confederation of warrior bands ever assembled on the plains . . . now forced to watch the Bear Coat chip away at his alliance. For the most part the Bull was alone now. And Johnny Bruguier knew what alone meant.

He had been running since the end of last summer, ever since killing a white man near the Standing Rock Agency. A sure-as-hell dance at the end of a rope for a half-breed like Johnny. So he had stolen a horse in Whitewood City and scampered off to the west—heading for Injun country, where the law and posses would not dare come looking for him. On down that outlaw trail he discovered the chaps tied up behind the saddle on that stolen horse, the chaps he had been wearing when he had bravely ridden right into the Hunkpapa village and dashed into what he had hoped would be the headman's lodge.

It turned out to belong to White Bull, the nephew of Sitting Bull himself.

"If you are going to kill him, then kill him," Sitting Bull had said to the angry Hunkpapa warriors that first day last autumn. "But if you are not, then feed this man and make him welcome."

The Lakota had made a home for Johnny, and because of those chaps he wore, they had come to call him Big Leggings. And on more than half a dozen occasions his ability to speak both Lakota and the white man's tongue proved invaluable. But now, like all the rest of Sitting Bull's once-great confederation, he was on the run again.

Not long after fleeing the Bear Coat's soldiers on the Yellowstone, Sitting Bull's thirty lodges had moseyed north to camp some twenty-five miles south of Fort Peck in the valley of the Big Dry Creek. With him were Four Horns and Black Moon, all three bands hoping to trade with the Yanktonais and Red River Slota, who traditionally hung close to the agency.

In addition, another 125 Hunkpapa lodges—under chiefs Long Dog, Crow, Little Knife, and Iron Dog—had eventually marched north after the Cedar Creek fight and camped together a few miles below the agency in the Missouri River bottoms. Poor in clothing and shelter against the coming winter, the chiefs reluctantly gathered in council with agent Thomas J. Mitchell to discuss peace terms.

As Johnny listened, Mitchell's interpreter told the Lakota, "The agent cannot offer you anything but complete surrender. You must turn over your weapons and all government booty taken from the soldier dead at the Greasy Grass."

Angrily the Sioux leaders argued among themselves for much of that day, but in the end they guaranteed Mitchell they would surrender their people, arms, and ponies. In turn the agent distributed some rations as night began to fall, then instructed the chiefs to have their people return in the morning for the actual surrender. The chiefs had barely gotten to their feet when a runner from downriver at Wolf Point burst into the crowd, jabbering so excitedly that Johnny had trouble making sense of his electrifying news at first.

"Soldiers! They come up the river on the house that walks on water! Many soldiers come this way!"

Sure enough, the following morning of 1 November, Colonel William B. Hazen and 140 of his Sixth Infantry from Fort Buford docked their paddle-wheel steamer at Fort Peck to unload supplies and forage for Miles's column expected up any day from Tongue River. Hazen left Second Lieutenant Russell H. Day and a company of thirty-one soldiers behind with Agent Mitchell, then turned the paddle wheeler about and started downriver to return to his post at the mouth of the Yellowstone.

No matter.

The damage to Mitchell's efforts at diplomacy was already done. Moments after the news burst through the nearby camps, there wasn't a Hunkpapa lodge left within miles of Fort Peck.

But Johnny Bruguier had stayed behind.

Having been raised by his mother on the Standing Rock, Bruguier thirsted to see this Fort Peck, to hear the familiar sounds, smell the familiar fragrances, maybe cure a little of his own homesickness. For more than a week now he had stayed among the agency Indians, neglecting to return to Sitting Bull's camp, eating and talking, singing and flirting with the young doe-eyed women.

For many years the place had been a fur-trading post before becoming the agency for the Yanktonais, Gros Ventre,

Assiniboine, and any assorted Lakota bands who wandered about in search of buffalo north of the Yellowstone in Missouri River country. Rough-hewn log cabins stood fortresslike on the riverbank, themselves shadowed by the bluffs towering more than a hundred feet over the stockade walls. Mitchell provided annuities for more than seven thousand Indians, not to mention the recent additions who were scattering to the four winds, fleeing the soldiers in this year of the Great Sioux War.

Curious, Johnny watched the arriving soldiers work from dawn to dusk that Wednesday and Thursday snaking their supplies to their bivouac on the south bank using a rope and baskets suspended from a system of pulleys because the river ice was not yet thick enough to support the weight of loaded wagons. Then on Friday the white men continued their labors as a small band of riders came down to the bank to cautiously cross the Missouri's frozen surface.

The closer the soldiers came to the stockade, the more certain Bruguier grew that he had seen some of those bearded fur-wrapped white men during those Cedar Creek parleys.* Especially the long-haired white scout, those two dark-skinned half-breeds who rode with him, and that tall soldier chief now known among the Lakota as the "Bear Coat." Johnny snorted, readily recalling just how angry the soldier chief had become during the inconclusive, roundabout talks with Sitting Bull and the other Lakota headmen.

At least the Bear Coat was true to his word, Johnny brooded. The soldier chief had promised the Sioux they would get no rest. He had promised he would make war on them again soon if they did not go in to their reservations, even if it meant fighting through the coming winter.

Bruguier adjusted the blanket over his head and watched the soldiers approach from the shadows he made over his face. As the group ascended the icy riverbank and approached the stockade's open gates, the long-haired scout gazed in Johnny's direction. Then looked away. And then glanced again. But the white man did not stop as the horsemen passed on by. Instead, it looked as if the long-haired one murmured something to the two half-breeds who rode on either side of him.

* A Cold Day in Hell, vol. 11, The Plainsmen Series.

Johnny waited for the riders to enter the gate before he turned to follow, keeping to the shadows as the wind kicked up the old snow around his wool leggings. He stopped, hugging the stockade wall as the soldiers dismounted. Then his belly flopped. Bruguier grew frightened as the long-haired scout handed his reins over to one of the soldiers and stepped up to Bear Coat, saying something as he nodded toward Johnny.

The soldier chief turned slowly, raising a hand to shade his eyes, and peered at the gate they had just entered. He said something to the scout, and together the two of them started in Bruguier's direction.

With his heart rising in his throat, Johnny's eyes flicked this way, then that—not certain where he could go or how he would escape.

Now the rest of the soldiers in the group were following the Bear Coat, their hands on their belt weapons. If Johnny tried to run, it was certain one of them would shoot.

Perhaps that fate was better than hanging at the end of a rope for killing a worthless white man.

As Bruguier was slipping his hand inside the blanket, wrapping his fingers around the butt of the big army pistol he had stuffed into his belt, the soldier chief said something to the scout.

Gesturing, the long-haired civilian shouted in English, "Bruguier! Is that you, half-breed?"

Beneath the folds of his blanket, Johnny pulled the long barrel free of the belt and began to click back the hammer.

"By Jupiter—it is him, isn't it, Kelly!" exclaimed the Bear Coat.

And he was smiling. The soldier chief was smiling!

"Bruguier!" the Bear Coat bellowed, yanking off a mitten and holding out his hand as he came up. "You're just the man I could hope to see!"

Chapter 3

Waniyetu Wi 1876

All the good that Bear Coat Miles had done at Cedar Creek was gone—evaporated like a puff of smoke in this Winter Moon.

First Hazen's soldiers had scattered the Sioux bands right at the very moment they had decided to abandon Sitting Bull and surrender. And now Miles himself had shown up in that Fort Peck country—convincing the chiefs that the government spoke with two tongues: agent Mitchell with one voice, promising blankets and bacon . . . while the soldiers crept up to speak with the throats of their weapons.

So just about the time Sitting Bull was feeling the most isolated and disconsolate with his thirty paltry lodges of loyal followers, suddenly there were more than four times that number camped with him in the valley of the Big Dry as the Fifth Infantry reached Fort Peck. Once again Gall of the Hunkpapa, Lame Red Skirt, Small Bear, and Bull Eagle of the Miniconjou were convinced that instead of surrendering, their only hope lay in running, their only salvation lay in fighting.

"We will never give up," Sitting Bull told them solemnly when the chiefs informed him of the soldiers' arrival at the agency. "Even if it means that we keep running all the way north to the Land of the Grandmother. No matter that it may mean I will have to live on the scrawny flesh of prairie dogs—I will never surrender!"

The shouts, war cries, and death songs grew deafening in the valley of the Big Dry that night as the sun went down and the wind came up.

Those who had been fortunate enough to tear their lodges down before the Bear Coat's soldiers invaded their camp at Cedar Creek had been taking in all of the very old and the very young they could shelter, while the rest simply made do under bowers of blankets and robes—anything at all that would turn the hoarfrost and even the light snow of another night of winter-coming.

These were a wounded people. They had been robbed of all the greatness that had been theirs for so long. But we will survive, Sitting Bull vowed in private. As long as we do not allow the *wasicu* to divide Lakota against Lakota.

"The people, they are hungry," Gall tried to explain, a man who had lost wives, whose children had been killed by soldiers. "So many little ones with their empty bellies."

The Bull looked at the muscular war chief who had lost so much to the pony soldiers at the Greasy Grass, and felt a sharp pang of sadness for his old friend. "From the very same moment of my vision of those soldiers falling into camp—I warned our people not to take anything from the dead. I told all who could hear my voice that we must not take any of the spoils from that battle."

Lame Red Skirt bent his head, and his eyes did not meet Sitting Bull's when he admitted, "I remember."

"I told all who could hear that *Wakan Tanka* instructed me not to plunder those dead soldiers. That we had defeated them, that we had killed them all, was gift enough."

"What happens now?" asked Bull Eagle. "What's done is done! What happens now that so many of our people did take the soldier spoils from the Greasy Grass?"

For some time Sitting Bull thought and thought, staring at the fire while he heard the sounds of dogs and children at play in the cold, women at their work with supper fires and boiling kettles, the faint rustle of the wind through the bare branches of the cottonwoods outside his smoke-blackened lodge. An infant crying. An old woman keening softly as her man slipped beyond into death. He listened to these sounds of his people before he listened to what he knew rested in his heart—put there as a gift from the Great Mystery.

"Now that so many have disobeyed *Wakan Tanka*," he sighed, "our fate is sealed. We will be driven before the winds like the down of the cottonwood tree. Without a home in our own land."

"But we can hunt the buffalo that will make us a strong people once again!" Gall cried out in growing despair, his face flushed in anger. "These soldiers cannot follow us for all of winter!"

Quietly the Bull replied, "Bear Coat's walk-a-heaps do not need to hunt buffalo to survive as we do. They carry what they need in their many wagons. Because of that they can follow us right on into the winter—giving our warriors little time to hunt, our women no time to dry meat and scrape hides."

"We can gather the bands once more and be strong as we were in the summer moons. We can defeat these soldiers!" Gall screamed in sheer desperation, his eyes glistening.

"Once we could defeat all those *wasicu* soldiers, yes," Sitting Bull admitted dolefully. "When we did as *Wakan Tanka* told us to do—He was on our side. Now some small Lakota chiefs have even sold away our sacred hills, the He Sapa.* Now it hurts my heart to see how many of the people in this camp have turned their backs on the Great Mystery and robbed the soldier dead. They are so proud of their trophies that they forget my warnings!"

Lame Red Skirt pleaded with the Hunkpapa mystic, "What are we to do now that so many turned their faces away from the right?"

"Without the Great Mystery to help us," Sitting Bull said gravely, as quietly as the crackle of the cottonwood fire at their feet, "we will be driven before the wind for the rest of our days."

"But, General," Simon Snyder groaned, "Bruguier's a wanted man!"

Miles turned from the captain of F Company and looked

---

* The Black Hills, often incorrectly transcribed as Paha Sapa, which means "a black hill."

at the half-breed as he said, "So what say you, Johnny? Will you come work for me and the army?"

Bruguier's eyes narrowed. "You know the white man wants to hang me—"

"General," Captain Edmond Butler protested, "this is the very man who was helping that outlaw Sitting Bull make a fool of you during your parley with the Sioux at Cedar Creek! This breed's nothing more than an opportunist who will tell you anything you want to hear—then abandon us at his first opportunity!"

"Perhaps even betray us to his Sioux brethren!" Snyder cried.

"Hush! All of you!" Miles snapped. "What think you, Kelly? Can I trust this man?"

Luther Sage Kelly turned from staring out the window at the swirling snow kicked up by the wind blustering past the small cabin where Nelson Miles had taken Johnny Bruguier for a conference that Friday morning, the seventeenth. He regarded the half-breed a moment longer, then said, "The way I see it, General: both of you have something the other needs."

"Poppycock!" scoffed Frank Baldwin.

Aide-de-camp Hobart Bailey snorted, "What does this redskin have that General Nelson A. Miles could possibly need?"

"Information on Sitting Bull and the rest of the roaming Sioux," Kelly replied, stepping between members of the colonel's staff to move closer to Miles.

"I have no doubt of that," Miles said before any of his officers had a chance to sputter their protests. "So, tell me, Kelly—what do I have that Bruguier needs?"

Luther gazed at the half-breed's dark face, those flintlike eyes gazing back at him evenly, without betraying what might lie behind them. "To begin with, General—Johnny Bruguier here is trusted by Sitting Bull. Trusted enough that he was the old warhorse's own interpreter. Isn't that right, sir?"

"Yes—so what are you driving at?" he snapped impatiently.

Kelly continued. "Because of his important status to Sitting Bull and the rest of the hostiles, I imagine it would not be an easy thing for someone like Johnny to turn his back on all that and come over to the army side . . . would it, Johnny?"

For a moment the cramped cabin grew quiet. Then, still clearly bristling at the officers' doubt of him, Bruguier stiffly responded, "No, not easy to help the soldiers."

"A man might even feel he was committing suicide if he became a turncoat like you're asking him, General."

"What's your point?" Baldwin demanded.

Kelly looked directly at Miles, saying, "I figure there's where you can make things right by Bruguier if he betrays Sitting Bull."

"How can this soldier chief make things right by me?" the half-breed challenged suddenly, his eyes haughty. "The army does not have enough money to make me turn my back on Sitting Bull. A man the Lakota called the Grabber did that before*—and his life is worth nothing now. One day soon, I hear, his scalp will hang from a Lakota lodgepole."

"But I doubt you'll ever see that scalp hanging from some warrior's lodgepole, Johnny," Kelly said confidently.

"Why you so sure?"

"You'll be dead—hanged at the end of a white man's rope."

Luther watched the half-breed swallow hard, as if he might be imagining the fierce struggle to breathe as he danced at the end of a hangman's noose. Then some of the fire smoldering in Bruguier's eyes faded.

Kelly continued. "General, if you could help Johnny here clear up his murder charge with the civil authorities . . . I bet he'd have a reason to come over and see your side of things."

Kelly watched the light come on behind the colonel's eyes. With Crook and Terry bumbling and bungling things north and south, it was evident Miles had himself a clear shot at getting something done to end the Sioux War, and thereby earn his general's star. If helping a half-breed turn his back on his mother's people would assure him that star, Kelly had a good suspicion that Nelson Miles would likely jump at the chance.

"What would you say to that, Bruguier?" Miles asked. "When we brought you in here a few minutes ago, you babbled that you didn't kill that man in cold blood. You said it

---

* *Blood Song*, vol. 8, The Plainsmen Series.

wasn't your fault. So tell me: if I help you get this matter straightened out—will you help me with the Sioux?"

The half-breed's eyes widened, then narrowed. "You say you make it so I'm a wanted man no more?"

Miles straightened, running a hand down the brass eagle buttons on the front of his tunic. "Yes—that's my pledge to you. I'll do all I can to make sure an innocent man does not get himself hanged."

Bruguier slowly turned on his heel, parting the officers as he stepped to the window, where he gazed at the wind-driven snow. After a minute he turned to Kelly, as if he might trust only him. "The soldier chief here—he can take the white man's rope off my neck?"

Kelly glanced at Miles. The colonel barely nodded.

Luther asked, "Can you see that Sitting Bull surrenders at the Tongue River post?"

"Yes. I think I can do that," Johnny replied, putting a hand at his collar, fingertips laid across his throat. "There aren't many left with him now—chiefs and warriors. Will the Bear Coat help me?"

Without waiting for Miles to answer, Luther said, "Yes. The Bear Coat will see to it there is no rope waiting for you."

In those next two days Johnny Bruguier began to pay for having that hangman's noose taken from his neck.

The first item of business for Miles was the matter of some Indians the two Jackson brothers said they learned were camped up north of Fort Peck along Porcupine Creek. From Big Leggings the soldiers learned the band was not Sitting Bull's Hunkpapa, but agency Yanktonais instead. So Miles sent Bruguier off to visit the various camps of agency Indians in the surrounding area, to tell them that their leaders must come the following morning for a meeting with the soldier chief.

On the eighteenth Miles held his audience with the Fort Peck bands, gleaning from them some idea of just where the soldiers might find Sitting Bull, as well as seeing for themselves the shabby condition of those winter roamers who once more clustered around the great chief instead of returning to their agencies. They told the Bear Coat that their horses were poor and they hadn't had much time to hunt buffalo for meat and the hides needed to replace those lodges abandoned after the Fifth Infantry's attack at Cedar Creek.

Kelly figured it would clearly be a long, hard winter for the hostile bands if Miles did indeed push and harry the Sioux as he had vowed he would do.

That Saturday night, after conferring with his officers, scouts, and Bruguier about dividing his command for the coming chase because of the vast amount of territory they would have to cover in the pursuit, Nelson A. Miles composed a letter to Sherman:

> We have divided Sitting Bull's people and . . . his strength and influence is fast breaking down. . . . Give me command of this whole region and I will soon end this Sioux War. . . . I would be very glad to govern [the hostile bands] afterwards.

In addition he once more boasted that he had done it all without the aid of cavalry—the horse soldiers that Terry and Crook had so unsuccessfully depended upon throughout the summer and into the fall.

> I can hunt them down on foot. . . . [But] it is not easy for ten small Infy companies with broken down mules & four scouts to confine the whole Sioux nation.

And Miles was quick to tell his uncle-in-law that such an accomplishment as that would justifiably merit him either the command of a department of his own or perhaps even a stint at secretary of war in Washington City.

But he refrained from telling Sherman of the anger and disgust his men felt as they were forced to watch some of the very chiefs and warriors they had battled at Cedar Creek walking about the grounds of Fort Peck as smug and cocky as could be, carrying Henry and Winchester rifles in one hand, while in the other the Sioux clutched a ration card that guaranteed them food from the same government they had been fighting for the better part of a year. That irony wasn't lost on many of Miles's officers after the privations they had suffered in their cold march up from the mouth of the Tongue.

Essentially, the army knew there were three groups still

out as winter closed its paw on the countryside: the Northern Cheyenne under Dull Knife and Little Wolf; the Southern Sioux, who banded with Crazy Horse and were said to be wintering south in the Powder River country; and these northern hostiles who loosely banded around Sitting Bull.

"If we don't round them up and herd them in now, this very winter, Mary," the colonel said quietly, speaking to his wife far, far away that night, "these same bastards will be out again come spring: resupplied, rearmed, with their ponies fattened on the government dole."

As he went to sleep that night, Nelson A. Miles vowed he would do everything in his power to see that such a spring would never come for the Sioux.

The following morning, the nineteenth, Bruguier learned from some of the loose-lipped agency Indians that Sitting Bull's lodges were camped about forty miles above Fort Peck in the Black Buttes region south of the Missouri. This exciting news caused Miles no small measure of pride, thinking that his presence had turned the Hunkpapa back, away from the march they first appeared to have started, heading for the Canadian border.

That afternoon the colonel split the Fifth Infantry into two battalions. He planned to ride out personally to the west at the head of six companies—A, B, E, G, H, and I—as well as taking along the Napoleon gun, a heavy fieldpiece firing a twelve-pound shell. He spent the better part of that day ferrying over the men in those six companies to the north bank of the river and distributing rations.

At the same time Miles deployed Captain Simon Snyder to command the other four companies—C, D, F, and K—along with a small party of civilian scouts and the Rodman ordnance gun on a countermarch to the southwest, back up Big Dry Creek, where he would expect to rendezvous with Miles at the Black Buttes in eight to ten days. After Luther Kelly's party of scouts was done scouting downriver, Kelly was instructed to rejoin Snyder's column near the Buttes.

"My sources tell me there's only two ways into that rugged country, Captain."

Snyder nodded with a grin beneath his shaggy mustache. "You'll come in the front door . . . and I'll come in the back."

"Precisely," Miles replied, closing his hands like the jaws of a trap. "With Sitting Bull caught napping between us."

At dawn on the twentieth both battalions were off.

In the cold, chilling darkness Miles led his men up the high ridge behind the agency buildings and onto the freight road that would lead them up the Missouri to Carroll City. But before midmorning he had his scouts turn the column away from the road, leading his battalion south by west to follow Willow Creek upstream into a barren, windswept, austere country where nothing but greasewood and cactus could survive. Under granite skies time and again the soldiers had to chop and saw tree branches they used to corduroy the creek bottom so they could make themselves a ford suitable enough for their wagons.

Back and forth they repeatedly crossed the twisting Willow, splashing up to their knees in the icy slush and soupy, sandy quicksand more than twenty times in the next two days. Up one icy hillside they would scramble, then slip down the snowy, frozen far slope as the air turned colder.

Lieutenant Baldwin rode up and halted his mount near Miles as the column below them slowly slogged its way up the convolutions of Willow Creek. "I've seen some bad country down on the Staked Plain before, General," he admitted. "But I've never encountered anything as desolate and godforsaken as this."

Miles took the field glasses from his eyes and nodded. "About as barren as an abandoned barn's floor, Mr. Baldwin."

On Wednesday the battalion awoke to find a thick, cold fog shrouding the entire countryside. With their visibility cut to less than a quarter mile, William Jackson was reduced to leading the soldiers with the aid of his compass. Early in the afternoon near the headwaters of the Willow, Baldwin requested a brief leave from the column to climb a high and prominent butte, where he pulled out his penknife and scratched into the sandstone: 5th Inf., Nov. 22, 1876.

"What do the Sioux call this place, Bruguier?" Miles asked late that afternoon after his troops had put nineteen exhausting miles behind them and were going into bivouac in a place far from the protection of the cold wind.

"Not for sure," Johnny answered. "Maybe this is the creek

Sitting Bull's people call The Creek Where the Women Were Killed.*

Robert Jackson inquired, "How'd it get its name?"

With a shrug the half-breed answered, "Story goes the Blackfeet killed some Sioux women here years back."

The sun rose gloriously on the morning of the twenty-third, dispelling the last remnants of chilling fog and raising the men's spirits. That day they pushed southwest into the lush, grassy valley of Fourchette Creek, long favored by buffalo and all manner of game including grouse, prairie chickens, and sage hens. From time to time that afternoon herds of antelope would halt atop a far hill and gaze for a moment at the column of soldiers—some of whom thought the four-legged pronghorns in the distance were Sioux horsemen preparing their ambush and attack.

That night the temperature dropped all the way to twelve degrees, but by midafternoon on the twenty-fourth the temperature had climbed to fifty-eight, causing the men to sweat as they marched along the grassy banks of the Fourchette. By four P.M. Miles had them establishing camp for the night after making another twelve miles in their chase.

At breakfast on the twenty-fifth, having struggled more than a hundred miles from Fort Peck, Miles called Andrew S. Bennett to his fire.

"Captain."

"Good morning, General."

"I'm reinforcing your company to the strength of fifty-two men, Captain."

"You have something in mind for me to do?"

"I want your B Company to proceed on down this freight road to Carroll City."

"Yes, sir," Bennett said with enthusiasm. "What's our assignment?"

"Some of the agency hang-abouts at Fort Peck told our half-breed interpreter that a trader was supplying ammunition to Sitting Bull's hostiles there."

"And you want me to take that trader into custody?"

"No," and Miles shook his head. "Just see that you seize every last cartridge the son of a bitch has."

* Present-day Timber Creek.

"How much might this trader have?"

With a shrug and a scratch at his cheek Miles said, "I have no idea, Captain. But I'll assign you a half dozen of our wagons to carry the ammunition."

"Where shall I rejoin you, General?"

"You will find us in the Black Buttes area—where I plan for all of us to rendezvous with Captain Snyder's battalion."

Chapter 4

That Saturday afternoon of the twenty-fifth, after Bennett's B Company departed for Carroll City to confiscate that trader's ammunition, the rest of Miles's column reached the banks of the Missouri River itself, directly opposite the mouth of Squaw Creek a little below the Musselshell River. Here the command established its bivouac across a rich, fertile bottomland where grass grew thick not only for their livestock, but for an abundance of buffalo, elk, antelope, and deer.

One problem with the varying weather, besides the trail becoming soggy for the foot soldiers, was that the Missouri River itself was no longer a solid sheet of ice. Instead the rolling surface of the wide river was pocked with huge, bobbing chunks of ice the size of immense boulders, crashing and crushing against one another with a constant, noisy, grating rumble.

Assessing the situation upon reaching the north bank that Saturday, Miles called for his most trusted subaltern.

"Mr. Baldwin, I'm putting you in charge of constructing a raft suitable for moving the troops across."

"I'll move the men and you'll caulk and float the wagons, General?" Frank inquired.

"That's right. But we need a raft big enough to move a good number of the troops across at a time."

"What dimensions do you recommend?"

Miles gazed up at the cottonwoods that lined the banks. "As big as you think your work details are capable of, Lieutenant."

All through that cold night the soldiers labored within a ring of bonfires that gave them light and provided some measure of warmth as they sweated: chopping, hewing, hammering, and lashing—voices joking and buoyant as the men worked or slept in relays. By the following morning, the twenty-sixth, Baldwin was ready. Not only had his crews constructed a rope-and-log raft eighty feet long by twelve feet wide, but they had cut down several long cottonwood saplings they would use to pole their way across the river. In addition, another group of soldiers had removed one of the wagon boxes from its running gear, nailing waterproofed canvas over the box itself to make the craft more riverworthy in floating numbers of the men across the Missouri.

But that morning as the sun emerged into a gray sky, the Missouri appeared to be running all the faster, all the more crowded with the noisy, jarring rumble of ice floes. Nonetheless, at that point Miles would not be deterred. He was not about to be kept from reaching the south bank, where he could continue his pursuit.

"Simply put," the colonel told Baldwin, "the Fifth must push on in its hunt for Sitting Bull, no matter the obstacles thrown in our way."

With a great shout and hearty exclamations from those hundreds watching on shore, more than ten soldiers threw their shoulders against the huge raft, shoving it across the thick ice frozen against the north bank to launch the craft into the slushy Missouri. Accompanying Baldwin on that maiden voyage was Miles himself, Lieutenant James W. Pope, and a dozen foot soldiers, nearly every one of them equipped with a twenty-foot-long sapling. In a matter of moments those poles proved themselves totally worthless against the increasing depth and speed of the current that hurled huge chunks of ice against the upstream side of the raft, where the icy river began to lap over the men's feet, then washed around their ankles, and eventually swirled crazily around their calves the farther they went.

Just shy of the halfway point the raft lurched with a sudden jar that nearly toppled most of the men. Scrambling to hold on to the ropes, the men cried out in fear and surprise, cursing their luck. As the craft slowly came around with the persistent force of the current, the huge cottonwood timbers groaned threateningly.

"Pole men!" Baldwin ordered, fighting to keep his footing as the raft wobbled, one end free and bobbing in the current, the other snagged on a submerged tree. "Hold 'er! Hold 'er!"

The ropes strained and creaked. Cottonwood timbers grated and shuddered against one another. The river flung ice into their frail craft.

"We're stuck fast, General!" Pope cried.

Miles demanded, "You saying we've gone aground?"

"I think we're caught on a sawyer," Baldwin decided. "A snag. Something huge, just below the surface that's keeping us from going on."

"And from going back too," Miles said, assessing their precarious situation.

"All right, men," Baldwin cheered. "Let's put our backs into it! Heave!" he grunted along with the others shoving against their poles, pushing with the power of their legs against the mighty river's current. "Heave! Heave!"

As suddenly as they had been jarred by the snag, a rifle shot cracked the cold air. In that heartbeat every man onshore turned to look this way and that. A second rifle shot rang out from the pickets Miles had thrown around their bivouac. In a moment it began to strike home that they might well be under attack.

Miles stood clumsily, steadying himself against the bobbing of the icy current. Flinging his voice to the north bank, he demanded, "What's the meaning of that firing?"

A voice onshore cried, "Indians coming!"

Beside the Missouri his soldiers milled, called out to one another, turned this way and that as the officers began to shout their commands.

"Damn it all!" Miles grumbled as he sank to his knees on the rocking raft.

Baldwin couldn't agree more. Here they were, caught at

midriver, helpless and without weapons while the main body
of the column was damn well caught with its pants down
watching this river crossing.

"Fall in!" Miles shouted through the gloves he cupped
round his mouth. His red face showed his frustration and
growing anger. "Fall in, dammit!"

Captain Ewers shouted, "Assembly, General?"

"Damn right," the colonel replied, cupping his hands to
hurl his voice at the north shore once again. "Bugler—sound
assembly. Look lively! Look lively, now!"

Confined as they were to their position on the river below
the steep banks, Baldwin could see nothing beyond those
soldiers right on the bank, men darting here and there to
begin forming up company by company, their lieutenants and
sergeants barking orders before the first outfits started scrambling up the shelf onto the prairie itself, where another shot
rang out just then.

Just one. Still no general firing, no yelps and war whoops.
Yet Baldwin knew those cries of battle could come at any
minute when the warriors swooped down on the main body
of the Fifth.

But as quickly as the first shot had surprised them all, the
first half-dozen soldiers onto the prairie turned back against
the flow of the hundreds, waving their arms, shrieking above
the panic as they split the ranks to trot down among the
general's nervous staff onshore. In less than a minute Bailey
was at the water's edge, shouting out to the raft.

"What's he say?" Miles demanded of the men around
him.

Baldwin repeated, "Bailey's saying it's only a false alarm,
General."

"No Indians?" Pope inquired.

"Says it was elk," Frank explained with a wag of his head.
"One of the pickets started shooting at a herd of goddamned
elk."

"Who announced that it was Indians?" Miles growled.

"Some nervous Nelly," Baldwin said, then chuckled.
"General, I sure as hell wouldn't want to be in that man's
shoes when you get your hands on him!"

"Damn right," Miles growled. "Here we are without
weapons, at the mercy of this blessed river—"

The raft suddenly convulsed against the powerful current, shifting a little more to the side as it came around and stopped—even more firmly locked against the snag.

As the following minutes rolled by, the men found their raft beginning slowly to list even more to one side in the ice-laden current, forcing more of the slushy river over the sides of their raft, pushing a swirl of bitterly cold water up to froth around their knees. Clinging to the ropes for their lives, the soldiers began to shiver, their teeth chattering as Baldwin and Pope shouted back and forth to those on the north bank.

It wasn't long before some of the men in Wyllys Lyman's I Company had the canvas-covered wagon-box boat down the shore and into the water, a complement of soldiers kneeling inside at the gunwales, using army spades as paddles. Again, sheer muscle was pitted against the growing strength of the river's frightening ice floes. As the rescuers bobbed close, one of Baldwin's soldiers tossed the end of their longest section of rope to those in the wagon box. Lyman's men promptly tied it off before the wagon boat was carried on across the Missouri's current.

Struggling against the powerful current and the battering of the huge grating ice chunks, the soldiers from I Company finally paddled their way to the south shore, where Private Thomas Kelly leaped over the gunwale and waded through the chilling water that boiled up to his armpits, dodging hunks of ice to clamber eventually onto a section of solid ice. Once there, he crabbed onto the bank. On firm footing at last, Kelly shook himself like a dog before his trembling hands fought to tie off the other end of the long rope around a cottonwood of generous girth.

That task completed, the men of I Company pulled themselves to the south bank, where several of the soldiers remained behind in the hope that the rest of their regiment would soon be joining them before nightfall. Then those left of the wagon-boat crew turned around inside their craft and dipped their spades into the river once more, pushing back toward the raft as the hundreds on the north bank erupted into a spontaneous cheer.

When Lyman's soldiers reached Baldwin's raft, the lieutenant tossed them the end of another length of one-inch rope he had secured to his tilting craft still snagged near the middle of the river. As the wagon boat slipped away into the current, its crew paddling for the north bank, a soldier slowly played out the rope connected to the raft. Thunking, scraping, groaning—more and more ice chunks smacked against the side of the wagon box, slid along the side with a noisy, frightening racket, then bobbed free, floating on downriver.

Of a sudden the solitary wagon-box soldier reached the end of that rope. "Goddammit—help me, for the love of God!"

Nearly all the rest of the paddlers dropped their shovels into the bed for those next desperate moments at midstream, every one of them clutching the rope as the current shoved against them, starting to urge them downstream in a bobbing arc.

"There's no way we can do this, General!" Baldwin shouted above the cries of the men on both shores who watched helplessly, the soldiers trapped in both rivercraft wobbling with the icy current. "They just don't have enough rope to make the north bank!"

"Tie it off there, men!" Miles commanded the wagon-box sailors, pointing to a large snag that poked its thick branches above the surface near the bobbing craft.

"Secure it to that sawyer!" Baldwin echoed.

As half the men in the wagon boat returned to their paddles, fighting to bring their craft back toward the snag against the power of the current, the rest held on to the waterlogged rope with the last of their strength, blue hands and soaked mittens gripping for all they were worth.

Meanwhile onshore several of the officers recognized the dilemma and ordered another wagon box taken from its running gear and quickly wrapped in oiled canvas. After more than an hour and a half of watching the crews of both the raft and the wagon boat barely holding their own against the mighty Missouri, the second wagon boat was shoved into the current by some men of E Company, loaded with several long sections of rope, the end of which was attached to a cottonwood on the north bank.

Here at midafternoon, with Miles, Baldwin, Pope, and their dozen soldiers still stranded on the rocking raft and water continuing to swirl up to their knees, men on both banks began to cheer, for it appeared the rescue was about to take place . . . just as bigger and bigger ice floes began to bear down the river's surface. Rubbing, jabbing, creaking against one another—blocks as big as boulders. The Missouri was beginning to fill with ice scum once more as the temperature continued to drop, and with it the late-autumn sun.

"Sweet God in heaven!" one of the men of I Company in the nearby wagon boat shrieked.

The rest of the soldiers on the raft and the second wagon boat looked upstream where he was pointing. Better than a mile away they could see it coming, tumbling slowly, roiling on the river's surface: a chunk of ice as big as a cabin itself. It's dirty luster bobbed in the current, easily filling a third of the Missouri's span.

"Don't panic, men!" Baldwin cheered them. "We don't know for sure where it will go! Just hang on!"

"Cut the rope!" came the immediate cry from the second wagon boat as the soldiers squirmed in fear while that huge chunk of ice bore down on them.

"Cut the goddamned rope!" another rescuer shouted.

Then another bellowed like a stuck calf—crying that they had to save themselves.

"No—don't do that!" Lieutenant Pope ordered. "You can't abandon us!"

"Steady, men! Steady! Pull yourselves in here!" Baldwin demanded. "Now, heave against that line. Hurry! Hurry!"

Inside that rocking second wagon boat the frightened men scrambled for their spade paddles, dipping deep and sure into the river, trying their best to steady the craft as Private Richard Bellows of E Company seized the rope securing them to the north bank and began to fight the waterlogged knot. Alone.

"No—cut the son of a bitch!" one of his companions cried.

Instead, Bellows hunched over his work with numbed fingers, struggling.

The others began to take up the chorus. "Cut it! Cut the line now!"

The ice chunk rumbled closer and closer.

With the danger no more than twenty-five yards away Bellows finally got the knot untied in the waterlogged rope, looped it around both his trembling hands, and hunkered down in the bottom of the wagon box, where he braced his legs against the creaking gunwale just as the huge chunk hit them.

As the box spun around, two other soldiers threw down their spades and leaped to Bellows's aid, each of them grabbing hold of the rope to join the courageous private. They grunted as the ice groaned and banged against the side of the wagon box.

"We can't hold it!"

"Let go of the bastard!"

Then Baldwin shouted above the noise of men onshore and the rumbling clatter of ice whacking and creaking against the raft and wagon boats, "Let go and save yourselves! For God's sake—let go and make for shore before you're swamped!"

Just then the three soldiers on the line were jerked to their feet as another side of the tumbling ice chunk keeled around and slammed into the wagon box.

"Let the damn thing go or we'll be broken to splinters!"

The two soldiers released their hold on the rope and instead locked their arms around Bellows, who struggled to maintain his grip. With an agonized cry of pain as the rope burned through the cold flesh of his hands he freed himself, and their raft, into the mercy of that merciless current.

"Row, goddammit! Row for shore!" Miles shouted above the crash of ice against wood.

As Private Bellows sank exhausted to the bottom of the wagon box, the rest of the men dived to take up their paddles, bending to their knees, rocking forward again and again as they forced their spades into the ice scum while the box swung slowly around and around, swept downstream in the midst of those growing chunks of ice. They were struck again by a huge lump of ice, then a patch of clear water appeared above them, upstream. That would be their one chance.

All the chance brave men would ever need.

Now the drenched soldiers sank their oars in deadly earnest, gradually turning the wagon box against the current that frothed over the sides of the gunwales as they brought it crosswise. Slowly, demanding the last bit of strength from their bodies, the last flicker of sheer grit from their will, the soldiers inched their wagon box toward the north shore as they were tossed downstream.

More than a mile later those men of E Company reached the willow and some cottonwood saplings against the bank. Two of the soldiers, then a third, lunged over the sides of the box, into the freezing water that lapped at their waists, each one helping shove the box into the shallows, where they no longer were subject to the will of the powerful tug that was the Missouri's current.

A spontaneous roar erupted from their mates upstream as men jumped up and down in joy, slapping one another in celebration of what bravery they had just witnessed from the dozen men aboard that second wagon boat.

"General—it's high time we get the hell out of here ourselves," Baldwin suggested quietly at Miles's shoulder.

"I couldn't agree with you more!" the colonel replied resolutely. "All right, boys—let's cut ourselves free of the south bank there. Just cut the damned rope . . . that's good. Now, pull away for all you're worth! Make for the north shore!"

As the rope attaching them to the south bank was freed, the ungainly raft rocked against the river's surface all the more, listing at an even more precarious angle in the strengthening current. Baldwin's dozen began to scramble into position as the huge craft bobbed. Ahead of them the soldiers in the first wagon boat dipped their spades into the river and began their crawl toward the north shore—slowly, steadily slaving over their exertions as the river ice bore down on them.

"Pull now!" Baldwin ordered as the men on the raft came up and took their places along the ice-coated rope securing them to the north bank. "Pull as if your life depended on it!"

There wasn't a man there who didn't realize their lives did depend on it.

"There's no one else going to free us from this snag now," Miles reminded them as he took up his own place along the line. "We must do for ourselves, boys!"

Hunching over their work, the soldiers fought for balance on the rocking raft while water splashed and danced up to their waists. Then came the first loud creaking.

At first Baldwin feared their flimsy craft was breaking up—the strain simply too much for that wood and rope. But in that next moment the raft lurched sidelong in the current, pitching some of the soldiers to their knees, sliding toward the icy current as others on the raft shouted, every man holding out his hand to another. Together those fifteen kept one another from being hurled headlong into the river.

Into the frozen, slushy Missouri—where a man might have as little as half a minute, no more than two minutes at the most, to fight alone against the river before he was too cold to struggle any longer. Each of them knew if they were swept into the current that it would be a sure, quick sentence of death.

The minutes crawled past as Baldwin's men strained beyond human endurance at their icy rope, Miles and Pope in among them—no officers and enlisted here. They were all in it together. Either they would reach the shore as one, or they might well drown in the cold Missouri, one, by one, by lonely one.

"Goddammit—pull you sonuvabitch!" one soldier grunted, then quickly glanced up to find the colonel was the one to whom he had just given that profane order. "B-beg pardon, Gen'ral!"

"Apology accepted, s-soldier," Miles grunted with the rest. "The rest of you bloody well heard this man! Now, pull—goddammit!"

Foot by foot felt like inch by inch as the surface seemed to rise about them and the edge of the raft came free of the sawyer. Now they were level once more on the surface of the Missouri, no longer captive of that huge cottonwood snag embedded in the river bottom. Now it was just the fifteen against that raging, icy river. What strength those soldiers still had in their aching shoulders, their trembling arms, the burning muscles in their legs that cried out in protest and quaked as the men braced themselves against the overwhelming roll of the powerful river . . . and what indomitable will.

Yard by yard now they were beginning to make some headway.

"That's it, boys!" Baldwin cheered, feeling the burn of tears at his eyes.

A final third of the river's width to go.

Onshore the hundreds of soldiers and civilians were jumping, cheering, calling out their encouragement, waving, pounding one another on the back, darting here and yon in a growing, swelling crowd that began to surge downstream, slowly following the raft as it was relentlessly whirled down-river by the current. Already at least half a hundred were sprinting in among the frozen willow and cottonwood sap-lings, helping the soldiers in the second wagon boat leap ashore, securing the box to the bank with those icy ropes.

There were still fifteen on the river.

"Ho—for General Miles!"

The cheer went up as the raft inched closer.

"Hurraw for our shipwrecked general!"

Suddenly there were two dozen or more splashing into the current as Baldwin's men inched toward the bank. Slowly they worked their way out toward the raft—water up to their knees, then waists, and finally icy chunks bobbing at their armpits as they lunged out to help.

Not for a moment did the men onshore stop cheering as the first in the water reached out and grabbed hold of the blue, frozen hand offered by one of the soldiers on the raft. They clasped, then cheered themselves. In a heartbeat others were there, pulling and pushing on the raft as Baldwin's men wearily unlocked their cramped, cold, icy fingers from the rope and sank back with a sigh, and some with tears in their eyes, as around them men danced in the shallow water and slapped their backs, laughing at the jokes many made of this biblical flood and how flimsy was this Noah's ark.

Baldwin dragged a hand beneath his nose as he jumped into the shallows and turned, sputtering his thanks to all those soldiers who together had brought that raft in to shore here late in the day after they had been imprisoned midriver since morning.

"Huzzah!" Frank croaked with emotion above the noisy clamor.

"Huzzah for our shipwrecked general!" came the cry from a nearby enlisted man.

Baldwin tore his sealskin cap from his head and whirled it aloft. "Hazzah for the Fighting Fifth!"

Chapter 5

Waniyetu Wi 1876

When the Bear Coat's soldiers reached Fort Peck, the foxy old Sitting Bull instructed some of the agency Indians to give the army scouts some bad information.

"Tell them the Hunkpapa are fleeing west," he ordered.

They did just that, and the scouts believed them.

But when the Yanktonais hurriedly returned to the Hunkpapa village, they carried news that cut Sitting Bull to the core.

Big Leggings had turned against his mother's people and agreed to help lead the Bear Coat on Sitting Bull's trail.

"The half-breed says he has not turned against you, Uncle," declared White Bull, his arm still aching from the bullet wound suffered at Cedar Creek. "Big Leggings tells the agency Indians that he is only helping the Bear Coat so he can talk you into surrendering."

"Why should he want me to surrender?"

White Bull scoffed, "Because Big Leggings thinks it is a good thing for our people."

He stared at the fire a long, long time, watching blue flames lick along the dry cottonwood limbs.

Finally the Bull spoke. "Sometimes I am not always right."

"What is not right now?"

"People," he replied morosely. "I get fooled by people."

"The *wasicu*?"

With a sad, mirthless grin, Sitting Bull shook his head. "No—I always expect the worst from a white man, always expect that he will not tell me the truth . . . and I have never been disappointed."

White Bull leaned closer, asking, "If not the *wasicu*—then who have you been fooled by? The agency Indians?"

"No. By the half-breeds. The ones who have their Lakota blood fighting their *wasicu* blood. Men like the Grabber."

Leaning back, White Bull nodded. "You saved his life that snowy day long ago."

"I thought I did right, even when he ran away from the Hunkpapa and made a home among the Crazy Horse people."

White Bull nodded. "His *wasicu* blood is evil: he brought the Three Stars down on Old Bear's Shahiyela last winter—and he stays with Three Stars's soldiers all through the summer."

"Yes, I saw him with the soldiers at the Narrow Buttes,"* Sitting Bull admitted. "And now . . . another half-breed I trusted has turned his back on me."

White Bull took his good arm to draw a thumb across his throat. "You could have killed both of them."

"Yes," Sitting Bull replied, his eyes lit with a cold fire. "One day I may still have the chance to do just that."

So it was that while part of the Bear Coat's army marched west and the others marched south by west up the valley of Big Dry Creek chasing nothing more than a planted rumor, Sitting Bull turned about and led his hundred-plus lodges all the farther to the east, on past the soldier stockade at Wolf Point, still farther downriver to the mouth of the Redwater, which flowed into the *Minisose*† from the south. In those frosty days at the heart of the winter moon they ascended the high tableland to the forks of the Redwater—far from the soldiers, where his people could hunt, make meat for the coming cold, scrape the hides for the many lodges needed by those

---

* The term used by the Lakota Peoples for Slim Buttes, *Trumpet on the Land*, vol. 10, The Plainsmen Series.

† The "Muddy Water River," the Missouri River.

who had lost all at the Cedar Creek fight. For the time being Sitting Bull had more than 250 of his people crammed into no more than three lodges and some ninety-two shelter tents they had scraped together since the glory days of the previous summer.

As the weather began to warm again, the thick ice in the *Minisose* began to soften and crack, then finally started to splinter, breaking apart into chunks larger than a council lodge. This is good, the Bull thought. If the soldiers cannot recross on the ice, they will be stranded on the north side of the *Minisose*. It was the first favorable sign to happen to his people in a long, long time.

Hadn't he warned them after the great victory at the Greasy Grass? Warned them not to touch the soldier spoils? But like children, his people had not listened to the words of the Great Mystery. So for some moons now they were being scattered and driven across the prairie before the winds. First they had been harried east to the Narrow Buttes, where the soldiers had found one of the villages and killed American Horse.

Then they had fled north to the valley of the Elk River*—where the Bear Coat had found them, decided to fight instead of talk, and the *wasicu* impoverished the Lakota once again.

Now the army was marching for another winter. And Sitting Bull was sure the Bear Coat would keep on marching after his people until he had taken them across the Medicine Line† into the Land of the Grandmother.#

There was little choice but to run.

Wakan Tanka had warned them there would be a terrible price to pay for disobeying.

Now there could be no doubt that *Wakan Tanka* had turned His face from His people.

Given his orders by Miles at Fort Peck before the colonel had departed with the lion's share of the regiment, Luther S. Kelly and three others—Jim Woods, Billy Cross, and the old

* The Yellowstone River.
† International border.
# Canada.

mountain man John Johnston—headed down the south bank of the river to search for any Sioux villages that might be in the neighborhood, coming in off the trail to join up with Sitting Bull. After all, the Hunkpapa were reportedly fleeing west, away from the army.

As soon as Miles had locked up his agreement with the half-breed named Bruguier, Kelly and the rest recrossed the softening ice on the frozen Missouri on the nineteenth and started east to look for Sioux. A day later Captain Simon Snyder started up the Big Dry with his four-company battalion.

The fat gray clouds that rolled in on the nineteenth began dropping snow before dawn on the twentieth. Accumulating rapidly, it soon obliterated any hope of finding old trails leading in to the Fort Peck country. On they slogged for more than fifty miles following the twists and turns of the Missouri until they reached a point opposite the old trapping post of Wolf Point. It was there Kelly's men smelled a faint hint of smoke on the cold wind, searched cautiously for the cause. Down among the trees along the south bank they discovered a cottonwood stump still smoldering, the snow melted away for some distance all around. There were enough foot-and-hoofprints, as well as cooking fires to account for as many as four lodges of Sioux. Where they had gone in the last day or so, Kelly's scouts had no way of knowing.

The snow had done well to cover the Indians' trail but was tapering off now to nothing more than a few random flakes. Frustrated, Kelly turned to gaze across the river. Firelight glowed red-orange against the low-hanging cloud bellies—a sure sign there was life within the Wolf Point stockade.

"Jim, you and the rest make us a fire. I'll see who's to home and be back shortly," Kelly said as he stuffed an ice-caked buffalo-hide moccasin back into the stirrup and raised himself to his saddle.

With the temperatures moderating over the last few days, the river's ice was beginning to soften enough that it proved to be some tricky business making that crossing any time of the day—much less here at sunset. Luther urged his mount onto the ice, whereupon the animal immediately fought the bit, struggling against its rider.

After those first few steps it was clear to Kelly that the top layer of the ice had thawed during the warmth of the afternoon, leaving behind huge puddles of water and slushy ice scum that extended all the way to the far shore. Better to go afoot, Kelly figured—to be out of the saddle if the horse took its own head, or the ice splintered below them. Freeing his lariat from the saddle, Luther tied a crude hackamore around the mount's head and muzzle, then set out for the north bank on foot, tugging on the lead rope.

Man and horse waded cautiously through the water and slush, picking their way through the deepening twilight. Every place he found the ice beneath his moccasins too spongy, Kelly turned back and made a slow, looping detour until he was once again walking on something a little more solid. It was growing dark by the time they reached the north bank and finally stood on firm footing among the bare, frost-coated branches of cottonwood and willow.

From the pair of white traders operating inside the crude stockade Kelly got some coffee and learned that three families had crossed the river that morning, scampering to the north because of word the army was marching along the south bank of the Missouri. It was black as the pits of hell by the time Kelly again stood on the bank, attempting to measure his chances of making it back across in the dark. A lot harder, he thought, to see the thin patches of soft ice without any moonlight to speak of. But, on the other hand, the ice might thaw all the more by morning—making a crossing even more difficult.

In the end the scout convinced himself that the cold nighttime temperatures would harden the spongy ice and improve his odds come first light. Besides, he decided as he turned back to the stockade, it would be good to share the evening with the two new faces, their Assiniboine wives and half-breed children, to hear new stories and to talk over the problems with the Sioux.

"I'm one glad sonuvabitch the army's finally getting around to taking care of those red bastards," grumbled the older of the pair, pushing some long greasy hair out of his eyes as he turned to spit into a crude corner fireplace.

" 'Bout time too," the other agreed with a nod. He was busy removing a thick crust of dirt and animal fat from beneath his fingernails. "Mebbeso them red-bellies'll stop bothering the good Injuns and turn out for some good once the government can make 'em into farmers."

The following morning one of the trader's sons led Kelly down to the bank to show him where the three Sioux families had crossed to reach the north side, although the recent snow had blotted out any sign of just where they had ended up going from there.

Staring at the river, disgusted to find that the water and slush were even deeper than they had been at sundown the day before, Kelly asked the boy, "How you figure the ice?"

Without speaking a word the youth touched fingertips to his lips and shook his head.

"Don't speak no English, eh?" Then Kelly looped the hackamore back over the horse's head, which freed both his hands to sign his question this time.

Watching the scout's hands carefully, the boy grinned and nodded, then pointed at the ice. "*Suta. Suta.*"

"*Suta,* is it?"

"*Suta.*"

"I don't have me no idea what *suta* means, lad," Luther muttered. "Assiniboine, ain'cha?"

But as quickly the youth signed that he was volunteering to lead Kelly across the softening ice.

"No," and Luther emphatically wagged his head. "I can't let you do that. Better for me to go out there and take care of myself—don't care to be responsible for no one else."

He turned the boy slightly and pointed up the bank to the stockade. "Now, go. Go on back to your folks."

Letting the horse have a good lead on its rope, Kelly stepped down into the several inches of icy slush that washed past his ankles. The ice had indeed softened, but the water was clear, and he now had enough morning light to see down through the water and scum to the ice itself, detouring here and there around a thin patch. By the time he neared the south bank, the others were stomping out their fire, having saddled their horses when they saw Kelly returning.

He glanced up at the sky and nodded to the trio as he brought the skittish horse to a halt. "Weather looks to fair up today. Let's see how much ground we can cover to catch up to that Captain Snyder's bunch."

·   ·   ·

"How long you figger to sit here watching 'em?" William Jackson asked his brother, Robert.

"As long as there's a good show."

William settled beside his brother on the side of the bluff and laid his army rifle across his legs. Together the scouts watched the struggles of the soldiers on the riverbank below. "Think they'll ever get us all across?"

Robert shrugged. "Maybe by spring."

The two Blackfoot half-breeds born and raised in the far Upper Missouri region had been watching the officers and soldiers with growing amusement and sometimes consternation over the last two days. Twice each day the pair went out to scout in this direction or that, looking for sign of the Lakota camps, to read the wind for smoke, the ground for travois trails, and to see if they could sight anything of Captain Snyder's battalion coming in from the south, or Bennett's outfit returning from Carroll City to the northwest.

But much of the time they sat and watched the growling, grumbling, frustrated army officers struggling to fight the Missouri—a river cold enough to kill a man in mere seconds, but not yet frozen solid again to attempt a crossing with laden wagons. Why, it was turning out to be some of the best entertainment they'd had in a long time: witnessing Soldier Chief Miles argue with his lieutenant named Baldwin.

Then, on Monday morning, the twenty-seventh, following Sunday's disastrous attempts at crossing the river, Baldwin's men finally did accomplish the improbable and managed somehow to string their line of ropes completely across the river to the south bank.

Now Miles gave the order to the rest of his officers. "Prepare your companies! We're going across!"

The big raft that had stranded Miles and Baldwin for most of Sunday was manned with the first dozen courageous soldiers. They pushed off, to the buoyant cheers of the rest. Every man on the raft pulled their craft into the Missouri's current, hand over hand on that inch-thick lifeline connecting them to both banks. Away from the bank, as the river grew all the stronger and the ice floes became all the larger—that rope might as well have been a strand of spider's silk.

The dozen were no more than a third of the way across the Missouri, steadying themselves, straining to keep control of the unwieldy raft against the chunks of ice colliding with their craft, when an unusually large piece bobbed to the surface upstream, spun around slowly, and began making its way for them. While the men on the raft grunted their exertion, those on shore cheered their efforts to pull themselves out of the way in time.

Then the ice struck with a terrible clatter, spinning itself and the raft around, to strike the raft on the opposite side before it started to creep and screech its way upon the raft as the soldiers scrambled, hanging on to the rope with their cold, frozen hands, shoving frantically at the block of ice with their feet.

To William Jackson the whole scene was comical in a way—to watch those soldiers fighting to keep that huge block of ice off the raft, struggling against the current that sought to shove it atop their raft. Comical indeed, had it not been that the lives of those twelve men could well be in forfeit at any moment.

Then, suddenly, the long raft gave a shuddering twist, its end dipping into the river as three of the men were left swinging helplessly from the rope, their legs dangling in air; the huge chunk of ice the size of a freight wagon groaned against the timbers, sliding off the raft.

As quickly the raft righted itself; the men on board lunged this way and that, slipping and falling in their struggles to bring it back under the shore-to-shore rope while others lunged out with their arms to grab hold of their comrades dangling from the line. Upstream more ice appeared, and the warnings were given from most every throat on shore. Then Baldwin himself was in the river up to his knees at the north bank, waving for all he could, signaling the raftsmen to turn about and return before lives were lost.

The dozen need no special urging. They pulled and groaned, struggling to haul themselves back to the north bank, where cheers erupted. But in the midst of the celebration Miles immediately went to Baldwin's shoulder, giving suggestions about how he would accomplish the crossing if it were up to him, offering advice on making changes in the raft's design, becoming the sort of nuisance that made William and

Robert chuckle as they continued to watch the comic opera for the rest of that afternoon.

In the end no further attempts were made to reach the south bank that Monday, but by twilight Miles turned away from Baldwin in frustration and ended up the day by calling together his own crew to begin construction on a raft of his own design.

At dawn on Tuesday the men continued their raft building as more snow began to fall. The surgeon reported that the thermometer had dipped to three below through the night, but the heavy layer of snow clouds helped the air rise above freezing by late afternoon.

Near midmorning the impatient colonel sent one of his staff with Robert Jackson and instructions to ride up the snowy road toward Carroll City to make contact with Captain Bennett's command. Later, despite the rising river and the increasing danger of large ice floes, Miles launched his raft. After a supreme test of muscle, might, and courage, the soldiers reached the south bank and deposited four of their number with orders to scout up Squaw Creek for sign of the hostiles.

On the twenty-ninth the combined efforts of Miles and Baldwin succeeded in getting no more than two loads of soldiers across the river with their rations and ammunition. After all that time and all that effort, fewer than fifty men built their fires, boiled their coffee, and prepared for the long winter night on the south side of the Missouri.

That evening beneath a cold, frigid sky twinkling with a million points of light, a courier arrived with word from Lieutenant Russell H. Day, garrisoned at Fort Peck with a contingent of messengers from the Sixth Infantry. From the way the general stomped and fumed there around his roaring fire, it was clear to William that the news was not good.

"Damn it all!" Miles bellowed to his officers and those gathered within hearing. "Appears that Sitting Bull's pulled a fast one on us!"

"Is he south of the river, where Snyder can get to him?" Baldwin inquired.

"No. This report says the Hunkpapa never moved west at all!" Miles fairly shrieked in fury and dismay. "The Yanktonais told Lieutenant Day that the Sitting Bull camp is some thirty miles *below* Fort Peck."

"Downriver?" asked Second Lieutenant Charles E. Hargous.

"Damn right. Somewhere on the Redwater. About halfway between Peck and Buford!"

First Lieutenant George W. Baird stated, "Then that means Snyder won't get a chance at them either."

"Exactly," Miles fumed, crumpling the foolscap message in his hand. "There's reports that Sitting Bull's at least a hundred seventy lodges strong now, expecting to hunt buffalo between the Missouri and the Yellowstone all winter. But what's worse than Sitting Bull pulling a fast one on us is that the Fort Peck Indians say the Hunkpapa village is moving south from our country toward the Powder."

"That's where they say Crazy Horse is wintering!" Baldwin cried.

"Exactly, Lieutenant. And if those two ever get together again, we'll have hell to pay," the colonel growled, flinging the crumpled dispatch into the fire. "Even if they don't rejoin . . . the fact that Sitting Bull is moving south, perhaps seeking to cross the Yellowstone, can bode no good for the Fifth."

"Why, General?" asked Hargous. "Shouldn't we be happy that we've made sure that Sitting Bull hasn't started north for Canada?"

Miles's eyes narrowed into slits. "No, Lieutenant. Because if Sitting Bull slips south of the Yellowstone, whether he joins Crazy Horse or not . . . it means that neither of them will be my prize. Instead—they'll likely fall right into the lap of George Crook!"

The following day the soldiers cheered one another at their breakfast fires with something William Jackson knew nothing of, banging their cups together and otherwise making merry beneath clearing skies.

"Happy National Thanksgiving Day!" they shouted to one another in celebration around the flames.

"A day to give thanks!" others would cry.

William looked at the Lakota half-breed named Bruguier and shrugged. "I'll give thanks they ain't asked me to go across that river."

"Not yet, they haven't," Big Leggings said.

Just after breakfast Miles called for scout George Johnson to carry another dispatch to Bennett at Carroll City while the rest of the command waited for the ice build up in the Missouri. Then around noon Robert Jackson and Lieutenant Bailey returned from Carroll City, having met Johnson on the road. Captain Bennett informed Miles that he had been successful in securing the trader's ammunition and would start back the following day, a Friday.

But the best news on that National Thanksgiving Day came from an unexpected source. Within the hearing of Nelson Miles, half-breed Robert Jackson just happened to mention to others that the Missouri was frozen solid no more than eighteen or so miles upriver.

Miles whirled on his heel, asking, "No farther than that?" Enthusiasm was back on his face.

Robert nodded.

"Must be near Fort Hawley," William instructed.

"Right near there, brother," Robert agreed.

"What's this Fort Hawley?" demanded the colonel.

"Old fur-trading post," William explained.

Miles asked, "Anyone still there?"

Wagging his head, William said, "Not recent. Everyone's been gone a long time. All gone. Empty place now."

Slapping his mittens together, Miles wheeled back to some of his staff. "Officers' call, Mr. Bailey! Lieutenant Baldwin—help Bailey get everyone in here now! We must make ready to break camp!"

"Where to, General?" Baldwin asked when he trotted up.

"Upriver to an abandoned post called Hawley," Miles declared, smiling in that dark beard of his. "I'm told the river's solid up there and we can cross tomorrow."

"C-cross tomorrow," Baldwin sputtered. "What about the rafts we've built—all that work . . . the men we've shipped to the other side, sir?"

"Yes, well," and a look of consternation clouded Miles's face. "Yes: see that we signal word for them to march upstream along the south bank, and we'll soon be reunited once we reach solid ice!"

Chapter 6

22 November–7 December 1876

Wasn't a lick of sense in pushing on east, Luther Kelly figured. Not with all the new snow falling to obliterate the tracks he and the other three had been following to see just where the Sioux might be scampering off to.

That Wednesday, the twenty-second, the four of them put Wolf Point at their backs and pointed their noses west, intending to do what they could to eat up that distance between them and Captain Snyder's battalion somewhere up the valley of the Big Dry.

Climbing the ridges to the south of the Missouri, the scouts kept to the high ground—the better to see over the surrounding countryside for great distances: watching not only for the soldier column, but wary for any of the Sioux sure to be in the area. But the only thing moving besides them that gray, somber day were some antelope cavorting atop the snowy heights.

Shadows were lengthening late that afternoon when Jim Woods spotted a half-dozen buffalo grazing down at the bottom of a bowl where a few cottonwood saplings promised the men would find a spring at best, some seep at worst. When Kelly's men agreed that there would be nothing finer than buffalo meat to roast at that evening's fire, Woods loped on down and dropped a two-year-old bull.

"Can't be too wise for us to be moving on now," John Johnston said.

Luther nodded, regarding the west. "Sun's headed to bed, and it sure wouldn't be healthy for us to show ourselves along the skyline after Jim's shot. We best camp in here."

After pulling the saddles and blankets from their horses, the men took out their small camp axes and began chopping down the smallest and most tender of the cottonwood saplings. From them the scouts trimmed the branches, then laid the trunks in a pile before their horses. Although cattle would most times chew on cottonwood buds in the spring, they wouldn't gnaw on the bark itself the way a horse would when hungry enough.

Stepping back, Kelly crossed his arms in satisfaction as their mounts took right to nibbling on the cottonwood. "Nothing a horse likes better than this here green bark of the yellow cottonwood, boys."

While Kelly and Billy Cross scrounged through the cottonwood grove for some squaw wood and kindling, Woods himself went to work on the butchering. Plainsman tradition dictated that the tongue and hide went to the man who had killed the animal. So with the tongue laid near the fire pit, Woods staked out the green hide near their fire, fur side up, right where he planned to make his bed for the night—then spread his blankets on that layer of thick insulation that would protect him from the cold ground.

By the time the first stars were twinkling into sight, the scouts had their peeled cottonwood wands prepared. From the ends of them hung juicy red pieces of buffalo the men suspended over the merry flames, grease dripping and sputtering into the fire. After dinner the coffee was boiled and the pipes came out as the air continued to cool, sliding past the freezing point.

The following morning the four were off at dawn without making breakfast, taking with them some of the cooked meat left over from last night's hearty feast. Upon reaching the valley of the Big Dry itself, Kelly's bunch finally discovered Snyder's trail poking its way up a northern branch. At that point the scouts decided they would rest some, giving their horses a

chance to graze on the thick bottomland grasses and themselves an opportunity to work on the cold meat in their sad-
dlebags.

Resuming their march up the branch of the Big Dry, they
entered a flat section of country, where they soon spotted a
distant horseman sitting still upon a ridgetop, watching their
progress. The scouts waved, hoping to receive some sign of
friendliness in return, but instead the horseman disappeared
over the far side of the hilltop.

"Injun or white man?" Woods asked.

"Weren't no Injun," Johnston surmised. "No feathers.
Didn't see me no shield."

Luther said, "White man would've come on down—don't
you figure, fellas?"

"Likely so," Woods agreed. "Best we keep our eyes
skinned here on out."

Not long after pushing on up Snyder's trail, at the base of
the ridge where they had spotted the lone horseman, the
scouts entered a rough, broken country slashed with brushy
ravines and cutbanks jaggedly scarring their way down from
the high ground.

A single shot suddenly rang out . . . then a ragged volley of rifle fire spat orange from nearby bushes just ahead of
them.

It was all Kelly and the others could do to control their
horses at that moment as the animals reared and kicked, doing
their best to twist about and flee. Cross and Luther were the
first to get their rifles up and pointed at the brush where the
gun smoke hung among the leafless branches. Both of them
fired.

From the vegetation across the coulee burst at least five
figures, breechclouts swaying like flags, feathers flapping as the
warriors turned tail and fled up a wide ravine.

Likely they've got their ponies hid up there, Luther
thought.

For the next few minutes the scouts loped up and down
that piece of broken ground, trying to find some way round to
get at the fleeing warriors—but in the end could not because
the ravine was too wide and deep to cross.

"They picked their spot good," Woods announced
breathlessly as they gathered once more.

Their eyes were still watchful and wary, their weapons still at the ready.

"Bet that son of a bitch we spotted back up yonder on top of the ridge give the rest of 'em the word we was coming through," Cross declared.

"A good spot for an ambush," Kelly agreed. "Place where they could get us close enough to do us all in—and be quick at it."

Johnston said, "I figger one of 'em got a itchy finger afore we was all in their trap."

"You can thank your lucky stars for that," Kelly told them. "If they'd all been patient men—"

"We'd all be *dead* men," Woods interrupted.

"C'mon, fellas," Kelly said, sawing his horse back to the northwest again. "Time we pushed hard to catch those soldiers. This country's turned out to be a mite less than friendly."

They didn't catch up to Snyder's battalion until the following evening, Friday, the twenty-fourth, far to the northwest up that tributary of the Big Dry. And for the next three days the column marched and camped, marched and camped, suffering the slush and mud during the day, then enduring the galling cold at night, without once encountering an Indian trail nor any sign of the warriors who had ambushed the scouts. On the twenty-seventh Snyder's battalion finally reached the rendezvous site at Black Buttes.

"It's like Sitting Bull's village just up and disappeared," Billy Cross said the night of the twenty-seventh at their fire.

"Maybeso they crossed over the Missouri," Johnston declared.

"We'd a'seed the place where they crossed, don't you figger?" Jim Woods argued.

"Doesn't make much sense, that much is true," Kelly explained. "If the Sitting Bull people were running west, why—one of these battalions should have bumped into 'em by now."

Woods slapped his knee, saying, "At least seen some hide or hair of 'em!"

On the following day, Tuesday, the twenty-eighth, Snyder ordered F and K companies to remain in camp while Irish-born Captain Edmond Butler was directed to lead C and D on a patrol up that north fork of the Big Dry with Kelly as their guide. Just past noon it began to snow, then quickly thickened into a howling storm before Butler's detail turned back to their bivouac, emerging ghostlike out of the whipping, cavorting snow behind their scout, who successfully brought them in without losing his way in the blizzard.

"You find anything?" Woods asked as Kelly dragged saddle and blanket to the ground.

Luther collapsed right beside his gear. "Not a feather, Jim. Can't tell you what we might've seen if the weather hadn't closed in on us."

Cross walked up to ask, "You think Sitting Bull's out there?"

Luther took a moment, then wagged his head. "I don't think we'll find him. Maybe Miles will. But as for us—I got a strong feeling we're poking down the wrong rabbit hole."

The fierce wind had sculpted the snow into huge icy drifts by dawn the following morning. Nonetheless, Snyder was of a mind to try to break a trail and continue his push north. His column struggled no more than two miles in more than five hours of grueling march. The captain conferred with Butler, then decided they would bivouac right there. At the order weary men fell to either side of their narrow foot trail hammered through the snow, collapsing back into the icy drifts, exhausted, shuddering with the tremendous cold as a relentless wind continued to blow ground snow about them.

On Thursday, the thirtieth, National Thanksgiving Day, Captain Snyder called Luther over to his windbreak formed by an outstretched gum poncho.

"Kelly, I want you to pick two men. Leave the others with us."

"You want me to go back out to scout for the Indians who aren't there?"

"I understand your position perfectly," Snyder replied. "And, frankly, I'm beginning to agree with you."

"Where are you sending me, if not to look for the Hunkpapa?"

"Find Miles," Snyder requested. "Maybe he's bumped into the hostiles north of the river for some reason and can't rejoin us here as he planned."

"You afraid he might have pitched into something more than he could handle?"

Snyder looked away and shrugged slightly. "All I know is that the time for our rendezvous here at Black Buttes has come and gone—and I have no idea where the general is."

"How long can you hang in here, Captain?" Kelly asked.

"My quartermaster sergeant tells me we're running low on everything. I can cut the men's rations—but we're damn well out of forage for the stock already."

"Which means you'll have to turn back for the Tongue before too long."

"Give yourself two more days, Kelly." Snyder said it almost like a prayer as he shuddered, pulling his blanket more tightly under his chin. "Go see what you can find out about Miles—then get back here by December second."

On the evening of the thirtieth of November, Colonel Miles separated his command from a battalion he would have led by his most trusted officer. That night Frank Baldwin and Companies G, H, and I camped apart with their scout, Vic Smith. Just after sundown they drew their rations and the forage for their complement of six-mule teams, loading it and their ammunition into thirteen wagons, then spent their first night apart from the rest of the regiment.

Before dawn on the following morning, 1 December, Lieutenant Frank D. Baldwin led those three companies of 112 men beneath the light of a full moon, their noses pointed east on a chase after Sitting Bull's swelling camp of hostiles last reported to be gathering somewhere on the Redwater River . . . even if that chase would take him all the way to Fort Buford at the mouth of the Yellowstone.

There were no written orders. After seven years of serving Miles on the southern plains, the commander of the Fifth Infantry trusted Baldwin's judgment implicitly in the field. After all, Baldwin was a non–West Pointer, like himself. Forget all that politics and book learning, Miles believed. If he wanted a job done, turn it over to a man like Frank Baldwin: pure gumption, grit, and fighting tallow.

In the meantime Miles himself planned to continue upstream with the remaining two companies, A and E, along with the Napoleon gun, making for Fort Hawley, where he would cross the Missouri ice to the south bank, explore the upper drainage of the Big Dry until his rendezvous with Snyder's battalion. Together the two battalions would then march south to the Tongue River Cantonment for resupply.

Sloshing through thick mud, which at times turned into a quagmire of quicksand, forced to hack their way through a thick maze of brush and deep snowdrifts in those rough breaks north of the Missouri, Miles's battalion finally limped into bivouac late that Friday night after a torturous nineteen miles. At dawn the next morning the command continued on upstream, cutting a path through the underbrush for their wagons and digging out a serviceable road until they reached a point opposite Fort Hawley, abandoned for some seven years. After they had corduroyed the riverbank, the wagons and men crossed the groaning ice to the south bank.

For a few moments Miles dismounted to stand among the ruins of the post—now nothing more than a few charred timbers sticking from the new snow like blackened broken bones jutting from a wound, an iron stove broken and turning to rust, and the fort cemetery. Nelson removed his hat and silently mouthed the words of a short prayer as he stared at all those faded, graying, faceless wooden headboards leaning a'kilter between earth and sky.

With the crossing of the frozen Missouri at the Hawley ford complete, the column was immediately faced with a new predicament. On the south side of the river the banks rose like an abrupt wall before them.

At first Miles tried hitching a double team of twelve mules to one of the nearly empty wagons to get his supplies up the bluffs. Yet the animals could not struggle up the sharp-pitched trail. Left with little choice, the soldiers emptied the wagon beds once more, then removed the boxes from their running gear—so box, running gear, and small loads of supplies could be dragged up on ropes by the men working in concert with the mule teams. Even as cold as it was, what with the way the wind blustered at the top of the bluffs, the soldiers sweated their way through the lion's share of that day and into the coming of night.

By ten P.M. the battalion finally settled into their bivouac on the top of the prairie, high above the Missouri River among the pine and cedar that provided a little windbreak to their cookfires, where juicy slabs of venison roasted, in a spot the foot-sloggers affectionately named Camp Elevation.

As twilight deepened into night, the pickets were the first to spot some fires glowing on the north side of the river.

"In the morning," Miles told William Jackson, "I want you to find out if that is friend or foe."

"I think your captain—the one my brother Robert took to Carroll City."

Miles nodded glumly. "Yes, I suppose you're right, Jackson. What with the reports of Sitting Bull being far to the east of us, it's not very likely that he's camped over yonder, is it? Not when he's eluded me a second time in as many months."

Nelson was morose enough that night that he found it hard to sleep—thinking and rethinking how Sitting Bull had outsmarted him not just once, but twice now—brooding how chasing the Hunkpapa was like chasing after wisps of winter smoke. Close enough to smell his prey, near enough to see, perhaps, but nothing to grab hold of—not a damned thing in your hand once you opened it.

At dawn the next morning the men found the view glorious from that lofty plateau above the rugged Missouri Breaks. Everywhere ran the deepest of ravines and coulees, perpendicular bluffs and cotton-topped ridges, every landform striated with varicolored sandstone and draped in winter white. Here and there long borders of pine and cedar in emerald-green threaded across the landscape. Far to the northwest rose the snowcapped Little Rocky Mountains, while to the south and west in the cold, clear winter air stood the magnificent splendor of the Judith and Moccasin Mountains, beyond them the ever loftier Snowy range.

On south by east Miles led his column, trudging through the ankle-deep snow and icy drifts along the twisting ridgetop above the aptly named Crooked Creek before the column was forced into the valley to cross and recross the creekbed many times during the day. Curious deer bounded up along both sides of the march as the men continued downstream. Late in the afternoon of the fourth Captain Bennett's B Company finally rejoined Miles, having crossed the Missouri upriver that morning. Camp was made that night where the men could find shelter from the wind.

Late the following morning of the fifth, Miles reached the

mouth of Crooked Creek in the lush, timbered, grassy valley
of the Musselshell River. While hunting details were sent out,
Miles dispatched the Jackson brothers to press upstream to
determine the best route while the colonel saw the column
across the thick ice on the Musselshell.

Early in the afternoon the half-breed scouts delivered
their disappointing news to a frustrated Miles. Because of the
ruggedness of the country and the snow depth they had encountered farther up the Musselshell, the soldier column
would have to turn back to the Missouri. Once on the south
bank, they would then continue along the river until reaching
the mouth of Squaw Creek.

It was there that the going became even tougher. Not only
were the teams and wagons breaking through the thin ice
crusting every little shaded slough, but now some of the men
were forced to use spades and picks to carve a crude road out
of the side of a bluff for their wagons, while the rest of the
soldiers unloaded those wagons and hauled on their backs
what supplies they had left them up the steep sides of the bluff
like a team of industrious ants at a country-fair picnic. Other
men somehow persuaded the balky mules to pull the wagons
up the precarious slopes by sheer muscle and rope power
alone. It took the last of them until after sundown to reach the
top of the prairie once more—putting no more than seven
short miles behind them for the day.

On the sixth the men dropped down into more solid terrain in the Squaw Creek drainage, realizing that their forage
for the wagon stock was running desperately low. Miles overheard a lot of the grumbling as both officers and enlisted men
worried with the darkening skies, knowing that they weren't
prepared to sit out any more bad weather, realizing that another snowstorm just might do them in.

Shortly past midday on the seventh, Miles brought his
command into sight of the Black Buttes rising just beyond the
grassy, wooded valley of Big Dry Creek. Here the Jackson
brothers returned with more depressing news for the colonel.
They had discovered evidence that Snyder's battalion had been
there—and gone. From the swath cut through the thick, tall
buffalo grass, it was clear that Snyder's four companies had
already turned southeast from the Buttes and were making for
the cantonment.

That night as the wind howled and smelled of snow, Nelson Miles trudged through the camp where there was little cheer and not nearly enough firewood. While the men did what they could to clear away more than a foot of snow, the temperature continued to plummet. It was clear his soldiers were weary of the march, exhausted after the superhuman effort to cut roads and haul wagons up the sheer face of the ridges, hungry and tired and depressed in spirit.

As the first few icy flakes danced through the air, Miles decided he could ask no more of his men.

Come morning, he would lead them back to the Tongue River.

Chapter 7

2–7 December 1876

Yellowstone Kelly didn't end up finding Miles on Crooked Creek in those two days that Captain Snyder had allotted him. That night of the thirtieth he slept cold and alone before starting back for the battalion in the gray light of dawn that first day of December.

On the second Kelly led the battalion out at first light, pushing south by east for the valley of the Big Dry, where Snyder abandoned a wagon because of a broken axle and worn-out mules. Herding the balky animals on with his little column, the captain pressed the men to put as much country behind them as they could, what with the dwindling rations and forage staring them in the face.

Over those next three days the mules and men visibly slowed their pace not only due to the deepening snow and rugged nature of the country, but to their worsening health as well. The march dragged slower and slower until Snyder grew extremely alarmed that he would not be able to force-march the men and animals all the way back to the cantonment.

"Kelly—grain up the best pair of horses we have," the captain told the scout on the fifth. "Pick another man sure to make it with you . . ."

"Just in case one of us doesn't, Captain?"

Snyder nodded. "We still don't know where the hell Sitting Bull is, and you two might run right into a pack of them. I want . . . These men all need one of you to make it back to our base."

"What do you want me to tell them at the post?"

"Just to send back with you all that they can spare in the way of rations for man and beast, Kelly." Then the captain's hollow eyes began to mist over as he held out his hand. "I wish you God's speed."

He shook Snyder's hand and smiled in that bushy, unkempt beard. "Don't you worry none now, Captain. I won't need any luck. You just keep an eye out for me on the skyline. I'll get those supplies for you. Don't you worry none about that."

Leading his two orderlies, four mounted soldiers, thirteen wagon drivers, and ninety-three foot soldiers, Lieutenant Frank D. Baldwin and his scout, Vic Smith, had backtracked uneventfully with his weakening mules all the way to Fort Peck, where on the afternoon of 6 December he learned from his advance scout, Johnny Bruguier, that the Hunkpapa were camped no more than fifteen miles east of the agency on Porcupine Creek, north of the Missouri. Although the sun would soon be setting, Baldwin immediately decided to press on.

His quarry was within reach. No more than a matter of miles and hours now. If he could only be the one to capture Sitting Bull—

What a feather in his cap that would be!

"I want you to carry word to General Miles," he instructed the half-breed as he scribbled out a hurried message.

If I thought you could arrive here in time I would wait . . . but [I] am afraid the chance will be lost. . . . I shall start this evening and endeavor to reach the main camp in time to pitch in early in the morning.

Slit-eyed, Bruguier asked, "Soon the Bear Coat takes the rope from my neck, right?"

For a moment Frank studied the half-breed's face, feeling almost sad for the man who was wanted for murder among the white people, a man who had just turned his back on the Indians who had taken him in as one of their own.

"Yeah," Baldwin replied. "You've done what you promised you would a few days back. Now the general will do what he said he would—since you've told me exactly where I'll find Sitting Bull."

As the shadows lengthened, Baldwin watched Bruguier and scout Billy Cross mount up and head west with his message to Miles that he was about to engage the Hunkpapa. Then the thirty-four-year-old veteran of the Civil War went against the strong feelings of his officers and prepared for his assault on the Sioux.

"All due respect, sir," said Second Lieutenant David Q. Rousseau, "we don't know what size of opposing force we're going to confront."

Baldwin bristled at the criticism from the West Pointers. He glared at the rest in turn. "What say the rest of you?"

"Permission to speak honestly?" asked Second Lieutenant Frank S. Hinkle.

"Permission, Mr. Hinkle."

"Considering the condition of the men and the weather, not knowing the strength of our enemy"—and then he paused—"I would recommend we send out scouts first, sir."

Baldwin boldly asked them, "Do any of you agree with me that we should strike before Sitting Bull's village slips away?"

None of the other three officers spoke up.

"Very well, then," Baldwin sighed. "You have your orders. We're going after the Hunkpapa—tonight."

In the next hour he had his men unhitch the wagon teams and off-load eighteen thousand rounds for the Springfields onto his mule train. In addition he supplied a hundred rounds to be carried by every one of his 112 men. After putting his last three bags of oats for the mules in the packs, he issued two days' rations for the men to carry in their haversacks suspended over their shoulders.

By eight P.M. the lieutenant climbed back into his saddle, formed his foot soldiers into column, and headed east in the dark, forcing their way through more than two feet of snow. If he managed to make good time crossing that winter wilder-

ness, his three companies could attack the Hunkpapa camp
sometime just after dawn.

As a young man from Michigan, Baldwin had enlisted in
the Union Army in 1861 and quickly won a commission. He
had served in Sherman's campaigns down in the Carolinas
and in Georgia. At one point he was captured by the Confederates, held for a time at Libby Prison in Richmond, then was
released in a prisoner exchange. He went back to active service, fought on, was captured and released a second time.

After Appomattox a restless Baldwin was assigned to various stations in the west until he found a home with the Fifth
Infantry and Nelson A. Miles. Time and again during the Red
River War against the southern tribes, he served Miles as chief
of scouts, winning numerous commendations for gallantry,
and received several brevet promotions. It was Baldwin's gutsy
wagon-train raid on Gray Beard's camp at McClellan Creek
that secured the release of the two youngest German sisters in
November of 1874.

But even that would pale compared to the glory to be
heaped on the shoulders of the man who captured Sitting
Bull. How proud his Alice would be of him, though she had
repeatedly begged him to leave the army. Yet in Baldwin flickered the same desire that burned bright in Miles. Not to mention all those hopes and dreams Frank committed to the pages
of his shirt-pocket diary every day.

As cold stars twinkled overhead, the men trudged through
snow some two feet on the level, an icy crust scraping and
gouging their shins. On into the deepening darkness they
struggled, following the Missouri down to the mouth of Milk
River. In the starry darkness about seven miles east of the
agency on the Fort Buford Road the column suddenly confronted several small bands of friendlies frightened by Sitting
Bull's swelling village and the arriving soldiers, hurrying now
toward Fort Peck.

Baldwin grew elated at the prospect of finding the
Hunkpapa camp on the north side of the Missouri. As they
marched on through the night, the freezing air carried with it
the faint hint of woodsmoke. The hostile camp could not be
far now.

Baldwin was certain he would soon be staring Sitting Bull
in the eye.

•   •   •

"The soldiers are near!"

Sitting Bull scrambled to his feet at that first cry from outside, but he was barely standing when his lodge door was thrust aside and in leaped his adopted brother.

"Jumping Bull!"

"My brother," the warrior said breathlessly, "forgive my discourtesy."

His eyes quickly darted around the crowded circle. In this lodge, as in every lodge and every tent the Hunkpapa bands still possessed, the people were hunkered close this winter. And in the last few days even more had come to stand with Sitting Bull as it became clear the soldiers were once more come to raid and burn and kill. Just three suns ago, ten-times-nine more lodges had joined the growing camp.

Sitting Bull asked, "Do you bring this alarm of soldiers?"

"Yes," Jumping Bull replied, pulling his hands from the two wool-blanket mittens and rubbing them over the fire. "The soldiers—they must know where we are. They are marching right for us."

"The one you trusted," growled Lame Red Skirt from the far side of the fire. "Big Leggings."

"Yes," Sitting Bull said dolefully. "I should have let you kill him when he came among us."

Jumping Bull whirled on Lame Red Skirt. "You were an old woman ready to surrender when Sitting Bull was standing alone against the Bear Coat. Your anger at Big Leggings does nothing to help us now, Lame Red Skirt!"

Sitting Bull watched the words strike the war chief like a quirt lash across the cheek. Lame Red Skirt's eyes flared, but the Bull put out a hand to motion him to keep his seat. "Tell me where the soldiers are."

"South," Jumping Bull declared, his eyes coming back from the humiliated war chief. "They are near the mouth of the Milk River."

"How is it you know this?" Black Moon demanded.

"At sundown last night the soldiers talked with Big Leggings at the agency."

"Were you there?" Lame Red Skirt asked.

"No, but some Yanktonais were," Jumping Bull said.

"They came in search of me, found me out hunting, then told me the soldiers were marching—even now into the dark of night."

"That never means any good will come of the next few days," Sitting Bull commented quietly. His fingers slowly played up and down one braid.

"I went to see for myself, brother," Jumping Bull continued. "In the dark at the agency, and bundled in my blanket coat, I must have been taken by the soldiers as one of their own scouts. I came up behind the *wasicu,* rode past the long string of their walk-a-heaps, and even passed right by the soldier chief leading them this way."

Suddenly Sitting Bull was decisive. "Let there be no delay! Tell everyone we are leaving. Now! Take down the lodges and tents. Men must ready their weapons to protect the women and children if the soldiers find us while we escape in the dark."

Already the chiefs were moving from his lodge with the Bull's instructions. In minutes the covers were slipping from the lodgepoles and the travois attached to rib-gaunt ponies were loaded with what the Hunkpapa still possessed.

In less time than it takes for a hungry man to eat his breakfast, the warrior bands who owed allegiance to Sitting Bull had slipped away from the mouth of Porcupine Creek, following the east bank of the Milk toward the frozen *Minisose.*

There in the predawn darkness of 7 December they planned to cross to the south bank a few at a time, horses and dogs, women, children, and old ones first. As the temperature had continued to drop over the last few days, new ice had formed on the river. For now the black of night rumbled with the muffled sounds of frightened children crying, women wailing their despair at being driven from their homes once more, and old men resolutely chanting their strong-heart songs to give courage to the young ones who would cover their retreat.

Those sounds seemed to be swallowed by the cold, clear night, buried beneath the creak and groan of the new snow as it strained beneath the weight of so many hooves, so many moccasins.

As the warriors took up positions in the timbered breaks

overlooking the crossing so they could delay the soldiers sure to come . . . the first of the Sitting Bull band stepped out of the skeletal trees, onto the icy *Minisose* River, and began to flee south toward the rugged, broken countryside, into the darkness, into a frightening unknown once more.

"Why the hell didn't any of you say anything?" Frank Baldwin demanded, feeling his gorge rise.

He glared at his junior officers and noncoms, those men who nervously shifted from foot to foot in the cold and the snow. The rising wind was brutal, and it smelled of even more snow here after midnight in the darkness of 7 December as Baldwin's battalion stood shivering on the north bank of the Missouri River.

He grew more frustrated because of their silence, because of the darkness of the night, because of this bone-numbing cold that made even a strong man want to lie down and go to sleep and never wake up again . . . because he had just been told by one of his new scouts, eighteen-year-old Joe Culbertson, that they had likely passed by the enemy village in the dark less than an hour ago.

"All right," Baldwin said quietly, fighting down his own despair at letting the Hunkpapa slip through his fingers. "Let's turn this battalion about and see if we can't still catch the Sioux napping."

Culbertson and Edward Lambert, hired on by Baldwin just hours ago at Fort Peck, both led the column toward the bottomland where the Porcupine dumped into the Milk River. Even in the snowy darkness as Baldwin led his cautious troops into the village, they could tell it was abandoned. The cold, quiet night made the men spooky about an ambush. So quiet that Frank knew better. Plain too that the Hunkpapa had fled in very great haste. Fires still smoldered and some actually burned. Camp gear and hides lay scattered and abandoned on their route of retreat.

Baldwin glared into the distance along that trail taken by the fleeing Sioux toward the Missouri—a path more than thirty feet wide—knowing his quarry expected him to follow. Sensing the irresistible urge to go charging after . . . knowing that sort of thing had killed many a soldier and their impetuous officers.

"Look there, men!" he called out above the soldiers as his horse stamped and pawed at the snow, snorting jets of frost from its wide nostrils. "We can see where they've gone. A wide trail for us to follow. Put out flankers and see that we aren't surprised. Move out!"

G, H, and I companies found the going much easier on the trail now, what with all the hooves and feet that had beaten down the snow in that hasty retreat toward the frozen Missouri. Baldwin marched them until they reached the Milk River just after three A.M., where he allowed them to fall out and prepare a meal. If he was going to keep his men up and possibly pitching into a fight, then they best have something in their bellies.

Just before dawn, as the lieutenant stood staring at the faint outline of the bluffs on the south side of the river, yelps and screeches made the hair stand on the back of his neck.

At first fearing they had stumbled into an attack, he ordered his officers to prepare the men to face a frontal assault, moving some soldiers here, deploying others there, to protect his flanks. But for all the alarm it turned out to be only a dozen or so cocky warriors racing past the column in an attempt to spook the mules in his supply train. Rifles cracked and men bellowed as the warriors sang out their courage. While mules brayed, the last of the shots died and the warriors were gone. At least one of them lay across the withers of his pony as the Hunkpapa disappeared through the timber.

"We got one, sir!" a voice in the darkness boasted.

"I saw it, soldier," Frank replied. "Son of a bitch is riding off."

"Must'a got us two of 'em, Lieutenant," an old veteran asserted. "The boys cutting the hair off a body back yonder right now."

"We got two of 'em, did we?" Baldwin said, taking what small satisfaction he could.

Still, he could not allow his men to tarry long. Baldwin got them re-formed and moving out once more within a matter of moments, pushing on for the river. They didn't have far to go.

At the banks of the frozen Missouri he halted his battalion and gave them permission to fall out, to make themselves as comfortable as they could without starting any fires in these

coldest moments of the day. Then Baldwin turned to look east
a moment, searching the horizon for that gray band foretelling
sunrise.

"If we're going to catch Sitting Bull," Baldwin vowed,
"then let it be this day, gentlemen."

A horseman loomed out of the darkness. Culbertson.

"General—the Yanktons—there's at least four camps of
'em back there to the north."

"What of them?"

"Figgered you oughtta know," the young man replied.
"There's Injuns you're hunting, and Injuns you're not."

He chewed his lip in frustration. "How close?"

The young scout threw his thumb over his shoulder. "Not
far."

Muttering something to himself, Baldwin called his officers together and gave them a final, strict order. "I've just
learned we've got some friendly agency bands camped nearby.
Inform your men that there'll be hell to pay if they fire on the
Yanktons. Make sure of your enemy. Dismissed."

After deploying his 112 men along the riverbank—G
Company taking up the left flank and I on the right, with H to
act as the rear guard—the lieutenant waited for the sky to
lighten, for the Sioux to do something, anything. Pacing and
watching the eastern horizon, he would then turn and gaze to
the west for a few minutes.

He didn't have long to wait.

Baldwin and some others suddenly saw them—out there
on the ice. Dim forms moving slowly in the murky dawn light:
the rear guard of the Hunkpapa still making its crossing of the
river.

Now his men were beginning to stir. In the ashen darkness they could just begin to make out the ghostly, shadowy
images of the enemy too. Farther still, beyond the warriors,
against the stark grayish-white of the hillsides, Frank could
discern the winding caravan of the women and children: the
rest of the village on the run.

Sitting Bull was at hand!

Baldwin turned so fast, so suddenly in the snow, that he
nearly stumbled. His eyes shooting over the men, his officers,
determining who was closest to the bank.

"Battalion!" he bellowed as he lunged into the saddle,

then leaped his horse down by the edge of the ice himself, waving them on as he rode parallel to the river—pointing at the Hunkpapa rear guard. "There's the enemy! Follow me—on the double!"

At once the entire line of his skirmishers were hustling out of the trees back to the trampled Fort Buford Road, trudging, stomping, stumbling upriver through the snow. As he neared the mouth of Bark Creek, the lieutenant halted his men, watching the village scurrying into the bare timber on the far side of the frozen Missouri.

"Culbertson," he instructed, "I want you to take these two men—make a crossing and see what you can find out about the enemy's position on the south bank."

He watched the scout motion to the pair of mounted infantrymen, then move down to the trampled crossing.

Baldwin said to his officers, "Tell your men they may fall out and fix breakfast while we're waiting for our scouts to return."

Chapter 8

7 December 1876

As the soldiers began to snap dry branches off the bare cottonwood, the lieutenant turned to watch the three horsemen cautiously pick their way across the ice. Minutes passed as Culbertson followed in the wake of the Hunkpapa village. Then, just as the trio neared the south bank, rifle fire erupted from the far trees. Orange flames spewed from the Sioux guns as the three riders fought to control their horses, wheeling and whipping them back across the frozen river.

Frank Baldwin was back up the north bank himself, yelling among the men clambering to their feet, scooping up their weapons. "Companies form up, goddammit! Volley fire by platoon! First squads into position—*now!*"

As soon as the initial dozen soldiers from G and I dropped to their knees, threw those long Springfields to their shoulders, and pulled the trigger on command, the rest of the two companies spread out in a ragged skirmish formation, prepared to move forward and fire their volleys.

"H Company!" Baldwin hollered. "Lieutenant Hinkle!"

"Sir?" the officer came huffing up.

"Bring your men up through the lines and advance across the river at all possible haste. Smith—I want you with them!"

Hinkle glanced at the civilian scout, then at the south side of the Missouri, before turning back to gaze at Baldwin. "Charge the far bank, Lieutenant?"

"Yes, by God! Drive those goddamned redskins from the timber over there!"

The constant crack of the lighter carbines was growing now, broken by the intermittent boom of the infantry Long Toms—heavy .45-caliber weapons that could shove a lead bullet across a good distance, and with impact.

"Very good, sir!" Hinkle replied, turning and wheeling away. "H Company—form up!"

"Keep at them, boys!" Frank bellowed as he wrenched the horse around, kicking it back up the bank toward the other two companies, who formed a disorderly line of foot soldiers clustered in the cottonwoods. "Pin those bastards down until H can cross the river!"

North and south the firing continued as the other officers barked their orders and the men shuffled back and forth along the skirmish line on their frozen feet. Frank Hinkle's H Company pushed through them on the right, moving onto the ice, double-timing it across the Missouri, still wobbly on cold, unforgiving legs, muttering their curses or their thanks to be moving again. For whatever reason it was, they were sure to be warm again real soon.

The timber on the south bank exploded with even more fire as H Company advanced, returning fire. Then slowed to a walk now as they ejected one shell and slammed home another. Slowing more, reloading, inching forward as they reloaded. Then, as Frank Baldwin watched, Hinkle's men were scrambling up the south bank.

By damn, they must have driven the warriors off!

At that moment Baldwin became certain his battalion could overwhelm this rear guard and have those warriors routed. That accomplished, it would only be a matter of chasing after the fleeing village scattering in those hills yonder. A footrace . . . just him and Sitting Bull.

More confident now, Baldwin brought I Company together to his right and G to act as reserve for H Company in the thick of things.

The minutes passed, and the firing grew hotter. Then the better part of a half hour slipped by before he suddenly heard a massive amount of rifle fire erupt from the far bank. Within moments he saw the first of Hinkle's men appearing again out of the timber, slowly being forced back to the river again. From the sheer number of muzzle flashes, it was easy to tell that the rear-guard warriors had been reinforced—now that the women and children were safely on their way.

"Pull back!" he hollered across the Missouri.

But he didn't have to give that order to the men of H Company. They had been in the timber and against the hillsides, close to the enemy. Baldwin didn't need to tell them this was their one and only chance to pull back or be swallowed up whole.

Hell—with as many warriors as there were swarming down the ridges toward the river crossing, streaming out of the timber after Hinkle's men, Baldwin felt his stomach pinch with genuine apprehension.

From the looks of it, at that moment the Sioux had him outnumbered four, maybe as many as five, to one. And they had his men on the run.

Baldwin was in among I and G, ordering the rest of his men to fire over the heads of H Company to try holding back the countercharging Hunkpapa. Screaming warriors. Screeching red devils. Yelping as they drove the soldiers across the ice. The first few of Hinkle's company were getting close enough that Baldwin could see the fear on their faces.

"They laid a trap for us!"

The panic was quick to spread through the battalion.

"Trap us like they done to Custer!"

In the gray light of predawn the shadows of the enemy horsemen and those warriors fighting afoot on the frozen river seemed ghostlike and ethereal to Baldwin: unreal, with a quality of everywhere at once as the bullets from their weapons smacked through the snow-laden branches of the cottonwood and yellow pine.

More and more of that red rear guard exploded off the far bank, lining themselves along the shore as they advanced, returning shot for shot in a brisk firing that bogged down Baldwin's battalion for the rest of that morning near the mouth of Bark Creek. Not getting to chase Sitting Bull nettled Frank like an itch he couldn't scratch. His stomach churned in fury just listening to that rifle fire from the enemy on the far bank.

Winchesters, Henrys . . . government-supplied rifles, firing government-supplied ammunition.

Hour by hour, ever so steadily, that pressure from the Sioux continued to mount. All along his front Baldwin listened to the reports of his officers as the skirmishing heated up. The Sioux were too strong. As simple as that. And now in the gray light of early morning he could see that the enemy was intent on crossing over, upriver and down, slinking past his battalion on both flanks.

"Sir!"

Baldwin wheeled on his heel.

The soldier reported, "Sir, the Yanktonais—they just showed up at our rear!"

"They're shooting at us?"

"N-no, sir. No shooting yet."

"Damn," Baldwin muttered. "Tell Lieutenant Rousseau to turn his men around and hold those Yanktonais where they are. Let there be no doubt that he will fire on the Yanktonais if they do not withdraw immediately. I repeat: if they make any trouble—shoot. Understood?"

The soldier nodded, saluted, and dashed off through the deep snow that swirled up in cascades around his knees.

Now not only did he have the Hunkpapa hostiles to worry about on his front, but he had these Yanktonais to worry about at his rear. Although they were considered friendly upriver at their agency, he wasn't about to gamble that the red bastards wouldn't leap at this chance to help out their distant relatives.

"Damn!" he muttered under his breath.

He had been surprised, a third of his men caught in the open on the frozen Missouri, with no telling just how many were facing him and no telling how many ready to jump his rear.

Jesus! What a dilemma.

If he pursued, he had only two companies to engage the hostiles, because one company had to watch their rear for the Yanktonais.

And if he countercharged and forced his way across the frozen Missouri, engaging the hostiles in close quarters . . . what if it turned out he had bitten off more than his three companies could chew? After all, he remembered suddenly, there had been rumors at Fort Peck that Sitting Bull now had close to two hundred lodges gathered around him once more—which made for some six hundred warriors.

After he had limped away from the Yellowstone with no more than thirty lodges only a month ago!

The firing was growing steadily heavier on his front. The Sioux were again attempting another sweep across the Missouri on his left flank, but I Company was holding strong. For how long, no man could say right then.

What if he pushed back and got his men over to that south bank, then got them pinned down and the river ice broke up again? His battalion would be cut off from their supply base at Fort Peck—burdened with their wounded and hamstrung by a limited supply of ammunition. It could be a Little Bighorn all over again.

"Holy Mary, Mother of Grace."

Baldwin listened to a nearby soldier from Lyman's I Company begin reciting his rosary. And then Frank knew what he had to do.

He had no choice but to retreat.

The very word caught in his throat the way a chicken bone might get stuck in a dog's gullet.

He turned and looked upstream, then down. And once he had spotted the right place, he remembered that his duty lay not just to his commander; he was the sort of soldier who knew his duty rested with his men.

He could hear them cry out in fear or frustration, hear the old files curse, doing what they could to buck up the shavetails as the bullets whistled in among them. Frank owed these men more than to let them get chewed up like Custer's bunch.

"Withdraw!" he suddenly bellowed, whipping his horse around and shouting it again.

Many of the men turned around to look at Baldwin, surprised.

Pointing downriver, he gave his order. "To the high ground!"

"The high ground!" a sergeant repeated somewhere upstream on the right flank. "You heard the lieutenant—now, get your ever-living arses humping for the high-by-God ground!"

•   •   •

By some favor of fate's fickle hand, Baldwin's battalion made it to that thumb of high bluff on the north bank, fighting their way through the thick, leafless brush as much as they fought a rear-guard action against the warriors who dared venture out on the ice and those who kept up a continuous barrage from the far bank.

At the top the lieutenant spun around on those first few who followed him. "Breastworks!"

That one-word order was immediately taken up by other officers, the sergeants directing their men to drag what logs, deadfall, and river trash they could get up the icy slope behind them. In less than twenty minutes they had themselves a substantial barrier that would stop many of the Sioux bullets.

Yet as good as that accomplishment made him feel, Baldwin took a good look at his men. They had now gone more than twenty-four hours without sleep, without much rest to speak of. And their march hadn't been a country walk, either. If these men had been on their feet, they had been moving, and moving meant struggling through snow anywhere from their ankles all the way up to their knees.

No two ways about it—this battalion that had jumped the rear guard of Sitting Bull's fleeing village was at the end of its string: no sleep nor food in more than a day. There seemed to be no end to the torture as the temperature continued to drop.

"Gentlemen," Frank quietly instructed his fellow officers as they gathered about him, most kneeling wearily on one knee, "rotate the men in your companies. Put half at picket duty at the breastworks. Relieve the others for an hour to build fires and eat what they still have along in their haversacks."

"Thank God!" Lieutenant Hinkle gushed in a whisper. Then his eyes found Baldwin's, and there was a smile where before there had been only despair.

"Yes," Frank croaked, his voice cracking with emotion. The wind burned his eyes, making them water. "Thank God we got here when we did, gentlemen. If the men wish to sleep during their hour at ease, they can do so—but in an hour we rotate to allow our pickets to have a chance at the warmth of the fires, and something hot in their bellies."

"A little sleep," said Lieutenant Rousseau, "some coffee, and a hot fire. Why, there ain't nothing can go wrong now, sir!"

Throughout the rest of that morning and into the afternoon the Sioux ventured forth from time to time to try the stalwart soldiers in their riverbank fortress. Most times the warriors scampered back out of range whenever a platoon here or there fired a volley, scattering the enemy like a covey of flushed quail. It was cold work, lying there in the snow, hunkered down behind the cottonwood deadfall, watching the icy river and that far bank, shivering with one's rifle cradled between one's arms—teeth chattering uncontrollably as the thermometer continued to slide past zero.

Then, at midafternoon, the worst that could happen loomed on the lowering western horizon. For long minutes the soldiers watched the dark front race closer and closer as the sky seemed to drop visibly with that incoming wave of grayish-white clouds. The first flakes they spat were icy, like shards of splintered glass hurled against the men, stinging their faces and flesh as they hunkered down in the collars of their wool coats, making themselves as small as they could behind the breastworks walls as the wind gave its call.

In the space of twenty minutes a prairie blizzard suddenly howled about them.

Should a man find he could stand to open his eyes in that gale of icy splinters, he discovered his visibility cut to less than ten feet, if that far. Frosty, frozen snow built up layer by layer on the western side of their fortress, thickly crusting the windward side of every hat, face, and coat until it looked as if Baldwin's battalion had been given half a coating of whitewash.

By the time Frank stared down at the face of the turnip pocket watch trembling in his mitten—seeing the hands closing on five o'clock in the waning daylight—he finally realized it had been more than half an hour since the Sioux had last fired at his position.

"Companies, report your status!" he cried out against the wailing of the rising gusts, turning his back to the wind that shouldered him this way, then that.

"I Company, left flank, Lieutenant," Lyman's voice cried out downstream. "No sign of the enemy from here!"

"Company G," came the call from Rousseau near the center of their breastworks. "No firing on our position, Lieutenant!"

"H Company, sir!" Hinkle's voice sang out from Frank's right as Baldwin turned slowly into the wind now, the better to hear the report. "Not a goddamned redskin in sight."

Then an old sergeant hollered from among H Company's soldiers, "And we ain't seen one of them bastards on the far bank in over a hour—pardon my French, sir!"

"You're damn well excused, Sergeant!" Baldwin declared. "Officers' call! Officers' call!"

They came out of the swirling, brutally icy mist to surround him like half-white, half-woolen ghosts, shivering and stamping, slapping their arms around themselves, most faces no more than a pair of eyes peeking out from above a wool muffler.

With one of his muskrat gauntlets Baldwin pulled down his thick scarf so he could speak again. "Gentlemen—I'm of the mind that the Hunkpapa are no longer a threat should we elect to retreat from our breastworks."

"W-where to, Lieutenant?" Hinkle asked plaintively.

"Only one place to go, men."

Rousseau inquired, "Back to Fort Peck?"

He turned to answer the officer. "That's right. We don't have near enough food, nor did we bring any shelters along. I'm afraid our fires won't last much longer in this wind. And our steward tells me the mercury in his thermometer's frozen at the bottom of the bulb. That means it's forty below . . . or worse. So I've come to the decision that if we don't move now—we never will get out."

"N-never . . . never get out?"

Baldwin spoke more quietly now. "I don't want any of you to alarm your men, but I've been told these high-plains blizzards can last two—maybe three—days."

Hinkle tucked his head against the wind, saying, "W-we'd be dead by then, sir!"

"That's why I want you to prepare your men to move out," Frank explained. "The first thing is for your companies to use what fires we still have going so the men can cook and eat all the food that's left among your outfits."

Rousseau shook his head. "You want us to eat, sir? B-begging pardon—"

"Yes, every man must stuff himself until he can eat no more," Baldwin said emphatically. "Your lives may depend upon just how much food you have in your belly to keep the furnace going inside once we start our return march . . . which means facing into that wind."

The officers knotted around him began to murmur and nod, understanding.

"And . . . ," Baldwin started, then paused a moment as he struggled with the thick ball of sentiment at the back of his throat, "I want each of you to tell your companies how proud I am of them this day. How *damned* proud I am to be leading this battalion."

"P-proud, s-sir?" Rousseau asked in a quaky voice, teeth chattering.

"Yes," Frank replied. "Tell all the men they can be most proud of themselves for driving the enemy out of its village and into this terrible storm. Tell them they've held off the warriors who butchered Custer's command. And . . . tell your men they've started the beginning of the end for Sitting Bull and the rest of Custer's murderers."

Chapter 9

7 December 1876

Ever since the death of his friend, Mitch Bouyer, at the hands of the Lakota last summer at the Greasy Grass, Tom Leforge had been performing the duties of guide and interpreter around the old Crow agency. Like Bouyer, Leforge was a squaw man, known to his adopted tribe as Horse Rider.

In early fall he had ridden with "Braided Beard" Crook when the army went looking for the Indians who had slaughtered Custer's soldiers. But after the sour-tasting victory at Slim Buttes, when Crook's campaign fizzled in the relentless autumn rains and they had to survive on horse meat, Tom had ridden back home to his wife, Cherry.

Now he poured himself another cup of that awful rebrewed coffee the soldiers made for themselves here at the Tongue River post. Leforge carried it to the frosted window and peered out at the winter night, blowing steam off the top of his coffee tin. Outside, a real prairie norther was whipping itself up. Folks from back east would call it a blizzard.

But out here they just called it winter hell.

As Leforge blew on the surface of his coffee, the window-pane clouded up momentarily, and when it slowly began to clear, the first thing Tom saw was his reflection in the glass.

Yes, some might call him a squaw man. But those were

the sort of men who had never come to the Yellowstone Valley, never spent any time among the River Crow, the sort of man to whom money was more important than happiness. Tom Leforge was a happy man with a beautiful wife and a young son to boot.

That autumn in Montana Territory the days were balmy and the nights crisp in preparation for winter. While Cherry crushed the chokecherries, pit and all, within her seasoned meat to make her special pemmican, Tom rocked their boy and talked over war exploits with warriors who visited their lodge—just generally busting at the seams, so happy was he.

Then a few weeks ago Second Lieutenant Charles E. Hargous had shown up with an impressive escort from the soldier post down the Yellowstone at the mouth of the Tongue.

"Leforge, I am looking for you!" the officer called out as soon as he spotted the squaw man among those crowding the agency grounds.

Not all that sure why the soldier would be looking for him, Leforge asked suspiciously, "What I supposed to done?"

"Seems you haven't done enough, Leforge," Hargous replied.

"I ain't done enough?"

The lieutenant licked his lips and said, "General Nelson Miles is requesting more Crow scouts. And I knew you'd be the man to act as interpreter—perhaps even lead the brigade yourself. If it makes any difference to your boys, General Miles says it's all right with him for 'em to bring their women and young'uns along too."

"Who you gonna fight this time?" Tom asked.

"Same as last time, Leforge—the Sioux."

"Got more soldiers than Custer this time?" he asked. "Got enough to kill off with hunger like Crook done?"

Hargous had just grinned at that, his eyes dancing over the buffalo-hide and canvas lodges a moment before coming back to rest on Leforge. "You don't need thousands of soldiers when you got the right man leading you. We've got the right man this time, Leforge."

The lieutenant went on to explain that Crook had retired from the field after his disastrous horse-meat march and might well not be putting another column into the field that season. Which was just as well, Hargous claimed, because the

Fifth Infantry was on the Yellowstone now and would stay on through the entire winter. They planned to pursue the hostile bands of Sitting Bull, giving the Sioux no rest. But to do that, Miles needed some scouts.

"How many?" Tom asked.

"How many can you round up quick?"

"Army pay the same as before?"

Hargous nodded. "Yep."

"Shouldn't take me more'n a day or two. You care to wait?"

"I'll wait, Leforge. You get me some good scouts for General Miles."

Two days later the whole outfit started for the Tongue River Cantonment to work for the Bear Coat and his walk-a-heaps. A few women ended up coming along with their men, but Cherry had decided to stay behind at the agency, with the boy being so young and all. Tom had been lonely for her ever since.

Working with the army had its good days of scouting and fighting, and it had its bad days of poor food, lousy coffee, cold and drafty cabins, and long periods of next to nothing to do. Back among the River Crow he could be chewing on a buffalo rib and drinking good agency coffee, not to mention that Cherry kept their lodge warm and homey no matter how hard the wolf-winds howled outside at the smoke flaps.

But here he stood at the frosted window, the winds beginning to whip and howl outside, thinking on the young Crow scout named Curly—remembering how the youngster had shown up across the river from Colonel John Gibbon's troops after the Greasy Grass fight, saying he was one of the last to see Custer alive. And that made him think again on his good friend—Mitch Bouyer, gone the way of the Star Road now, killed with Custer's bunch in the Long Hair's last fight.

Had it not been that Tom was nursing a broken collarbone, Gibbon would have chosen him to go off with Mitch and the other Crow scouts who had ridden with Custer into that hot valley . . . that one very good friend never rode out of.

Chances were, Tom knew, he would not be standing here this cold winter night looking through that pane of isinglass at the snow swirl across the sky, blotting out a thin rind of moon. Chances were damned good he would never dream of seeing Cherry ever again—much less holding her.

Chances were . . .

What the hell was that out there coming down to the ford on the north side of the river?

With his bare hand he quickly swiped the fog and frost from inside the windowpane. Tom blinked, squinting, trying to focus across the distance in those first terrifying moments of a winter blizzard settling upon the land.

A lone horseman!

Leforge watched him dismount stiffly and wave. And when he hadn't gotten the attention of the soldiers operating the ferry in the cold and the dark, the stranger pulled out his pistol and fired. The muzzle flash was bright as a falling star in that darkness. He fired again—then things began to happen. A trio of soldiers yanked and pulled, getting their ferry over to the north bank, where the horseman stepped on, then pulled his reluctant horse on behind him. The soldiers turned right around and started pulling for the south bank of the Yellowstone.

Over his shoulder Leforge called out, "Coffee, soldier."

"What's that?" asked the man with a three-day growth of beard.

"Get me another mug of your rotten coffee."

"Rotten, you say?"

Tom drained the last of his and slammed down the tin on the plank table behind him. Wiping his mouth with the back of his sleeve, he held out his other hand to receive the steaming cup the unkempt soldier had just poured. "Damn right it's rotten. But your coffee might just be what that rider out there needs right about now."

The horseman caused no little stir with his surprising arrival late that cold night as the blizzard thundered down upon the Yellowstone country. Soldiers bundled in their long coats, or with wool blankets pulled over their shoulders and heads, appeared here and there at the doors to the log barracks, some holding aloft candle lanterns and Betty lamps whipped in the sharp wind.

Then the rider's voice croaked from the darkness, "Word from Captain Snyder!"

"Snyder? Same Snyder out with General Miles?"

The horse and rider came closer. "The same, soldier."

Then an officer pushed into the flickering light to demand, "Who carries this word?"

"Kelly."

A moment more and the rider stepped into the light of lamps and a single sputtering torch wavering in the icy wind. Shards of frozen snow blew sideways. No longer was it coming down. It was snowing sideways.

Funny, Tom thought now. All along he had it figured for Yellowstone Kelly. Wasn't many a man who had the bottom and the grit to tackle a prairie blizzard. The horseman's entire face was a layer of ghostly frost, pale as a civilized-folks' bedsheet—eyebrows and eyelashes frozen solid. That huge bearskin hat of his was pulled down about as far as he could get it. Only the chertlike eyes were visible above the frost-caked beard until the horseman pulled away the length of muffler wrapped from chin to nose.

"Here—you could use this, Kelly." Tom stepped through the others, holding up the coffee tin, a wispy banner of steam trailing off the dark, glittering surface of the liquid.

Dropping his reins, Kelly accepted the tin, cupping it in both his horsehide gauntlets. Blowing the steam off quickly, he brought it to his lips as the snowstorm grew in intensity around them and the soldier fiddle-footed in the cold, anxious to know what was news with Miles and his bunch. The steam went a long way to melting the frost on his mustache, turning it from white to auburn, drops of water forming on the whiskers, then spilling into his cup.

"B-bless you, Leforge," Yellowstone said. He sighed, his eyes half closing. "Ahhh, m-my kingdom for some c-coffee."

"A mite cold out, ain't it?" Leforge asked.

Kelly blew across the surface of his cup. "Just a mite. Is it true what I heard from the general?"

"What's that?"

"You were to bring in some Crow."

"I'm that man," and Leforge smiled.

Sipping at more of the coffee, Kelly asked, "How many you bring with you?"

"Enough to go chasing a war party or two of them Sitting Bull Injuns."

"When'd you get here?"

"Almost two weeks ago, the soldiers tell me."

"Hasn't been busy around here, has it, Leforge?"

"If you call picking soldier lice out'n my clothes keeping busy—we ain't been real busy at all."

Kelly smiled and kicked his right leg to the left, dropping out of the saddle, still cradling the coffee cup with both hands. "See to my horse, will you, soldier?"

The young private leaped at the opportunity. "Glad to, Mr. Kelly."

Now the scout stopped, turned to pat the animal's neck with one glove. "Grain him down good, for he deserves the best of care. I was afraid he wouldn't make it all the way in here with me."

"I'll treat him right, Mr. Kelly!"

They watched the soldier lead the snow-crusted animal away; then Tom pointed, and the two of them turned toward the low-roofed mess hall with a small gaggle of others. Leforge asked, "How far you come to get here so long after dark—and in this storm?"

"Been riding for two nights and a day," Kelly replied with a weary shudder. "Snyder's battalion needs forage in a bad way, so I came riding. Wasn't all that terrible most of the way. This blizzard just hit a few miles back."

Quickly they all retreated into the sudden warmth of that log hut, where Kelly tore the bearskin hat from his head and shook out his long hair, ice crystals showering like spun sugar.

Leforge settled on the closest half-log bench, saying, "Listen, Kelly—you tell me just where we can find them soldiers, I'll send some of my Crow out with that grain for Snyder."

Waiting until he had forced down the last of the hot liquid, Kelly declared, "Bless you, Leforge. And your Crow boys too. For that would be a curse of a ride for any man to face on a turnabout."

Leforge leaned over to slap the white scout on the back. "You sit, eat, and warm yourself. We'll get these Paddy soldiers up and about getting Snyder's grain ready. Then my boys can ride out at first light."

An older officer appeared at the doorway and stomped into the mess hall, pulling a sealskin cap from his head. "Heard you was back, Kelly. All this hubbub you stirred up."

"Colonel Whistler," Kelly replied, standing to accept the lieutenant colonel's hand. They shook.

Whistler dragged a hand over his face to sweep some of the icy snow from it and said, "We'll have your battalion's feed ready shortly. Say, are you a voting man by any chance?"

Luther Kelly looked up from his coffee. "What's to vote for, Colonel?"

"Not no copperhead, are you?" the officer asked, one eye squinting suspiciously.

Kelly held up his cup in his red, trembling hands as the grizzled soldier filled it with more coffee. "Blue through and through, that's me. I fought for the Union cause and would fight again if the call came out from my president."

"Then you'll likely be mad as me," Whistler grumbled. "Word just in from downriver has it the Democrats put Tilden in the White House."

"Tilden?" squeaked a soldier rubbing his bottom by the fireplace.

"Samuel J., soldier," continued Whistler, who turned to the squaw man. "Those boys you send out to find Snyder, you make sure to tell him about Tilden when they carry that grain out come morning, Leforge."

"Why tell Snyder that?" Kelly asked.

"Because he's a mossback like me, and I'd love to be there to see the look of disgust on his face when he hears another Democrat is going to rule in the White House!"

The soldiers had forced his village of 190 lodges to the south side of the river in those first blustery moments of the blizzard. Perhaps that was a good thing, Sitting Bull wanted to think. Maybe if he could keep them moving south, they would get themselves out of the storm, escape its fury.

Here in the Midwinter Moon he was sure all these terrible happenings were part of *Wakan Tanka's* warning not to remove any of the belongings of the soldier dead from the battlefield at the Greasy Grass. His people had been warned—he had told them himself when he'd awoken from his startling vision at the foot of the Sun Dance pole beside the Deer Medicine Rocks.

But they did not listen—and so time and again, ever since

the Lakota had been forced to run for their lives with little but the clothes on their backs and a few lodges to hold all of them.

Maybe if they kept going south to the Elk River, across and beyond . . . maybe they would eventually locate the camps of the Crazy Horse people. The Hunkpatila and Bad Faces should be wealthy this winter. They had not been fighting the soldiers all through the autumn.

Across the last few weeks Sitting Bull had been trading with the Red River Slota for what he needed even more than blankets and food—rifles and bullets, along with more than twenty mules to carry the fifty heavy boxes of ammunition his warriors would use to fight the soldiers to a decisive conclusion come spring.

So with those mules and those bullets and guns, with his people and their few meager belongings, Sitting Bull had headed away from Fort Peck, crossing the frozen river and plunging into the breaks south of the *Minisose,* back toward the Redwater River country. Day by day they would have to march south and east, climbing toward the divide that would eventually drop them into the valley of the Elk River. From there it would be a few short sleeps until they found Crazy Horse somewhere on the Powder, perhaps on the Tongue.

Then, with the ammunition and weapons the Hunkpapa had traded from the northern *metis,* the reunited Crazy Horse and Sitting Bull bands would be ready for that final war against the *wasicu* soldiers come the spring, when the new grass filled the bellies of their fattened horses and brought the buffalo herds back once again.

Chapter 10

7–8 December 1876

———※◉◈———

"Get up, soldier! Stand up, damn you!"

Hearing that curse from one of the old files behind him, Frank Baldwin stiffly turned his horse about and moved back down the line of soldiers painfully trudging into the howling gale. For these few moments, at least, he would have the hurling snow at his back.

There out of the darkening mist as the last layer of daylight seeped from the western horizon, Baldwin spotted the group. Two older soldiers hunched over a third, pulling the man to his feet with a struggle.

"Lemme . . . lemme be," he pleaded, flinging his arms about like a stocking doll.

"Naw, I ain't gonna lea'f you, faith," one of the men explained, his voice softer now as he attempted to cradle the reluctant soldier beneath his arm.

"Not me neither," the other said, sweeping a long arm around the third man's waist, and with a mighty heave raised the soldier nearly off the ground between them. "Couldn't live with myself knowing I left you out here."

"Don't! Don't take me," the rag doll pleaded. "Lemme sleep."

"No sleeping—Baldwin's orders, faith," the old graybeard

said, scooping up the young soldier's rifle out of the drifting snow, then stepping up to shove his shoulder under the failing infantryman.

Baldwin said, "If he falls again, give him the point of your bayonets."

Both of the older men jerked up in surprise to find the lieutenant all but upon them as they stumbled to a halt there on the trail so many feet were carving out of the snow.

"Beggin' pardon, sir," one of the two chattered, fighting to keep his misshapen kepi on in the stiff wind as he peered up from beneath the rumpled brim at the lieutenant on horseback, "I cain't bring my own self to jab a fellow Fifther with me bayonet. I save such a punishment for them blooming redbellies."

"Jab 'im, soldier," Baldwin ordered. "If that's the only way to keep the man moving—give 'im your bayonet. Is that understood?"

Both men swallowed, glanced at each other and the soldier between them, then nodded.

"Understood, sir."

Baldwin started to turn, hearing more growling and yelps from back up the line of march, but instead turned round to the trio once more. "Listen, men—I don't cotton to using the bayonets either. But you must understand. If you don't keep every last one of us moving till we reach Fort Peck, then some might just lay down and die right here. How do you men want it?"

"Sir—beggin' pardon?"

"You want half the men in your company falling out to die along this road? Or will you use your bayonets as I've ordered you to do?"

"W-we'll bring 'em all in with us, sir," the old graybeard replied. "Trust in that, Lieutenant. Trust in that."

"I will," Baldwin said. "Because I know what you're made of, soldier."

Then the lieutenant turned away and urged his weary horse to plod back up the line of stumbling, wobbly men hunching over to shove their way into the stiff, changeable wind that was blowing an icy mix of wet snow and dry crystal right into their faces. Not a moment passed that Frank did not watch a man collapse to a knee, perhaps to both. By and large most men waited a few seconds to rest, catch their breath as others trudged, stumbled, fell around them on the trail, then pull themselves slowly up, hand over hand on their rifles until they stood on wobbly pins once more. Again they would lean into the wind, forcing their legs to follow somehow.

All round them voices begged to be left behind so they could just sleep. Others pleaded to die right then and there—since it was clear they were all going to die anyway before Baldwin's lonely battalion made it back to the safety of Fort Peck.

Yet there were more voices, stronger voices, deeper and more confident voices from those who shouted down the naysayers, who suffered this same unthinkable torture but fought back by grumbling and grousing and cursing up a blue streak in the raw, unrelenting face of that Montana blizzard. The sort of man who might often complain himself about lack of sleep or the poor rations of sidebelly and old crackers not fit for a man in prison, the sort of man who would grumble about putting in fatigue duty back at the Tongue River Cantonment, or curse his superiors when he had to dig a new latrine or corduroy a bank for the wagons or chop down trees to somehow construct just one more bridge across one more nameless goddamned creek.

But it was just that sort of double-riveted soldier who rose to the need and pulled lesser men out of the snow now as the wolfish wind howled, pulled others not quite as strong out of the frozen snowdrifts that might otherwise be their graves. The sort of man who pushed and yanked and even poked with his bayonet to be sure that every other soldier in front of him kept moving.

Just to keep all of them moving together into the teeth of that brutal storm. One crippling step at a time.

The sort of man who was bound and determined that every last one of them would make it back to Fort Peck alive. All. Without the loss of a single man.

At the head of the march the men in charge of the pack train had their own problems with the balky mules. Baldwin had put them up there for a purpose: to break trail through the deepening snow and near-insurmountable drifts. With the snow and that cursed wind blowing head-on against them, the men were far past numb. And with numbness begins the creeping fatigue, the irrepressible drowsiness that convinces a man he needs only to sit down, curl up, and rest awhile—then he'll be fit enough to march on, invigorated and refreshed.

Frank wondered if his own brain were growing cold, and slow, and just might not be as sharp as he needed it to be to get these hundred-plus men back to safety. If he failed them, they might well all die.

"Get that man up!" the lieutenant bellowed, the ice cracking on his cheeks and beard, sprinkling the front of his dark wool coat with moonlit glitter. "Get him moving—jab 'im if you have to!"

This new bunch of soldiers looked up at Baldwin; then one of them pulled his bayonet from its scabbard and prodded their fellow with the sharp tip. The soldier down and floundering in a snowdrift tried again and again to shove the long knife aside whenever it jabbed him.

"Awright!" he hollered, grabbing on to the muzzle of another man's long Springfield, raising himself painfully with his own rifle as a crutch. "I'm standing, Lieutenant! I'm standing, by God!"

"Standing isn't good enough—I need you to march, soldier!" Baldwin shouted, his words hurried on by the rising wail of the wind. "March! Fast or slow . . . I don't care. Just stay on your feet and keep moving!"

It had been that way since dark. How many hours ago now?

Just before they had set off into the raging blizzard, as the last of the men were stuffing themselves with their rations, Baldwin had gone from company to company, ordering each commander to choose the eight or ten who were strongest of body and will to walk at the rear of each outfit with the officers, all of them with their bayonets fixed.

Their situation grew all the more desperate as the night wore on. Sometime well past midnight and after miles of grueling march—Frank could not get his turnip watch freed, for his pockets had frozen shut—he ordered those hearty soldiers assigned the pack string to lash all the unused rope to the sawbucks and string the lines out to the rear. Then the call was made up and down the column of wobbly, weaving, near-dead men.

"Every one of you who believes you can't possibly go on

under your own steam—grab hold of the rope," Baldwin instructed each group within the sound of his voice as he yelled against the keening wind. "And hold on for your life."

He knew the next few miles and hours might well be their lives.

There were times when he had to coax what he thought would be the last bit of strength out of his horse, prodding it to the front of the column repeatedly, where he would give his order to those soldiers with the mules who were following a half-dead Vic Smith.

"By damn, boys! It's a sad, sad sight back there. This walking isn't near enough. For fifteen minutes we've got to trot these beasts!"

"T-trot 'em, Lieutenant?"

"Trot 'em, soldier," Baldwin snapped. "At a walk is no longer good enough. The men are fading on me—I must get their blood moving! Keep these dumb brutes moving at a trot. Now!"

With stiff salutes the first half-dozen soldiers turned back to their duty, whipping the balky, braying animals until first one, then another, and finally the rest of the snow-crusted beasts lumbered into a rolling trot, yanking on the ropes that pulled the hapless, frozen, blizzard-beaten soldiers along through the snowdrifts being broken by those hooves.

On and on Frank went, in and out of the saddle himself, up and down the line, many times pulling his flagging horse behind him just so he could stir up his own circulation by walking, so he could show them that he wasn't above busting through the icy, crusty snow himself. Baldwin wasn't sure just when it happened, so numb was his mind, so splintered was his judgment—but he stood among a half-dozen men, lending a hand to their struggle to hoist one half-dead man atop Baldwin's horse when—

"Listen, sir!"

Frank turned dumbly, blinking, his face so cold, his eyelids barely moved in the swirl of snow.

"I don't hear anything, goddammit!" one of the others grunted, holding up his share of the soldier's weight as they shoved the unconscious man across the lieutenant's saddle like a wet sack of oats.

A nearby voice cried, "That's all of it!"

"Exactly!"

"The wind . . . ," Baldwin whimpered with exhaustion, so tired he didn't even have the strength to cry with relief. "It's stopped."

Another man yelped with glee. "The gol-danged storm's gone and blowed over us!"

All around them men began to lumber to a halt, slowly able to stand straighter now that they did not have to hunch over against the gale-force winds, able to open their eyes fully and peer out beneath the frost-crusted eyelashes. Slowly each one came to understand, causing some to pound one another clumsily on the backs, croaking their cheers and congratulations with cracking voices.

Then near the front of the march the men started demanding quiet, silence . . . like a flow, the call rippled back along the column as every one went dumb, listening.

There, every now and then beneath the rustle and shove of the dying wind, they heard a gunshot. Distant. So far away the gunshots were almost muffled.

"That's gotta be the fort!" one cried out.

The rest celebrated all over again. To be within hearing distance of Fort Peck.

Baldwin didn't have the heart to tell them it might well be nothing more than the ice thickening in the river, no more than the cottonwoods popping in the brutal, soul-numbing cold.

Somewhere deep inside him he knew he had to let them go on believing they were nearing the post. Keep them moving . . . and believing that it was just beyond the next hill, perhaps. So he reminded them. Then, when they were beyond that rise and the fort still did not loom into sight, Frank told them he was certain the post lay just around the next big bend in the Missouri.

"Yes, yes," one of the soldiers cried. "I remember it 'sactly that way. Same's the lieutenant said!"

And so they somehow continued to stumble on through the darkness, and into the coming gray of day.

The sun never appeared at sunrise that Friday, the eighth of December. Nothing more than a dull lightening patch at the horizon behind the fury of the storm rumbling east. On through the snowdrifts they persevered, mules pulling the weakest among them, soldiers prodding their fellow soldiers, Baldwin clutching the horse's reins for dear life so that he himself would not fall there beside the trail. Praying that the stumbling horse would not go down.

Not until they reached Fort Peck.

Images danced and swam in front of him with the stark-white landscape: the spiderwebs of leafless brush and tall cottonwoods, the stark outline of ridge and bluff top against the graying sky here two, maybe three, hours past sunrise. Dim mirages leaped out of the darkness at the periphery of his vision so sudden, they scared him, bringing him instantly awake. So otherworldly was it all that Frank wondered at times if he was still alive.

Each time he worried, Baldwin worked up the strength to call out to the soldiers around him, to hear his own voice, mostly, before he slipped completely away. "C'mon, men! Just a few more yards! Yes—I think I see it now!"

Frank found himself longing to see the post materialize out of all that white more than anything since he had wanted sweet, pretty Alice Blackwood to marry him during the insurrection of the Southern states. Trying so hard to remember her face with his cold, numb mind while he licked at his frozen lips that cracked and oozed—how did her mouth taste on his . . . then heard the soldiers up front with the mules shout.

He looked up, expecting to find Alice before him, hoping she could wrap her arms around him and make him warm again.

But it was only a group of buildings swimming dark and shadowlike out of the frozen mist that coated every branch and rock. Buildings. Logs stacked on top of one another. At first he could smell the smoke, then saw each curl rising from the stone chimneys.

"W-we made it, boys!" His voice cracked with cold and emotion as he turned, nearly stumbling in the deep snow as his horse continued on without him.

Baldwin jerked in a grotesque, wild motion to free his frozen, cramped hand from the reins so he could lurch back along the column, hollering at the top of his lungs.

"We made it, boys!" he bellowed. "I see it! There's fires and food and shelter. Keep going! Keep going!"

Later that morning after the men had shed their empty haversacks and dumped weapons in the corners of every cabin within Fort Peck's stockade, the battalion gave Baldwin three cheers, and then three more for those men who had kept the mules pulling the ropes, and finally three cheers for the old files so good with their bayonets. And when the cheering died down and the men had wiped their eyes dry once more, those three companies of the Fifth Infantry roared their huzzahs to Frank Baldwin for pulling them all through that blizzard.

Not an animal down. Not one man lost.

Chapter 11

8–14 December 1876

As soon as it was light on the morning of the eighth, Leforge and Lieutenant Colonel Whistler dispatched a party of ten Crow warriors with what pack mules Quartermaster Randall could spare, each one loaded down with enough grain and forage to see Captain Snyder's column all the way in to the Tongue River Cantonment. They even carried sketchy and inaccurate news claiming Samuel J. Tilden had been elected president back east.

Snyder's battalion would not drag into base until the afternoon of the tenth, having put more than 330 miles behind them in their month-long hunt for the roaming Sioux.

After recuperating for a day and most of the next night, Luther S. Kelly himself pulled out again early on the ninth with two more of Leforge's Crow scouts, this time starting north on the trail hoping to locate Miles's battalion. Chances were good they would be found somewhere on the divide above Big Dry Creek.

Early on their second morning out, Kelly and the two Crow trackers were heating up some coffee and broiling some antelope flank steaks when they heard a pair of distant shots come to them on the wind. Without a word he immediately kicked snow into their fire, gave sign, and the three of them quickly saddled. Mounting up, they cautiously pushed north more than a mile, keeping to the ravines and coulees so they would not be caught against the skyline.

On a patch of ground lying in the gentle saddle between two rounded knolls, it was clear even from a distance that the snow had been disturbed. They waited a few moments there, smelling the air, listening for more gunshots, watching the hilltops. Only then did they inch forward to stop on that patch of ground where it appeared a small herd of buffalo had sought shelter during the recent blizzard.

One of the Crow motioned the others over, pointing to the ground across the side of the hill. A recent set of boot prints. Then a second set, the tracks coming around the brow of the hill to join the first.

These were definitely white men. And Luther figured the only white men out and wandering about had to be soldiers.

After mounting up and pushing on with the Crow for close to a mile, Kelly found he could smell woodsmoke before he ever saw its wispy trail rising beyond the ridge. The three rode as close as they dared with the horses, then dismounted and crept in the rest of the way on foot.

Around the base of a low ridge crusted with wet, frozen snow, the three dropped to their bellies, staring at the distant figures. Slowly they made out the scene: no lodges; a heap lot of wagons and mules; and the men all wore soldier clothes. It was clear from all the activity around the wagons, what with the teams being backed into their hitches, that this bunch was preparing to break camp.

"Bear Coat," Luther said out loud as he stood, his hands making sign.

The Crow followed him back to their horses, where they mounted up and rode on in to the soldier bivouac, frightening the first of the outlying pickets as they appeared at the top of the snowy hill. In a moment more soldiers were being deployed, readied for attack, until they realized there were only three horsemen coming slowly toward the camp.

"Kelly!" roared Miles as the three approached. "By Jupiter, it's good to see you!"

"Haven't froze yet, General," Luther replied. "Though it wasn't for want of a blizzard trying."

"We were caught in it too. Had to leave a few of our

mules behind, but we didn't lose a man in all that muck," Miles explained, extending an arm to point at one of the last fires still going. "Care for a cup of coffee?"

"Don't mind if I do, General."

"How's Captain Snyder's battalion faring?"

"We lost a lot of our stock. But he was just a day shy of making it back to post when I lit out to find you."

"You came from Snyder's battalion?"

"No," Kelly replied. "He sent me on in for grain. I've come out from the cantonment."

Miles sipped at the last of his coffee. "You and Snyder have any luck—any contact with the Sioux?"

"Nothing, General."

Miles wagged his head. "Damn. I was sure you'd catch him in the Big Dry."

"Not so much as a track. No sign."

"So with Snyder going in—how do you come to be out here, Kelly?"

Luther smiled. "Come looking for you, General. Started on your backtrail."

Rubbing his bare hands over the fire, Miles said, "How'd you find us?"

"We—that pair of boys and me—were having our breakfast when we heard gunshots from this direction."

"Likely the hunters I've had Captain Ewers send out this morning before we put back on the trail." The colonel glanced at the two scouts standing by their ponies, watching the white men at the fire. "What band are they?"

"Crow."

Miles clapped his bare hands exuberantly. "So Hargous got me some Crow, did he?"

"Tom Leforge brought 'em in. Couple weeks back now."

"How many, Kelly?"

"I was told Leforge brought eighty warriors with him. There's a few women came along."

Miles waved a hand for the pair of scouts to join them at the fire. "That's what I told Hargous to convince the Crow to join us: bring their women and families if need be. If that's what it took to bring in some Crow, then so be it."

"You need that many scouts?"

"Hell, I don't need any of 'em for scouts, Kelly," Miles said, holding out his tin for more coffee.

Luther watched the colonel's dog-robber pour coffee in all four cups, then asked, "If you don't need 'em for scouts, why did you send for the Crow?"

"Fighting men, Kelly. Simple as that: fighting men. Congress has cut the army's budget again—so Washington's cut down the total number of scouts to less than three hundred."

"How you going to pay them?"

Miles grinned over the edge of his tin cup. "There's plenty of Sioux ponies and plunder to raise—plenty of Sioux scalps for the taking, I figure. For Leforge's Crow that ought to be pay enough."

Kelly nodded. "True enough that there's many winters of bad blood between the Crow and Lakota," Kelly agreed. "So you don't figure you have enough soldiers to take on Sitting Bull fixed just the way you are, General?"

"Never know," Miles admitted. "And that's the rub, Kelly. The army sure as hell won't send me the help I've requested. Not cavalry. Not a proper battery of artillery. And they sure as hell aren't shipping me reinforcements."

"You s'pose they need those men somewhere else?"

Miles licked the drops of coffee off his mustache and said, "I hope the men I need aren't being sent to help George Crook and Ranald Mackenzie . . . that's for damned sure!"

The army's strength the previous spring had been a little over 25,000 men out of a U.S. population of 46,246,000. Then came the Custer disaster—which meant that the call went out for more enlistments and larger company strength. Throughout the summer "Custer's Avengers" signed on, enthusiastically trained at places like Jefferson Barracks near St. Louis, then marched off to fight Sitting Bull and Crazy Horse.

Within weeks a nervous Congress got into the act.

Since they had ultimate control over the purse strings for Sam Grant's and Bill Sherman's army, Capitol Hill started paring things down. With as bad as the economy was suffering in the country, one sure way to save was to hack away at the size of the army. After all, Congress believed they were doing nothing more than carrying on the long-held American predisposition against standing armies. Unlike Britain, Prussia,

France, and Russia, the U.S. had never had itself a need to support a large "peacetime" army.

Finishing his coffee, Kelly declared, "Despite the miles and the weather, these men look to be in fighting trim, General."

"Yes, I suppose we're fortunate that we've come through the last weeks as well as we have, considering. What else is news down at Tongue River?"

"Lakota and Cheyenne horsemen raided a couple of nights back," Kelly explained. "Rode in right after the blizzard."

"Raided? What'd they come for?"

"The beef, General. That herd you had brought down the Yellowstone from Fort Ellis came in. The civilian wranglers had it near the post."

"All of the beeves?"

"Maybe half."

"Damn," the colonel muttered. "Where'd those warriors come from—"

"Riders coming in, General!"

Interrupted, Miles stood immediately, accompanied by Kelly and the Crow trackers as he moved away from the fire. "More riders?"

A soldier turned and shouted, pointing. "From the northeast, sir!"

Turning quickly to Kelly as the two horsemen appeared on the crest of the nearby hill, Miles said, "I'll bet that's some word from Mitchell. He's agent up at Fort Peck. I told him to let me know as soon as he had any news on where Sitting Bull was going . . . where I could find that red son of a bitch."

Kelly squinted into the glare, asking, "General, isn't that the half-breed?"

Miles shaded his eyes with a hand as he peered into the middistance, watching the two horsemen approach. "Half-breed?"

"Bruguier."

The dark rider called, "General Bear Coat!"

The colonel sang out, "Johnny Bruguier? Is that really you?"

The half-breed and his companion came to a halt nearby but did not immediately swing out of the saddle. "Johnny

Bruguier. Here to tell you I done what you wanted from me, Bear Coat."

"How's that?"

Bruguier pointed back to the north. "At the fort I told your soldier chief where he would find Sitting Bull before he send me here to find you."

"My soldier chief?" Miles asked. "You mean agent Mitchell?"

Kelly interrupted, "I figure it must've been Baldwin, General."

"You told Baldwin where Sitting Bull was camped?" Miles asked with gusto. "Hot damn!" He slapped his hands together again, then went back to rubbing them over the fire. "He go pitch into 'em, right?"

With a shrug Bruguier replied. "Maybeso. He send me here with these."

Miles watched the half-breed reach inside his coat and bring out a small, flat leather parcel he handed the colonel. Untying the rawhide strings, Miles pulled out the two sheets of paper and began reading.

"By Jupiter—Baldwin's probably got that old warhorse already rounded up by now!" Miles exclaimed, shaking the papers once he was done reading.

"Baldwin went after them, General?" asked Hobart Bailey.

"Damn right. He says here that after Bruguier told him where the Sitting Bull camp was to the east on Porcupine Creek, he was planning to march straight for it and engage the hostiles. Tells me to expect word as soon as he has destroyed the village and has something conclusive on the disposition of Sitting Bull himself."

Kelly turned to Bruguier, asking, "You fellas want some coffee?"

They both nodded, starting out of the saddle while Miles motioned forward his dog-robber with a pair of cups. "Have you boys eaten lately?"

"Last night," Johnny admitted.

"Here, eat what's left here," Miles offered. "We're breaking camp, but I'll see that my mess sergeant issues you two some rations for the next four days."

"Four days?" Johnny asked.

"Yes," Miles replied. "I'm turning you right around with a message I want you to take back to Baldwin. Besides, Bruguier—I can't wait to hear what's become of his attack on Sitting Bull!"

That morning of the eleventh, before he put his battalion back on the trail to Tongue River, Nelson Miles composed his dispatch to Lieutenant Frank Baldwin, known to be somewhere east of the Fort Peck Agency.

If you meet with ill-success I can take the responsibility of the movement; if you are successful it will be very creditable to you.

Then, knowing how the Sioux villages always fled once attacked, he urged that Baldwin notify him as soon as the lieutenant might know the direction the Sitting Bull people were taking in their escape.

If I get the information in time [I] will endeavor to intercept them.

"Get these back to Baldwin as soon as you can, Bruguier," he instructed the half-breed. "You've been on the army payroll since the middle of November—so I expect you to keep on earning your pay."

"I take this for the Bear Coat to the little soldier chief."

"You find him and tell him to stay on Sitting Bull's tail until I can rendezvous with his battalion to help."

With a nod Bruguier and the other scout rose to their saddles and reined away.

"All right, gentlemen!" Miles bellowed, kicking snow into the fire pit of hissing limbs. "Let's get this column back to Tongue River, where we can reoutfit ourselves to surround Sitting Bull!"

The following day they awoke to another heavy snowstorm. Breaking camp without taking time for fires and coffee, the men pushed on through the cold, dancing veil of white. The clouds continued to lower throughout the morning, but they nonetheless managed to locate Snyder's in-bound trail early that afternoon of the twelfth. Miles's foot soldiers fell grimly silent as they began to pass by one dead animal after another, all abandoned where the creatures had dropped out of hunger and utter exhaustion. As the storm thickened, the Jackson brothers and the staff officers often resorted to using their compasses to stay their course homeward.

Twilight came and still Miles pushed on. When darkness fell the trail became more difficult to follow, every man having nothing more to see than the soldier in front of him. Miles kept marching, with William and Robert Jackson to lead them south through the swirling darkness. From time to time the scouts would fire their pistols in the air to signal those coming behind at the head of the command. And so the firing would continue back along the column, other men clinking their noisy tin cups to alert those following on their rear in the dark.

Through most of that day and into night's woolly cloaking of the land, the first men marching at the front of each company would plow through the snow until they became absolutely weary. Then they would fall to the rear of their company, and the next pair of men would break the icy snow and waist-deep drifts for the rest to follow. On and on in that way the men moved up to take their turn, falling back when they had little strength left them.

By eight P.M. the colonel himself grew too weary to sit the saddle or spell his horse by walking beside it. They had reached the divide above the headwaters of Sunday Creek. Here Miles gave the order to bivouac where they were. Those men not so utterly done in scrambled through the greasewood and stunted pine of that high country to scrounge up what firewood they could. While the snow tapered off sometime after midnight, the wind continued through the night, torturing man and beast and playing havoc with their sputtering sagebrush fires.

That Tuesday they managed to put another twenty-four torturous miles behind them by forging on through the howling storm without once stopping nor slowing their grueling pace. But the lack of proper forage was plainly telling on the livestock. Later that night, after the snow stopped falling, Miles heard one of the drivers boasting with his gallows humor that his team of mules had grown so thin, he could almost read a newspaper through them.

Not long after the men pulled themselves out of the

snowbanks the next morning and rolled up their blankets for the day's march, moving off below the clouds hovering over that divide, Miles was plodding through the deep snow when he heard the Jackson brothers fire pistol shots beyond the nearby hills. His heart hammering with dread, the colonel immediately kicked his horse into motion, getting no more than a rolling lope out of the weary, ill-fed animal. More pistol shots, followed by a ragged volley; then the firing tapered off. Dread became fear: certain that his forward scouts had been caught in an ambush.

Quickly looking behind him, Nelson found some of his staff on their own poor horses, straining to keep up with him as he reached the top of the hill, pistol drawn, prepared to signal the column of the attack.

Instead—farther down the slope of that branch to Sunday Creek, he spotted his half-breed trackers circling their horses: both of the Jackson brothers whooping, waving their hats in the air. And on the far side of the valley, another group of horsemen did the same, brandishing their pistols in the freezing air, gun smoke drifting above them all in tattered remnants. Men on horses. In the next moment, there at the ridgetop, appeared the first team and its wagon. And another. Then a third, all of them escorted by a line of foot soldiers slogging along on either side.

Miles wanted to yell the announcement to those behind him but found his voice could only croak, so thick did he find the ball of sentiment in his throat. Soldiers. His own gallant foot soldiers. Bringing out from Tongue River those wagons that would keep his battalion alive until they reached the post.

Now the cold mattered little. Let the skies rage and drop even more snow on them. For now the men would have more than hardtack to eat. Now his battalion's poor animals would get the grain that would keep enough of them alive to pull the emptied wagons back to that cluster of cabins and stables on the south bank of the Yellowstone.

He wiped his eyes hurriedly as his staff caught up to him on the hilltop. And before he knew it, they too were whooping and hollering. A small group of four horsemen broke from the head of the far column and headed his way behind William and Robert Jackson.

"Captain Dickey!" Miles roared, saluting, his eyes misting with the cold and the relief.

Charles J. Dickey of the Twenty-second Infantry returned the salute and smiled. "General! Reporting as requested, sir! We have rations for your men and forage for your animals, as you asked." His arm swept to the far side of the creek valley, where the wagons were beginning to wind down the side of the slope—escorted by men from D and I companies, Twenty-second Infantry, who had been left to garrison the cantonment during the Fifth's absence.

"By damn, if you aren't a sore sight for these eyes!" Captain Andrew S. Bennett yelled exuberantly as he saluted and held out his hand to shake with Dickey.

"General Miles"—Dickey turned back to the colonel—"with your permission I'll halt my train there in the valley below and we can bivouac—the better to allow your men to eat while my battalion feeds your stock."

"Perfect, Captain!" Miles replied.

"I regret to inform you that a load of potatoes you had brought over from Bozeman City arrived completely frozen."

"That's a loss I didn't count on," the colonel grumbled.

Dickey went on, "But Major Hough's delivered tons of hay brought upriver from Buford and Glendive to feed the stock."

Miles clapped his hands once. "Forget those spuds. With that grain at Tongue River, Captain—I can continue to chase Sitting Bull."

The men ate and drank coffee at fires where they joked, learned of news from the east, and raised their spirits. The soldiers of the Twenty-second moved among them as they fed the stock, reminding the Fifth that they were close to home. Just a few more miles down Sunday Creek. Just one more night on the trail . . . and then they would be back in those leaky, cold, mud-chinked log cabins that they called home.

At noon the following day Miles and his column of wagons and foot soldiers limped on down to the north bank of the Yellowstone and began the long process of ferrying across to the cantonment. In that five long weeks of fruitless search and endless wandering, suffering blizzards and murderous ice floes, running desperately low on food and forage, Nelson

Miles's battalion had logged more than 558 miles under their boots and wheels and hooves.

But now they were home again.

How sweet it was to hear the men cheer and yelp as they came in sight of that ferry, as they looked across the Yellowstone at those squat log cabins these brave men called home.

Chapter 12

Wanicokan Wi 1876

How he yearned to be without the responsibilities of a Shirt Wearer. Let He Dog and the chiefs of the Hunkpatila Oglalla find another to carry on his shoulders such a burden.

Better it was, Crazy Horse thought, to hunt and fight and couple than it was to have so many look up to him with their hungry eyes.

Again the Shahiyela had come trudging through the deep snows to find his camp close by the mouth of Otter Creek.* Again the soldiers had made war on them, driving the Shahiyela into the winter. And again the Crazy Horse people did what they could—but his Hunkpatila had so little to share compared to last winter after the attack on Old Bear's camp.† Not near enough dishes and needles, much less robes, blankets, and lodge skins, to go around, to shelter these visitors from the wrath of winter.

Now Crazy Horse not only had the responsibility of holding his people to the old way, to prevent them from fleeing back to the agencies, but he had to protect the Shahiyela of

* Near present-day Ashland, Montana.
† *Blood Song*, vol. 8, The Plainsmen Series.

Little Wolf and Morning Star. Sometimes he wondered if it would not have been better if he had died from No Water's bullet winters ago.

But such a thought always made his veins run cold with fear . . . because Crazy Horse would remember that his vision had told him he would not die in battle with the *wasicu*—but at the hand of one of his own people.

Six hundred lodges* allied themselves with him now. Although winter usually caused the *Titunwan* Lakota† to take separate trails due to the scarcity of game, each band finding its own place out of the wind along some river valley, this winter was far different. Last autumn, after it was learned that Three Stars was marching his soldiers here and there north of the Bear Butte country in search of villages,# many of the warrior camps began to come in search of Crazy Horse on the *Maka Blu Wakpa,* or Shifting Sands River.@

Not long after that it was reported that the soldier chief who many called the Bear Coat started to talk peace with Sitting Bull while his soldiers came marching up to fight.^ From all that was going on around the Crazy Horse people, it was plain to see the soldiers would not rest this season of cold. They would continue to make it hard to hunt, difficult for the Lakota to live the old way.

With so much relentless pressure, most of those chiefs who had been in the Sitting Bull village when Bear Coat attacked quickly promised the soldier chief they would go into their agencies as soon as their horses were strong enough and they made enough meat to last them through the cold moons. But, instead, within days those same chiefs grew too frightened to consider surrendering their people. Once out of sight of Bear Coat's soldiers, they promptly scampered south into the country of the *Tatonka Ceji Wakpa,* the Buffalo Tongue River, where their wolves reported they would find the swelling camp of the Crazy Horse people.

Old Lone Horn, head chief of the Miniconjou, had died

---

* As many as thirty-five hundred people.
† The Seven Council Fires of the Teton, or Prairie Dwelling, Lakota bands.
# *Trumpet on the Land*, vol. 10, The Plainsmen Series.
@ The Powder River.
^ Battle of Cedar Creek, *A Cold Day in Hell*, vol. 11.

just before his people had started their journey south to unite with the Hunkpatila. Now his sons each had their own band: Touch-the-Clouds, Spotted Elk,* and young Roman Nose. Not to mention the Miniconjou clan of war chief Red Horse, a veteran of many battles against the *wasicu* soldiers.

They, as well as a growing number of his own Oglalla, had begun to talk openly about making peace.

Especially Packs the Drum.

A few winters older than Crazy Horse, Packs the Drum had been one of the bravest of the young warriors who had joined in their attack on the white settlement of Julesburg. Then again at the fight with Caspar Collins's soldiers at Platte River Bridge.† But over the last ten summers, this courageous Oglalla warrior had been listening more and more to the *wasicu* agents. Why, the white man had even taken to calling him "Sitting Bull the Good," to contrast him to Sitting Bull the Hunkpapa, who wanted nothing to do with whites.

Packs the Drum even became one of the Oglalla leaders at the White River Agency.# As such, he had been taken back east just last year to visit the *wasicu's* Great Father on a long journey. He returned with a repeating, lever-action rifle engraved with his name, presented to him by the Great Father Grant in appreciation of his good work with the white man's government.

But despite his long history of friendliness, Packs the Drum vigorously opposed the sale of the Black Hills. Although others like Red Cloud, Old Man Afraid, and Spotted Tail had touched the pen and given up the sacred *He Sapa*, Packs the Drum grew disgusted, and a little ashamed of his trust in the white man. So ashamed that he had packed up his family and abandoned the White River Agency. Late last summer in the north country he joined the wanderings of the Crazy Horse village.

It hadn't taken long for many of the chiefs in Crazy Horse's camp to see that the soldiers were not going to rest for the winter. In a short time Packs the Drum became the

---

* Who would one day change his name to Big Foot and in December of 1890 lead his band of Miniconjou to its fate at Wounded Knee Creek.

† July 11, 1865—*Cry of the Hawk*, the Jonah Hook Trilogy.

Red Cloud Agency.

leader of those who believed that the Oglalla should surrender to avoid the fighting that invariably killed so many women and so many of their children.

As more and more of the chiefs began to listen to the persuasive arguments of those who suggested making peace with the *wasicu,* Crazy Horse spent more and more of his time away from the camps—preferring to be alone, sleeping in wickiups he constructed himself, or in caves and bear dens he found in the surrounding hills.

At that moment Crazy Horse sat on the hillside looking down on the huge village, the thick fur of the buffalo robe brushing his cheek, tickling his flesh in the wind. How could he blame them? Crazy Horse thought. The Bear Coat was doing all that he could to drive a wedge between the *Titunwan* Lakota peoples. It wasn't only just Packs the Drum, but men like Pretty Bear and Tall Bull, Yellow Eagle, Two Elk, and Poor Bear too—yes: Sans Arc, Miniconjou, and even Four Horns's Hunkpapa—they all had talked with the soldier chief and believed he would give them a good peace.

As inconceivable as it sounded, the Bear Coat had promised the chiefs that he would establish an agency for them at the forks of the Cheyenne River, east of the sacred *He Sapa.* The soldier chief even vowed they would have a soldier for their agent and that he would understand their needs. The Lakota would soon see that the Bear Coat could be trusted to treat them generously.

Were there no warriors left who would stand steadfastly beside him? Crazy Horse brooded. How long must he go on bullying his own people so they would not slip away to the agencies?

It had come to that. So many in this great camp feared the soldiers would come without fail that winter, so many suffered from lack of meat and the brutal cold, that the Bear Coat's words actually began to make sense to the Lakota heart.

Filled with anger, Crazy Horse had ordered his *akicita** to soldier the villages, throwing a wide cordon around them, allowing no family to escape back to the *wasicu's* reservations.

---

* Camp police.

It was but another reason he spent so much time away from the camp. Only a man with a heart of stone could remain untouched when he looked at the ribs of the women, when he stared into the hollow eyes of the children, when he saw how the once-proud warriors cast their gaze on the ground like sick horses about to die.

Crazy Horse had allowed the first few to go. They took down their lodges late at night while the rest of the village slept, slinking away in silence with their meager belongings, often lashing their possessions to travois left some distance from camp so others would not know until long after they had gone. Those first like those who would leave now if they could: all of them frightened of this terrible winter as much as they were of every soldier scare. So scared, they chose to flee to the little deserts the white man had made of the reservations, where the mighty Lakota would be forced to eat the moldy flour and the rancid pig meat, because they no longer had a choice. How heavy it made his heart to know that if his people went in to the agency, they had to surrender their ponies and their weapons.

They might as well turn over their whole way of life. Without ponies and weapons—no more would they be *Titunwan* Lakota.

Just what had happened to Red Cloud and Red Leaf at the White River Agency?

Hoyay! What was a man without his weapons, without his pony? Was he still a man?

Last autumn when Three Stars asked who among Red Cloud's warriors would go with the soldiers in search of the hostile bands—Crazy Horse's old nemesis, No Water, was the first to volunteer. Crook gave the traitor a rifle, pistol, and a pony to use when they came looking for Crazy Horse. No Water, the turncoat—the very same husband from whom Crazy Horse had kidnapped Black Buffalo Woman winters gone before.

It had come to this: Lakota against Lakota!

Only the *wasicu* would drive a wedge between the hearts of the People.

Back and forth Crazy Horse felt himself begin to waver again like the willow blown by a strong autumn wind that strips it of all leaves. Day by day he grew more frustrated and angry; then in a rage he finally sent his police after those who had already abandoned his village. Once and for all he decided that if he did not stop the escapees, more and more and all the more would leave.

Soon none would be left with him.

"Break their lodgepoles!" he ordered his *akicita*. "Cut up their lodges so they are useless to anyone! Break the bows of those men who refuse to turn back with their families! Kill their ponies if you have to, and bring in the meat to feed our people!"

But just when Crazy Horse was beginning to wonder if he himself had the strength to hold the Hunkpatila and others to him by force, if he himself had the heart to inflict such pain on his people for their own good . . . he saw how the sour ball of anger swelled in their bellies once more when they watched the crippled Shahiyela stumbling through the snow, making bloody prints in the snow, most clad in little more than the green frozen hides they had peeled from the carcasses of ponies sacrificed so that the little babes could be placed inside the temporary warmth, so that old ones could stuff their hands and feet into the steaming gut-piles.

Just to cast their eyes on the pitiful Shahiyela made the bile rise again in the throats of Lakota warriors. Again the *Titunwan* talked of making war on the soldiers so evil they would drive helpless women and children into the winter.

"But where will we find the ammunition and more rifles we need to fight the *wasicu*?" asked Two Elk.

"After hunting to feed our families and fighting the soldiers all summer and into the autumn," explained Red Horse, one of the Miniconjou who had been advocating making peace with the white man, "we do not have enough bullets and weapons to make war for the winter."

Each time the chiefs and headmen talked, Crazy Horse could see the anxious fear on all the faces. It was written there as plain as was the fear in the eyes of a new-foaled mare when she scented a nearby mountain lion. His people were wavering. But how could he blame them? He himself was beginning to have his own doubts.

"Perhaps we can steal what bullets and rifles we need

from the log villages in our sacred hills,"* Poor Bear suggested.

"How can we decide to do that?" Yellow Eagle scoffed. "Our ponies are poor, and most will not be ready to ride into battle until the tender grass of spring has shown its head on the prairies."

Working hard to maintain his composure, Crazy Horse said, "Doesn't a warrior fight on—even when the pony beneath him has been killed?"

"Crazy Horse! You were my enemy in battle," declared the stocky shaman who now carried the name *Pehinhanska*, Lakota for "Long Hair." Last autumn, after the roaming bands learned who it was they had defeated at the Greasy Grass, this war chief had begun using the name—stating that the warrior spirit of the dead soldier chief talked through him daily. "But now I am your brother in death."

All eyes turned to Long Hair. Patiently, Crazy Horse said, "What do you have to say to me this day, Long Hair?"

In that hushed lodge the stocky warrior half closed his eyes and spoke his words in an unfamiliar, high, and reedy voice. "You must not give up. Fight until you die. You are a warrior, Crazy Horse. As I was a warrior in life. A warrior must die as a warrior. Make your people understand there is no life at the agencies. Fight on, Crazy Horse!"

In the growing clamor and hubbub Roman Nose whirled on Crazy Horse. "Fight on? What if we have no bullets to put in our guns?"

"I will make bullets for you!" Long Hair shouted the others down.

"Make bullets for us?" Crazy Horse demanded.

"Yes. Each morning you will find that my two hands are filled with bullets for our guns. *Wakan Tanka* will provide, if you do not lose heart!"

How he desperately wanted to believe.

So the next morning at the middle of camp Crazy Horse waited with hundreds of others for Long Hair. Eventually the shaman appeared from his lodge, stopping in front of Crazy

* The Black Hills settlements of Deadwood, Whitewood, Custer, and Crook City.

Horse to hold out his hands. Then he slowly opened his fingers, and out poured the shiny brass shells.

"Use these to kill soldiers!" the shaman bellowed as proud as a prairie cock. "Kill all *wasicu* soldiers who march against us with Three Stars or with Bear Coat!"

That morning Crazy Horse distributed the bullets. And for the next seven mornings. Then on the eighth day Long Hair did not appear. Within two more days the camp learned the shaman had made fools of them. Not only had they the winter and the soldiers to fight, the cold and the hunger to battle . . . but the Crazy Horse people now had despair to fend off as well.

Once more they became like panting rabbits run to the end of their strength by the coyotes, forced to seek shelter in some tiny hollow, hiding with eyes wide, watching, waiting until the coyote eventually found them. These—the people who had reveled that bright summer day on the *Onjinjintka Wakpa* or Red Flower Creek* against Three Stars, again at the Greasy Grass against Long Hair's many, many dead! To rise to such greatness with *Wicokannanji,* the Midsummer Moon.

Now to collapse to such ruin with the arrival of winter.

As much as he tried to keep the thought from his mind, Crazy Horse himself had begun to fear that soon there would be no more buffalo. Only soldiers.

Crazy Horse returned to the hills. He had to flee the village—the empty eyes, the shrunken cheeks.

All around him the children coughed. And some of those would not last out this winter. There simply was not enough buffalo to feed and shelter all who needed that meat and those robes. There were simply too many soldiers. They kept coming and coming.

And coming.

So the doubt first planted itself in his heart.

Could it be true, he began to fear: no more were the *Titunwan* Lakota a mighty people. Had they already lived their finest days? Were those summers of greatness gone the way of breathsmoke on a sharp winter wind? Without counting the boys and old men, Crazy Horse had no more than six hundred warriors he could count on to fight. He knew that

* Rosebud Creek.

six-times-ten-times-ten was not near enough to hold back the *wasicu* forever.

Would Sitting Bull stay to fight beside the Crazy Horse people? Or would the Hunkpapa medicine man flee with his warriors to the Land of the Grandmother, leaving Crazy Horse to fight on alone?

And in the meantime, how many of these children and women and old ones would die needlessly? How many of these blank-eyed people who looked to him for help would not live to see spring because he himself clung to a warrior's pride and vowed to fight on?

Looking down at the village from the snowy hillside where the wind swept past him, Crazy Horse fully realized how those people had put their lives in his hands. They trusted that he would do right by them to save the Oglalla from the white man's devastation. To save them from starvation . . . and soldier bullets.

Why must things be so hard? he brooded. It had not always been this way—not always difficult to decide what was best for his Hunkpatila. It had all begun with the Little Chief Grattan coming after a sickly Mormon cow and continued with the boasts of Little Chief Fetterman crossing Lodge Trail Ridge. No longer could the Lakota just try to stay out of the way of those *wasicu* passing through.

No, the white man had to own everything he saw, everything he touched, even that which could never be his.

Yet now the enemy was everywhere. Try as they did, the Lakota and the Shahiyela had not been able to hold back the mighty tide. Now the buffalo were disappearing from the hillsides.

With a sigh Crazy Horse resigned himself to listening . . . at least listening. Just the day before, two powerful Miniconjou chiefs had reached the village, come here on a long journey all the way from the agency at Cheyenne River. Important Man and Foolish Bear brought gifts of tobacco so they could talk of peace between the Crazy Horse people and the government.

"Your people and Morning Star's Shahiyela must surrender before all your warriors are killed," Important Man had told Crazy Horse last night.

"Before all your people starve," Foolish Bear had added.

They had said the Hunkpatila would have to do as Red Cloud had done: turn over their ponies and their weapons too. In return the *wasicu* soldiers would not punish them for killing the Long Hair at the Greasy Grass in the Midsummer Moon.

He hadn't slept for so many nights now. The weariness had seeped all the way to his bones. Why should this happen to him? He was nothing more than a warrior. They called him a Strange Man, but he was no more than a man who had begun to wonder, to despair for his people, and finally to doubt.

Perhaps, as the others claimed . . . perhaps the day had come to see what terms of surrender he could wrest from the Bear Coat. True was it that Three Stars was retreating from Indian country. He would not be back until grass grew green. But the offer made by the soldier chief at the mouth of Buffalo Tongue River for a reservation of their own in the Shifting Sands River country was beginning to sound like something his people would have to live with.

Crazy Horse bowed his head there in the wind scudding along the side of the hill above the upper Buffalo Tongue where Otter Creek joined the icy flow. He thought of nothing but the hollow eyes and the sunken cheeks of his hungry people. Not today—he could not bring himself to limp back to the village like a wounded man today. So maybe tomorrow . . . he would gather the chiefs and they would talk . . . about going to see the Bear Coat.

Go to the mouth of the Buffalo Tongue to make the best peace they could before they all died of empty bellies, or soldier bullets.

Or broken hearts.

Chapter 13

Big Freezing Moon 1876

BY TELEGRAPH

**The Mississippi Closed by Ice
at St. Louis**

ST. LOUIS, December 9.—The river at St. Louis is blocked solidly opposite the city and for six miles below. Pedestrians crossed yesterday, and if the cold weather continues teams will cross to-day or Wednesday.

At long last, eleven suns after fleeing Three Finger Kenzie's pony soldiers—soldiers guided to the *Ohmeseheso* village in the Red Fork Valley by their turncoat Indians—Morning Star's advance scouts came racing back to all those people stumbling across the hills on frozen feet, yipping with their exciting news in the bitter cold that had killed old ones and tiny babes . . . those nowhere strong enough to endure this greatest of winter hardship.

Descending from the high mountains where the *ve-ho-e* dared not follow their bloody footprints, down past the Big

Lake,* over to Crow Standing Creek,† finally to the Tongue, where they marched north to the mouth of Otter Creek. Following the east fork, Morning Star's *Tse-Tsehese*# crossed the high divide, where it was said they should find their friends and relations among the Lakota.

Morning Star's heart leaped in his chest—like a pink-bellied fish breaking the surface of a high-country stream. How he hoped for succor, for relief . . .

At the head of that sad procession of the *Ohmeseheso*@ lurched the two Old-Man Chiefs, Morning Star and Little Wolf, coming to a clumsy halt on their frozen legs, the new snow nearly reaching their knees.

"There! Beyond that hill!" one of the three young riders cried joyfully as he came galloping up to the old men. "We have seen the Crazy Horse people!"

As that news shot back through the cold stragglers, many of the old warriors began to sing once more those strong-heart songs that had sustained them during the recent battle with the pony soldiers. Even though they had few robes and blankets among them, everywhere now the women joined in celebration, trilling their tongues in joy. Once more *Ma-heo-o* had delivered His people from the hand of disaster.

Trudging stiff-legged to the crest of that low hill, where he caught his first whiff of woodsmoke on the knife-edged breeze that made his eyes seep, Morning Star peered down, his limbs gone wooden with the terrible cold. There . . . below . . . along a bend on the east side of the upper waters of Box Elder Creek,^ among the leafless cottonwoods where the Lakota sought shelter from much of the winter's cruel wind, sat the hide and canvas lodges—smoke rising from each blackened crown of poles. Headed their way already was a handful of young Oglalla warriors and camp sentries, their strong ponies plowing through the deep snow, while behind and below them dark antlike forms of the Crazy Horse people emerged from

* Lake DeSmet.
† Present-day Prairie Dog Creek.
# "Those Who Are Hearted Alike."
@ The Northern Cheyenne.
^ Present-day Beaver Creek.

their lodges, coming out to see for themselves what was causing all the excitement among the camp guards.

"Come, Morning Star," Little Wolf said quietly as he reached his old friend's side and tugged on an elbow. "Let us go tell Crazy Horse that the *ve-ho-e* soldiers have attacked us again."

For the longest time that winter afternoon the *Tse-Tsehese* leaders sat with Crazy Horse and the other Hunkpatila headmen, discussing Three Finger Kenzie's attack on their Red Fork village. As the sun began to set on that cold land, they talked over the why and asked the Oglalla to consider just what they could do for their close cousins, the *Ohmeseheso*—just as the Crazy Horse people had done last winter before eventually deciding to go in search of Sitting Bull's Hunkpapa.

But this time Morning Star believed he heard a different sound come from the throat of Crazy Horse. This time the Oglalla Shirt Wearer did not speak with the same voice as he had when the pony soldiers attacked Old Bear's village beside the Powder last winter.

This time there was a chiseled hardness on the face of Crazy Horse. And nothing soft in the eyes of the Oglalla war chief.

"We have little," the Lakota leader explained icily to his people as well as to their *Tse-Tsehese* guests. "After soldiers have chased us from camp to camp to camp since summer—forcing us to stay on the run all the time—there aren't many hides to give you to replace your lodges. And we do not have enough meat to feed your people."

For a long time Morning Star was stunned into silence. Then he finally asked, "What can your people give us?"

Wagging his head icily, Crazy Horse said, "I do not have enough to feed my own people . . . so how can I feed the *Ohmeseheso* as well?"

"What would you have us do?" demanded an angry Little Wolf, the Northern People's Sweet Medicine Chief, a warrior wounded six times in their recent battle with the pony soldiers.

Drawing himself up, Crazy Horse explained to his old comrades in war, "I will give you what my people can spare . . . for three days we can take you in and feed you, shelter you. But no more."

"For three days," Morning Star repeated. "After that, where will we find Sitting Bull?"

"Yes," Little Wolf said, his dark face suddenly beaming with hope. "Sitting Bull will help us again if you cannot. Tell us where we can find him!"

As the Oglalla leader's eyes crimped into resolute slits, he replied, "Sitting Bull is no longer in this country."

Morning Star asked, "Where can we find him?"

"You will not," the Lakota mystic answered. "For he is long gone—many days' ride from here."

"Where?" Little Wolf demanded sharply, hope replaced by suspicion.

"Far to the north of the Elk River*—where my scouts tell me he is running away from the Bear Coat's soldiers . . . fleeing for the Land of the Grandmother."

So the *Tse-Tsehese* rested for those three days, sleeping in the crowded lodges among their close relatives, the Oglalla, eating what the Crazy Horse people had to spare. Once more the two peoples shared the same despair.

In those moons come and gone since the big fight at the Greasy Grass last summer, some of the Hunkpatila had journeyed in to visit friends and relations at the White River Agency, where they learned the soldier chief they had wiped off the earth was none other than Yellow Hair, known to the *Tse-Tsehese* as *Hietzi*—the very same *ve-ho-e* who had destroyed Black Kettle and driven Rock Forehead's band in to their cramped reservation on the southern lands.

Then, on the fourth day, when Crazy Horse said the *Ohmeseheso* were to be on their own, the Oglalla chief suddenly called another council, his face no longer as hard as chert.

"Our people are like two streams that run down the same mountain," he told the refugees from the Red Fork Valley. "We have always looked to one another's welfare."

"Do your words mean we can stay on with you?" Little Wolf demanded, the iron edge of a warrior to his voice.

Finally Crazy Horse answered, "We no longer have much

* The Yellowstone River.

food to share with you—but my hunters tell me there are buffalo to the south, along the Buffalo Tongue. Your men can make meat and gather robes—"

Morning Star put out his hand to quiet Little Wolf and the angry warriors the moment they interrupted the Oglalla Shirt Wearer. "We will take our people there, Crazy Horse—and hunt for ourselves."

Little Wolf growled angrily, "We cannot go south! It would be sheer lunacy! Three Stars is marching north from the Powder to look for us!"

Then, as Morning Star opened his mouth to explain to his embittered chiefs that they had no choice but to look to their own safety, Crazy Horse spoke again.

"My village will go with you," he explained to the *Tse-Tsehese*. "We too must hunt for meat and hides. Like you, the soldiers have not given us much rest this autumn so that we could hunt for the winter. My warriors are almost as desperate as yours to feed our people. Unless our hunters make meat, I am afraid many of the Hunkpatila will be forced to go in to the White River Agency to fill the bellies of their children."

"But what of Three Stars's soldiers?" Wooden Leg demanded. "What of Three Finger Kenzie's prowling pony soldiers?"

Crazy Horse turned to the young warrior, saying, "My wolves who have been keeping an eye on those soldiers tell me they have turned around and are going south again, back to their warm forts. Once more the Great Mystery has watched over us and the soldiers haven't found us here in this country."

"But don't you believe that once the soldiers have new supplies," Morning Star asked, "they will return to search for us?"

"No," Crazy Horse asserted. "Together we will go hunt buffalo on the Tongue. Our women will scrape hides for new lodges to replace those the soldiers have destroyed. We will dry meat so that our people will not want for food this winter. No, my *Ohmeseheso* friends—I don't believe the army will march against us again this winter."

Fully a quarter of Baldwin's men lumbered into Fort Peck suffering from frostbite: ears, noses, or cheeks blackened with dead, rotted flesh. Little wonder, Frank thought, what with the mercury in his thermometer having frozen at the bottom: forty-two degrees below zero. And that was without the wind.

What was more, every soldier in that battalion suffered from want of sleep. In the past two days the hardy foot soldiers had marched more than seventy-three miles through snowdrifts and a howling blizzard, grabbing five minutes of sleep here, ten minutes of rest there. In fact, many of the battalion were so fatigued that they had suffered hallucinations on that brutal march that had meant the difference between survival or death. In his report to General Alfred Terry at department headquarters, Frank wrote:

> Some thought they were riding in steam cars . . . others thought they saw parks, lakes and cities when there was nothing but the vast snow-covered prairie before them.

In that dispatch Baldwin even confided, "I never experienced such suffering. . . . I myself got to sleep and fell off my horse." One of the men had to use his bayonet to prod the lieutenant out of a snowbank—an act for which Baldwin said he would recommend the soldier for a medal.

But it had been an excruciating ordeal that he had not mentioned that night when he quickly penned a letter to Alice. Instead, he had chosen to boast to his wife: "Just think your old man whipping Sitting Bull & driving him across the river when he has set at defiance 2 Brig Genls all summer."

From some of Mitchell's friendly Yanktonais camping the winter near the agency, Baldwin learned that afternoon of 8 December that Sitting Bull had stopped long enough to send a threat to the soldier chief that his Hunkpapa warriors would attack the walk-a-heaps once they started south for the Tongue River, then would turn about and destroy Fort Peck itself. Quickly composing a report that would be carried by one of his mounted soldiers ordered to locate Miles somewhere between their backtrail and the cantonment, Baldwin suggested that the colonel's battalion march east immediately for Bark Creek, and together they might just capture the elusive Sioux between them. If for some reason the colonel was unable to act in concert with him, Frank requested that supplies be forwarded down the Yellowstone to meet him.

Then he told his commander that in another three days—with his men rested and reoutfitted with rations—he planned to start again for Fort Buford as originally ordered. Frank disclosed that he planned on hiring a number of Indian scouts from the Fort Peck Agency, men who would provide a great service because they knew the surrounding area intimately.

But first there was the matter of empty soldier bellies and bone-numbing fatigue to be reckoned with. Frank's battalion immediately consumed one whole buffalo brought in by the Yanktonais; then the men promptly fell asleep. They awoke later in the afternoon to eat even more. Never had a warm meal and a place out of the winter wind meant so much to the men of the Fifth Infantry. Baldwin himself finished his first reports, ate every bite he could get his hands on, then collapsed into a deep slumber.

Not stirring until the following day, 9 December, Frank called his company commanders together to begin planning their next moves to trail, surround, and capture Sitting Bull's village. Their first item of business was to learn where the Hunkpapa had gone. From the direction taken by the fleeing Sioux, their best guess had the enemy moving south by east toward the timbered bottoms along the Redwater. To determine with more certainty, the lieutenant sent out Left Hand, an agency Assiniboine mustered onto the rolls the previous day.

"Mr. Baldwin, I'm sure that I speak for more than just myself when I say that some of the men are concerned that we might again run into the same situation with the Sioux attacking us in force," said I Company's Second Lieutenant, James H. Whitten.

"If we only had some artillery," grumbled David Rousseau.

Slowly, the grin came across Baldwin's face. "Why, gentlemen—we might just come up with something that will work."

"You can get your hands on a c-cannon?" asked Whitten.

Frank nodded. "I bet I can show you something we can put to good use."

"Jumping Jesus, sir! Show us!" exclaimed Frank Hinkle. "If we had a cannon—then those redskins never would get the upper hand on us!"

Frank immediately led the other officers to the north side of one of the agency buildings, where under a partial pile of firewood and a battered sheet of canvas rested an old mountain howitzer.

"But, Mr. Baldwin!" Whitten griped. "One of the wheels is broken beyond repair."

Rousseau joined in, "And the goddamned thing's got no limber, Lieutenant!"

"Hell, if I listened to you two, I might well never got our battalion back to the agency night before last!" Baldwin snapped. "Mark my words, and heed them, gentlemen: nothing was ever done by a man who said it couldn't be done!"

After he sent Lieutenant Hinkle to chase down the agency carpenter, Baldwin and the others tore off the canvas shroud and dug the howitzer out of the snow. The first step was to assign a work detail to detach one of their wagon boxes from its running gear. The next stage saw the soldiers unhooking the front truck of the wagon's running gear so that it could be pulled along by a team of mules much like a cannon's caisson or "limber"—that detachable front part of a gun carriage that usually serves to transport a large chest of ammunition for the twelve-pounder going into the field.

At the same time, a detail of soldiers laid in a store of dried buffalo meat while others repaired their own thirteen creaky wagons and readied another nine from the agency so that the six-mule teams could transport the foot soldiers this trip out.

At midday on Sunday, the tenth, agent Mitchell returned from Wolf Point with fifty Assiniboine he had enlisted, having learned that, once again on the south side of the Missouri, Sitting Bull had again taken his village east to the Redwater country.

The enemy was clearly moving farther and farther away. And very well might be headed for the Yellowstone country. If the victory was to belong to his battalion, Frank knew he had to act.

In his anxiousness to be on Sitting Bull's trail, the lieutenant decided he would have to overlook his battalion's need for replacement clothing, as well as the additional rest he'd planned for the men after what he'd put them through in the last few days. To replace the bootees and shoes that were falling apart—stitching coming loose and soles peeling off—many of Baldwin's men fashioned some crude but serviceable footwear from the green hides of those buffalo recently killed near the fort to feed them.

That afternoon Frank wrote another letter to Miles, this time explaining what he was about to embark upon, stating that though he apologized for not pursuing his attack upon the overwhelming numbers of Hunkpapa at Bark Creek, he nonetheless had every intention of herding Sitting Bull's village south toward the Yellowstone, where Miles himself might have a crack at them.

Having solved his problem of fatigued men by loading them onto his wagons, Baldwin put Fort Peck behind him on the eleventh. In addition to Mitchell's fifty Assiniboine, and those two new scouts hired to help Vic Smith—a young Joseph Culbertson and half-breed Edward Lambert—Frank had even convinced Second Lieutenant William H. Wheeler of the Eleventh Infantry, stationed at the agency, to join in their chase. Pushing east through the snowdrifts crusted along the ice-rutted Fort Buford Road, no more than a half mile beyond the site of the Sioux crossing and their fight of the seventh, the battalion went into camp for the night.

Overnight a Chinook wind blew in and, with the "snow-eater," temperatures moderated enough to turn the frozen, snowy road into a muddy quagmire. Late the afternoon of the twelfth Baldwin's wagons rumbled into Wolf Point, where the battalion acquired some sacks of oats for the stock, as well as some flour and hams for their own rations. While they were taking on supplies, the Assiniboine went off to visit their families camped nearby, but a local Assiniboine war chief named White Dog promised Baldwin that his fifty warriors would indeed continue in the search for Sitting Bull. However, by the time the battalion was crawling into their blankets that night, the Assiniboine had not yet shown up.

Nonetheless, later that night White Dog returned to give the lieutenant a report that the Hunkpapa had left the Redwater and were pushing south across the high divide toward the Yellowstone—just what Baldwin had already figured Sitting Bull would do. But the Assiniboine war chief went on to explain that news from the Lakota camps indicated the Hunkpapa intended on rallying and uniting other Indians to their cause on their way south . . . south toward the Powder River country, to reunite with Crazy Horse.

On the morning of the fourteenth, with no more than three sacks of grain for 150 animals and a paltry three days' rations for his men, Baldwin's battalion began moving across to the south bank of the Missouri—without White Dog's fifty Assiniboine warriors. Because of the warming weather Baldwin could no longer trust the ice beneath the heavy wagons. Instead, he unhitched the teams and sent the mules across first. That done, he had teams of men station themselves on the south shore to drag the wagons across by rope in the event their weight broke through the softening crust. Successfully reaching the far side, the mules were rehitched and the battalion was again on its way for that Thursday, marching up the boggy bottoms to the headwaters of Sand Creek, where they ascended the low divide that eventually took them over to Wolf Creek and finally down to the drainage of the Redwater.

Here the weather began to turn again, forcing the weary, shivering men time and again to cut passage for the teams and wagons through the snowdrifts still untouched by the recent thaw. By their Herculean efforts the battalion managed to put more than sixteen difficult miles behind them before they went into bivouac, built fires, and huddled beneath a frightening wind for the night.

By dawn on the fifteenth the wind of the previous night brought with it a thickening blanket of snow. With heads bowed the determined battalion marched another fourteen miles, yard by yard by yard at a time through a barren, high, exposed piece of country. At last, near sunset, Baldwin located some sparse vegetation, where his men squared their wagons, brought the mules within the corral, and struggled to build their pitiful greasewood fires in the keening winds that again buffeted them while they tried vainly to sleep.

In his pocket journal that night Frank noted that he had taken an assessment of his rations and found them once more running dangerously low. He began to hope they would encounter some game along the way. In addition, the unshod mules were having a hard time of it finding proper footing on the icy terrain, tiring quickly in their exertions.

Through the sixteenth the conditions only worsened; then, near midday on the seventeenth, scouts Smith, Culbertson, and Lambert finally located an Indian trail of unshod ponies and travois they figured to be no more than a week old. Through the rest of that day the temperature continued to drop, sliding quickly and refusing to rise above zero. That day Baldwin finally lost his last shred of hope of sighting game. Chances were not good, Vic Smith informed him, that they would find any deer or elk up and about during the brutal storms. Besides, the young eighteen-year-old Culbertson reminded Baldwin, what game there might have been in that country was more than likely either already harvested, or it had been driven out as the Hunkpapa had passed through only days before them.

"I have no other choice," Frank confided his private thoughts only to his journal that bitterly cold Sunday night. "We're somewhere between Wolf Point and Tongue River. Countermarching offers me little hope of accomplishing anything. I have but one option open to me now: I'll take the battalion on into this storm, keeping my nose to the enemy's trail—and trust Providence to provide for the men what I cannot."

Then he said a prayer asking that God grant him just one more crack at Sitting Bull.

Chapter 14

Wanicokan Wi 1876

In those first days of the Midwinter Moon, Spotted Elk joined the other chiefs and headmen of those bands of Shahiyela, Hunkpatila, Sans Arc, Miniconjou, and Hunkpapa who chose to stand shoulder to shoulder with one another that winter—against the soldiers, against the great cold, against starvation, as they continued their hunt for buffalo in the valley of the Buffalo Tongue.

Some young warriors from the migrating camp rode north to learn what they could of the soldier fort. In two days the riders returned, driving before them a small herd of cattle and some soldier horses. It was a good thing, because the farther the village wandered up the river valley, the fewer buffalo they encountered. As strong as they felt together, Spotted Elk knew no man could remain untouched by the sight of the hungry children, their gaunt wives, the way the once-proud war ponies hung their heads in starvation.

Not even the great Crazy Horse.

So it was that by the time the village reached the mouth of Suicide Creek,* even the stoic Strange Man of the Oglalla went along with the rest of the headmen in deciding they would at

---

* Hanging Woman Creek, site of present-day Birney, Montana.

least talk to the Bear Coat, who was making war on them from his Elk River fort. With the hunting become so poor and the cold grown so deep, it surely could not hurt for a delegation of their people to go look the Bear Coat in the eye and see if this soldier chief spoke the truth when he did not just demand their surrender but offered the *Titunwan* Lakota peace on a reservation of their own at the forks of the Cheyenne River.

Spotted Elk, middle son of Old Lone Horn of the Miniconjou, knew his father would expect nothing less of him—for it was a chief's first responsibility to care for his people.

"I will go to the soldier fort," Spotted Elk told the assembly of chiefs deciding on who would join the delegation.

Packs the Drum nodded approvingly. "This is good. What other brave men are there who will join me on our journey into the land of Bear Coat's soldiers?"

Hollow Horns volunteered, "For the Sans Arc I will go."

"And for my band of Miniconjou, I will join you," declared Fat Hide.*

In the end Red Cloth,† Tall Bull, and Bull Eagle agreed to go for their Miniconjou clans. Then two more stood to offer themselves.

"I must go with you," Bad Leg told the council. "But I will go along to take back the stolen horses to the soldier fort at the mouth of the Buffalo Tongue."

The Yearling stood in agreement. "Just as Crazy Horse and He Dog have said today: we are honorable men and cannot go talk with the *wasicu* about peace so soon after we have stolen his horses. We must return those animals."

In the end more than two-times-ten joined Packs the Drum that blustery morning when they dressed in their finest, mounted their strongest ponies, feathers fluttering in the steady wind, buffalo robes tugged tightly about them, and set off north to talk peace to the Bear Coat. Even Crazy Horse and He Dog decided they would ride along to represent the Oglalla.

Oh, what a glorious morning that was for Spotted Elk! The women pouring from their lodges into the bitter cold to

---

* Also known as Fat on the Beef in historical literature.
† Sometimes referred to as Lame Red Skirt.

trill their tongues, making good wishes upon this endeavor all hoped would bring an end to the slow starvation. Children raced about, laughing for the first time in so, so long as they dodged in and out among the delegates' ponies.

Stoic but expectant friends watched from the hillside across the creek while the village said its farewells. When the delegates had moved out of the tall, stately cottonwoods along the banks and were heading down the Buffalo Tongue, Bad Leg and The Yearling, along with four others, filed in at the rear, keeping their soldier horses bunched together in the deep snow.

From early morning, when the cold was its most bitter, until the night sky turned completely dark overhead, the peace delegates pushed toward the soldier fort on their mission of great urgency. How weary the ponies became on that journey, carrying these men a long way each day, animals forced to dig down through the snowdrifts at night in search of grass to eat. Four long days . . . but on the morning of the fifth Spotted Elk and Tall Bull reached the low rise of a bluff and looked down upon the valley of the Elk River.

Below them stood the squat log huts gathered in among the old cottonwoods. Wagons stood about, mules and horses grazing nearby or clustered in their corrals. And between that fort and where Spotted Elk sat on his pony stood some hide lodges, more than two-times-ten of them scattered among the trees and brush south of the soldier huts, a thin column of smoke rising from each one.

"They must be the soldiers' wolves," Tall Bull explained, his eyes quick to hide any worry.

"Eyes and ears for the Bear Coat, eh?" replied Spotted Elk. "Who do you think they are?"

"Corn Indians,"* Tall Bull answered. "Maybe some Yankton, come down from the Fort Peck Agency."

"Then they are Indians who will know us," Spotted Elk said. "We have nothing to fear."

Tall Bull nodded in agreement, but his eyes showed fear. "What if they do not know us?"

"There is no reason to fear an honorable warrior," Spotted Elk declared with a grin. "Even if he is your enemy."

---

* Arikara, or Ree, Indians from the Upper Missouri country.

"We will have the white flag flying above us?"

Spotted Elk reached out and laid his hand on Tall Bull's arm. "Packs the Drum wants to have the honor of going toward the soldiers first."

Tall Bull tried to smile bravely, saying, "And he wants me to be among those who join him."

"We have been friends a long time, you and me," Spotted Elk said. "So I want to come with you."

Shaking his head, Tall Bull said, "I think . . . you should stay back with the others and ride behind us."

Spotted Elk swallowed hard, sensing the other man's dread. "Are you expecting trouble?"

Tall Bull's eyes went first to those delegates coming up the slope behind them now. Then he gazed at the open ground between them and the soldier huts. "No—I am not expecting trouble. Those soldier wolves must surely be honorable men . . . and the Bear Coat's soldiers will see our white flag and know that we come in peace."

As the entire delegation of chiefs and soldier horses proceeded down the bluffs to the banks of the Buffalo Tongue, they came across a wood-cutting party, then a small group of men watching over a herd of cattle. Alarmed at first by the sudden appearance of more than a dozen warriors, the *wasicu* prepared to fight until they saw the two white flags carried by Hollow Horns and Tall Bull at the end of their lances. With that, and by other signs, the Lakota made it known that the white men had nothing to fear, that they were on their way to the post to talk to the Bear Coat about surrendering, to talk over making a strong peace between their peoples.

The winter sun was climbing near midsky by the time Packs the Drum stopped them all to form his forward delegation. The five he chose would ride in ahead of the others, who would stay behind a respectful distance, accompanying the horses being returned as a gesture of goodwill.

"I will wait behind with the others," Crazy Horse declared.

This was good, Spotted Elk believed. For a man of the Shirt Wearer's status to allow five others to go ahead on such an important mission was a good omen.

"And I will wait with him," Bad Heart Bull added. He urged his pony up beside that of Crazy Horse, taking a piece of stiff rawhide and some charcoal sticks from a parfleche he had slung over his back. "I will draw the picture story of this day when our chiefs go with such great hope to the Bear Coat so that our people can survive."

"We will show the *wasicu* that we are as honorable in peace as you have been in war," Packs the Drum confirmed to Crazy Horse, then ceremonially unwrapped his pipe from its otter-skin bag and placed it across his left arm, requesting the other four who would ride with him to do the same with their pipes.

"We will not only have the white man's white flags flying over our heads to show we come in peace," Tall Bull now explained to all the delegates, "but we will show them that we do not carry any weapons—only our pipes."

At Packs the Drum's signal Tall Bull brought his pony up on the leader's right side. Then Red Cloth positioned himself at Packs the Drum's left arm. On the far left rode Red Horses, and at the far right rode Bull Eagle, both men not only clutching their pipes and reins in left hands, but holding aloft their lances with smaller makeshift white flags fluttering in the stiff breeze nuzzling down the valley of the Elk River.

"Stay here until we have gone the distance of an arrow-shot," Packs the Drum requested of the others. "Then you are to follow."

Spotted Elk, Hollow Horns, and Fat Hide remained behind with Crazy Horse, He Dog, and the others, while the five set off about the time a knot of more than a dozen warriors emerged from the lodges erected along the riverbank. The Miniconjou chief did not feel good about the way the strangers suddenly showed themselves with great martial bluster, advancing with a swagger, all of them shouting and yelling—shields strapped to their upper arms, their right hands filled with weapons.

"This is not the way a man greets a warrior he honors," Hollow Horns warned.

"Who can these men be?" Spotted Elk asked, worry making wings flutter in his belly. "Who are these strangers who act with such poor manners when we show that we come in peace?"

"*Aiyeee!*" gasped Fat Hide, who clamped a hand over his

mouth. "Perhaps these are the *Psatoka** from beyond the Greasy Grass country!"

"Look at them!" Hollow Horns grumbled angrily. "If these are *Psatoka*—they act like insolent children before our warriors!"

Spotted Elk turned to look at Crazy Horse a moment, finding the war chief's eyes crimped into narrow slits of hate. The *Psatoka* had been enemies of the *Titunwan* Lakota back into many generations. Could such bad blood be set aside now? he wondered.

As the dozen strangers got closer and closer to the peace delegation, Spotted Elk's heart began to thump all the faster in his breast, like the beating of a wounded bird's wing. He glanced beyond the strangers, finding some three or four soldiers advancing on foot in the distance—trotting, in a hurry. There was much activity taking place at the first fringe of log huts beyond those Indian lodges erected on the right, where even more warriors stirred now, clearly a few women too, all of them beginning to emerge from the trees and leafless willow onto the open plain.

Too many of the strangers . . . more than ten-times-ten. Back and forth they shouted to those who came hurrying on foot to confront the five delegates. If they were indeed *Psatoka*, thought Spotted Elk, then there was reason for him to fear for Tall Bull and the other delegates.

For winters beyond his count the *Psatoka* had allied themselves with the *wasicu*. For many winters the *Titunwan* Lakota had been making forays deep into traditional *Psatoka* hunting grounds. Many were the scalps Lakota warriors had carried home from the enemy's country. Hard and cold must be the hearts of the *Psatoka* warriors against all Lakota. Even Lakota coming in peace, with their pipes out, with the *wasicu's* white flags fluttering over their heads.

"Perhaps there is nothing to fear," Hollow Horns suddenly said, hope rising in his voice.

"Yes, look!" agreed Fat Hide. "The *Psatoka* are showing their hands to our men."

"They want to shake hands!" Hollow Horns cheered.

---

* The Crow, or Absaraka, tribe.

Spotted Elk nodded, his heart leaping, and said, "This is a good sign!"

Just as the frost from those last two words hung in the cold air before his face, Spotted Elk watched one of the strangers clasp hands with Packs the Drum, then suddenly jerk, yanking the man off the back of his pony. As quickly, other extended hands locked on to Lakota arms and dragged the remaining four delegates to the ground, where all five disappeared in a swirl of horses' legs, a flurry of blows, the bright glint of sunlight on metal blades, along with the lusty blood-cries of those who had ambushed the delegates.

From the trees to the right burst a sudden cry as the many *Psatoka* who had been watching burst into the clearing, sprinting past the ambush toward Spotted Elk and the others.

Crazy Horse yanked his Winchester from beneath his buffalo robe, trying to steady his prancing horse. "They are murderers!"

"We cannot save them!" Hollow Horns shouted as he wheeled his pony, jabbing heels into its ribs.

Quickly trying to stuff his pipe back into its sacred bag, Spotted Elk fought to pull his bow from its wolf-skin quiver with a handful of arrows. He would stay with Crazy Horse and He Dog as long as there was a fight.

"No!" Fat Hide snarled. "There are too many!"

Spotted Elk nocked an arrow on his bowstring. "We cannot leave them—"

"They are lost!" He Dog growled, shoving Spotted Elk as the many on foot closed the gap on them.

"Turn the horses! Turn the horses!" Fat Hide ordered Bad Leg and The Yearling.

All was confusion now. In the middistance a handful of soldiers were shouting. Spotted Elk could hear their voices, see the breathsmoke puffing from their tiny mouths as they came racing toward the scene. The delegates' ponies were bolting, scattering in fear to the four winds, being chased by some of the enemy warriors and their women.

Oh, how those *Psatoka* screamed and screeched at the Lakota fortunate to escape, *Psatoka* holding aloft Lakota pipes in one hand, the scalps of those five honorable men they had just murdered in the other.

Spotted Elk glanced over his shoulder, finding more

soldiers were coming now. Behind them a soldier horn was blowing too. *Wasicu* coming from many directions now. It was a wholesale ambush! The soldiers broke from hiding, running to help the *Psatoka* murder all the Lakota.

Those left with Crazy Horse wheeled about and kicked their ponies into a hard gallop, heading back to that low rise of ground where they had first looked down upon the soldier fort. Where they had first spotted the enemy lodges back among the trees along the Buffalo Tongue River.

For a few heartbeats He Dog halted them, throwing up his arm and bringing his pony around in a tight circle. Down on the flat ground they saw the soldiers reaching the scene, guns in their hands. At that very moment Spotted Elk watched a *Psatoka* warrior disappear into the tall willow with the two white flags, carrying away those signals of peace as the soldiers arrived.

"We better go before the soldiers follow us!" Fat Hide cried out.

Already Bad Leg and The Yearling and some others were frantically driving the horses hard through the deep snow, down off the high ground, heading south, racing back up the Buffalo Tongue River toward the Crazy Horse village.

He Dog waved the rest on, waiting to be the last to flee with Crazy Horse. But Spotted Elk reined up beside them, all three waiting a breathless moment longer, gazing down at that scene . . . realizing that there were no survivors, knowing the soldiers' *Psatoka* wolves had killed all five.

No man could still be alive after that treacherous butchery.

"There, Mr. Leforge!" Nelson Miles screamed at the civilian, ripping the two white towels from the hands of Hobart Bailey, his adjutant. The colonel roughly yanked up Tom Leforge's hand and stuffed the flags into it.

"G-general—"

"There, by Jupiter! Your goddamned Crow are guilty of unprovoked and cowardly murder!"

"I can't believe—"

"There—that's your evidence!" Miles roared. "What have you to say to that?"

Leforge could do little more than stare down at the flags

and wag his head in disgust. One of the towels was even stained with a little blood. Sioux blood.

"Bull Eagle! They even killed Bull Eagle!" Miles screeched, wagging his head violently. Then his voice suddenly quieted. "He was one I took a real liking to, figured I could trust his word." Then he was screeching again, "And now your bunch of cowards have murdered him!"

Leforge gulped, then said, "I know most of them what done this—"

"You know the sons of bitches, do you?"

Shrugging, looking back up into the flinty glare of the colonel, Leforge admitted, "Don't know what come over 'em to do anything like this."

"A little too late to figure that out, don't you think, Mr. Leforge?" Miles was seething. "Why—just yesterday I had you warn that bunch of yours that I would hang any one of them if they killed one of my Yanktonais couriers riding between here and Buford or Peck. Now they've killed Bull Eagle!"

Leforge pleaded, "Sir, they told me them Sioux fired on their women as they was riding in."

"Bullshit!" Miles roared, slamming a fist down on his flimsy desk. "You and I both know those five didn't come riding into a soldier fort shooting up your Crow camp!"

"The women . . . they'll tell you—"

"Shut your lying mouth before I shut it for you, Leforge!" Miles fumed. "I have witnesses—soldier witnesses—that tell me different. I for one could not believe the Sioux would ride in here under a flag of truce, shooting at your women!"

Leforge swallowed hard, then nodded grudgingly. "General—there's most of 'em wanna try to make it up to you—"

"Make it up to me?" Miles interrupted Tom Leforge. "Don't you understand that just a month ago Bull Eagle showed up here, came riding right in here while I was gone chasing Sitting Bull? That's right—he came in under a white flag—just like the ones your Crow tried to hide—came in to get some rations because he trusted me, because I told him he could trust that white flag!"

Leforge stared at the floor. "I can't defend what they done, General."

"Bull Eagle was the sort of man doing what was best for

his people," Miles stormed. "He alone was more of an honorable man than a hundred of those cowardly Crow of yours!"

Never before had Luther Kelly seen the man so angry. Make no mistake, Nelson A. Miles was an emotional, volatile man. But this . . . this treachery and attempt at cover-up had the general right on the edge. Miles was shuddering as he tried to contain his fury, his fists clenching and unclenching. As the general slowly brought both fists up, Kelly became afraid Miles would do something he might well regret.

Luther instantly stepped between Miles and the squaw man. "General—if I may. Let's try to sort out what we can do about all this right now."

"What we can do right now!" Miles shrieked. "We had five Sioux chiefs ride in here to surrender their people to me. Our efforts at convincing the enemy that we will continue to make war on them is finally beginning to bear enough fruit that Bull Eagle and his emissaries come riding in here under two goddamned white banners of peace . . . and they're butchered within sight of my post!"

Miles lunged at the two grease-stained white towels Leforge held across his open hands, but Kelly was there first, tearing them away from the squaw man.

"Any reason why your Crow would kill the Sioux chiefs without warning?" Kelly demanded, glaring into Leforge's eyes.

"Any reason?" Leforge answered. "How 'bout lots of dead relatives—if one reason's good as another for you."

Miles grumbled something under his breath, turning slightly before he roared, "They're cowards, Leforge! All of them who had any hand in this! I'm not sure I shouldn't string you up while I've got my hands on you! Just to show your bunch what I think of cowards!"

Kelly watched Leforge flinch and swallow hard at that imaginary noose tightening around his throat.

The squaw man bravely said, "If that somehow evens things, General—then string me up."

Miles began to sputter with frustration. "You know goddamned well it won't do me a bit of good with the Sioux, Leforge! Those other riders who watched your Crow kill the five helpless chiefs, why—they're halfway back to Crazy Horse right now . . . off to tell him that my word can't be trusted!

Your back-stabbing sonsabitches have gone and shattered months of my hard work trying to hit the Sioux solidly while talking straight to them at the same time!"

"I ain't got no idea what you want me to do now, General," Leforge pleaded.

Miles leaned in to ask, "You said the dozen or so responsible for the murders have already escaped?"

"They took off about as soon as your soldiers started showing up."

"Cowards!" Miles shouted as he whirled on his heel and stomped back to collapse behind his desk in the canvas chair. "Those Crow are supposed to be warriors! Warriors don't kill unarmed enemies under a flag of truce!"

Feeling almost like a traitor himself, Kelly had to declare, "General, the Sioux had weapons under their blankets—just like at Cedar Creek."

"But they didn't have those weapons out and ready to use, by God!" Miles blustered. He turned to glare at the squaw man. "What will become of those responsible, Leforge?"

"They've took off for the agency, General."

"And you'll never get your hands on them," Kelly admitted. "The rest of the tribe will protect them, harbor them."

"Yellow-backed cowards," the colonel fumed. "I don't think I can trust one of your mercenaries now, Leforge." Miles turned to Charles Dickey. "Captain, I'm hereby ordering you to disarm the remaining Crow scouts and send them packing."

"Yes, sir," answered Dickey. "Anything more?"

"I want you to dismount them, Captain—then I'm going to send those ponies to the Sioux, along with a few pounds of tobacco and my word that I had nothing to do with this. Yes—I'll send those ponies back with a couple of the friendly Yankton couriers. By Jupiter—that ought to make the Crow think twice about pulling this kind of yellow-backed thing again."

"General," Leforge began to plead, "the rest of 'em ain't to blame."

"Did they stand and watch?"

Leforge shrugged. "I s'pose they did—"

"Did the rest of your goddamned Crow stop the murders?"

"No," and he wagged his head.

"I can't trust any bunch who will kill someone coming in under a flag of truce, Leforge," said Miles. "I don't want your Crow around here anymore."

The squaw man said, "I'll pull out in the morning."

"No, not you," Miles said. "You're not going anywhere."

"N-no, sir?"

"You're staying right here, Leforge."

"Why are you sending all the rest back to the agency and you're keeping me here?" Leforge asked, his eyes filling with worry. "You making me your prisoner?"

"No, you knuckle-brained son of a bitch. You're my guide, my tracker. Kelly knows what lies north of here, but you know more about this country south of the Yellowstone than any scout I've got on the payroll. Tomorrow I want you to pick two of the most trustworthy Crow you can find—then send the rest packing."

"Just two, General?"

"Two, Leforge. That's all. So, believe me, I'm going to get my money's worth out of *you.*"

"You're really keeping me on to scout for you?"

Miles pointed a big finger at the squaw man. "Damn right I am. While you might not be my prisoner—I do in a way consider you my hostage."

"H-hostage?"

Miles went on. "You brought those Crow here, squaw man. Those Crow probably just killed any chance I ever had of getting the rest of the Sioux to surrender to me. Not to Crook, but to *me!* So now you're staying put, and when this outfit's ready to march again in a few days, you're going to take me south, Leforge."

"South?"

This time Miles turned to his chief of scouts, asking, "That's where the hell those Sioux came from, wasn't it, Kelly?"

Luther nodded, grim-lipped as he answered, "South, General. Probably camped along the Tongue."

The colonel slowly leaned onto his desk, rising out of his canvas chair. "And Mr. Leforge here is going to make up for the murder of those five peaceful Sioux by leading me up the Tongue after the one Sioux warrior we all know won't ever give up and make peace."

"C-crazy Horse?" asked Leforge.

"Goddamned right," Miles grumbled. "If those Sioux don't accept my offer of peace after what your Crows did, Leforge—you're gonna be the one who takes me right into the lap of Crazy Horse himself."

Chapter 15

17 December 1876

**Steamers Crushed in the Ice
at St. Louis**

Etc., Etc., Etc.

MISSOURI

**Ice Jam at St. Louis—Steamers Caught and
Crushed.**

ST. LOUIS, December 11.—A reporter lately up from
the arsenal gives these additional particulars of the
destruction of steamers this month. It appears that
nearly all the boats of the Keokuk Northern line were
in winter quarters near the arsenal and supposed to
be secure from damage. When the ice started these
steamers were forced from their moorings and carried down stream. The War Eagle and Golden Eagle,
two large and valuable boats, were forced on shore
opposite the arsenal wall in such a manner as to

block the passage, and the other boats crowded and caused a complete jam. . . . At 2 P.M. the ice again moved, crushing the boats still closer together, and doing additional damage. Again at 4 P.M. there was another movement of ice which pressed against the boats with terrific power and forced them still farther down, crushing guards, upper decks and wheels and doing great damage. . . . The hull of the Mitchell was stove in and she filled, but her position prevented her from settling to the bottom.

Headquarters Cantonment at Tongue River
December 17, 1876

To
Philip H. Sheridan
Assistant Adjutant General
Department of Dakota
Saint Paul, Minn.

Sir:
I have to report the occurrence of an unfortunate affair at this place, yesterday. . . .

Those killed were believed to be Bull Eagle, Tall Bull, Red Horse, Red Cloth, and one other prominent Chief of the Sioux nation. I am unable to state the object of Bull Eagle's coming, but am satisfied he came with the best of motives. I can only judge from the following: When he surrendered on the Yellowstone, after the engagement on Cedar Creek, he was the first to respond to my demands, and, I believe, was largely instrumental in bringing his people to accept the terms of the Government.

[Bull Eagle] seemed to be doing everything in his power for the good of the people, and endeavoring to bring them a more peaceful condition. He appeared to have great confidence in what I told him. I gave him five days to obtain meat; during that time he lost three favorite ponies which were brought to this place. During my absence he came in, bringing five horses that had strayed or been stolen from some citizen in the vicinity, and requested his own. . . .

[The five murdered Sioux] were within a few hundred yards of the parade ground, where they were deliberately placing themselves in the hands of the Government, and within the camp of four hundred Government troops.

[This whole affair] illustrates clearly the ferocious, savage instincts of even the best of these wild tribes and the impossibility of their controlling their desire for revenge, when it is aroused by the sight of their worst enemies, who have whipped them for years and driven them out of their country. Such acts are expected and considered justifiable among these two tribes of Indians, and it is to be hoped that the Sioux will understand that they fell into a camp of their ancient enemies, and did not reach the encampment of this command.

> Very respectfully
> your obedient Servant
> (sgd.) Nelson A. Miles
> Colonel 5th Infantry
> Brevet Major General U.S.A.
> Commanding.

Seamus Donegan took a deep breath—so deep, the cold air hurt within his chest. He nudged the roan and kept the gelding's nose pointed north.

Down the Tongue all the way to the Yellowstone.

Seamus had been there before. Last summer with Crook and Terry, after Custer got half his regiment wiped out. About the time Nelson A. Miles got itchy to break loose from the senseless thumb twiddling of the two generals and headed toward the Tongue for the winter.

It wasn't just cold in this country anymore. No. This had become pure hell: one day after another of endless, soul-thieving cold. Then yesterday he was certain the temperature played a card off the bottom of the deck on him. Instead of warming through the day, it got even colder. Mercilessly cold.

And the wind never stopped.

Tugging the thick, wide wool scarf up to the bridge of his nose, Seamus used it to swipe quickly at the tears seeping from his eyes because the galling wind was strong enough, stubborn enough, to sneak inside every gap of his clothing—despite the Irishman's best efforts to pull his head down inside the big flap collar of his wool-and-canvas mackinaw like a turtle, turning his face to one side as he fought to keep one eye on some landmark off in the distance. North by west.

One eye that constantly watered from that wind beneath the long gray frosted hairs of the wolf-hide cap.

"It's your'n now, boy," old Dick Closter had told him that Sunday morning at Crook's wagon camp on the Belle Fourche. "I'm going back to post—put up my feet and play some cards by the stove. So I figger you need it more'n me."

"Swear I'll get it back to you soon as I come down through Fetterman."

The old mule packer's eyes had softened beneath the two bushy white beetles nestled on his brow. "You just keep it, son. And remember me as your friend when you wear it."

Behind him whipped the wide-brimmed hat attached only by that wind string knotted around his neck. Tossed this way and that, it would again one day provide shade from a blazing sun or protect his eyes from the piercing glare off winter snow. Seamus snorted. No glare these last few days—why, the sun had been no more than a buttermilk-pale button in the sky, if that. What with the way the storm clouds danced past one right after the other, day after day. Seamus sniffed and dragged the horsehide gauntlet mitten under his sore, reddened nose.

For three and a half days he had followed Three Bears and the other Lakota scouts, who had led him northwest to the mouth of the Little Powder. He had wanted to push right on down the Powder itself, rather than chance the arduous cross-country journey. But Three Bears had advised against it. To ride the Powder in the wintertime was a gamble: the Crazy Horse people preferred its valley at this time of the year. Upstream or down, a lone white man was taking a very, very big chance.

So just as the Lakota warrior had scratched out on his map in the snow, Seamus bid the scouts farewell and pushed on across the Powder, then slowly ascended the high divide that carried him over to Mizpah Creek. Many were the times Frank Grouard had told him stories of the Powder and

Mizpah country. Prime hunting ground for the Hunkpatila of Crazy Horse and He Dog, that was.

That's when it had struck him—remembering something Grouard had told him about the lay of the land. Something that just might take a day off his trip.

Cold and feeling more alone than he had in a long, long time, Seamus knew full well what a warm fire and new faces could do for his half-numb soul. A little hot coffee and something more to eat than dried meat and army tacks.

That's when he decided that there would be no question if he should chance cutting at least a day off his ride to that post at the mouth of the Tongue. He would accomplish that by cutting north-northwest, cross-country after leaving the Mizpah, until he struck Pumpkin Creek. After another day and one more freezing winter night Donegan reached the mouth of the Pumpkin . . . to stand, finally, on the banks of the Tongue, far below where he would have struck the river had he not gambled on the shortcut.

On his left, back to the south, lay Otter Creek; beyond it was Hanging Woman Creek. Grouard had often talked about the warrior bands making camps in that country.

Donegan shuddered and turned down the Tongue.

For the better part of a week now he had been dozing in fits, too cold to get any real rest. What he did more often than not was to pull his head beneath his blankets, his breath warming the skin on his face there in his cocoon, and remember the touch of her fingers on his cheeks. Recalling the sweet smell of the babe's breath after the child had finished suckling at its mother's breast and Seamus would rock the boy to sleep. So lonely and cold, it was nothing he could call sleep.

So he poked his warm wool mittens down inside the stiff horsehide cavalry gauntlets and stuffed each of them beneath an armpit, trying to remember just how warm he had been back at Fort Laramie. Just how safe and secure and warm a man could feel in the arms of a woman.

Donegan discovered that his fire had gone out when he awoke in the shapeless early light that eighth morning. With one hand he pulled the two thick blankets back over his head and closed his eyes. Not going to worry about a puny fire now. He would have to be on his way soon enough. Down in that burrow of darkness he listened to the rattle of the wind as it hurtled over him, tormenting the leafless branches of the alder in the cottonwood grove he had chosen last night when the moon and stars had begun to cloud over.

Then he heard the roan snort.

Likely thirsty, he thought.

Cold and shuddering in the dark, Seamus had been forced to camp where there was shelter out of the wind, but no open water, in a copse of saplings and brush near the Tongue.

Slowly, stiffly, he pulled himself out of the wide sack of oiled canvas where his blankets kept him from freezing. Standing, revolving his shoulders to work some of the kinks out of them, Donegan trudged over to the gelding, patting its muzzle.

It took a few minutes, but he found a spot along the bank where the ice didn't gather so thick. He smacked at it with the butt end of his camp ax, then bent his head over the hole to plunge his chin into the icy cold. His beard quickly freezing as he struggled to his feet, Seamus stood back and let the roan have its first long drink of the day.

To the east the invisible sun was just then beginning to turn the underbellies of the low clouds to an orange fire, pink above. By the time he had saddled, tied his bedroll behind him, and pushed on down the Tongue another five miles, he could see that the thick clouds stretching from horizon to horizon were destined to blot out the sun again for another day.

All around him the wind skipped, whittling its way across a desolate country scarred by winds of a thousand centuries, a thirsty land veined by the erosion of countless springtimes that brought moisture, only to have that moisture sucked right out of the ground come the bake-oven summers.

Plodding slowly, letting the roan pick its own way, Donegan kept the Tongue to his left, winding northward into that afternoon, sensing the path the sun took at his back all the while, until it finally rested for another day near the far, far mountains somewhere beyond the back of his left shoulder. A Sunday, he had figured out. One long week since he had finished that letter to Samantha in those moments before he'd ridden away from the Belle Fourche with Three Bears.

At the muffled crack Donegan pulled back hard on the reins—so hard, it startled him, realizing he must have been half-asleep in the saddle again. A dangerous thing to do, even in this cold. A man who counted on its being far too cold to bump into a hunting party of Lakota might well be a dead man in this country.

Nudging the horse into the trees, where he might have a chance to see them before they saw him, Seamus waited and listened. Another muffled crack. Then more, all muffled, in a ragged rhythm. And in the space between some of those cracks, he imagined he heard voices.

Straining his eyes through the bare, snow-slickened branches of the trees, he studied the far side of the Tongue, the slope leading up from the river. The sounds came from beyond that rise of ocher earth mantled in patches of dirty white. He decided he had to know.

Leading the horse out of the brush, Seamus moved to the riverbank, plopped one boot down on the ice, thumped it good with a heel to test it, planted both feet down and jumped several times, then yanked on the reins. Slowly, deliberately, measuring each step, Donegan began to cross, eyes flicking from the opposite bank to the place where he would plant each foot. Yard by yard he moved across the opaque, shimmering ice, where he could sometimes make out the Tongue River bubbling beneath its thick, protective coat.

Now the voices grew louder, one voice more so than the others, sternly snapping; then more of that clack-clunk of wood against wood. In minutes Seamus was at the top of the hill, brazenly putting the skyline at his back because he knew, he remembered, he recognized those sounds. Donegan held his breath as he stared down on the wood detail. A dozen soldiers wrapped in heavy buffalo-hide or wool coats, muskrat caps tied under their chins, axes and saws in their mittens, and a sergeant standing up on a pile of wood in the first of two wagons, bellowing his orders as the men finished filling the bed of the second wagon up to the gunwales.

Each of those resounding clunks of wood like a step taken closer to home for a lonely wayfarer.

Then he blinked, not really sure his ears weren't playing tricks on him. Suddenly those faint, brassy notes floating his way on the cold wind.

"God-blessit!" the sergeant bawled in his mass of gray-and-black whiskers. "I tolcha idjits! Said they'd blow retreat afore you'd get this detail done, din't I, you slackards! Now we have to bust our ever-livin' humps to get back afore dark!"

Again the trumpet blew those homecoming notes. And Seamus felt the cold tighten his throat, remembering the sound of that call at Fort Laramie just before they would fire the sunset gun. Retreat for the day. Which meant supper, and shelter for the coming of night.

Below him now sharp commands cracked above the six-mule teams, whips snapped, and the loads groaned as wagons lurched into motion with a creaking rumble across the hard, icy ground. Beside both wagons the dozen soldiers strung out on both sides, having laid their long Springfields at a shoulder now.

Grabbing hold of the horn, Seamus swung himself into the saddle with an ungainly grunt, settled his coat and the thick buffalo-hide leggings, then hurried the roan into motion along the ridgetop, watching the first of the soldiers at the back of the procession turn to look up his way, suddenly stumbling, regaining his footing, and pounding on the back of the man in front of him.

They both whirled about, beginning to yell and point, and a moment later the wagons shuddered to a halt as the whole outfit turned about to watch the lone rider lope down the hillside, cutting this way and that around the snowy turnip heads of greasewood.

"S-sojurs!" he sang out as loud as he could in joy, finding his voice a croak after so many days of not using it.

"Just who the hell you be?" the slit-eyed sergeant demanded. "Keep a eye on this'un, fellers. And that hill too. Might be more of 'em."

"Just me," Seamus pleaded as he reined up. "Donegan's the name."

"Where the blazes you come from?" asked the soldier closest. "Up from Glendive by the south bank?"

With a wag of his wolf-hide cap Donegan grinned, for the moment just letting his eyes dance over the faces raw and chapped by the brutal wind and cold. How good it was to see such faces, men, soldiers. Even if they all had guns pointed at him.

"No, not Glendive," he answered with an unused voice. "Over from the Belle Fourche. And the Crazy Woman Fork of the Powder far to the south. Beyond that—I come all the way from the Red Fork Canyon where Mackenzie's Fourth drove the mighty Cheyenne into the snow."

"Y-you from Crook's bunch?" the sergeant squeaked in disbelief. He wiped a dribble of tobacco juice from his lower lip.

"None other," Seamus said, sliding out of the saddle clumsily with those thick buffalo-hide leggings. He stomped over to stop in front of the sergeant, pulled off his horsehide gauntlet, and held out his bare hand in the cold. "I've got a letter from Crook for your General Miles."

They shook and the old file muttered, "I'll be go to hell, boys . . . if this feller don't look like he's come through hell to get here."

"You really come from Crook?" another soldier gasped, shuffling up close to look the Irishman up and down as if he had to be an apparition.

With a shudder of his head the sergeant asked, "That ain't no bald-face? It true you come right up through all that country down yonder?"

"I been eight days doing it, fellers," Donegan replied, licking an oozy lip, then shoved the wolf-hide cap back from his forehead a bit. "And I sure got me a hankering for a hot cup of coffee right about now."

"By God, if we all don't have such a hankering our own selves!" roared an old soldier who shoved his way into the knot around Donegan.

"Lookee there under his hat, Sarge!" another man piped up. "He come up from Crook's country . . . an' still got him his hair!"

The sergeant's eyes finally began to twinkle as he pounded the Irishman on the shoulder. "So, you gol-danged civilian—maybeso while we finish our li'l walk back to the post yonder . . . you can tell us how come your scalp ain't hanging from Crazy Horse's belt right about now."

Chapter 16

18 December 1876

BY TELEGRAPH

THE INDIANS

The Latest from General Crook.

CHEYENNE, December 14.—NORTH FORK BELLE FOURCHE, December 10.—Crook's force left Buffalo Springs on the 6th, arrived here on the 9th, and is now in camp here. The train leaves to-day to bring up rations and forage from Buffalo Springs. The trail over which the army marched was a very bad one. There is no information as to the exact location of the hostiles. Crook will remain here several days to rest and recuperate the animals, and then move to the mouth of the Little Powder. Weather mild, and not much snow has fallen.

After a miserably cold night suffered down in the snowy bottomland of Ash Creek, Lieutenant Frank Baldwin had the men of his battalion awakened for their breakfast of quarter rations. That meant they ate not much more than a corner of one of their hardtack biscuits and a bite or two of frozen salt pork the soldiers could let thaw inside the warmth of their mouths, savoring the taste of the animal fat and grease.

As the last of his lieutenants came up to form a tight knot around Baldwin, each man huffing a thick cloud of hoarfrost, Frank quickly looked at the half-breed who had walked his horse up to the pickets in the subfreezing darkness some two hours before dawn. Johnny Bruguier had just covered a lot of country in a very short time.

After taking Baldwin's message to Miles, whom he found in the country north of the cantonment, the scout turned back around with a dispatch from the colonel. He found Baldwin's battalion already gone on its chase across the Missouri when he reached Fort Peck. By that time scout Billy Cross was all but done in and elected to stay behind at the agency while the half-breed mounted up to follow the soldier trail east, slipping south across the frozen river, then cross-country to the Redwater, traveling fast, and damn near nonstop.

"Bruguier here comes with word from the general," Baldwin announced to his officers now, once they were gathered close. "Miles confirmed our orders to track Sitting Bull and pitch into his camp. The general reports that he'll bring the rest of our regiment up to support. So I'm sending Bruguier back to Tongue River, where the general was taking his battalion."

"When do you suppose we'll find the Sioux?" asked Lieutenant Hinkle with an edge of impatience.

"Smith and our other scouts tell me chances are good we'll run onto the village sometime in the next two or three days," Frank said in a way calculated to buoy the flagging spirits of those men who had spent long days of marching and long nights of cold, all in an attempt to catch up to the warriors who had nearly wiped them out ten days before.

Looking at their faces for a moment that gray dawn of the eighteenth while the battalion stomped around to work up circulation in their feet and legs, Baldwin added, "And that village should be somewhere this side of the Yellowstone if we're lucky."

"I want to have a crack at them myself, sir," said Lieutenant Rousseau. "Sooner us than the companies with General Miles."

The rest of the officers echoed that sentiment.

Ever since they had crossed the Missouri near the mouth of Bark Creek, those three companies of foot soldiers had been slogging through the snow and frozen mud in the wake of Sitting Bull's Hunkpapa village. For all that they had endured in silence, Baldwin prayed it would be theirs to capture the greatest of the Sioux chiefs and drive the rest of his people back to the reservation.

His men deserved it for all they had suffered, for all they had gone without, for the way they had stood off the Hunkpapa back on the seventh.

Just past seven A.M. he watched Bruguier climb back into the saddle and point his nose south by west, toward the Tongue River Cantonment, carrying word to Miles of Baldwin's present location, his direction of travel, the battalion's condition, and their disposition to fight any and all Sioux encountered. With the half-breed on his way, Frank ordered the men out, on Sitting Bull's trail once more.

Through that morning they first marched east, then eventually south, keeping to the bottoms of the tiny tributaries feeding Ash Creek, doing all that they could to stay hidden from any enemy rear guard. Despite all their efforts after some five hours, close to one P.M. a solitary horseman appeared on the brow of a hill ahead of the column, watched the soldiers for a few moments, then disappeared.

Frank was certain they had been discovered.

"Keep up the pace now, men!" he cheered them. "This is the time to show the enemy what we're made of!"

Within minutes a flight of ring-necked doves burst from the leafless branches of a nearby grove of cottonwood saplings, causing Baldwin to notice the sky beyond the hilltops. "Look there."

"I see it, Lieutenant," replied Lieutenant Whitten.

A few columns of smoke poked wispy fingers into the air.

His throat constricting, Frank held up his arm and gave the command to halt the column. "Perhaps it's not too much to hope for," he told the officers at the head of the march.

Hinkle asked, "What's that, sir?"

"I'm praying that smoke means they haven't broken camp and fled when they learned we were coming."

"If that scout of theirs spied us," Rousseau warned, "and the village isn't running . . . that can only mean they're lying in wait for us."

"And have an ambush ready," agreed Whitten.

Baldwin nodded. "What say I go have a look for myself?"

Taking only Whitten with him, Frank crept ahead on foot a quarter of a mile, a half mile, then reached the brow of a ridge close to a mile from the head of his battalion. At that point the two officers were less than two miles north of the divide that separated the drainages of the Missouri and Yellowstone rivers.

Here above the frozen, sandy bottom of Ash Creek the two officers lay on their bellies—surprised to look down at Sitting Bull's village.

A few horsemen moved in and out of the cluster of 122 lodges situated beneath a bluff on the east side of the creek, women going about their work and children staying close to the camp circle that midday. None of the canvas or hide lodges and tents were coming down in a panic to flee. Indeed, Baldwin was shocked to find that there did not seem to be any great anxiety or alarm in the village.

Perhaps they're not afraid, Baldwin thought as he looked over his enemy. They figure they beat us once, so they can do it again.

"It's no wonder the Sioux would feel like they could whip us on a rematch," Frank whispered to Whitten at his side. "When we last heard of Sitting Bull's strength after Cedar Creek, all he had was thirty lodges."

"And look at them now," Whitten said. "Enough warriors in there to make this a good scrap for us, sir."

"I'll wager every last one of those warriors is loaded for bear."

Baldwin and Whitten hurried back to the column, where the lieutenant quickly issued his orders for the attack, then had young Joe Culbertson and Lambert lead the battalion around to the left, where he could approach the camp from the more favorable ground northwest of the village. He deployed his three companies much as he'd prepared for his attack against Gray Beard's Southern Cheyenne at McClellan

Creek: with one company attacking as skirmishers in front of his wagons advancing four abreast, his other two companies deployed along either side of the train, with a small rear guard to protect his supplies and ammunition from a flanking maneuver by the Sioux.

Culbertson and Lambert rode at the point of attack with Baldwin, all three of them growing even more astounded to confirm they had crept up on the village—so certain had they been that the lone horseman had galloped off to raise the alarm.

"Bring that caisson and limber up!" Frank ordered the moment the tops of the lodges came into view.

Beyond the trees the village began to bustle now.

They must surely know we're coming, know we're at their door, he thought as the artillery crew dragged the Fort Peck howitzer around the wagons, right up to the head of the columns, where some of the crew unhitched the pair of mules while others scurried to wheel the cannon about in a half circle.

"Gauge elevation the best you can, men," Baldwin ordered as his gun squad went through its paces, loading the cannon's throat with a satchel of black powder and a solid ball weighing twelve pounds.

"Ready, Lieutenant!"

Frank glanced at the nearby lodges. "Fire!"

Punk was laid against the touchhole, where it fizzed; then the howitzer suddenly belched spears of bright-orange flame from its muzzle, heaving itself backward off its makeshift carriage.

"Help me get that back up there, dammit!" the gunnery sergeant growled at his crew.

In less than a heartbeat a half-dozen men were scooping the howitzer tube out of the snow, shuffling forward to perch it atop its wobbly carriage once more.

Frank cried, "Fire two more, Sergeant!"

The old file cheered, "That oughtta soften the red bastards up, sir!"

"Damn right!" Baldwin replied, turning to the commander of his front line. "Mr. Hinkle! Prepare to pitch in when the third salvo is fired!"

"Very good, Lieutenant!" answered H Company's lieutenant.

Then the second shot belched from that cannon, which
again pitched itself backward off its wooden carriage with a
great, spewing, tumbling velocity. Suddenly small arms
cracked to their left and right upstream. Not that far away.
Enemy guns.

Frank whirled to look in that direction, finding a trio of
warriors on horseback cresting the top of a hill to his left. He
snapped off a shot with his pistol as the three bolted out of
sight, just as the yelling and screeching exploded from the
camp upstream.

The last of those three howitzer shells whined in over the
snowy brush, crashing in among the village, sending up a
spray of ice, water, and creek-bottom sand.

Women and children were screaming as the cannon's roar
faded from the nearby bluff.

"Come on, men!" Hinkle yelled to his company.

At long last Baldwin felt at the marrow of him that it truly
was to be their day. Time for him to pitch into the enemy.
Seize the day, once and for all. Just as he had at Gray Beard's
camp on McClellan Creek.

"C'mon, men!" Frank hollered at the rest as Hinkle's men
started away. "Remember the seventh of December!" He
waved his pistol overhead. "Now we can pay our respects to
Sitting Bull himself for that terrible day!"

As the first warriors appeared in their front, Hinkle's skirmishers slowed their advance until Rousseau's G Company
came up. Then they noticed how the horsemen began to fall
back under the pressure.

In the village beyond, pandemonium reigned. Screaming
women and crying children scattered like dung beetles from
beneath an overturned buffalo chip on the prairie, all of them
beginning to scurry upstream through the waist-deep snowdrifts toward the far end of the elongated camp.

Less than fifty yards out from the first of the Hunkpapa
tents, Baldwin ordered his wagons to halt. Leaving a small
force of Whitten's I Company behind for the protection of
their dwindling supplies and that precious ammunition, Frank
quickly moved the bulk of G and I companies forward in

support of Hinkle's H. Back, back, slowly back the warriors
fell.

All too easily, Frank feared.

Trying his best to fight down his suspicion of an ambush
that might well immobilize his advance, cut him off from his
wagon train and ammunition at a crucial moment, Baldwin
worried that he could see far too few warriors attempting to
hold back his troops. Where were the others?

His skin prickled with apprehension as Hinkle's men continued into the village.

Looking about, he decided there were simply too many
lodges and tents and wickiups covered with blankets and green
hides for these few warriors. Perhaps no more than a hundred
making a valiant but feeble stand against his soldiers when
there had been at least five times that number just days ago. As
the seconds crawled by, Frank grew more convinced it simply
had to be a ruse to pull his battalion into the village, where the
Sioux would snap the jaws shut on their trap.

Swallowing down his doubt, he hollered out encouragement to his men again and again—shouting down his private
fears each time his threatened instincts began to whisper in his
ear.

There among the wagons he saw the first of them from
the corner of his eye: a pair of soldiers lifting themselves from
their places in the wagon beds assigned to bear the sick, the
frostbitten, the severely fatigued—any of those men so done in
they could no longer move about on their own. But there those
two were, lumbering over the rear gate of one of those
wagons, calling out to their comrades to join them.

Then a handful of others in three more wagons shoved
aside their blankets, fighting to get to their knees, clutching
their rifles to spill over the back gate onto the snowy, trampled
ground. They cheered one another, waving the rest of those
forty ailing soldiers out of the wagons.

"C'mon, boys!" cried one of them. "You won't have another chance like this'un!"

"I'm a'comin'," shouted a soldier who wobbled shakily
on leaden legs, righting himself against a wagon bed. "To hell
with my frozen feet—I'm gonna shoot Sitting Bull in the ass
for myself!"

One by one the others rose from the wagon beds now to

rejoin their units, bringing a sour ball of pride to the back of Baldwin's throat as he watched those sick, injured, hurting men tumble out to join the attack. Frank turned away, knowing at that moment they had won the day. No matter what the Sioux might throw at them—if these men refused to give up, if these men fought so selflessly, then Sitting Bull had better be on the run.

He turned back to the village to find Culbertson and Lambert loping toward the column driving at least a dozen ponies and mules before them.

"The rest of the men must be out hunting!" Culbertson announced with boyish enthusiasm as he came skidding to a halt in the icy sand near Baldwin.

"Out hunting?"

"Best time of a winter day," the youngster replied. "Your soldiers attacked at dawn, or late in the winter afternoon—this village be crawling with fighters." Culbertson grinned widely. "You're one lucky man, Lieutenant Baldwin!"

In less than a half hour after the first cannon salvo, the village was deserted. Sitting Bull's people had squirted out of the south end of camp, then crossed to the west bank of Ash Creek, fighting the deep snow every step of the way, floundering and falling down in the crusty drifts, scrambling back to their feet again as they clambered into the icy bluffs beyond. Now that the women and children had escaped, the few warriors were falling back. And back. Crossing the creek themselves. Following their families—none of the Hunkpapa carrying very much, no more than what they had on their backs and what little they could snatch into their arms when that first shot was fired.

For the next three hours, until the last shreds of light began to fade at sundown, some of Baldwin's battalion rounded up more than sixty Indian ponies and mules while other soldiers pulled weapons, ammunition, dried buffalo meat, and blankets from the lodges and tents. Then they began their destruction of Sitting Bull's camp. First one fire, then a second, and finally more than twenty pyres were blazing, each with its ring of soldiers merrily pitching tons of agency-issued goods—sugar, tea, flour, and calico—into the flames that warmed those soldiers for the first time in days.

It was about time he allowed himself some of the congrat-

ulations too, Baldwin figured. Although they still had to worry
about their livestock suffering without army grain, the battalion no longer had to concern itself with running out of food.
Sitting Bull's Hunkpapa hunters had seen to that. His hearty
infantrymen could sustain the rest of their campaign chasing
the Sioux all the way to the Yellowstone.

But what gave Frank the deepest sense of pride was the
fact that in another forced march of at least a hundred miles
after departing Fort Peck, his three companies had routed the
fierce warriors who, eleven days before, had forced his battalion to fort up and fight for their very lives. On top of that was
the fact that Baldwin's battalion had put the entire village to
flight, forcing the Sioux into the wilderness without food,
robes, blankets, and very little clothing in subzero weather.

"If anything, Father Winter might well finish the job
we've started here today," Frank told his officers late that afternoon as the mercury began its hoary descent, eventually to
fall beyond forty below after nightfall. "Though we only killed
one warrior in our fight—the enemy has no choice now but to
scamper on back to their agency, where we damn well know
the Indian Bureau will feed and clothe and protect these murderers until we can catch up to them again."

Chapter 17

18 December 1876

"The hand of God Himself delivered you through that Sioux-infested country, Mr. Donegan!" Nelson A. Miles roared as he motioned for the tall Irishman to take a seat on one of the half-log benches in the colonel's cramped, crude office. "Wouldn't you agree, Kelly?"

The regiment's chief of scouts stepped forward, holding out his hand. "Luther S. Kelly."

"Some call him Yellowstone," Miles announced as he himself settled in his canvas chair behind his cluttered desk awash with maps, far too many sheets of foolscap, scattered ink packets and bottles, as well an assortment of nibs, pens, and pencils lying about in the utmost clutter.

"Seamus Donegan," he said, shaking the handsome Kelly's hand as he pulled off the wolf-hide cap.

"That's a nice head of hair you have there, Mr. Donegan."

"Yours ain't so bad either," Donegan replied. "Call me Seamus."

"Yes, Seamus," Kelly said with a grin. "So how did you manage to keep so much of it on your ride north along the Tongue?"

Donegan liked the civilian immediately. Standing there, he could not remember having met a man more handsome than Luther S. Kelly. "Didn't come all the way down the Tongue."

"That explains it, Kelly," Miles snorted. "Where'd you strike the Tongue, Mr. Donegan?"

"Mouth of Pumpkin Creek." Seamus watched Kelly wag his head. He grinned with those huge teeth of his. "Damn luck of the Irish, t'ain't it?"

"I think what we're trying to say, Mr. Donegan," Miles began, "just yesterday we had ourselves . . . an ugly incident with some Sioux who came in to talk over terms of surrender with me."

"Let's call it what it was, General," Kelly said abruptly with that rare impatience of his, turning to Donegan. "The Sioux camps south of here along the Tongue sent in some chiefs to talk with Miles."

"And?" Donegan asked. "What's the incident?"

"Some of our Crow scouts got to five of the Sioux before they reached the post," Miles admitted morosely. Then he raised his face, his eyes lit with a smoldering fire. "Damn, if I could have gotten my hands on just one of Leforge's yellow-bellied Crow."

"Did . . . did any of them Sioux escape?"

"Most," Kelly replied. "Right after they watched the five get murdered in cold blood. They turned right around and hightailed it back up the Tongue. So you can understand our amazement: here you just slipped downriver while they were escaping upriver to their camps."

Miles asked quickly, "Yes—did you see any sign of Indians?"

"No, none." Donegan's head swam, thinking that it had been only a matter of a day that Providence put between him and those escaping Sioux. "The Crow killed the chiefs coming in to talk surrender?"

"Some damned good men among those delegates," Miles said.

Kelly added, "And now the Crow have skedaddled back to their agency—what ones the general here hasn't already punished."

"Punished?"

"Taken away their army weapons and horses."

Scratching at his thick beard, Donegan said, "Damn, if

that ain't rotten luck, General Miles. You get them Lakota ready to listen to terms of surrender—then your Crows cut up five of their chiefs. By the saints! There's gonna be hell to pay now."

"Ain't that the gospel?" Kelly concluded.

"I couldn't blame them if they didn't trust me enough to talk peace, to come in and surrender to us now," Miles admitted quietly, staring at the floor a moment until he suddenly looked up at Seamus. "So what of this message you say you have from General Crook?" Miles asked, the fingers of one hand drumming rhythmically atop the clutter on his desk. "Verbal or written?"

"Written, of course, General," Donegan said, politely using Miles's brevet rank.

"Let's see it."

"Of course," and Seamus reached inside his three shirts to where he carried the flat leather dispatch envelope against the last layer of clothing, a gray wool undershirt. He watched Miles rise, take the leather envelope, then sit again to work at the leather thong.

"Perhaps Crook is planning on waging a campaign again this winter?" Miles asked as he spread apart the leather flaps and pulled the folded pages from the case. "He wants me to operate in concert, I suppose."

"He was . . . er, has already waged his campaign," Seamus corrected himself.

"Don't say?" Miles muttered, concentrating on the pages he was unfolding. He looked up momentarily. "What do you know of Crook's last fight?"

Seamus straightened. "I was there, General."

"I see," the colonel replied, his eyes returning to the pages covered with Crook's scrawl.

Kelly inquired, "You say Crook *has* waged his campaign?"

"Over and done. Likely the outfit is already back at Fetterman by now."

"Getting ready for Christmas, I'll wager," Wyllys Lyman said.

Donegan said, "I figure there won't be any celebrating for Mackenzie's Fourth Cavalry until they reach Fort Robinson again."

"Ranald Mackenzie?" Miles asked as he looked up from

the papers. "What I wouldn't give to have his cavalry! What I couldn't *do* with his cavalry along!" Then the colonel went back to reading his messages.

"We pitched into a big village of Northern Cheyenne the last week of November," Donegan explained to Kelly and the other officers. If he hadn't had the room's attention until then, the Irishman sure had it now. The place became hushed.

Hobart Bailey asked, "Cheyenne?"

"Little Wolf, Morning Star," Seamus answered the aide-de-camp's question. "Proven warriors and veterans, all. That was a long day in hell, it was."

"No doubt," Kelly replied.

Miles looked up again. "Says here Mackenzie drove them off before he destroyed the village that fell into his hands."

"We drove the survivors into the mountains, and Mackenzie's boys burned everything to the ground. But before they did, we found more than enough plunder from the Custer fight to show that village was at the Little Bighorn when the Seventh met its fate."

Miles laid the messages down atop his maps with a dry rustle and slowly rose from his canvas chair. "Damn, but I'd give a year's salary to have a regiment of cavalry like that at my disposal. And now Crook tells me he's booking it in for the rest of the winter, when I could put those soldiers to bloody good use."

"Going in for the winter is just what I hope to do my own self," Donegan said.

Miles came to the side of his desk. "Plan on heading south, are you?"

"I'll stuff myself with all the warm food and coffee I can, sleep for a good twenty-four hours, then get what dispatches you want me to carry back to Fetterman for you, General."

Miles looked at Kelly. "Is that a wise course?"

"No, sir," the chief of scouts replied, his grin fading as his face went somber. "Not by a long shot."

"It's your choice," Miles declared, staring at Donegan as he settled back on the side of his desk. "I take it you're on Crook's payroll."

"Yes, General."

"Then you can decide, Mr. Donegan. I won't seek to advise you one way or the other—"

"But I will," Kelly interrupted. "Listen, Donegan. You go south up the Tongue, by yourself or with a battalion of soldiers . . . you're going to run into trouble. That's where the Sioux are."

"Then I'll jump east to the Powder," Donegan argued. "It's a better route for where I need to go anyway."

Miles crossed his arms and asked, "Back to Fetterman?"

"Then on to Fort Laramie from there," Seamus answered, watching Kelly wag his head and turn to the window.

"So, Mr. Donegan," Miles said, "does this mean you're giving up scouting for the army?"

"Didn't say that, General. It's just . . . there ain't all that much work for a man when Crook's got his army disbanded for the winter. And, besides . . ."

"I should have known you'd be the kind of man who would have a sweetheart tucked away down there!"

"No, sir. A wife."

The colonel's eyes softened. "Children too?"

"A babe. Our first. A boy—born seven days into October."

"More than anything you'd love to see him again, wouldn't you?" Kelly said suddenly, turning abruptly at the window to fix Donegan with his stare. "More than anything to hold that woman of yours in your arms."

Donegan swallowed hard. For a moment he thought he was reading something in the civilian's eyes that had the look of brass-cold certainty. Trying hard to keep his voice from cracking, Seamus replied, "I can't think of anything I could ever want more than to hold the two of them."

Kelly declared, "Then you don't dare ride south from here alone."

"But I told you I come north alone."

The chief of scouts asked, "From where?"

Instead, Miles answered, "From the Belle Fourche."

"East of here, isn't it?" Kelly asked.

"That's right," Donegan replied.

"Which is why you wouldn't make it riding south from here by way of the Tongue or the Powder or the Rosebud or any of the rest of them," Kelly said emphatically, pounding a fist into his open palm. "You didn't lose your hair because the route you used to get here from the Belle Fourche took you around the country where the Crazy Horse bands are wintering."

Seamus felt that first pinch of despair. "I want to go home."

"Home, Mr. Donegan?" Miles asked.

But that despair quickly turned to the first flare of irritation at the colonel and his chief of scouts. "Fort Laramie, General."

"From what I can tell—it's the closest thing you have to home, isn't it, Mr. Donegan?" asked Kelly.

"Where my wife and boy are—that's where home will always be . . . yes."

Miles pushed himself away from the rickety desk. "You want to live to see them?"

"Yes—"

"Then you'll pay heed to what Kelly here has to tell you," and the colonel turned back to his canvas stool behind the desk.

"Seamus, you strike me as a man smart enough to read sign," Kelly said, taking a step closer.

"I had my first fight with the Sioux on the Crazy Woman in the summer of 1866,"* Donegan told the room. "I've seen my share, Kelly."

"Call me Luther or call me Yellowstone," the civilian replied. "So if you've seen your share, you ought to take it from another man who knows, Seamus. Take it for gospel from a man who'd like nothing more than to have a family of his own one of these days. Because of that—I can't stand by and watch you ride off to the south by yourself."

His empty belly pinched in warning again, rumbling for lack of fodder. How he wanted that promised cup of coffee a young soldier had been sent to fetch minutes ago as they'd walked into the colonel's office. As that long, wide scar itched in apprehension across the width of his back, Donegan's mind tumbled round and round with despair and dilemma at having all that he had planned upon suddenly dashed upon the rocks of—

"Ten years of scouting for the army out here?" Miles asked.

* *Sioux Dawn*, vol. 1, The Plainsmen Series.

"Off and on, General."

Kelly turned to gaze at Miles. "Can I put him to work, General?"

"I want to go home," Seamus groaned, closing his eyes and wagging his head.

"You'd never make it," Kelly echoed.

Then Miles said, "You'll be on *my* payroll, Donegan."

"Yours?"

"Already on Crook's, aren't you?"

"It's the dead of by-God winter," Seamus growled, wanting to protest in the worst way as he settled back to the half-log bench. "What in hell do you think you're going to accomplish against the Sioux with your infantrymen between now and spring?"

"I'm waiting on my last battalion to make it in from the field," Miles explained, pointing off across the Yellowstone. "Baldwin's men have been chasing Sitting Bull down."

"Any luck?" Donegan asked, sensing a twinge of excitement flutter within him as he looked from Miles to Kelly.

"We nailed him once on Cedar Creek, back in October," the civilian explained to Seamus. "And already Baldwin's caught the old fox back up near Fort Peck."

"He slip through your fingers?" Seamus asked.

"Through mine," Miles admitted, "and a second time through Baldwin's grasp."

"A courier brought me word from the lieutenant that his battalion has been following Sitting Bull south from the Missouri and they expected to engage his village within a matter of days," Miles declared proudly.

Looking down at the mucky floor below his boots, Seamus said, "So you'll keep hammering away at them, no matter that it's the dead of winter."

Miles brushed the question aside, saying, "Mr. Donegan, I'll pay you scout's wages, but understand that Kelly here will make you work for that pay."

Drawing in a deep breath, he let half of it out slowly, the way he would when he was trying to squeeze off a tough shot. "If that's the way it's to be, I'll stay on till I stand a chance riding south again."

"You can head home before spring."

Donegan looked at Miles with sudden hope. "I thought

you just told me the country south of here was crawling with Crazy Horse's warriors!"

"They are," Miles said, pushing himself erect from the desk, rubbing his two big hands together.

"Mother of Christ—I'd promised my wife I'd be back by Christmas," Seamus explained with a doleful wag of his head. "New Year at the latest. Now you wanna promise me I'll be heading home before spring?"

"As soon as Baldwin gets his battalion in here and we've reoutfitted this regiment, I plan on letting my men celebrate a merry little Christmas right here," the colonel instructed.

Not understanding, Donegan shook his head and shuffled his feet, stretching his aching, cold, saddle-hammered back muscles. "I don't know how that can help me ride south before spring, General."

"Mr. Donegan, before the New Year has arrived," Miles said as he came up to put one hand on the tall Irishman's shoulder, "I plan on marching my Fifth Infantry, with you joining Kelly and his company of scouts . . . the whole lot of us headed south to corral Crazy Horse once and for all."

Seamus began to grin within his thick beard. "Once you've beaten Crazy Horse, then I can ride back to my family."

Miles grinned in turn. "Once I've beaten Crazy Horse, Mr. Donegan . . . you can damn well ride anywhere in this country you bloody well want!"

Chapter 18

18–23 December 1876

Having finished the fiery destruction of some ninety canvas and hide lodges abandoned by Sitting Bull's people close to sundown, Vic Smith, Joe Culbertson, and Edward Lambert led Frank Baldwin's column south, following Ash Creek into the coming twilight. Just shy of the Missouri-Yellowstone divide the lieutenant gave the order to bivouac at dusk.

After drawing their wagons into a square and bringing within its protection their mules and some sixty captured Sioux ponies, the men pulled from the wagons everything they could use for breastworks: their last sacks of grain and crates of hardtack. That done, the captured buffalo robes were hastily distributed among the companies as the men settled in the snow around their greasewood fires, the sky above cold and clear as a bell jar, black as tar and sprinkled with a million frosty pricks of light. Once every man had a robe for himself, the extra hides were laid over the backs of the bone-weary mules.

Late that night of the eighteenth the Hunkpapa fired into the soldier camp from long distance and without causing injury to Baldwin's men. Just before dawn on Tuesday, Frank and his officers inspected the captured ponies and from them selected enough to replace what mules had died of exposure or want of grain.

"We'll kill the rest before we push on," he explained.

"Shoot them, Lieutenant?" asked Joe Culbertson.

"Only the ones my soldiers can't hold still enough to slash their throats," he said dryly. "I won't turn my fighting men into herders, and I sure as hell won't turn these ponies loose for the Sioux to get their thieving hands on again."

Mounted warriors, and many on foot, were spotted in the middistance along the hilltops as soon as there was enough light to see. No telling how long they had been waiting through the cold night to look down on the soldier camp.

An hour later more than fifty horse carcasses lay on the bloody snow, going cold in the wind on that high, treeless divide as Baldwin's men finally pushed south that cheerless Tuesday morning. On the far side they located a narrow gap for their wagons and rumbled on down an upper fork of Cedar Creek toward the Yellowstone Valley. Their spirits buoyed to be nearing home, the soldiers reached the Tongue River–Fort Buford Road on the north bank of the Yellowstone late that afternoon.

Warriors had been in sight all day, dogging the path of the column, always staying to the hills at a respectful distance from those far-shooting Springfields. But just before sunset as the soldiers began squaring their wagons for the night, the Sioux rushed in from the nearby ravines and coulees, screaming and firing their weapons.

Though gallant, their effort was too little, too late.

Baldwin quickly formed his companies into squads and turned away one halfhearted charge after another before the attack was over less than twenty minutes after the warriors had launched it.

Well after moonset Baldwin shook hands with Lieutenant Frank S. Hinkle and scout Vic Smith as the two stood beside the strongest animals left with the battalion.

"Mr. Smith here figures we ought to be at the cantonment by sunrise," Hinkle said.

" 'Pendin' on the road, snow, an' Injuns," the civilian added.

Baldwin turned back to Hinkle. "Just get there when you

can—safe and whole. Doesn't do us any good if you don't make it—we don't get word to the general about the grain."

"I'll see to it that the corn for the animals is sent back to Custer Creek just as you're requesting," Hinkle replied, then stepped back and saluted. He clambered up to his saddle, then quietly urged his mount between two wagons where a pair of soldiers held aloft the long wagon tongues as the two riders disappeared into the snowy darkness.

"God be with you both to see you through," Baldwin said almost under his breath. "And God be with us if you don't."

It was to be another near sleepless night for the lieutenant. Like those gone before on this expedition, he was up and moving about, always prowling, walking the perimeter, checking on his pickets to assure they hadn't fallen asleep, making sure they wouldn't freeze.

The following morning Baldwin's men continued their struggle to hack a way through snowdrifts and to block up the wagons to keep them from careening down every slippery slope as the sky began to spit an icy snow down at them. Throughout the day the column had to halt briefly now and again to free a broken-down mule from its harness, each time turning the animals loose before they pushed on. By midafternoon the weary battalion had reached the banks of Custer Creek, where Baldwin ordered them to bivouac. When it wasn't snowing that night, the wind was howling, making it next to impossible to keep their fires going.

"Tell your men to keep warm," Baldwin ordered the morning of the twenty-first. He was more weary than any of them. "We're laying to."

"You trust that Hinkle got through to Tongue River?" asked Lieutenant Rousseau.

"Yes," Baldwin answered with some of the last of his optimism. "The grain will get here, or we'll have to abandon the rest of the mules and wagons where they are. I don't think there's a single one of these animals can make it on in to the cantonment—"

They all turned at the rapid, scattered gunshots downriver, coming from the direction where Joe Culbertson and a mounted soldier had gone in search of those mules abandoned the previous day.

In less than five minutes Baldwin was in the saddle and

leading a mixed company of men out at double time along their backtrail, heading toward the sound of the guns. They hadn't gone more than a couple of miles when two horsemen appeared ahead on the road, whipping their animals for all they were worth.

As the pair drew closer, Frank recognized Culbertson's youthful face, saw the graying fear written clearly on the young soldier's. On the road just behind the scout and soldier suddenly materialized more than two dozen mounted warriors screeching after their quarry.

"Skirmish order! Full left!" Baldwin cried, wheeling his horse and watching the infantrymen—for the moment no longer cold—scurry into formation across the width of the snowy Fort Buford Road.

"Second and third squads, prepare to advance," Frank ordered, struggling with his anxious horse in the deep snow. "First squad—*advance!*"

After he had marched them only another five yards, Baldwin watched the warriors emerge from a wide bend in the road beyond some leafless cottonwood. Just as the Sioux spotted his soldiers, they hurriedly began to rein up in confusion and surprise.

"*Fire!*"

That first volley ripped through the center of the horsemen, causing ponies to rear and men to scream in pain. But by and large most of the warriors had pitched to one side or another of their horses and were now turning their animals around on either side of the trail.

"Second squad—*advance!*"

Following their corporal, those soldiers raggedly trotted up and knelt just beyond the first squad, going to their knees to steady the long rifles.

"*Fire!*"

Baldwin did not have to call up the third squad that late Thursday morning. Already the Sioux had retreated beyond the trees at the bend of the road, pulling back to a safe distance from those soldier rifles.

With no mules recovered Baldwin moved his men back to their bivouac at Custer Creek to continue their wait for relief, which meant enduring the intense cold through the rest of the day. An hour before sundown the pickets on the west side of their camp began hollering out. Over a hundred men stood shivering in their buffalo robes at their smoky fires and watched expectantly as the first forms appeared out of the west, where the sun was falling in a frosty haze.

A handful of horsemen accompanied by the squeak of some twenty wagons hoved around the bend of the road leading from Tongue River. Captain Ezra P. Ewers led a detail of forty soldiers to man and escort those wagons carrying grain for Baldwin's ailing battalion.

Frank was certain it was the fact that he was facing the cruel west wind that made his eyes begin to tear as he watched his comrades and friends coming to the relief of his men.

"Lieutenant Baldwin!" Ewers cried out as he brought his prancing horse to a halt and saluted. Then he held down his hand. "Well done, sir. Well goddamned done!"

"T-thank you, Captain!" Baldwin replied self-consciously.

"From Mr. Hinkle we hear it was just like McClellan Creek!" Ewers gushed with enthusiasm.

"I'm very proud of my men," Frank boasted, really feeling the sting at his eyes.

"And well you should be," Ewers replied while Baldwin's battalion lumbered forward to greet the new arrivals who marched in two rows down the extent of the short wagon train. "We hear you drove Sitting Bull into the night without food or shelter!"

"Yes," Baldwin said as Ewers dropped from his horse. "I only wish I could have gotten my hands on that flea-bitten scalp of his for the general."

Ewers declared, "He wants you to return immediately."

"Im-immediately?" Frank stammered.

"To report to him personally," the captain answered. "Hinkle told him some of the story, but the general gave me orders to have you start out posthaste. We'll take the strongest horses I have with me." Then the captain handed Baldwin a folded note.

I am delighted to learn that you have been successful in your engagement & without loss. I sent Capt Ewers out with supplies for you. I want to see you as soon as you can get near enough. Take what mounted men you want and come in in the night.

Frank looked up from that note written by Miles. "Now?"

"Yes, goddammit!" Ewers roared, slapping a hand on Baldwin's shoulder. "The general couldn't be more proud of you!"

"The men," Frank tried to explain.

"Yes—he's most proud of your battalion. None of the rest of us has done near what you've accomplished, Lieutenant. Just think of it: if Sitting Bull doesn't starve this winter . . . he'll damn well have to make a run for Canada of it!"

Just past sundown Baldwin mounted the horse he had named Redwater several days before and rode west with Ewers and a small escort, reaching Tongue River at five A.M. on the twenty-second to find that Miles had left orders to be awakened as soon as the "fightingest lieutenant in the Fifth" had arrived. Over hot coffee and more food than Frank had laid eyes on in a month, Baldwin told the colonel and that crowd of soldiers everything about that first fight where he'd ordered a retreat to save the lives of his men, and then told the group how not one of his battalion had given up when they'd fought that blizzard all the way back to Fort Peck.

Told them how his men had hitched up their britches, straightened their backs, and pitched back into the wilderness to track down Sitting Bull again. How they'd caught the Hunkpapa sleeping that time and destroyed everything the band owned.

Late the following afternoon of 23 December, Companies G, H, and I of the Fifth Infantry limped into the Tongue River Cantonment, slowly parading down a long gauntlet of clapping, shouting, hurrawing soldiers who couldn't wait to pound on the back those heroes of the prairie winter and welcome them back home.

Not one man lost.

It brought a sting of sentiment to the throat of Frank Baldwin as he watched his loyal troops march proudly back among their fellows, three full companies who had suffered unspeakable cold, men who gaped and smiled and laughed now despite the blackened, frostbitten flesh every one of them suffered, men who had empty grain sacks, pieces of green hides, and bands of rawhide thongs tied around their feet to hold together their shoddy army boots.

Men who had marched more than 716 miles on short

rations, across some of the most unforgiving terrain on the entire continent, right through the very heart of winter.

Soldiers who nonetheless had still beaten Sitting Bull.

By bloody damn: they had beaten the man who had orchestrated the destruction of Custer.

Now all they had to do was find Sitting Bull's most powerful general . . . and destroy the Crazy Horse bands forever.

Chapter 19

Wanicokan Wi 1876

BY TELEGRAPH

Gen. Crook's Opinion

WASHINGTON, December 19.—Gen. Crook, in his
annual report, says the miners in the Black Hills did
not violate the Sioux treaty until the Indians had
ceased to regard it. He also calls attention to the fact
that his command, less than a thousand, fought and
defeated Sitting Bull's band on the Rosebud, a week
before the Custer disaster. He thinks the government
has treated the Sioux with unparalleled liberality,
which they have repaid by raids along the border of
reservations.

The heart of Crazy Horse turned cold.

Just when he was beginning to believe the other
chiefs that they could trust the Bear Coat, the soldiers' Indian
scouts murdered five Lakota leaders.

"Do you see now what peace means to the *wasicu*?" he

roared at the many who hastily gathered as soon as the entire delegation raced back to the village days after the killings.

His heart had never been colder, here in the Midwinter Moon. Never had it been colder to the white man.

Spotted Elk's eyes were sad. "We cannot trust the word of the soldier chief."

"He sends his *Psatoka* out to kill our peace talkers!" yelped He Dog, barely able to contain his fury.

"Packs the Drum was a good man," Crazy Horse told them. "He believed he was doing right by our people. But he made the same mistake we have made time and again: he trusted in the *wasicu*."

"And that was his undoing!" bellowed Roman Nose.

"Bull Eagle!" whimpered Touch-the-Clouds, wagging his head. "They murdered Bull Eagle when he came to talk peace to the soldier he trusted!"

All about them now women shuffled aimlessly through the snow, pulling blankets over their heads to hide not just their red-rimmed eyes, but the ashes of mourning they had scooped from fire pits to smear on their tear-streaked faces, some of the young and old angrily ripping knives from their scabbards and screaming at the sky while they slowly slashed their arms and legs, each row of crimson ribbons not taking long at all to freeze in the shocking cold of that winter afternoon. Dogs barked, wailed, and whimpered—not knowing the cause of this great disturbance. And all the while children cried, hugging the legs of their mothers, or standing alone and abandoned, quietly sobbing as the adults around them poured forth their bitter, private fury, their unrequited rage welling like a fevered boil.

"They will not die in vain," Crazy Horse explained to the crowd.

Young Bad Leg shouted, "Let us attack the soldier fort!"

But Red Cloth disagreed. "We could not force the *wasicu* out to fight us. They would be like gophers in their burrows. So many tunnels that the wolf cannot ever catch one."

"Red Cloth is right," Crazy Horse declared. "The soldiers would hide behind their log walls, and we would never dig them out."

"Then we must lure them out!" Long Feather suggested.

"Yes, that is just what we should do," Crazy Horse replied, his voice rising in hope. "We can lure the white men out—just as we lured the *wasicu* soldiers to their death at the Battle of the Hundred in the Hand ten winters ago."*

No Neck asked, "With some decoys?"

"Yes, I will pick five-times-ten of them myself," Crazy Horse replied. "And we will ride to the soldier fort, where we lure the *wasicu* out, taunting and teasing the Bear Coat all the time as he brings his soldiers south farther and farther until we reach the place where all of our warriors will be waiting to crush the Bear Coat's puny army."

"But the soldiers must not come close to the villages!" protested the old Rising Sun.

"They won't have a chance of getting close to our villages," Crazy Horse snapped, anxious to shut off all debate.

"It is good to keep the soldiers far from our village," He Dog declared. "The women and children, our old and our sick, would panic if they knew the soldiers were close to our camp!"

"Bear Coat's soldiers will never reach our village," the Horse repeated. "We will lure them to the place *we* want to fight, where we will have our warriors waiting. There the task of our decoys will be over—and the killing can begin!"

"You will lead the decoys yourself?" asked The Yearling.

"No, this time I will pick a young warrior," Crazy Horse answered. "As I was given that honor by Red Cloud and Afraid of His Horses when I was a young warrior."

"They have become tired old women now!" shouted Bad Leg.

"Yes," No Neck agreed. "Both of them are like old women before the *wasicu*."

"Whipped dogs!"

"But they were not always whipped dogs!" Crazy Horse attempted to defend his old friends. "They drove the soldiers away from the Pine Woods Fort,† and from the Mud-Wall Fort# in those days. Remember what they did—because the

---

* The Fetterman Massacre at Fort Phil Kearny, as told in *Sioux Dawn*, vol. 1, The Plainsmen Series.
† Fort Phil Kearny, Dakota Territory.
# Fort C. F. Smith on the Bighorn River in Montana Territory.

Titunwan Lakota have never again forced the soldiers to empty any of their forts."

"They may have been powerful warriors once," said Rising Sun. "But now they take the white man's scummy meat and his thin blankets. They even gave up their horses and their weapons to the soldiers!"*

Spotted Elk cried, "We will never give up, will we, Crazy Horse?"

"No, a warrior never gives up his pony. Never lays down his weapons. The old ones too frail, the little ones too small, the sick ones too weak to fight—these we must protect from the *wasicu* chief and his soldiers, who lie to us about peace."

"You will lead us in this fight?"

"I will lead you," he promised them.

His words were answered by an immediate and thunderous roar as both men and women screeched, shouted, trilled their tongues and cried out their praises to the blue sky above, frost lying in a wreath about every head.

"This soldier chief Bull Eagle trusted," Crazy Horse told that great crowd of his Lakota people and the wounded Shahiyela, "the one Bull Eagle called the Bear Coat . . . he talks to you of peace with one hand while his other hand grips a war club that he swings at your head. I think we should convince this Bear Coat that it is time to leave Lakota country forever."

Again the crowd roared its approval, women shaking their knives in the air, each blade coated with a frozen film of blood, the hundreds of warriors rattling guns and shields.

"Yes, it is time that we teach this Bear Coat what we taught the Hundred in the Hand, what we taught Long Hair and his soldiers at the Greasy Grass!"

"Remember the Greasy Grass!" came the echo from that great assembly.

But as he turned away, Crazy Horse knew there was no prophetic vision the likes of which Sitting Bull had experienced last summer at the Deer Medicine Rocks.

Perhaps it was only a matter of time until there were more soldiers in Lakota country than there were Lakota. One sum-

* Mackenzie's raid, 23 October 1876, *A Cold Day in Hell*, vol. 11, The Plainsmen Series.

mer soon . . . perhaps one winter very soon—his people would not be able to hold back the *wasicu* any longer.

But for now Crazy Horse would do as his people wanted, as they expected of a Shirt Wearer: lead them against this Bear Coat and his soldiers—cut a swath up and down the Buffalo Tongue River to avenge the deaths of the five chiefs. Perhaps even drive the soldiers from their fort on the Elk River. For now the heart of Crazy Horse beat strong once more. For now Crazy Horse would again be a war chief.

And when the time came for him to hand over his pony and his weapons . . . as he knew that time would come, down in the marrow of him . . . Crazy Horse hoped he would again have the courage to do what was best for his people.

As brave as he had been in battle, could he be just as brave in surrendering?

Perhaps, if he was fortunate, Crazy Horse decided as he led the chiefs back to his lodge—he would never have to find out.

Perhaps this would be the winter to die as a warrior, fighting the *wasicu* soldiers, defending his people to the last.

Come the winter to die as a warrior.

BY TELEGRAPH

More Murders by Indians on Hat Creek

THE INDIANS

More Murders in Wyoming—A Coloradan among the Victims.

HAT CREEK via CHEYENNE, December 20.—Four freight teams accompanied by five men were attacked by Indians in camp on Indian creek, six miles north of this place, about 9 o'clock last night. Three of the party escaped and arrived here at midnight barefooted and half clothed. A detachment of soldiers and a party of citizens repaired to the scene of the fight early this morning and found the bodies of two men—B. C. Steppens of Salt Lake, and a German named Fritz of Colorado—terribly mutilated with a butcher's cleaver taken from one of the wagons. The contents of the wagons were scattered over the ground, the flour and corn in piles as it had been emptied from the sacks. The horses were missing and over forty bullet holes were in one wagon. The dead were brought here and buried.

Two hundred and forty-eight Arapahoes and Sioux scouts from the agency, in charge of Louis Richards, a half breed, passed here on Sunday, en route to join General Crook.

Samantha found her tea had gone cold the next time she sipped it.

There was so much going on around her there with the officers' wives in hand-knitted shawls, and buffalo-coated soldiers whirling in and out of the parlor, through the dining room and out into the vestibule, that she really hadn't noticed that her tea was growing cold, the cup sitting there nearby on the tiny table made from an old crate.

Samantha was simply paying all her attention to the child on her lap.

She had wrapped the boy as warmly as possible before coming downstairs just after dawn this Christmas morn. It had been near impossible to sleep last night—what for all the disappointment that had caused her to sob silently in her pillow, for all the memories of parents and home, of family and these special holidays. Remembering how her father always killed a big fat tom for National Thanksgiving Day, how he fattened a goose for Christmas dinner.

There in the cold and the dark just before dawn she had smelled it all the way up to her narrow rope-and-tick bed—those fragrances rising from the kitchen below her tiny room with the single frosted window. Someone was up early, baking already, loading kindling into the stoves, closing the iron door with a muffled clang. Samantha recalled how she and Rebecca would lie in bed side by side on Christmas morning, waiting impatiently to hear the sounds their mother would make in her kitchen. Then it was finally time to scurry out to greet parents with hurried hugs and kisses before they would sip hot tea and eat tiny rum cakes around the tree they had decorated just the night before with tinsel and tissue and a paper star on top.

And each time Samantha had remembered those holidays of the past, she had sobbed all the harder . . . until she would again put her hand beneath the pillow, and her finger-tips would touch the two folded sheets of paper.

They had been carried south to her from that land where he had written those words trying to explain why he would not be keeping his promise to be home by this special day—their son's first Christmas. Time and again Samantha read each word, each line, every sentence to wring from those two spare pages all that they had to tell her about the what and why of his not coming back with the rest of the Bighorn and Yellowstone Expedition that Crook was disbanding.

If the generals were sending the men back to their winter quarters, then why wasn't Seamus among them?

Each time that question tore at her heart, each time she thought about this child's first Christmas, Sam told herself that she must trust in him. Trust that her husband would always do what was right by them all. Not just what was right for country and flag . . . but what was right for his own family. She decided some time ago that she could do nothing less than trust in him.

As well as trust in God to bring Seamus back alive.

The child was beginning to squirm and fuss, what with all the noise from happy children and the singsong voices of those adults calling out their merry wishes to loved ones and good friends all. She probed a finger into his diaper and found that he wasn't wet. Perhaps he was getting hungry. Samantha would have to take him upstairs soon, where she would nurse him and he would fall asleep with his tummy once again filled with warm milk.

But for now she prayed he would not grow too fussy and would allow her to stay down there among the noise and the warmth and the celebrants moving in and out as they visited the houses and quarters at Fort Laramie this cold, cold Christmas Day.

It helped to keep her mind off Seamus and what he might be facing in that frigid north country. Helped her forget how much she had counted on his being home for their son's first Christmas . . . and it was beginning to appear as if Seamus might not even be home a week from now—the first day of 1877.

Her eyes misted, and she fought the sour taste her sobbing made at the back of her throat—fought back vainly, bouncing the boy on her knees, turning him so he could watch the room and people and flutting candles with her, all those colors and movement as he gurgled and chewed on a knuckle.

Oh, how she remembered Seamus's big-knuckled hands . . . so rough and callused, then grown so gentle and soft whenever they brushed her flesh.

"Merry Christmas!" she called out as another group burst in through the front door and stomped across the entryway, scattering snow and ice from their boots, bringing in that sweet tang of bitter cold on the coats and scarves, hats and mittens, they swept off and hung on the last of a long row of iron hooks imprisoned on the nearby wall.

From pockets came the tiny packages wrapped in red-colored tissue, or perhaps nothing more than homely newspaper if one could afford nothing else. Small presents from the heart, purchased from the sutler with a particular someone in mind. There wasn't all that much out there for folks to choose from at this holiday of gift giving. But now that she had been an adult for a few years, Samantha was coming to realize at last what this holiday was truly all about.

Not the tiny presents wrapped in scraps of newspaper. Not even those rare and fine presents her parents had wrapped in delicate tissue to present to her and Rebecca back home many years ago.

Christmas was about friends and gathering close to loved ones.

Christmas was about family.

The baby fussed, perhaps sensing her disappointment as Samantha's eyes glistened and the candle- and lamplight grew soft and fuzzy. Sam blinked to clear them, frustrated when she felt the tears spill down her cheeks.

"Oh, Sam," Martha Luhn said gently as she came up to her and knelt beside her chair, laying one hand on her arm, the other hand on the boy's tiny legs. "It's Christmas, and we are all here together. I know how you must miss him so."

She tried twice to say something, but the words would not come out. All she could do was swipe at her tears.

"He's safe. Trust in God, Sam," Nettie Capron cooed. "On this day especially. Please trust in God to watch over him . . . wherever he is right now."

"Yes," she croaked. How she wanted to believe.

The baby fussed, and she bounced him some more, blinking as the swirl of people and candlelight became fuzzy again.

"He'll be home soon, Sam," Elizabeth Burt said softly at her side. "He promised you before, and he kept his promise. Remember that. Seamus Donegan will move heaven and earth—and even hell itself—to keep his promise to you, Sam. You just remember that."

"Yes . . . I'll t-try."

"I'll bring you some cider, and then we'll gather with Lieutenant Bingham's wife at the piano. She does play so well, doesn't she?" Elizabeth asked. "And singing will brighten your spirits, won't it, now?"

Sam watched Mrs. Burt rise and move off into the knots of well-wishers and joyful celebrants that Christmas morning.

Swallowing down her fear the way she blinked back her tears, Samantha Donegan resolutely told herself that she would have to trust in God to bring Seamus back alive.

She would simply trust in God.

Chapter 20

26–29 December 1876

BY TELEGRAPH

Discredited Rumor of an Indian Massacre

Sitting Bull Driven Across the Missouri

New Plan for the Management of Indians

Sitting Bull Heard From.

ST. PAUL, December 21.—The following was received at headquarters department of Dakota to-day:

FORT PECK, M.T., December 8.—Yesterday, with a force of 100 men of the Fifth infantry, I followed and drove Sitting Bull's camp of 190 lodges south across the Missouri river, near the mouth of Bark creek. He resisted my crossing for a short time, and then retreated to the bad lands. Sitting Bull is in camp on Bark creek with over 5,000 warriors.

[signed]. FRANK D. BALDWIN
Lieut. Fifth Infantry, Com'dg.

A New Idea.

WASHINGTON, December 21.—At a meeting of the house committee on Indian Affairs to-day, Seelye submitted a proposition which embraces an entire revolution in the management of Indian affairs. It makes provisions for extending the laws of the United States over every Indian, giving to him the same status in the courts, conferring upon him the same rights and exacting from him the same duties as belong to any citizen or subject of the United States; abolishing the office of commissioner of Indian affairs, and transferring the entire functions of the Indian bureau to an Indian board or trust, constituted somewhat after the manner of great charitable and educational corporations. . . . It is the opinion of the committee that some change in the management of Indians affairs is indispensible, and that the transfer of the Indian bureau to the war department would be no improvement on the present management.

"**D**amn their red hides!" Nelson Miles bellowed again when the soldier huffed into the office to report a third raid on the cantonment's beef herd in the last two days. "Don't the Sioux understand they're cutting their own throats?"

"You can't blame them, General," Luther Kelly responded, then looked quickly over to the tall Irishman. "A few days ago the Crazy Horse bands came riding in here under a flag of truce to talk peace with you—and then your Crow scouts went and convinced the Lakota that your word was simply no good."

"No good!" Miles shrieked. "A day after the murders I sent two of my Yankton scouts up the Tongue with presents to find the villages. As a peace offering, they took twelve of the Crow horses, some sugar, and tobacco too—along with my letter of apology to tell them no white man had a hand in the Crow treachery."

"But those Yanktons came back in here five days ago, unable to locate the hostiles," Kelly declared.

Seamus asked both men, "Do you really think those Yanktons of yours made a full-hearted effort to find the Crazy Horse camp?"

Kelly shook his head. "Absolutely not, Donegan. I'll bet they laid low a little south of here until they figured they could come back in here with their story about not finding the hostile village anywhere close."

"Considering the foul mood the Crazy Horse people must be in," Miles explained, "I suppose I can't blame those Yankton couriers for not making much of an effort. But since they didn't succeed in getting my message and presents to the chiefs, Crazy Horse and the others have no way of knowing that those murders weren't the fault of this army. So now the Sioux are raiding and stealing again simply because they don't think my word is any good?"

Donegan pushed himself away from the log wall and said, "They've got nothing else to believe, General."

"Don't you think their spies would know that I've stripped near all the Crow of their weapons and ponies and sent even the innocent ones back to their agency with their tails tucked between their legs?"

This matter of the Crow ambush was still clearly a sore point with Miles. A day after the murders, the colonel sent a courier to the Crow agency with word that he demanded the arrest of those guilty, then requested the return of at least seventy-five of the innocent Crow warriors to serve as scouts.

"All the Crazy Horse camp knows is that they had five of their chiefs killed," Kelly repeated. "Which means they're going to do everything they can to avenge those deaths."

"If they don't see fit to trust me," Miles fumed, "then—by God—they'll taste my steel until they're good and ready to surrender!"

"I don't think surrender's what they have in mind, General," Donegan observed.

Miles's eyes narrowed on the Irishman; then as quickly the furrow in his brow softened, and he replied, "So be it. I'll be happy to oblige Crazy Horse . . . and give him the fight he wants."

Beginning early the day before on Christmas morning,

soldiers and scouts had started celebrating with what spirits the post sutler and a pair of whiskey traders could provide: some potato beer, a peach brandy, a heady apple cider, and a little cheap corn mash. By midafternoon the guardhouse was so overcrowded that Miles issued an order forbidding the sale of any more liquor on the post. The sutler and those two savvy entrepreneurs had only to pack up boards, barrels, and tent, then move their saloons a few hundred yards to put themselves beyond the army's reach—just outside the boundaries of the military reservation.

With what little hard money he had left in his pocket, Seamus had joined Kelly and the old plainsman, John Johnston, for a few drinks. While most of the conversations among the soldiers were consumed with topics of the East and the hotly disputed presidential election between Rutherford B. Hayes and Samuel Tilden, Seamus and other civilians talked more of hearth and home, of loved ones far, far away from this snowy, frozen land where the Sioux hunted buffalo and scalps.

Their holiday revelry was over all too soon, however, when horse-mounted warriors swept down on the snowy fields south of the cantonment that Christmas afternoon, successfully driving off a few horses and mules before the surprised soldiers gathered enough numbers and with their far-shooting Springfields scattered the fifty-some horsemen. A second attempt was made right at twilight.

From their manner of dress and hair ornamentation, it was plain to Seamus that the Sioux were not alone in that Christmas Day raiding party. "Luther, there's Cheyenne riding with 'em."

Kelly came jogging over as the last of the enemy disappeared into the fading light with another half-dozen army mules put out to graze and thereby recoup their strength after Baldwin's battalion returned from its long, cold march on the twenty-third. "I've heard the Cheyenne are particularly close to the Crazy Horse Oglalla. But how can you be so sure?"

"I was with Mackenzie, remember?"

With a nod Kelly said, "I suppose by now a fella like you would be able to tell the difference between a Sioux and a Cheyenne."

"What this means is that the bunch Mackenzie's Fourth

drove off into the mountains has somehow managed to survive, Luther," Seamus surmised. "Shows they've joined up with the Crazy Horse bands."

Kelly nodded. "Like they did last winter and spring before they wiped out Custer's Seventh."*

"And damn near rubbed out Crook's army a week before on the Rosebud."†

"Not a good sign, is it?" Kelly asked.

Donegan wagged his head. "A bloody bad omen, if you're asking me."

Then at dawn on the twenty-sixth the half a hundred horsemen were at their serious mischief again. Another strike at the mules and horses working hard to nuzzle the deep snow aside and crop at the autumn-cured grasses in that bottomland south of the post. A second foray near midday netted the warriors more than a dozen animals. Then, late in the afternoon, the Sioux and Cheyenne pulled off their greatest surprise.

This time they sent in about ten of their horse thieves to rustle, once again, more of the cantonment's riding stock. And after three raids the officers and soldiers performed exactly as the warriors had hoped they would.

As soon as the alarm was raised and the white men came rushing toward the scene of the attack in overwhelming numbers to fend off the decoys, the majority of the Sioux and Cheyenne had already slipped across the frozen Tongue River and at that moment were busy driving off more than 250 head of the white man's spotted buffalo. By twilight on that Tuesday, Crazy Horse's fifty warriors were headed south, herding before them more than sixty horses and mules in addition to those beeves.

Many miles and at least four days away on the upper Tongue River the chiefs and the village waited in the cold for their young men to make their way south once they knew for certain that the soldiers were following. More than anything—they wanted the Bear Coat and his men to follow them up the Tongue.

For Miles's Fifth Infantry the painful, throbbing heads

---

suffered in celebrating their lonely little Christmas with the trader's grain alcohol was all but forgotten there at the mouth of the Tongue River. With more than a foot of snow on the level before the wind began to drift it, once more the mercury in the surgeon's thermometers plummeted to thirty-five below zero—and no man stayed out in the wind if he could avoid it.

Besides, it soon became common knowledge that their commander was not about to keep them forted up. That very night after the beef herd disappeared into the bluffs south of the Yellowstone, Miles called together his officers and scouts to begin laying plans for following the thieves.

"Baldwin caught Sitting Bull twice," he told those gathered in that stuffy, smoke-filled cabin that served as his office. "And now we'll catch Crazy Horse."

As soon as Baldwin's wagons had returned three days ago, the colonel put his men to work using all those tanned buffalo hides the lieutenant's battalion had captured from Sitting Bull's camp to fashion heavy coats and leggings. In addition, on Christmas Eve a wagon train of supplies from Fort Buford at the mouth of the Yellowstone arrived. Among the cargo was even more winter-survival clothing.

While Miles and Baldwin had been chasing Sitting Bull's Sioux across northern Montana Territory, Colonel William B. Hazen's men at Fort Buford had been busy constructing winter overcoats, leggings, and mittens from tanned buffalo robes traded from Yanktonais villages at the nearby Fort Peck Agency. As autumn had approached, Miles was specific in placing his order with army quartermaster officials, stating that the coats he wanted for his men be made "of large sizes, long, coming below the knees, double breasted, and high rolling collar, such as can be turned up about the ears." The leggings, he ordered, were "to come above the knees, sewed at the sides, to buckle or tie over the instep and buffalo overshoes, and to be sustained at the sides and top by a strap attached to the waist belt."

In addition to buffalo caps and gauntlets, the soldiers of the Fifth Infantry sewed up crude underwear from extra woolen blankets. Snatching up the leftover wool scraps, many of the men cut masks or hoods to protect the bare flesh of their faces from the brutal windchills expected in the coming campaign to find and destroy Crazy Horse. From Quartermas-

ter Randall every soldier got his hands on at least two, and
sometimes three, pairs of trousers made from heavyweight
kersey wool.

And from those crates shipped up the icy river to Fort
Buford, then brought overland to Glendive, freighted west to
the Tongue River from there, the quartermaster issued each
soldier his regulation woolen mittens, buffalo overshoes, and a
visored sealskin or muskrat cap complete with earflaps. For
those foot soldiers who were not assigned the overshoes, they
were issued what the frontier army called "arctics," vulcanized
rubber boots.

Whenever a man could get his hands on an empty burlap
feed sack, he would immediately hide it away in his haversack,
where the coarse sacking would eventually be put in service:
cut up to wrap around his feet before they were stuffed into
his boots, the better to prevent frostbite.

Near midmorning on the twenty-seventh Miles watched
the first of his winter-clad soldiers start south up the Tongue
River in hot pursuit of the raiders. Following squaw man Tom
Leforge and the last two Crow scouts brave enough to stay on
with the soldiers, Captain Charles J. Dickey led his own Company E as well as Company F of the Twenty-second Infantry,
along with D Company of the Fifth.

Later on that afternoon Dickey's command managed to
catch up with the hostiles' rear guard moseying comfortably
behind the cattle herd. In a short, hot skirmish the soldiers
managed to retake more than a hundred beeves. Just after dark
the captain sent a courier north to inform Miles of the good
news.

Elated with Dickey's initial success, the colonel continued
with his plan the following dawn when he dispatched First
Lieutenant Mason Carter's K Company of the Fifth Infantry to
follow Dickey's trail with the bronze twelve-pounder Napoleon gun hidden beneath a sheet of canvas stretched over iron
bows to make it resemble a supply wagon. Buffalo Horn, a
Bannock, served as their scout.

And early on Friday morning, the twenty-ninth, Nelson
Miles himself started upriver with Companies A, C, and E, led
by the remainder of Kelly's scouts, these last troops bringing
the total of officers and enlisted to 436. In the last few days
Miles bolstered each company to a fighting strength of fifty-

eight men by drawing from the four companies Miles was leaving behind for garrison duty. While most of the soldiers walked south, some forty men commanded by Second Lieutenant Charles E. Hargous rode ponies confiscated from the Sioux during the Cedar Creek skirmish in October.

Owing to the poor condition of what mules the Sioux hadn't driven off, Miles was able to field only a few company wagons drawn by six-mule teams. To strengthen his supply logistics, he had recently commandeered a civilian bull train of eight wagons, each drawn by a team of a dozen oxen. Four of those huge freight wagons would be headed up the Tongue, laden with corn for the stock, rations for the men, and extra ammunition for the coming fight. In addition, Miles's battalion was accompanied by a second piece of artillery: the three-inch rifled Rodman gun, its carriage, like Dickey's Napoleon gun, fitted with canvas stretched over iron bows to make it resemble the company supply wagons. This ordnance rifle was placed under the command of Second Lieutenant James W. Pope.

"No matter this cold, gentlemen," Miles told his officers that frigid, blustery morning as a new snowstorm whipped into their faces and those last three companies were about to set off up the Tongue. "The Fighting Fifth Infantry has been stationed on the frontier continuously since the days following the end of the Civil War. That's a glorious heritage. And now we have the opportunity to add to our regiment's battle banners. Let it be understood by every man in your units that we'll follow the enemy until they turn around and fight . . . or they decide to surrender. One way or another—we'll damn well do our best to end this Sioux War before the next Chinook."

Through the morning and into the afternoon the column marched up the timbered valley that stretched about a mile in width between the tall, austere bluffs that bordered either side. Each time Seamus peered around him at the other scouts, the officers, and the foot soldiers, he wondered if he looked anything like them: pairs of dark-ringed eyes peeking out at him from beneath the brims of their fur caps, there above their thick, woolen mufflers slicked with a solid layer of thick frost. A dense, low cloud lay over the entire length of the column, man and beast alike. By and large that day's march was a quiet one, most of the soldiers trudging along, deep in their own thoughts.

And Seamus in his. Four days after Christmas. Two more until the New Year. And here he was again—marching through the snow after Crazy Horse. Would this third journey be his charm?

After struggling through occasional snowdrifts for some eleven and a half miles, forced to cross the frozen river twice during that long day while the temperature never climbed above fifteen below, the colonel's battalion went into bivouac among the cottonwood on the west bank just before three P.M. By twilight the cold began to seep into the bones of every man.

Seamus watched Kelly trudge up to the fire, stomp his thick pair of buffalo moccasins, then rub his mittens over the whipping flames that seemed to lose their heat immediately in the numbing cold and the stinging wind.

"Aren't you bunking in with the headquarters bunch tonight, Luther?"

The handsome scout shook his head. "Poor Tilton."

"The chief surgeon?"

"Right. He and most of the other fellas on Miles's staff just cracked their tents out of the shipping crates."

Seamus asked, "Not enough room for all of them?"

With a snigger Kelly replied, "Some dumb son of a bitch of an army quartermaster clerk back downriver shipped the Fifth Infantry summer-duty tents!"

"Summer duty?"

"Linen tents."

"Not heavyweight canvas?"

Kelly roared with laughter. "Summer duty, Irishman!"

"Sweet Mother of God!" Donegan declared. "If the weather ain't gonna be hard enough to deal with already. Them poor foot-slogging souls. My heart ached for 'em today as I rode to the top of each hill and looked back at the column, Luther. Step by step, they were dragging their haversacks, and rifles, and frozen canteens through this deep snow."

"I think Miles is working these men to death already," Kelly said quietly so his words would not be overheard. "First that campaign up to the Missouri River country. Now he's turned them around after no more than a few days of rest."

"We can both remember the war, Luther—when men fought day after day and units marched into battle bone weary."

"From what I can see of the soldiers who served with Baldwin's battalion," Kelly continued, "both men and officers are disgruntled."

Seamus grinned. "There's always a little grumbling in every army."

Luther Kelly wagged his head and stared at the flames for a long moment before he said, "I'm just afraid that if we meet up with all the warriors we know Crazy Horse has at his command, these soldiers just won't have any bottom left to make a fight of it."

Chapter 21

30 December 1876

BY TELEGRAPH

Reported Indian Massacre.

WASHINGTON, December 22.—No information has been received in regard to the reported massacre of Major Randall and party, but it is thought the report may be true. Major Randall is with General Crook's command, and it is feared may have been sent on a mission to obtain scouts and ran into Crazy Horse's band, for which Crook has been looking for some time past.

CHICAGO, December 22.—The report that Major Randall and entire party has been massacred by the Indians in the Big Horn mountains is discredited at General Sheridan's headquarters. The report is discredited from the fact that Randall was at Fort Reno on the 14th of December, 400 miles from Fort Fetterman from which point the report should have been first received had there been any truth in it.

Could Seamus be with Randall?

Samantha looked down at her trembling hands, the way they made the newsprint rattle so.

The instant she started to read that news story about the reported massacre, Samantha remembered how often Seamus had talked about Major "Black Jack" Randall—Crook's chief of scouts.

Stifling a sob, she quickly glanced at the babe sleeping in his tiny bed made from a crate Elizabeth Burt had talked the post quartermaster out of—afraid she had awakened the child with her anguished cry. Holding her breath, a quaking hand over her mouth, Sam waited, watching the infant.

When she saw that the boy still slept, Samantha turned away, her mind racing with the horror of possibilities. Then her eyes darted aimlessly here and there over the room. And at last, on instinct alone, she literally dived onto the tiny rope-and-tick bed, plunging her hand beneath the overstuffed goose-down pillow.

Her fingers touched it, seized the pages, brought his letter out into the light.

Barely breathing, Samantha opened the folds. Her eyes danced over her husband's words. Did he mention riding off with Randall?

How her heart leaped into her throat, her breath suddenly stilled like river ice in her chest as the seconds stretched into moments . . . as she desperately searched for some clue to just what Seamus was doing in that country, some mention that he might possibly be with Black Jack Randall's company of scouts.

> Valley of the Belle Fourche
> Wyoming Terr.

My Dearest Heart—
It looks to be we'll be here awhile. Crook's waiting for supplies to come up from Fetterman. We were supposed to have them before now. . . .

Her eyes searched farther down the page.

Don't fear that I'll grow bored here, Sam. Crook and
Mackenzie will see to that. They've got scouts going
out in this direction or the other all the time. Coming
and going. And they plan on having me out too.
While we are waiting here for rations and grain for
the horses, the generals want to know what the Indians are doing. Where Crazy Horse and Sitting Bull
are camped, or moving—

She bit down on her lip so hard to keep from crying out,
Samantha was sure she made her flesh bleed. Scouts with General Crook's command may have run onto Crazy Horse's
band!

"Dear blessed God," she whispered prayerfully, then ran
the tip of her tongue over her bleeding lip. "Holy Mary,
Mother of God."

Angrily she swiped at her eyes that darted over the words
she realized she had memorized by now, reading his letter over
and over again so many times the pencil scratches were all but
rubbed off the cheap army paper.

So the Indian scouts are being sent north toward the
Yellowstone, into the Powder River country. It's there
the Indian scouts say Crazy Horse and his warriors
have gone.

Closing her teary eyes, Samantha raised her face to the
low ceiling Seamus always came close to scraping with the top
of his head. Alone there in the quiet and the cold, she began to
whisper her plea.

But in the midst of her prayer, as she stuttered to a stop
mouthing the words, her heart reminded her of snatches of
what he had told her in that letter.

So at least I have something to do from day to
day. . . . Able to saddle up and ride out rather than
hanging about camp. . . . I'd rather be out on the
back of a good, strong horse that doesn't talk back.
Where it's quiet enough to hear my own thoughts.
    Where I can think about you. And our boy.
    It will be light soon and time to go to work for
the army. To mount up and ride out.
    It gives my mind a lot of time to think, and my

heart a lot of time to ache, Sam. But we both know I have a job to do while I'm here. There aren't many things I have the talent to do. I am a simple man with big, clumsy hands and a half-slow brain, but I can do army work. If this is how God wills me to put the food on my family's table, to put the clothes on your backs and a roof over your heads, then so be it.

I will always do what God sets before me, to the best of my ability—for there are those who are counting on me to see my way through all the trouble and travail thrown down in my path, for there are those who are counting on me to make my way back home to them.

If for some reason the army keeps me here in this far north country longer than that—I vow to do all I can to be home shortly after the coming of the new year.

Keep me in your prayers, Sam. Hold our son close morning and night for me too. Oh, that I could wrap you both in my arms right now, it is so cold here. So very, very cold here. For the love of God, please pray for me—pray that God will hold me in his hand and deliver me to you soon.

"Dear God," she whispered almost aloud. "Listen to every one of my prayers. Please listen to his too. And bring him back to us as soon as his work is done."

And remember what I've always told you. That God watches over drunks, and fools, and poor army wretches like me. . . . Watch the skyline to the north. One day I'll be there, big as life, come home to hold you both again.

Until then hug yourselves for me. And tell my son that his father loves him more than breath itself. Know that I love and cherish you more, much, much more than I do my own life.

Samantha crumpled into the overstuffed pillow, trying her best to muffle her whimpering sobs. This not knowing, this simple matter of just plain enduring day after day. . . . Was she strong enough to be Seamus Donegan's wife?

She cried and cried and cried some more that afternoon and didn't realize until the baby's cries awoke her that she had cried herself to sleep.

Quickly she went to the child's tiny bed, swept the boy into her arms, and clutched him to her tightly, tears streaming down her cheeks.

"Dear God," she whispered there as she cradled her child, "just as I am holding the son of Seamus Donegan in my hands, I pray you'll hold Seamus himself in yours."

She worked quickly at the buttons on the front of her dress, pulling aside the linen bodice to free one breast. The boy took to it eagerly.

"Keep Seamus warm," she whispered, laying her lips atop the child's warm, furry head. "Holy Mother, watch over your wayward child in the wilderness."

BY TELEGRAPH

WASHINGTON

The Black Hills Committee.

WASHINGTON, December 26:—The president today sent to the senate a message enclosing the report of the proceedings of the commission appointed to treat with the Sioux Indians for the relinquishment of their right to the Black Hills. He calls special attention to the articles of agreement by the commission. Among the other advantages to be gained by them is the right of citizens to go into the country of which they have taken possession, from which they cannot be excluded; ordered printed and tabled.

No one knew how long it would take for the Sans Arc runner to reach the Sitting Bull camp.

Many suns ago Crazy Horse had asked for a volunteer, a man who could ride day and night, switching back and forth between three ponies, galloping north to find the Hunkpapa people. He was carrying Crazy Horse's request that Sitting Bull trade for ammunition with the Red River Slota north of the Muddy Water River.* Trade for as many weapons as the Hunkpapa could get their hands on.

Then he asked Sitting Bull himself to bring the rifle cartridges to the Shifting Sands River,† where the Hunkpapa camp circle would rendezvous with the Crazy Horse people. And once more they would be strong enough to turn back, perhaps to wipe out, all *wasicu* soldiers—with enough bullets and guns, the *Titunwan* Lakota would never have to bow their heads in shame like those who had been driven back to the agencies.

Day after day Spotted Elk watched and waited for the runner to return with word that Sitting Bull was on his way, especially now that they knew the Bear Coat's soldiers were marching south toward the villages. With his slow wagons pulled by the plodding, lead-footed animals the white men were so fond of, it would take the Bear Coat many more days before his men were a threat to the women and children in the villages. Once the soldiers reached the ground Crazy Horse had selected for their battle, only then would the warriors ride out to engage them.

If the ammunition and guns arrived in time, then their war against the *wasicu* could go on, and they never would have to surrender, Spotted Elk realized. But if after he had delivered that precious cargo, Sitting Bull still desired to flee back across the Elk River, north beyond the Muddy Water River until he had crossed the Medicine Line into the Land of the Grandmother, then Crazy Horse would not try to stop the Hunkpapa visionary.

Then Crazy Horse would be on his own.

After the decoys left for the soldier post, the Horse ordered that the village move upstream from the mouth of Suicide Creek# to the sheltered mouth of Prairie Dog Creek, which flowed into the Buffalo Tongue from the west. With plenty of wood close at hand as well as a warm, seeping spring that did not freeze over even in the coldest weather, the camp raised their lodges, sent out small hunting parties of the younger boys, and kept wolves moving up and down the Buf-

---

* The Missouri River.
† The Powder River.
# Present-day Hanging Woman Creek.

falo Tongue day after day—watching the Bear Coat's army advance through the deepening snow.

Just as Spotted Elk watched Crazy Horse.

What were they to do as leaders? Because the hunters could find too few buffalo that winter, their people were hungry. There weren't enough hides to make lodges where every man, woman, and child would stay warm. And because this was the coldest winter any of the old ones could ever remember, many of the Lakota were sick.

Not just the red, raw noses sore and cracked inside because of the cold, dry air . . . but more and more were becoming truly sick. Even Black Shawl—the wife of Crazy Horse. In her chest rattled the dry rasp of death-coming. Spotted Elk never saw her without a piece of cloth she would use to cover her mouth each time she coughed, bringing up flecks of blood and tiny pieces of her lungs.

So Spotted Elk watched Crazy Horse, feeling sick in his spirit for the Shirt Wearer—for both of them knew it was only a matter of time before the woman took her last, painful breath.

Then no one knew for sure just what the Strange Man of the Oglalla would do.

Would he find himself another wife, who would be like a balm to soothe his mourning? Or would he be so consumed with grief that he would abandon his responsibility to his people and finally wander off from the village for good? So consumed with hate at the *wasicu* and his diseases that he would single-handedly attack the soldier column because he no longer wanted to live?

There really was no telling, Spotted Elk decided—because Crazy Horse was not acting like himself these recent days of endless cold. At one time Spotted Elk would have declared he knew what was held in the heart of Crazy Horse . . . but no longer was he so sure. Never before would he have thought Crazy Horse the sort of leader who would keep his people in the village by force. This was a strange thing for Crazy Horse to do: ordering his *akicita* to kill the ponies of those who tried to sneak back to the agencies, to cut up their lodges, break their lodgepoles, steal their powder and bullets.

Aiyeee! This was a strange and terrible time for the Lakota people who tried hard to remain steadfast in their loyalty to the great mystic of the Oglalla.

Maybe it was as Crazy Horse tried to explain. "You see," he told the other camp leaders, "I make it plain what will happen to any who attempt to return to the agencies."

"What are you so afraid will happen to those who go in?" asked Long Feather.

"The *wasicu* will shoot them," Crazy Horse declared.

Many clamped their hands over their mouths in amazement.

"This is not a strange or silly notion," Crazy Horse argued. "Just look what happened to our chiefs who went to talk to the Bear Coat about surrender."

"Perhaps Crazy Horse is right," He Dog said to that hushed council. "There is no life in surrender. Only death—death from the white man's diseases, from the starvation, perhaps even from the *wasicu's* bullets once the soldiers and agents have robbed us of our weapons and we can no longer protect our families."

For a time there even the Shahiyela wanted to break away. When Crazy Horse decided the village should head on up Hanging Woman Creek toward the eastern divide, Little Wolf, Morning Star, and the other chiefs stood their ground and declared that it was better to find game for their starving people if they continued due south, up the Buffalo Tongue River, as fast as possible to get as far as they could from the Bear Coat's soldiers.

Those had been hard days for Crazy Horse, with his friends wanting to desert the struggle, and hearing no word from the Sitting Bull camps. And now the Shahiyela were going their own way. Yes, Spotted Elk ruminated: it must have made Crazy Horse feel very lonely. With all the bands deciding to take their own trail, no more were they a powerful people able to withstand and even defeat the finest pony soldiers sent against them, time and time again.

They had watched Morning Star and Lone Wolf take the Shahiyela south along the leafless cottonwoods bordering the Buffalo Tongue. For three sunrises the Crazy Horse camp had moved up Suicide Creek while the great chief brooded more and more. Eventually, Crazy Horse turned his people around and went south in search of the Shahiyela.

Once rejoined, he told the *Ohmeseheso* that they would all continue up the Buffalo Tongue River to the warm spring near the mouth of Prairie Dog Creek. There they would choose the place where they would make a stand. Here among the bluffs they would await the soldiers.

Hunhunhe! Shameful the things that so strong a leader as Crazy Horse must do to hold together his fragile confederation at the moment the Bear Coat was marching his soldiers toward their village! What torment for a proud man to swallow his pride for the sake of a thankless people.

Enough shame and torment that even the strongest of Lakota hearts would feel small, cold, and on the ground.

Chapter 22

30 December 1876–3 January 1877

BY TELEGRAPH

MISSOURI

Another Radical Outrage

ST. LOUIS, December 27.—In accordance with orders from Washington, all ordnance stores at the St. Louis arsenal, formerly Jefferson Barracks, are to be removed, the cannon, over 800 in number, to Rock Island, and the guns, and pistols to the New York arsenal. The removal will commence at once. The arsenal here is to be converted into a cavalry recruiting station.

NEW MEXICO

Big Strike of Mineral at Silver City

SILVER CITY, December 27.—A large body of first-class ore was uncovered in the "Seventy-six" mine on the 23rd inst. . . . The first ten tons of ore were broken from the mass in a few hours by one drill, and is estimated to be worth from $500 to $1,000 per ton. . . . The miners and all the citizens of this place are greatly excited.

On Saturday the thirtieth the column was forced to cross and recross the frozen Tongue more than ten times. The order of the march issued by Miles dictated that the column begin its journey for the day shortly before or at first light. Each morning a new company would take its place at the head of the march in rotation, while other companies moved along the flanks, and a rear guard protected the wagon train.

That afternoon they forded Pumpkin Creek, which flowed in from the east, and made their bivouac for the night in a spot that not only offered water and wood, but was easily defensible if the Sioux should decide to turn about and attempt an attack. At each camp the colonel established a tight ring of pickets, allowed the animals to graze the best they could until dark, then brought the horses, mules, and oxen within the corral of wagons for the night, where the men continued to feed the animals on strips of cottonwood bark.

During their march on the morning of the thirty-first they found the valley growing wider, the spare, naked bluffs on either side of them now topped with stunted pine and cedar. Nonetheless, the twisting path of the Tongue required Second Lieutenant Oscar F. Long's engineering detachment to work far in advance preparing the banks for the supply wagons to cross the frozen river several times throughout that short winter day. Along the trail they passed more than a dozen dead cattle before finally catching up to Captain Dickey's and Lieutenant Mason Carter's battalions. At this point they had put forty-six miles behind them since leaving the Tongue River Cantonment.

That New Year's Eve there was little to celebrate, and most of the weary men were asleep well before midnight, quietly wrapped in their two blankets, back-to-back with their bunkie not long after dark had gripped the land. About all that any of them had cause to rejoice in before they fell into a cold, fitful, exhausted stupor was the fact that they were all together again—seven companies of infantry—along with those two pieces of artillery, a handful of scouts, and a hot trail left behind by the cattle thieves.

Miles had reveille sounded at four-thirty A.M. on the first day of 1877.

In that high-plains darkness most of the men stomped circulation back into their cold feet and legs around fires nursed throughout the night. Despite the bitter subzero temperatures most men did their best to act merry, toasting one another New Year's wishes with their steaming coffee tins. At five-thirty they were marching south beneath a brilliant moon still reflecting silver light off the icy-blue snow.

Not long after sunrise it was plain to every man that the wind had shifted out of the southwest, warming in the process. By midmorning the first of the gray rain clouds moved in, turning the frozen, snowy trail into a slimy slush. Man and animal alike fought for a foothold, sliding this way and that every yard they slogged up the valley of the Tongue. It was a wet and sullen bunch of soldiers that neared Otter Creek late that Monday afternoon.

As Seamus rode off the muddy slope of the ridge and back across the bottomland toward the column marching on the far side of the valley, he remembered none too fondly the endless days and nights of rain and mud and soul-sapping despair as he and others led Crook's stumbling, lunging command toward the Black Hills settlements. His stomach jerked with a twinge of nausea; those were memories that knotted a man's belly with the stringy taste of horse meat—

The first gunshot echoed like a dull crack from the far ridges across the Tongue. Then there came a scattering of shots. Donegan quickly looked over his shoulder at the hilltops behind him—relieved to find them empty—then jabbed his small brass spurs into the roan's flanks. The gelding burst into a lope, its hooves tearing up rooster-tail cascades of powdery snow.

On the far side of the frozen river he watched the lines of soldiers knot and unfurl, officers on horseback whirling and shouting, the wagon train brought to a sudden halt. Farther to the south at the head of the march, across the river past the naked willow and in among the cottonwoods, Seamus saw the flash of movement. Lots of horsemen. Now their foreign cries cracked the cold, bursts of frosty breath jetting from each dark hole in their faces as they screamed back at the soldiers.

Leforge and his last two Crow, along with Bruguier, were hammering heels to their ponies, darting into that cottonwood grove. From the south end of the trees exploded at least two dozen horsemen, feathers fluttering, shields clattering, voices yapping as they fled upriver.

Seamus yanked back on the reins with his left hand, and the roan shuddered to a halt in the snow. With his right hand he dragged the Winchester carbine from its leather boot beneath his right leg. Knowing there was already a shell in the breech, he dragged back the hammer with his thumb as he shoved the butt into his shoulder and peered down the barrel. Squeezing off a shot at the escaping horsemen, he levered another round into the chamber and fired a second time before he figured the Sioux were simply too far for him to make any good of a third shot.

On the far side of the river Kelly had Leforge and the Crow on the way with Bruguier and Buffalo Horn close behind, all of them yipping and yelling as if they were an entire company. Thirty yards to their rear Miles stood in his stirrups, watching expectantly, ordering some of Hargous's mounted company into the chase.

Then, flinging an arm to the right and the left, the colonel bellowed orders no more than a muffled echo to Donegan. But as quickly the nearby officers were scurrying like ants among their outfits. While some instantly spread their men into a skirmish line on that eastern side of the river, others led their men cautiously onto the ice, across, and up the snowy bank on the far side, where they deployed the companies in a tight skirmish formation extending across the valley floor and up the slope of some slimy, icy bluffs, each man no more than five feet from the next.

Occasional gunshots cracked upstream, and from moment to moment Seamus spotted a glimpse of either the Sioux horsemen or Kelly's outfit, all of the riders bobbing in and out of sight as they rode up and down the rolling landscape. Quickly dragging his field glasses from his off-hand saddlebag, Donegan twisted the wheel and attempted to focus on the far scene. More than a mile away, the enemy disappeared beyond a far bend in the river. The only riders visible now were Kelly and the rest. Luther flung his arm into the air, stopping those behind him as it appeared he bellowed out his orders to Leforge and the Crow in front of him.

"Good man, Luther," Seamus said in a whisper, his breath huffing in a great cloud above his face as a cold mist continued to fall. "Those red bastards suck you into a mess of quicksand before you know it."

He sighed audibly when he saw the entire bunch turn and head back to the column behind Kelly. Maybe there wasn't any coup to count this afternoon, but at least the Sioux hadn't sprung any trap—no ambush, no casualties, for that short, hot, running fight of it.

"By Jupiter, we could use Crook's cavalry, couldn't we, Donegan?" Miles roared as Seamus pushed the roan off the ice and into a grove of old cottonwood.

"As hard as these men might want to catch Crazy Horse," Donegan replied, "it's like a tortoise and a hare for your foot soldiers to stay up with red h'athens on horseback."

"Just give me Mackenzie's Fourth, and I'll show you better than he accomplished with the Cheyenne!"

"Mackenzie did all that Crook expected of him—and more," Donegan protested, suddenly sensing the immense, unflappable ego of the soldier before him.

Those words were just sharp enough that it appeared they brought Miles up short, stung by the civilian's observation. Chewing a lip for a moment, Miles finally looked north, finding his scouts returning.

When he finally turned back to Donegan, Miles said, "Then the Fighting Fifth will just have to do on foot what Crook failed to do with Mackenzie's cavalry."

"Find and catch Crazy Horse?" Seamus asked as more of the headquarters group brought their horses to a halt around them.

"You forgot one very important part of the equation," Miles corrected. "Find and catch—and *defeat*—Crazy Horse."

After suffering that cold night at the mouth of Otter Creek, where the rain soon turned into a frozen sleet that coated man, animal, and equipage with a layer of ice, Miles had his men up in the dark, gulping coffee and wolfing down their hard crackers. With the command up and about the colonel ordered that the teams of slow-plodding oxen not be hitched to their wagons.

"Mr. Bowen, it's my belief we can cover the ground a little faster if the oxen don't have to pull their wagons," Miles explained to the second lieutenant he had placed in charge of his supply train.

William Bowen asked, "We're leaving all the wagons behind, General?"

"No, Lieutenant. We'll take the company wagons along."

"The ones pulled by mules," explained Frank Baldwin.

"So what will become of the civilian's oxen?" asked Captain Casey. "Leave 'em behind?"

"I think it best that we don't," Miles replied. "Unhitch them and drive them along with the column. We might just need those big brutes for food before this chase is over."

"Damn right," grumbled Edmond Butler, a tough forty-nine-year-old Irish-born captain. "In a pinch tough beef is better than no rations at all."

Leaving behind the four huge freight wagons the oxen had struggled to drag through the snow, slush, and mud for the better part of four days, Miles trudged on, leading his infantry south on the trail clearly marked by the stolen cattle and all those unshod hoofprints. They had marched better than fifty-five miles already and would have at least that much more ground to cover before they reached the ground Crazy Horse had chosen for his battle.

"Was that a war party we bumped into yesterday?" Kelly asked the morning of the second after the blood-red sun began to rise low along the southeastern horizon. "Or was it only a hunting party?"

With a shrug Seamus replied, "Either way, Luther. I figure the h'athens knew we were coming—they have to have scouts hanging back to keep track of us."

"Yeah," Johnny Bruguier said, nodding.

"Or that bunch could've been out hunting to feed a lot of empty bellies," Donegan continued.

"A big village like Crazy Horse got," the half-breed stated, "it need lots of meat."

Kelly turned to Donegan. "And we haven't run across much in the way of any game at all, have we?"

"One way or the other, let's just say that bunch of Sioux

was out hunting," Seamus declared, shaking off a cold shiver as the wind picked up. "Hunting four-legged game . . . maybe hunting two-legged enemy."

Early that afternoon the advance party was forced to divert the line of march far to the eastern side of the valley, where the going wasn't so tough but where the men were forced to march some distance from the Tongue. It wasn't long before they came across an abandoned camp of rustic shelters erected from slabs of wood, poles, and rocks, along with some sections of sod and thick boughs of cedar and evergreen.* Here and there among the makeshift hovels lay the carcasses of butchered cattle.

"Smell that, Irishman?" Kelly asked.

Seamus put his nose in the wind and sniffed. Then sniffed again. "Tobacco smoke."

"That isn't soldier smoke," Kelly declared. "The column hasn't gotten anywhere close yet."

"Warriors were here this morning, I'd wager," Seamus replied.

"Keeping a close eye on us, aren't they?" Kelly asked. "Even returning here to these shanties to do it."

"What you make of this, Luther?" Donegan asked as they both climbed out of the saddle. He hadn't seen anything quite like these heart-wrenching hovels since he'd been a young boy in poor famine-ravaged Ireland.

"I figure you'd be the one to know better'n any of us, Seamus," Kelly answered as he knelt before one of the shelters and peered into its dark, snowy interior.

"How's that?" he asked, straightening as he bristled, thinking Kelly was marking him down because of his Irish roots.

The chief of scouts got to his feet and turned. "Why don't you tell me what Injuns with Crazy Horse wouldn't have their own lodges along?"

"Wouldn't have lodges?"

"What Injuns did Mackenzie run off into the countryside not so long ago?"

Donegan wagged his head dolefully, his eyes studying the pitiful hovels where human beings had actually taken shelter

---

* Near the mouth of Beaver Creek.

from the brutal weather. "Cheyenne," he answered quietly. "Morning Star's Cheyenne."

"A proud people," Kelly said with complete admiration, dusting the snow and mud from his knees and gloves.

"A damned *proud* people," Donegan said, almost choking on the words. His eyes stung. "They'd rather live out in this weather, eating jackrabbits and gophers, sleeping under rocks and brush, than go back to the white-goddamned-reservation. I'll say they're a damned proud people."

He turned away before his eyes betrayed him, and stuffed a big buffalo moccasin into the stirrup. Swinging into the saddle, Donegan said, "I'll go fetch up the general. He'll wanna see for himself just what sort of warrior we're following."

"What do you mean?" Kelly asked, catching up his reins. "What sort of warrior?"

"I think Miles needs to know that he's following a bunch of iron-riveted hard cases what can live out here under rocks and scrub brush, running about on foot, eating what they got when they got it."

Kelly nodded, his eyes fired with admiration. "Damn right I think Miles should know. He and his soldiers won't be going into battle with a bunch of young sprouts who'll fight only as long as it takes for their women and young'uns to pull out."

"No, this outfit we're scouting for is due for a fight of it, Luther," Seamus responded as he eased his horse around and Kelly came into the saddle. "Some of them ain't got nothing more to lose."

Kelly nodded. "And that makes a man one hell of a tough bravo in a fight—when he hasn't got anything left to lose."

"This bunch Crazy Horse has got around him now ain't the kind give up easy. These warriors are all breechclout and balls, Luther. I figure Crazy Horse is going to pick the ground where he'll stand and fight. Just like he done us at the Rosebud."

Kelly slapped the end of his reins down on the horse's flank to put it into a lope, saying, "And just like General John Buford picked the ground to make his stand at Gettysburg."

There had been times in the last five days when the scouts had turned about and reported to the head of the column that the easiest route was that provided by the river itself. Their slow, tortuous march of the second was again that sort of day where the foot soldiers and the wagons made their way off the bank onto the ice to follow every twisting curve and corkscrewed turn of the Tongue, always on the lookout for soft ice and narrow stretches of open water where a warm spring fed the otherwise ice-choked river.

Due to weakening ice the column was forced to cross the Tongue four times with their exhausted, played-out animals. In the end they put no more than another five miles behind them that second day of 1877. Perhaps because they believed the overtired stock were not likely to wander astray, Lieutenant Bowen's detail soldiers did not corral the huge oxen.

At dawn on the third it was clear they had made a mistake.

It was also plain from examining the tracks of the cloven-hoofed beasts that the oxen hadn't been stolen—they had merely wandered away on the backtrail through the night. In the dim half light Robert Jackson was assigned to lead four of Hargous's mounted soldiers back to the north to round up the wayward stock while the column formed up and pushed off for the day.

No sooner had the five horsemen disappeared downstream and the rear guard marched out of sight than some twenty warriors kicked their ponies into a gallop, streaking off the hillsides in a blur, thundering down on Jackson's roundup detail. Shots echoed off the snowy bluffs.

At the first crack of enemy carbines, Colonel Nelson A. Miles immediately ordered a halt, wrenching his horse around to gallop to the rear, where he sent that day's rear guard, Edmond Butler's C Company, back to the rescue.

"They got there too late," Jackson told the other scouts and officers who later on gathered around the trampled snow where the lone soldier had fallen from his horse.

Seamus rubbed his oozy lower lip with bacon grease and said, "Butler's men got here soon enough to keep the bastards from cutting up the poor lad."

Surgeon Henry R. Tilton had been kneeling beside the body of Private William H. Batty. He brushed his mitten across the young soldier's face one more time, clearing it of some of the icy snow that continued to fall, then got to his feet. The major said, "Let's get him buried."

While Batty's body was carried back all the way to the front of the column, Captain Butler had the men of his C Company begin working in relays on the frozen ground. The private had been one of their own.

Miles had his regimental adjutant, First Lieutenant George W. Baird, say a few words over the dark scar of earth in the midst of all that scuffled snow. After Butler's men had each tossed in a handful of sod, the colonel had other soldiers fill in Batty's final resting place and shovel enough snow over the grave to cover it from view. Miles ordered the march to resume.

Over that crude mound walked every foot soldier, rolled the wheels of their wagons, plodded the hooves of mules and oxen alike, obliterating all sign of the grave . . . in hopes of protecting it from predator and warrior alike.

After the brief service Donegan and the rest of the scouts led the wary troops south past the mouth of Turtle Creek. At noon the column was forced to recross the Tongue on ice softened by the recent rains. Beneath that heavy weight of the overburdened wagons the semisoft surface of the river groaned and creaked. But as much as the men feared the Tongue would swallow them, wagons and all, not one was lost in the crossing.

"Donegan!"

Reining up, Seamus turned to find Kelly riding up with Bruguier and Buffalo Horn, the lone Bannock.

Luther Kelly brought his horse to a halt beside Donegan's. "Wanted to let you know the three of us will be gone for the better part of a day."

"Headed where?"

With a nod to the west Kelly said, "General wants to know if there's any camps in the valley of the Rosebud."

"Just the three of you?"

Kelly replied, "If we have to make a run for it—best keep our outfit small." He smiled at Donegan in that handsome way of his. "You'll watch over the old man for me, won't you?"

"Miles?"

"Yep. Stay out front and make sure he doesn't run into an ambush before I get back."

Dragging off his mitten and holding out his bare hand in the cold wind, Seamus watched Kelly pull off his glove, and they shook. Donegan said, "I figure I know what kind of ground cavalry will want to use against foot soldiers."

"Even Crazy Horse's cavalry."

The Irishman smiled, the skin on his face tight and drawn in the bitter cold. "Bet your life that I'll know the ground that savvy bastard will likely use, all right."

Kelly started to rein away, tugging on his horsehide mitten. "I'll let you bet my life on that any day, Donegan."

"Keep your eyes peeled, Kelly!"

"Yup—and you watch your hair, you ol' horse soldier."

Chapter 23

4–6 January 1877

BY TELEGRAPH

OHIO

Hayes Confident of Success

NEW YORK, December 27.—The Graphic's correspondent at Cincinnati telegraphs that he has been informed on good authority that Governor Hays intends to resign the governorship of Ohio, on the re-assembling of the legislature next Tuesday, confidently believing that he will be peacefully inaugurated president of the United States on the 4th of March.

FOREIGN

War News and Rumors

CONSTANTINOPLE, December 28.—The prevalent opinion is that the port will not accept Lord Salisbury's proposals.

LONDON, December 28.—A special from Paris says
the sultan in answer to Salisbury's representation,
said his personal safety would be compromised if he
conceded all that the powers demanded.

MOSCOW, December 28.—The Gazette declares the
new Turkish constitution a mere mockery of the powers, and says the only way of improving the Christians in Turkey is efficacious occupation, and
granting to Christians the right to carry arms or de-
priving Muslims of this right.

VIENNA, December 28.—General Hanken, at the re-
view held in taking command of the Servian army
said, "in a week's time you will have an opportunity
to prove your courage before the enemy." A special
says that on Tuesday 500 Russians crossed the Dan-
ube from Thunzevenin. A cabinet meeting on the
eastern question will be held at Vienna to-day.

"Forget all that foreign gobbledygook!" Martha Luhn said
to Samantha as she smacked her palm down on the
paper spread across the tiny table in the fire-warmed kitchen.
"You remember just a few days back when this same Rocky
Mountain *News* had that headline story about the ore strikes
they were making down at Silver City?"

Yes, she had seen the story, read it, and thought of them
all fleeing south from Indian country. But it wasn't something
she was ready to admit—not just yet. Samantha gently pulled
the sleeping baby from her breast and laid him on her shoulder. As she began to pat his back softly, she said, "I usually
don't pay much attention to that sort of thing. Mostly looking
for any notices on the campaign—"

"Well, you should give it some attention," Martha said.
"More than any of the rest of us, you ought to feel like you
and your Mr. Donegan are free of the army. Which means you
can pick up and get right on out of this country. Say good
riddance to all this waiting and the terrors of army life."

"What are you trying to get at?" Sam inquired.

Martha replied, "Those silver strikes down in New Mexico—that's where they are, you know? Not so bad a place to
raise a family."

"If you don't have to worry about Apaches wandering away from their reservations!" Nettie Capron squealed.

Martha Luhn turned to Samantha. "You don't have to worry about such things. That's just the point I'm making." Her eyes dropped a minute to the dozing child Samantha was burping at her shoulder. "You've told me more than once that your Mr. Donegan first came west after the war to look for gold in the Montana diggings."

"Yes—well, but . . . he never got that far to try," Sam began to explain.

"Still wants to make his fortune in that precious ore, doesn't he?"

Samantha nodded less than emphatically. "Seamus has talked about it with me a time or two, yes we have."

"When he gets back this winter—you sit him down and convince the mister that it's high time for him to get back to what he intended to do ten years ago," advised Martha.

"Yes, digging for gold and silver must be a much safer occupation for a husband and a father than riding scout for Crook or any of the rest of them," Nettie added.

"It's really a single man's profession, Samantha—don't you see?"

"I . . . I never thought of it in those terms. It's just what I've come to believe he has to do—so I'll wait behind."

"And when he gets back," said Nettie, coming around behind Sam's chair to lay a hand on the young mother's shoulder, "don't you think it better for your child to grow up some other place where you're not in the middle of the comings and goings of Indian country?"

"It's what we both talked about . . . ," Sam began, feeling a little put upon by the others, who were taking far too much an interest in what Seamus should be doing with his life. That sort of thing was for a man to decide for himself.

"Just . . . just think about it, Samantha," Martha said, in her own way shushing the other women in the kitchen, all in flour-dusted aprons, as this was baking day for the week. "I'm sure it will all make sense to your mister when he comes riding back home to you."

Sam pushed herself up from the chair, adjusted the tiny blanket around the sleeping baby in the crook of her arm, and said, "Seems I better put Mr. Donegan's son down for a nap. I'll be back down to help later."

She heard their voices as she slipped out to the landing and began her climb up the narrow stairs. Women talking about this and that of no real consequence to her, bits of news from the papers just come to the post late yesterday, perhaps the latest rumor to find circulation among the officers and their wives, or the most recent tremor in relations with the Sioux up at Red Cloud's agency. All of it meant nothing much at all to her.

She waited only for news of Crook's army and its return to Fetterman. Then heard that Mackenzie's Fourth was moving back to Camp Robinson. But neither of those meant Seamus was coming back.

What did she have to count on? she asked herself as she laid the boy in his nest of blankets. Was she really being selfish to want Seamus with her more than he had been around her for most of their married life?

Oh, Samantha! she chided herself, catching a glimpse of herself in a faded, scratched mirror she had nailed above the tiny bureau. You have as much of your husband as any army officer's wife. Yes—he could be a store clerk or a blacksmith, or he could be a farmer gone all day to the fields like Pa.

"No, he couldn't," she whispered quietly.

And looked down at the child.

"You and I both know it, don't we, God? Seamus Donegan couldn't be any of those."

But maybe it wouldn't hurt—she thought—to look downstairs for that old paper with the news story about the Silver City ore strike. Just to have it here and ready when he did return home soon.

Maybe the lure of silver and gold and riches beyond imagination would entice him once more. God knows there'd never be any money in army scouting.

BY TELEGRAPH

More Indian Murders Toward the Black Hills

THE INDIANS

More Murders by "Good" Indians Near Red Cloud.

CHEYENNE, December 30.—A courier into Fort Laramie, from Red Cloud agency, reports that two couriers, a mail-carrier and a wood-chopper, left Sage creek early Christmas morning, and two hours before sundown they were struck by a party of thirty friendly Indians within sixteen miles of Red Cloud, who killed the two couriers, named Dillon and Reddy; also mortally wounded the mail-carrier, Tate, who had two sacks of matter, and likewise severely wounded the wood-chopper. The wounded men arrived at Red Cloud day before yesterday, and being exposed during the interval to intense cold, they were severely frozen. They report hearing more firing in their rear an hour after being attacked and it is supposed that other parties not yet reported were attacked. A party has gone out from the agency to search for the bodies.

They were gradually gaining in altitude the farther they marched up the valley of the Tongue. And for much of the time the wagons did not have too bad a time of it, what with the way the large Indian village had itself followed the trail made by some buffalo along the river. So many hooves, so many travois poles, so many moccasin prints in that snow gradually pounded down and hardened into a highway pointing south—toward the Wolf Mountains.

Just before dawn on Thursday morning, the fourth of January, Luther Kelly returned from his reconnaissance over to the valley of the Rosebud.

Seamus held out a cup of coffee in the gray light as Kelly stomped up to seize it eagerly. "You see anything worth making mention of?"

"Not a sign," Kelly admitted, then blew on his coffee and drank. "No trails, no tracks, no sign of buffalo over there either."

"What that tells me is that we're gonna stare the lot of them in the face here real soon, Luther."

He looked up at Donegan and nodded once before going back to his coffee and staring at the fire. "They're all together, aren't they? All those warrior bands."

"Used to be a man could figure they'd split up come winter."

"Not this bunch," Kelly said. "If it really is Crazy Horse, he'll hold 'em together because they know we're coming. Won't be any going this way or going that. They'll *all* be waiting for us."

"By gor," Seamus whispered harshly as he started kicking snow into the fire the moment the first orders were shouted around them to prepare to mount. "Looks plain as sun that Miles is going to get himself exactly what Crook his own self has been wanting for the better part of a year."

"What's that?"

"To get a crack at Crazy Horse—and have the bastard stand and fight."

"Just like he did at the Rosebud . . . right?" Kelly asked, then swilled down the last of the coffee in the tin.

"And nearly overran us three times, the bleeming bastard."

"Yeah," Kelly commented quietly. "Miles will get his own crack at them Sioux . . . just like Custer prayed Crazy Horse would stand and fight."

"This could be it, Kelly," Seamus said, dragging the reins off the ground and stabbing a buffalo moccasin into the stirrup.

"Could be what?"

"Maybe this will be the last battle Crazy Horse will ever fight."

Just about the time the scouts pushed out of the bivouac to probe the valley ahead of the soldier column, a fine mist began to fall. Within the hour that chilling mist became a continuous and galling rain that tended to soak man and animal to the bone, turning the wide trail to a mucky slush, hard going for the foot soldiers and wagons both.

From time to time that day Donegan and the other scouts came across recent sign of the retreating bands. Here and there among the cottonwood groves they found the crude frames for wickiups and the cold, lifeless black rings of dead fires. Clearly, all indications showed how bands of warriors were staying behind the villages, between their people and the soldiers, monitoring the Bear Coat's advance up the Tongue, falling back slowly, ever so slowly.

It was enough to worry any battle veteran. By any calculation Crazy Horse had more than enough warriors to take on Miles's infantry. So why didn't the Sioux stand and fight?

And another thing was just as galling: the soldier column was being watched, constantly. The two recent attacks had proved that. That could only mean that Crazy Horse was falling back for a specific purpose.

It made Seamus shudder. Maybe, after all, this was like what John Buford had done when he'd been the first to arrive on the outskirts of that tiny Pennsylvania town called Gettysburg. Buford knew Lee's Army of Virginia was coming—perhaps no more than hours away. So while he could, Buford chose the ground.

If a man could seize one advantage above all others, he must choose the ground where he would engage the enemy.

Crazy Horse was falling back, falling back . . . and when he stopped—that would be the ground where he would stake himself and go no farther. There Colonel Nelson A. Miles and his Fifth U.S. Infantry would have their hands full.

During the incessant rain throughout that day most of the snow melted. Only patches remained beneath the scrub cedar and stunted pine. Out where the army marched, the ground had become a quagmire. Late that afternoon the halt was called on the west side of the Tongue across from the mouth of Otter Creek.* After Miles set up his rotation of pickets, the weary men did their best to scratch around to find some dry wood for their smoky fires, then curled up in their wet blankets and fell fast asleep.

By first light on the fifth the column was off and marching again, plodding through a steady, driving rain that gusted at their backs and turned the trail into a sticky gumbo yearning to pull a man's boots off his frozen feet if he wasn't careful. Back and forth they were forced to cross the softening ice of the Tongue as the sandstone bluffs crowded in first on one

* Site of present-day Ashland, Montana.

side, then on the other, narrowing the valley once more as the river snaked and twisted much more than it did farther north. Animals and wagons became mired in the mud or broke through the spongy ice, requiring the men to plunge in themselves to yank, and haul, and tow everything free.

From time to time men fell out of line to drag off their soaked and shapeless bootees and socks, scooping up a handful of snow and rubbing it on the stark-white foot—hoping to startle circulation back into their frozen, plodding extremities. Lips turned blue and teeth chattered, that dull gray day as the rain continued to fall. There was no drying off; there could be no changes of clothes, no stopping for fires. Only more miles of march, more rain, more watching the horizon for mounted warriors, more waiting.

Off to the southwest beneath the low-slung gray drizzle the men began to make out the gradually ascending heights of the Wolf Mountains. Back along the column more and more men began to talk quietly among themselves, wondering if the Sioux were drawing them farther and farther downriver, eventually to draw the army into the rugged fastness of those mountains in the distance. There finally to make their play—finally to stand and fight among the heights.

Seamus brooded on it too. With all the sign they were beginning to run across, it was of a sudden causing the Irishman to recall the dogs he had so often noticed around the forts and outposts and frontier towns in the last ten years he had been in this western country. Crazy Horse's village of winter roamers was the bitch in heat luring Crook's, or Terry's, or Miles's armies to follow . . . follow, as the soft-headed, hard-dicked town dogs would always follow, fighting among themselves for the chance to be the first to crawl atop and hump the seductive, alluring bitch.

The farther they pushed that Friday, the more such a devilish plot on the part of Crazy Horse made sense to him. It seemed that with every hour, if not with every mile, they were marching past more and more recent Indian sign. More of the abandoned wickiups and war lodges. Here and there the trampled earth of lodge circles and fire rings. Meat-drying racks. Scattered and half-used piles of cottonwood bark stripped and peeled for their war ponies. More carcasses of cattle and oxen slaughtered in those migrating camps. Even a few live cattle contentedly grazing among the mud and boggy, grassy bottoms alongside the river, animals abandoned by the retreating village. A very large village that by necessity had spread itself for some distance along the riverbank.

Very late in the afternoon, after a grinding march of some fifteen miles at the mercy of a drenching rain, the column went into bivouac about the time the wind began to quarter around, for the first few hours of that night blowing out of the west. But just before dawn on the sixth the wind pounded at their backs, howling directly out of the north again, with the steely tang of snow in its bite.

Chapter 24

Hoop and Stick Moon 1877

Telegraphic Briefs

DAKOTA

Wild Bill's Murderer.

YANKTON, January 3.—In the United States Court to-day, John McCall, convicted of the murder of Wild Bill, was sentenced by Chief Justice Sponnon to be hanged March 1. He will carry the case to the supreme court. The only ground of defense is that he was intoxicated, so as to be unconscious of the act.

Wooden Leg watched the soldier column through those first fat flakes of snow as dry as alder leaves became in late autumn. The wind caught them, spun each one in a whorl, then scutted them along the ground. At times there was no sense in trying to shade one's eyes to peer into the down-river distance. But for a moment, perhaps no more than a heartbeat or two, the wind dance of the snow stopped as if the sky suddenly held its breath . . . while the young Shahiyela warrior could see clear enough to make out the shapes of the soldier scouts, walk-a-heaps, and wagons plodding out of the first pale light this stormy dawn.

"They won't give up," Yellow Weasel said dolefully.

Wooden Leg wanted to turn to the older warrior and tell him just how much of a fool he was for ever thinking the white man would give up.

But instead of angering Yellow Weasel, Wooden Leg swallowed down his youthful impulse and said quietly, "With my own eyes I have seen what the soldiers did to Old Bear's village on the Powder last winter. Understand that there is something that does not let these *ve-ho-e* soldiers give up their chase of our villages. No matter the distance. No matter the cold."

Wooden Leg would know. Born in the Black Hills near the Sacred Mountain, this was his nineteenth winter—having matured in many ways over the last three seasons of fighting the white man. Now a member of the *Hemo-eoxeso,* the Elk-horn Scrapers warrior society, he cast a long shadow upon the ground: there were only two *Ohmeseheso* warriors who stood taller than Wooden Leg.

How he would have loved to ask Yellow Weasel why any man could think the *ve-ho-e* would ever give up following the villages . . . but instead Wooden Leg bit down on his tongue. Sometimes it was more honorable not to say something than to show the foolishness of another.

"Go on now—*vo-ve-he,*"* Sits in the Night ordered Beaver Claws, one of the younger scouts in his pack of wolves. "Ride back to our village to tell Crazy Horse, to tell the chiefs. The soldiers come on this morning!"

They all watched the youngster leap onto the bare back of the spotted pony, then pull his blanket about him. Beaver Claws kicked the animal in the flanks and leaned far forward as it spurted off into the snowstorm. Wooden Leg breathed deep of the sharp air. He hadn't been able to sleep all that well last night wrapped in his one blanket and buffalo robe, cold as it was. They made themselves no fire, even after the whole long day of rain. Instead, the wolves had huddled in a cotton-wood grove through the night as the winds shifted and the rain changed to an icy snow.

* Run!

As soon as it grew light enough to see the far bank of the river, they moved out—quietly on the soggy, sodden, snow-covered ground. Watching the veil of snow and foggy mist until they saw signs of the *ve-ho-e* fires, listening until they heard the white men laughing, grunting, talking in their camp before they would continue their pursuit of the village for the day.

The weather this morning would slow the soldiers down even more, Wooden Leg thought. It was good, because the chiefs had calculated that the Bear Coat's men should be within attacking distance of the village by that very afternoon. But while the ponies and travois could disappear quickly over broken ground, up the mouth of a coulee and into the far reaches of a distant canyon, the *ve-ho-e* soldiers were invariably held back by their slow animals, by the sheer bulk of those wagons hidden beneath the dirty, oily canvas stretched tight over iron bows.

All the wolves had to do today was stay just out of sight, but right in front of the army in its worming march. Close enough to keep track of the Bear Coat's progress, but far enough away that they would not be discovered again as they had been a few days before. Those were their orders from Crazy Horse. In fact, Sits in the Night's wolves were instructed to build the fires in those campsites the soldiers had come across the last two days: let the scouts find the fire pits still warm; leave behind a few old ponies ready to die anyway . . . all those sorts of enticements that would draw the Bear Coat farther and farther into their trap.

The white man always went for the bait.

Wolf Tooth, another leader of their scouting party, threw up his arm just ahead of them. They all halted. Listening, straining their eyes into the snowy middistance. A thin layer of wispy fog clung to the leafless willow, surrounding the copse of cottonwood. They waited. Then suddenly Wolf Tooth pointed. And Wooden Leg saw.

There, not very far away, came the three, no four . . . now five horsemen—their animals with their heads bowed, plodding slowly into the fog and surging snowstorm.

"Go back," Sits in the Night ordered sharply.

The others turned their ponies quickly at the command. But Wooden Leg was the last. He wanted to get himself a little better look. After all, he hadn't seen such creatures since last winter on the Powder River.

Out of the swirling, wind-whipped gloom they appeared again. Just as they had on the southern edge of Old Bear's camp that morning only heartbeats before the soldiers had charged in with their pistols drawn.

Army scouts.

"*Hotoma!*" Wooden Leg whispered into the wind, calling upon the mysterious bravery medicine of a *Tse-Tsehese* warrior.

Oh, how he yearned for the trap to close!

Wooden Leg hoped that this time the ones who led the soldiers to the villages would be the first to die.

By the time it was light enough to see on that sixth day of January, it was plain there was a prairie snowstorm in the process of working itself into a lather up and down the Tongue River Valley.

Snow whirled in this direction and that—up, down, and sideways on a cutting wind that made it all but impossible to keep the fires lit. Men stood about in their blankets at breakfast fires—grumbling, stomping cold feet back into frozen boots that had never fully dried out, never come close to warming, snowflakes readily clinging to the damp weave of their wool coats or matting on the wet, stringy buffalo hair of their winter overcoats and those heavy leggings lashed to their belts. At least it warmed the blood to curse a man's officers, his commander, and perhaps even the unseen, taunting enemy who kept on disappearing farther and farther up the valley.

An enemy who was always just out of sight. Just beyond reach. Nothing more than a wisp of smoke—like that smoke needling off the puny fires they had eventually abandoned early that Saturday morning.

From time to time just below the hulking clouds Seamus got himself a glimpse of those distant gray-and-purple-shaded Wolf Mountains once more being dappled in white with the approaching storm. Throughout that morning and into the afternoon the column was again forced to cross the Tongue several times as the sandstone buttes closed in on one side; then a mile or so farther they shoved themselves close to the other bank. Hours were consumed with excruciating physical labor as relays of men were ordered up to join Lieutenant Oscar F. Long's engineering crew in chopping away at the frozen mud of the banks, to lay down as much deadfall as they could find to corduroy the approach, and to hack away at the creaking, splintering ice before the mule and ox teams were able to trudge through the shallow water of the Tongue with each crossing.

First one, then a second, and finally a third Indian camp they passed through. That dreary afternoon in the midst of the icy snowstorm, the scouts came across some gaunt, wolfish, half-starved Indian ponies the village had evidently abandoned. Nearby in the midst of some lodge rings a half-dozen small fires still smoldered in the driving snow.

Late in the day Donegan halted and stared south into the dance of white against the ever-changing background of leafless bush and striated sandstone butte. He watched the Crow trackers and Buffalo Horn disappear ahead of them in the white smear.

"Luther, there's a reason they're letting us get this close."

Kelly stopped beside him, for a long moment staring into the swirl of snow as he raked the hoarfrost from his mustache. "We're catching up with 'em, that's all. And they surely know we're on their tails."

Wagging his head, Seamus continued, "The ground . . . what Crazy Horse has chose to make his stand—it can't be all that far now—"

The sharp crack of carbines shattered the snowy stillness of the air, answered by a half-dozen yelps, cries, and squeals of surprise.

No more had Donegan and Kelly kicked their mounts into motion and yanked pistols from their holsters than two horsemen appeared in front of them, heading straight for the white scouts. Both the Irishman and Kelly raked back the hammers on the pistols as the two warriors started screaming while they kept on coming.

"Hold it!" Seamus hollered. "It's Leforge's boys!"

"Damn if it ain't," Kelly growled.

The pair shot past, crying out in their tongue, their long hair flapping out from beneath the wool hoods of the blanket coats.

Kelly shook his head, asking, "Where the hell's—"

Another shot, this time a pistol . . . then a second.

"Where's Buffalo Horn?" Donegan asked.

"Yep." Kelly smiled.

"That's one brave Injin got himself in a scrap," Seamus declared. "C'mon, we can't let him take 'em on all by himself!"

Jabbing spurs into their mounts, the two civilians shot into the snowstorm as the voices of the retreating Crow trackers disappeared behind them. More pistol shots, followed by what was clearly the ring of a carbine.

"That Bannock's having himself all the fun!" Kelly roared.

From behind them there came a clatter of hoofbeats. Turning in the saddle suddenly, not sure whether to expect an ambush by a war party of Sioux who had suckered them, or the arrival of the Crow trackers who had somehow worked up their nerve again, Seamus found John Johnston and Johnny Bruguier racing up on their tails about the time all four reached the edge of a small clearing.

There on foot near his skittish pony stood Buffalo Horn, the long reins looped around his left wrist, slowly levering one cartridge after another through his repeater. He whirled in a crouch at the sound of the hoofbeats, ready to fire at the white scouts; then a big smile cracked his dark face. He turned again and snapped off another shot at the ten or more horsemen disappearing into the blinding storm with a clatter of hooves and shouts to one another, taunts flung back at their enemy.

Snatching up his pony, the Bannock leaped onto the animal's bare back and rolled into motion to join the others as they all set off again at a lope after the Sioux. In less than a mile the ground started to rise. Ahead of them the enemy horsemen reached the brow of the ridge, halted in a spray of snow, and circled in a tight formation.

Just as the white scouts and Buffalo Horn reached the bottom of that slope, the sharp edge of the terrain above them suddenly sprouted more than two dozen warriors. He couldn't be sure in the snowstorm, but Donegan figured there had to be more than thirty-five or forty Lakota horsemen up there now—all of them pretty much motionless, eerily motionless, for some reason content for the moment to watch the bottom of the bluff, where Kelly hollered out for all of them to halt.

Then Seamus added, "Take cover, dammit!"

Instantly wheeling their mounts in a corkscrew, the civilians shot back some twenty yards into a tiny grove of old cottonwood. Among all the old deadfall Donegan was sure they could make a stand of it, once the guns started cracking and the bullets flying, until Miles sent a company of foot soldiers on the double time.

But no sooner had the scouts dismounted on the fly, sliding in the snow behind the thick cottonwood trunks that lay rotting across the grove, than the warriors on that snowy ridgetop disappeared into the snowy mist . . . as if they had never been there.

"You see what I saw?" Kelly asked.

Bruguier nodded. "They're sneakin' round on us?"

"We'll wait," Donegan said. "Keep your ears open."

They did wait, but heard nothing more than the snort of their horses, their pawing at the icy ground to find something to eat. Ten minutes, twenty, then after a half hour they finally decided that the Sioux weren't doubling back on them.

"I don't get it," Johnston said. "They wanted to sucker us into their trap with them damned decoys. Why didn't they just wait a shake more when they'd have us in a corner, then rub us all out?"

"They weren't out to do anything to us with no decoys," Donegan claimed as they mounted up and started back to the command.

"They had us dead to rights," Johnston protested.

"Wasn't us they was wanting," Kelly advised.

"That's right," Donegan agreed. "Not when Crazy Horse wants the whole damned outfit with one big fight."

Buffalo Horn nodded his head, but not a word did he say. He didn't have to; he showed how much he agreed with the big Irishman by suddenly sliding one flat mitten across the other—violently.

"That's right, Buffalo Horn," Donegan echoed. "Doesn't take a smart Injin like you to know Crazy Horse will be patient enough until he can rub us all out."

Just past four P.M., with the snowstorm still raging, Miles decided to call in his scouts, station his pickets, and go into camp on a relatively flat piece of ground just above Hanging Woman Creek. By sheer refusal to give in, the column had managed to scratch out another fifteen miles that day with the storm wailing at their backs.

As twilight closed around them, the wind came up and began to howl, bringing with it even more snow. By the time it was completely dark just past five P.M., the encampment was being battered with periods of sharp, icy hail, gusting and flying horizontally like the snow it accompanied. The men did what they could to find shelter out of the wind as the thermometer steadily dipped far below zero.

Try as he might, Seamus could not recall any such godforsaken weather in any more godforsaken camp pitched in any more godforsaken a patch of wilderness—wind, sleet, hail, and snow.

What, pray you, Sweet Virgin Mother of God, will you throw at us next?

"That's all I can feed you tonight," the corporal apologized. "General's already got us on half rations."

"I'll be fine, sojur," Seamus said, looking down at the soupy remains of the white beans in the cook's blackened kettle.

The soldier looked in both directions, then said, "Maybeso I could slip you another spoonful—"

"Nawww," Donegan interrupted self-consciously as he glanced around the camp. "There's more of these fellas been slogging through water and ice and mud today—they need them beans lot more'n me."

Instead of using his spoon this time, he brought the tin cup to his mouth and licked what he could of the bean juice from it, then abruptly handed it to the soldier. "You'll have some coffee for me when I get back, Cawpril?"

"I will, Mr. Donegan. Count on that!"

"Many's the time I've gone days with nothing but army coffee to eat a hole in me belly—so keep that pot steaming for me."

"I'll make sure to hold you some back!"

Seamus snapped a salute of respect to the old soldier with the peppered beard, then turned, slapping the front of his coat with one of his horsehide gauntlets, knocking some of the snow and ice from the thick canvas.

"How many?" Miles was asking as Donegan approached the colonel's fire.

Leforge asked his Crow trackers again. Then Buffalo Horn agreed in his pidgin English. The squaw man nodded to Seamus as Donegan came to a stop at the fire ringed by Miles's scouts. "They make it more than a thousand warriors, General."

"How much more than a thousand?" asked an anxious Frank Baldwin.

Leforge said thoughtfully, "Maybe couple hundred more."

"Twelve hundred," Miles repeated. "That many, eh?"

"That's got to be counting every two-legged critter with a man-sized prick big enough to handle a gun, and them who aren't too old to stay on his feet!" Kelly snorted.

"These here Crow been following the trail and walking through those damn villages same as the rest of us," Leforge defended his trackers, taking a step toward Kelly. "You got any better idea, go right ahead and tell the general what answer you wanna give to his question."

"Well, Kelly?" Miles asked after a moment of hesitation. "Do you think Leforge's Crow are far wrong on their estimation of just how many warriors we might be facing?"

It took him a moment, but Kelly finally shrugged and said, "I suppose it's always better for us to be prepared to fight off more than we'll likely ever encounter."

"I'll take a crack at it, General," Donegan declared suddenly.

The eyes turned to him. Miles said, "All right. How many do you think we're facing?"

Seamus said, "I don't figure Crazy Horse has no twelve hundred warriors. But I do figure you'll be facing at least two-to-one odds."

Miles turned slightly to acknowledge the appearance of the civilian. "So you agree more with Leforge than you do with Kelly?"

"Not taking sides in anything," Seamus explained. "Just speaking my mind. But like Luther said: be prepared for the worst of it. Either way, I'm only telling you what the sign tells me. That's what you hired me for, isn't it, General?"

"By Jupiter if it isn't," Miles replied. He banged his thick mittens together. "I suppose you all know by now that we might have to stretch out our rations some."

"Half rations already," Captain Casey added.

"Because this campaign's running longer than I figured it would at first," Miles explained, staring into the wind-whipped fire. "I had calculated hitting the village far north of here, exacting our punishment, then being on our way back to base. But it appears the enemy is retreating and we're playing catch-up."

"How long can we go, General?" asked Captain Butler.

"I'd like to tell you that we could go on till spring if need be . . . but that's not the truth," Miles admitted. "I'll be damned if my food shortages will force a premature end to this campaign!"

"The men will understand," said First Lieutenant Robert McDonald.

And Donegan thought, These poor soldiers have no choice, do they? They never do—because you officers always make that choice for them. If they don't like the choice you've made for them, then they can march on and grumble with the rest, or try to slip off and desert. But who in hell is going to desert in this country? And in a blizzard like this?

Miles suddenly seemed cheered. "I know we can whip them, gentlemen. We can whip Crazy Horse and the rest of his henchmen, even if they've got us down three or four to one!"

"Just give the men something to fight on, General," Donegan reminded. "Something, anything, in their bellies is better than an officer's empty promises when it comes to fighting these red h'athens."

Chapter 25

7 January 1877

BY TELEGRAPH

WYOMING

Military News and Orders

CHEYENNE, January 5.—The court martial for the trial of Colonel J. J. Reynolds and Captain Alexander Moore, both of the Third Cavalry, convenes here tomorrow. It consists of Brigadier Generals Pope and Sykes, and Lieutenant Colonels Bradley, Huston, and Beckwith.

Temporary headquarters department of the Platte are established here, and troops composing the late Powder river expedition are distributed from this point. The Ninth infantry goes to Omaha, Twenty-third infantry to Fort Leavenworth, battalion Fourth artillery returns to the Pacific coast, and the Fourth cavalry to Red Cloud agency, where Colonel Mackenzie will take charge of the Department. Headquarters of the Fifth will remain at Fort Russell and the Third at Fort Laramie.

As cold, weary, and miserable as the soldiers were, to Luther Kelly it seemed as if General Miles wasn't all that anxious to order them onto their feet in the predawn darkness. The continued subzero temperatures and half rations, along with the bone-chilling rain and hail that had soaked them to the skin in the past days, continued to wear away at every man's wick.

Luther wondered just how long this chase could go on—with Crazy Horse and his chiefs withdrawing the village farther and farther up the Tongue, making sure his scouts who kept a constant eye on the column's movements did not engage the soldiers . . . maintaining only enough contact to keep luring, taunting, seducing Miles and his officers farther and farther into the river canyons.

Maybe it was just as that tall Irishman had said: the enemy village will drop back, little by little, until Crazy Horse finds the ground where he will make his stand against a half-fed, half-froze, beat-down, ragtag bunch of soldiers too damned far from their supply base.

Later than usual, it was just past seven-thirty A.M. when Miles sent out his scouts and ordered his men into formation to begin their day's march through five more inches of new snow.

Twisting and turning, the river continued its relentless attempt to make things as hard as it could on the foot soldiers and their wagons. Hugging first one side of the valley, then the other, the Tongue confounded and tested the most tolerant man's patience. It took more than five hours to cover the first two and a half miles that snowy, blustery day—most of the time eaten up with the three crossings the men were forced to perform in that short distance.

With what had clearly become a growing sense of frustration, Miles ordered Kelly's men to probe ahead while he rested his column there at midday . . . now better than 115 miles from their Tongue River cantonment.

"Find me something—anything—that will tell me what the hell the enemy is doing besides retreating!" Miles growled with exasperation as he twisted the long leather reins in his leather mittens. "See if you can find out how far away they are . . . I've got to know if the hostiles are in striking distance."

"We'll push on ahead a few miles, General," Luther replied sympathetically. "See what the sign holds for us."

He led his scouts away from that cottonwood grove where the last of the wagons were coming to a noisy halt, mules braying and oxen grunting after that last cold crossing to the east side of the river. There in a loop of wide, sloping bottomland the soldiers were in the process of falling out right where they were in the snow, collapsing against trees and deadfall while a few began to scrape together some kindling, snapping twigs and branches off the leafless trees.

Several hundred yards to the south stood a long treeless ridge, at the middle of which rose a pointed, cone-shaped butte.

His small band of civilians and Indians rode through the gray, cold midday light in silence. From time to time across the next two miles Kelly signaled a halt at some high point of ground where the rest hunkered out of the biting wind to listen while Luther patiently scoured the country ahead with his field glasses.

The country all about them was awash with winter's brush, painted with a blur in a limited palette of colors. Beneath the monochrome gray of the low, ice-laden clouds, the monotonous white of the new snow was marred only by an occasional streak of ocher along the slopes of striated buttes, dotted by huge clumps of sage and those stands of fragrant cedar growing here and there in pockets where roots could be sent down deep.

He let out a sigh and pushed the focus wheel with a bare right finger. With the rising of the cold wind his hand was starting to tremble a little, so Kelly held the field glasses with only the left hand still encased in its wool mitten stuffed down inside the horsehide gauntlet. He was looking mostly off to the southwest, peering all the way to the distant foothills of the Wolf Mountains. He and many of the others expected they would find the Crazy Horse camps in that direction, figuring the hostiles were leading the army farther and farther up the Tongue, eventually around the southern end of the Wolf Mountains and on to the Bighorns in an endless, draining chase.

That is, if Miles didn't run out of rations and grain for his animals before then . . . if Crazy Horse hadn't forced the issue. A long chase it would be if the Sioux didn't choose to stand and fight—

As he was slowly scanning the far countryside from west to east, a beetlelike movement caught his attention, and he quickly moved his field of focus back to the southeast. There against the snow, inching along a hillside, black forms. Half a dozen?

Yes, at least six. Some were shorter—children, he decided. But at least some were adults. And those grown-ups would have answers to Kelly's questions.

Still, why were they on foot? Without ponies . . . perhaps they were part of the bunch who escaped Mackenzie's attack.

"Look at this, Seamus," he said, handing the field glasses across to the Irishman. "There, halfway down the slope. Better than a mile off, I'd say. Sight down from the saddle."

"Don't see what—"

"In the saddle," he repeated. "Look for some movement, about halfway down from that rocky outcrop that looks like a—"

"I see 'em," Donegan exclaimed in a gush. "But what the bleeming hell are they doing on foot?"

"Injuns?" asked George Johnson, flicking a grin at James Parker and John Johnston, who sat their horses on either side of him.

Kelly took the field glasses back from Donegan. "Yes—Injuns." Then he took one last look at the distant figures, just to be certain. "Fellas—that isn't a hunting party we've spotted."

Seamus nodded. "I'm sure as sun the general will want to talk with what Injins they are. Maybe they can tell us where we can find Crazy Horse."

In the background Tom Leforge was whispering from the side of his mouth, translating for his two Crow trackers, Half Yellow Face and Old Bear.

Kelly grinned. "Exactly what I'm hoping they'll be able to tell us, fellas." He got to his feet, immediately shoved sideways a step by the cold wind. Stuffing the glasses back into a saddlebag, he said, "Let's go round up some prisoners for General Miles."

With her head bent into the strong wind blowing at their faces, Old Wool Woman struggled on, breaking a path for the younger ones who followed her through the drifting snow—especially the two children. Each time the wind drew in its breath and she dared look up, the distant wisps of smoke she saw on the far side of the ridge in the valley of the Tongue promised that their struggle would soon be over.

It had been a tough journey on foot from the Pretty Fork* country near *Noaha-vose,*† where they had gone for a short visit among Tangle Hair's band of Dog Soldiers. Big Horse, a scout for Little Wolf, had come to visit friends and relations too. But, like Old Wool Woman, they all quickly came to miss their families and friends among Morning Star's people now traveling with the Crazy Horse village somewhere in the valley of the Tongue. Another widow, Twin Woman, as well as Old Wool Woman's own daughter, Fingers Woman, and her niece, Crooked Nose Woman, all decided to ask Big Horse if they could return with him when he started on his way back to their people.

Including Twin Woman's son and daughter, Red Hat and Crane Woman, along with an adolescent boy named Black Horse, the group set off overland on foot, what ponies they had each dragging a travois carrying their tiny lodge and other baggage. They did not have all that much after Three Finger Kenzie's soldiers had destroyed everything and driven them into the wilderness.

Following a grueling struggle, the little party finally reached the headwaters at the east fork of Suicide Creek. From there they trudged through the icy, crusty snow until they reached the divide and looked down on the valley of the Tongue. Far away, where they had expected they would find the village, they saw no lodges. But there was smoke rising from the distant trees, farther down the Tongue.

"I do not believe our people would move their camp such a short distance downriver," Big Horse warned from atop his

* The Belle Fourche River.
† The Sacred Mountain of Bear Butte.

pony. "It could be soldiers come looking for camps in the snow again." For a moment his eyes gazed at the boy, Black Horse. "Go on down this creek—but be careful, and watchful. I will go see whose smoke that is in the distance and return for you."

Old Wool Woman and young Black Horse watched the warrior move off into the wind and snow that swirled along the ground. In moments he was gone among the cold fog and clumps of cedar.

Sighing, she set off again at the head of the march, breaking snow for the rest of those who followed. The boy waited for the rest to pass, then protectively took up the rear of their march. Although this was her fifty-fourth winter, Old Wool Woman was nonetheless as strong as Fingers Woman and even Twin Woman, the widow of Lame White Man, who had been killed in the fight beside the Little Sheep River.*

Both of them were still young enough to be strong in body, but their will had never been tested the way Old Wool Woman had been tested in her life.

She remembered the taste of this wind—like laying her tongue on a piece of the *ve-ho-e*'s steel when the temperature plummeted. So sharp the metallic taste. So cold, it was hard to pull her tongue from the barrel of a pistol or the blade of the knife. So cold and so hard that her tongue kept the taste of that steel on it for a long time afterward. It had been that way when Black White Man had first come to live with the *Ohmeseheso*—when she and he were both children.

Many, many winters ago.

Almost as cold then as it was this day. So long ago that it was a time of few *ve-ho-e*, very few. What white men there were came to trap the flat-tails in the streams, or trade furs from the wandering bands of the northern plains. It was a time before those light-eyed creatures from the east pushed hard against the land and the herds and the migrating bands.

She was called Sweet Taste Woman back then. When the men came back from trading buffalo robes and fine furs to the *ve-ho-e*, often they brought small pouches of the white grains that were so sweet on her tongue, they made her mouth tickle, made Sweet Taste Woman giggle. She was so young then, less

* The Little Bighorn River.

than eight winters—now remembering how on one journey the warriors had brought back not just iron kettles and bolts of cloth, not just powder and lead and sugar . . . but in front of one of the war chiefs sat a strange creature. The whole village came out to gawk and whisper, some daring to inch close enough to touch the creature once the war chief dropped to the ground with the little dark person still wriggling in his arms.

How wide and filled with fear were the child's eyes back then as he looked around at all the *Ohmeseheso* who crowded about him. Finally one old man licked a finger and rubbed it hard across the creature's cheek. But the child's black paint would not wipe off!

"We stole him," the war chief announced. "I saw him at the log lodges where we went to trade. There was a grown-tall person with skin as black as this. But I wanted this little one for my adopted son."

He was thin and gangly, with strange pink palms and pink on the soles of his bare feet, but he learned quickly how to speak the People's tongue, quickly adopting the People's ways. And before long he went on his first pony raid. Then off for scalps against the *Ooetaneo-o.**

Moons and seasons and winters passed, and soon this boy they had been calling Little Black White Man was called only Black White Man.

He had come of age, and grown all the more handsome to the eyes and heart of Sweet Taste Woman. She had hoped the look in her eyes would tell him how much she wished him to come to her parents' lodge with his blanket after dark that late spring night she would always remember.

Spring ran into summer, and still he did not show . . . then finally one night she sat there beside the fire with her father and mother, with her younger sisters and brothers—and they all heard the flute. She remembered now as they struggled through gusts of cold breath from Winter Man's nostrils how she had closed her eyes and prayed that it would be Black White Man who was playing the flute for her outside their lodge door.

Sweet Taste Woman's father barely lifted the door flap and

* Crow or Apsaalooke people.

peeked out. Then he quietly let the door flap back down and went back to looking at the fire without saying a word. Only the crackle of the flames along the dry-split cottonwood in that quiet lodge . . . and the sound of that flute.

Finally her father looked at Sweet Taste Woman and spoke.

"I think there is a young man outside our door, playing his song for you. He is a good man and will make a fine husband for you. Go see if he truly wants to make you his wife."

For a moment she wanted to cry out, to ask who it was before she went out and made a fool of herself before the wrong young man. Instead she bit her lip and felt the tremble grow inside her until she could not move.

"Go ahead," she remembered her father saying gruffly, though his eyes twinkled with merriment. "He is a brave young man. I do not think he is a very rich young man with many fine ponies to bring us, but I am certain that one is brave enough to stand and play his flute all night long if you do not go out now to be with him, Sweet Taste Woman. Yes, I think he is bull-headed enough to stay until he gets what he wants. Go see to him so he will stop playing, because you know how I don't like to have my sleep disturbed. Go, daughter."

Sweet Taste Woman turned quickly now as she heard one of the young girls whimper behind her on the side of the hill where there was little shelter from the harsh wind. She motioned the child, Crane Woman, to her side, where Old Wool Woman put the girl beneath her arm, wrapping her there beneath the edge of her old blanket—so they could share their warmth. In that way they walked on, seeking the Crazy Horse camp where their relatives were staying this winter after the terrible battle with Three Finger's soldiers in the Red Fork Canyon.

Her thoughts drifted back to that warm summer night . . . how she had bitten her tongue, held her breath, and moved through the door. She stood in the darkness, waiting, so scared she dared not look for the flute player at first, looking instead at the other lodges lit up like lanterns aglow, the cool night wind brushing her skin. When a part of the night moved toward her, she jumped back a step. Then Sweet

Taste Woman saw his eyes shimmering like stars in that face so much like the summer night itself. Saw his teeth when he smiled as he took his flute from his lips.

Black White Man held out his blanket, and she came within his arms. They stood there that spring night beside the door to her parents' lodge, talking, feeling the warmth of each other's closeness, listening to and sensing the gentle throb of each other's hearts. Knowing that they would never be apart from that night on. How happy he had made her; he had given her many children and had become a strong and respected warrior of the *Ohmeseheso*.

A warrior protecting what was most dear to him.

So it was that despite his many winters, Black White Man had been one of the first to cut his way out of the frozen lodges when Three Finger's soldiers attacked, sweeping up only his rifle and cartridge belt, turning quickly to lay his lips on hers before he gently ran his fingers down her wrinkled cheek where the tears were already spilling. Outside, the shouts of the enemy were drawing closer; already the gunshots echoed from the canyon walls.

"I must go," he whispered, his eyes crinkling.

Sensing that this was to be their last parting, she had said nothing, knowing her heart clogged her throat—but held him quickly before she turned and stabbed her butcher knife into the stiffened hides at the back of the lodge, cutting a slash that she forced all the way to the ground. He took one finger and touched his lips, then laid it on her left breast, there over her pounding heart.

She closed her eyes, wondering how she would ever tell him what he had meant to her in their many seasons together—

In a whirl Black White Man was gone through that slash she had cut in the buffalo hides of their home. The home where they had coupled, where they had given birth to their babes and raised their children, laughed and cried, and now were alone—just the two of them.

Following his sturdy figure out through the slit in their lodge that morning, Sweet Taste Woman felt even more alone as she raced with the others up the coulee to the ridgetop where the women and children laid up rock upon rock for breastworks while the soldier trumpets blared far away across the snowy valley.

Down below them a band of valiant warriors ran crouched and half-naked in the teeth of that cruel wind, scurrying into the mouth of a ravine until they stopped halfway to the side of the canyon. Turned. And waited. Then rose up and fired point-blank into the faces of the charging pony soldiers.

When the surprise ambush at the ravine was over that terrible morning, there were many warriors who did not rise from the bloodied snow.

She remembered how she had wanted to die in that valley with him. How so many times during the day she had wanted to leave the breastworks and go in search of her husband—so she could leave her body beside his. But as the sun fell on her people, the other women pulled her on up the side of the mountain, wrapped her in a shred of old blanket, and forced her to walk with them that long, horrid night when babies died and many of the old, sick ones asked to be left behind, left beside the bloody footprints they tracked in the snow.

"You must be brave now—brave enough for both of us," his eyes had told her that morning before he had gone through the back of the frozen lodge skins. They were the same words his voice kept saying in her ear that first long night without him. Oh, how his voice came to speak to her each day of their march until they found the Crazy Horse people, his words making her brave enough to keep going one more step. One more step.

Yes, she had always been brave. But she was alone now. No longer was she Sweet Taste Woman, for she was no longer the wife of Black White Man. Others began to call her Old Wool Woman because of that shred of blanket she clutched around her shoulders, sheltering the children beneath it with her on that long march to the Hunkpatila camp.

Old Wool Woman was she now.

Stopping suddenly, she looked up, blinking her red-rimmed eyes into the icy lancets of blowing snow and wind that shoved her thin, frail body this way and that. Hoofbeats.

Perhaps that meant they were close to the village now . . . oh, where was Big Horse? She did not know how long the little ones could take this weather. Rain, and icy hail, and more snow—

Riders in front of them!

Not warriors.

"*Aiyeee!*" she croaked, trying to turn so quickly that little Crane Woman fell beside her, crying out.

Old Wool Woman spotted young Black Horse lunging up through the deep snow, a warrior's resolve chisled on his boyish face. Her throat tasting like bile, she managed to shriek, "*Ve-ho-e!* Run!"

Suddenly there were horsemen on either side of them. And there was no place to run. She looked around her and realized that young Black Horse, the boy, was not there bringing up the rear. It was good! He or Big Horse would eventually find the village. One of them would tell their relatives they had been captured by the soldiers' scouts.

Then the Crazy Horse warriors and the *Ohmeseheso* men would come to rescue them.

Chapter 26

Hoop and Stick Moon 1877

B ig Horse became afraid as soon as he saw the first outlying pickets, then some of the wagons, and finally all
those white soldiers in their camp. Not afraid for himself, but
afraid for Old Wool Woman and the others. If there were
soldiers in this country, then they would have their scouts
prowling about.

In going to see what the firesmoke was all about, Big
Horse ended up wandering down in a maze of coulees, which
caused him to go too far by the time he'd worked his way out
to the high ground with the exhausted pony. Urging the animal back up to that high divide to the east of the Tongue River
Valley, the *Ohmeseheso* warrior came to the skyline, then immediately dropped to his belly.

Down below in all that snow lay a camp of soldiers.

Now he slid backward, his heart in his throat. Big Horse
remounted and stayed as hidden as he could, racing the pony
back toward the place where he had left the women to continue on their own while he went to investigate the smoke. Too
many heartbeats later he crossed their trail of footprints. Getting down, Big Horse looked closely. The tracks were theirs,
both big and small, along with the two ponies with their
drags, the whole party trudging ahead through the deep,

crusty snow. He wheeled the pony to the right and hurried along their trail.

But Big Horse hadn't gone far—no more than two short ridges—before he reined up suddenly. Down the slope, three arrow-flights away, he spotted the women and children as they were surrounded by horsemen. Some of them looked to be *Ooetaneoo-o*, the Crow People, but not all. The way they moved, walked about, most of the riders had to be *ve-ho-e* scouts for the army. One of them waved his arms, and Big Horse saw Old Wool Woman tuck one of the children beside her and start walking away through the midst of the scouts. Knocked down into the snow by the enemy, young Black Horse scrambled to his feet, stood rooted defiantly a moment, then turned and moved off behind the others.

Moving downriver toward the soldier camp!

Wheeling the pony about again, Big Horse began to pray to the Four Sacred Persons as he took big gulps of the shockingly cold air, his heels pounding the pony's ribs. Down the side of the ridge, up the slope of another, kicking up cascades of powdery snow, he raced the weary pony toward the Tongue River. Somewhere upstream he would find the village.

The soldiers had camped down the Tongue.

It was plain they had not yet reached the camp of the Crazy Horse Hunkpatila and the *Ohmeseheso*, wounded by unending warfare.

Big Horse realized he must bring them word.

The soldiers were coming!

As they slowly encircled the women and children, Donegan realized that their prisoners had no idea they had been in any danger. Nor had these people really known where the village was located, much less that there were soldiers in the area. They had been moving along as if nothing but the horrid cold was of any concern to them.

The first woman had her blanket pulled over her head as she helped a young child along beneath an arm. She led the rest, who stayed back with their two ponies, into the head of the coulee and started down its jagged path, a course that would eventually take her to the river. Seamus didn't like the way the two Crow trackers were inching up on either side of the prisoners, talking privately among themselves. There was something not quite benign about the look on those trackers' faces. He remembered how furious Miles had been after the Sioux peace delegates had been killed—

"Leforge!" Kelly whispered sharply, waving an arm and ordering the squaw man over.

The squaw man grumbled haughtily, "What do you want?"

"You tell your Crow to stay back from these people. Got that?"

"Stay back?" Leforge growled. "That may be hard. Maybeso those women are relatives of warriors who killed these boys' relations in battle or raids—"

"I don't give a damn!" Kelly snapped. "They're women and children."

"You heard him," Donegan added. "Just keep them Crow back, and there won't neither of 'em need to get hurt. I'll just make you responsible."

"Me?"

"One of them prisoners gets cut, gets shot—same'll happen to you and your Crow," Seamus snarled. "Count on it, Leforge. Count on it till your dying day."

Leforge's eyes followed the Irishman's mitten as Seamus's hand went to rest on the butt of one of the big pistols in the civilian's belt. "What's a few women to you, anyway? You planning on making one of 'em your blanket warmer tonight?"

"G'won now!" Kelly ordered with an emphatic gesture of his arm. "Get up there and tell your Crow to stay back and not harm these—"

"Don't see why you two are so all-fired mad about nothing what's happened," Leforge said, shaking his head.

Kelly urged his horse forward until it was directly opposite the squaw man's. He planted a mitten on Leforge's arm and kept it there while he said, "I just remember that it was your Crow who killed those five Sioux right there at the post. That's what I call murder."

"Them two better not touch no women and children today," Donegan warned, turning to let his glare rest on the Crow scouts. "Or I'll see to it all three of you don't make it back to where Miles has raised his camp."

For a moment Leforge didn't budge in the saddle, didn't

utter a word; then Kelly suddenly turned his horse, wheeling away. He whispered instructions to Donegan and to Johnston as they split up. Kelly went forward while the other two went left and right. Behind Donegan and Johnston rode James Parker and George Johnson, along with the two Crow scouts, while Leforge followed Buffalo Horn at the rear of the procession.

As soon as Kelly moved toward the women, Donegan could see he began to gesture to the prisoners, making sign.

"They're Cheyenne," Kelly declared now that the squaws and children had stopped, clustering together with their two ponies the way a covey of quail would cower, looking all about them, seeing the ring of horsemen slowly coming in.

"Keep them Crow back!" Donegan warned Leforge.

Kelly turned to find Half Yellow Face urging his pony into a lope toward the Cheyenne women. Whirling his horse, Luther kicked it into a gallop, heading on a collision course for the Crow tracker, bringing his rifle to his shoulder. A scant ten feet from the chief of scouts, Half Yellow Face reined up sharply, holding aloft his yard-long coup-stick, shouting and cursing the white man in his own tongue.

"I'll drop this son of a bitch if he tries me again like that," Kelly said.

"He's just wanting to count coup on them Cheyenne," Leforge explained sheepishly. "Not do 'em no harm."

Donegan patted the butt of his pistol, saying, "Just keep them back and there'll be no trouble."

"I don't think you understand Injuns," Leforge spat at Donegan.

"I understand enough to tell you that there'll be three Crow widows singing their mourning songs tonight if either of these boys hurt one of our prisoners."

By the time Kelly got turned around again so he could talk with the women, they were crying out in fear, the children wailing pitifully. Slowly the scouts continued to tighten the wide ring around their prisoners until they halted their horses just feet from the captives. This close to the Cheyenne, Old Bear leaned forward, stretching as far as he could, and slapped one of the younger women on the back of the head with his stick, singing out joyfully as he sang his war song.

"Keep an eye on both of 'em for me, Seamus," Kelly ordered.

"I'll drop the first one of 'em hurts a woman or so much as looks cross-eyed at one of them young'uns," Seamus growled, mad enough now that he pulled his pistol and cocked it—just as Half Yellow Face whacked his coup-stick on the shoulder of the old woman who had been leading them all across the snowy prairieland.

None of the scouts could speak Cheyenne, but they did get the old woman and the rest started off down the coulee toward the river. Kelly motioned Buffalo Horn up to the front of the march with the old woman, where the Bannock made the prisoner understand they were being taken to the soldier camp. Once there, they would be fed and have a fire for warmth, and have no reason not to feel secure.

Donegan glared at Leforge's Crow as he asked the Bannock, "Buffalo Horn—you tell them they'll be safe with us?"

"Yes. I tell."

"Good. If these Crow do anything to hurt our prisoners—I'll let you have the first Crow scalp we'll lift."

Morning Star was sure they were under attack the moment the first shouts were raised late in the afternoon. But as it turned out, the alarm was only a lone rider, racing a weary, lathered pony through the snow up from the bank into the outskirts of the village.*

The horseman was howling like a wolf—that eerie warning cry. Four times he stopped, pointing his tired pony to the four winds to greet the Sacred Persons dwelling in each of the cardinal directions, and each time he howled at the top of his lungs. When he got close enough, he started to yell.

"The soldiers are coming!"

Women began to scream—both Lakota and Shahiyela. Children darted for their mothers. Then several of the war leaders hollered above the tumult for calm. No guns were being fired nearby. The camp guards had not raised an alarm of attack. Nothing more than a solitary rider come across the river.

* At the mouth of present-day Post Creek, seventeen miles upstream from the soldier bivouac.

Men began to gather about the lone horseman, helping him as he pitched off his pony, all of them asking questions of the man at once. Then Little Wolf and White Bull, Crazy Horse and Black Moccasin, were there with Morning Star to confront the rider.

Morning Star asked, "You are Big Horse?"

"Yes," the man gasped. "I am of Two Moon's people."

The chief held out his personal pipe and said to Big Horse, "Touch my pipe, and on its honor swear that you will tell me the truth."

The exhausted warrior wrapped his fingers around the long stem of the pipe and said, "I swear that I will tell you the truth of what my eyes have seen."

Then Crazy Horse shoved his way into the group, anxious, asking, "Where are these soldiers you are yelling at us about?"

Big Horse pointed, licking his cracked lips. "Down the river less than a half day's ride."

"The Bear Coat," Crazy Horse snarled, making it sound like a curse. "But he is coming slower than I had hoped."

Then Big Horse lunged for Morning Star. "They have taken prisoners!"

Morning Star gripped Big Horse's wrists. "P-prisoners?"

"Our people!" Big Horse replied, and that started the women and children wailing all the more around that circle of men. "Lame White Man's widow. And Old Wool Woman. Children are with them—"

"The women gone to Tangle Hair's camp at the base of the Sacred Mountain?" Little Wolf asked, his voice rising.

"Yes," Big Horse said, nodding. "The soldier scouts captured them. I saw the scouts taking them to the soldier camp."

"Who are these scouts?"

Big Horse turned to He Dog to answer. "Some are Crow People, but most are *ve-ho-e.*"

"It does not matter," Little Wolf snarled. "*Ooetaneo-o* or white man—we must get our people back!"

A loud roar erupted from the crowd.

"I call for a war council!" Morning Star shouted.

Lakota and Shahiyela alike agreed, war chiefs of all the clans stepping forward to follow Crazy Horse and the three

Old-Man Chiefs to the center of camp, where they would decide just what to do.

By twilight they had decided there was but one course of
action to take. For many suns now they had been slowly retreating up the Tongue River, drawing the Bear Coat's soldiers
farther and farther from their fort. They knew the white man
did not fight well far from his source of supplies. So they
would be patient and continue to lure the white men farther,
and farther.

But with their own people taken captive, they were now
forced to change their original plans. Now they must attack,
no matter the rugged terrain, no matter the wind and snow.

The first warriors ready before dark would follow the war
chiefs north to the soldier camp, where they would attempt to
create a diversion and free the prisoners. The rest of the warriors would come along sometime after the moon was high
and be ready to fight at dawn.

Dawn . . . when they would have the soldier camp surrounded.

"You'll see to this one first, won't you?" Seamus asked the
surgeon. He clutched the small girl across his arms tightly. The
child squirmed enough that it was a battle, so afraid of him
was she.

Dr. Henry R. Tilton evidently read the seriousness in the
scout's face and looked at the girl's legs and feet, covered by
frozen, icy wool leggings and skimpy moccasins. "Likely she's
got frostbite."

"This'un's worse off than all the rest," Donegan said. "See
to her first, I beg you in God's name."

Tilton smiled. "Yes. I'll see to her first. Take her into the
tent." Then he motioned the rest to follow the tall gray-eyed
civilian. "Bring the others into the tent too. I'm sure we won't
need to worry about them escaping tonight."

Donegan ducked through the flaps, went to the lone cot,
and laid the girl upon the blankets. She tried to rise immediately, swinging her feet off the cot, but he laid a firm hand on
her shoulder, stopping her attempts. With the other hand he
motioned the old woman to come over. She limped to the cot
and sat down, talking to the child in a calm, soothing voice.
Then the woman gazed up at Donegan and nodded once.

Reassured, Seamus turned and ducked out of the wall tent.

"Kelly!" he called out, spotting the chief of scouts.

"Donegan—you up to riding?"

"I s'pose. Set on going after that camp now?" He glanced into the afternoon sky.

"Maybe we can get a fix on where it is before nightfall," Kelly said. "At least we may end up finding out if these prisoners have any bucks coming along behind them. I've some of the rest going with me, but you're always welcome if you're up for more saddle work."

"Count on it," Donegan answered.

"You think we can get any more news out of those women?"

Seamus shook his head. "Not a chance. Those women are scared, but they're brave too. Those aren't just squaws, Luther. Those are wives and mothers of chiefs and warriors. They're not going to talk to us."

Kelly turned to one of the Jackson brothers. "William—see that those women and children have all the food they want to eat. Fill 'em to the brim. Maybe we can make all of them warm and happy enough that one, just one, will want to chatter a bit tonight when we get back."

"I'll feed 'em my own self," William replied before he turned away.

Kelly looked determined. "You ready to ride, Irishman?"

"Let's swing a leg over a saddle, Yellowstone."

That trip out, John Johnston, Tom Leforge, James Parker, and George Johnson rode along with Kelly and Donegan as the sun eased ever closer to settling behind the Wolf Mountains off to the southwest.

"You know they're all around us," Kelly said quietly as the horses plodded through the snow, picking their way among the sage and cedar.

"It's too late in the day for them to make a go at Miles," Donegan replied. "But I'd lay a full month of *your* wages that they'll be eye to eye with us for bacon and biscuits by first light."

"A month of *my* wages?" Kelly snorted. "Will you listen to that!"

John Johnston guffawed in that affable way of his, reaching over to slap the Irishman on the back of the shoulder. "Always been that sort of fella what'll play fast and loose with another man's wages, are you?"

"Long as there's a pot, I'll ante up—"

"Look there, by damn!" Parker cried, pointing at the ridge in their front and a little off to their right.

At least a handful of warriors sat atop their ponies, motionless as buckbrush, watching the scouts' advance.

"Keep your eyes peeled, boys," Kelly advised. "I'll bet a month of Donegan's poorhouse wages those aren't the only redskins close at hand."

Despite the fact that they were being watched from the heights, they kept on the trail that would lead them back to the place where they had captured the women and children. At the spot where they had surrounded the Cheyenne, Kelly halted them, dropping to the ground to study the backtrack direction of the captives' prints.

"Luther," Seamus said in a quiet voice.

Kelly rose from a crouch. His eyes followed Donegan's arm, where the other four were all gazing. On the nearby ridge sat at least ten, maybe more than a dozen, horsemen now.

"Never did like me no Sioux sonsabitches," grumbled George Johnson. "I say we give 'em a hoot and a holler and run 'em off."

"Maybe you'll get lucky and get yourself a scalp," Parker replied.

"A man can hope, can't he?" Johnson added. "What say, Kelly?"

"All right," Luther agreed after a moment's contemplation. "If they were up to something, I suppose they would have pulled their shenanigans by now. Let's give that bunch a how-do, then be about our business to find the village they came from."

"We run them off," Seamus explained, "why—they might even lead us back to their village, Luther."

"What are we waiting for, fellas? Let's give those redskins a little send-off!" Kelly cheered, lunging into the saddle and drawing his carbine out of the saddle boot.

Chapter 27

7 January 1877

In those next few moments Seamus thought it very odd that those mounted warriors stayed put right there atop that ridgeline, the wind scutting past them in sharp gusts, tugging at hair and feathers and horses' manes. Not a one of the Indians so much as moved an inch—just sat their ponies and watched the white men galloping closer and closer.

If he didn't know better . . .

Then the big scar across his back began to itch.

And there wasn't any time to scratch it.

When the scouts were no more than fifty yards away, one of the motionless horsemen suddenly shouted, at the same time raising a scrap of blanket high overhead at the end of his arm. Before Donegan and the others galloping across the slope below could react, better than fifty warriors burst out of the snow, leaping out from behind every other clump of sagebrush, behind every scrub of oakbrush and cedar. They all had rifles, and most of them already had cross sticks planted in the frozen ground—all the better to hold on a target.

Sweet Virgin Mother of God! he prayed as he sawed the reins savagely to the right, bumping against James Parker's horse as their animals made the sharp cut on the icy ground the moment the Indian weapons cut loose.

Lead sang through the air with the fine whisper of death hissing past a man's ear.

A second volley from those fifty-plus rifles spewing orange muzzle blasts no more than fifty yards away cut through the half-dozen scouts as they wheeled left and right, jabbing spurs and kicking heels into their mounts to escape that deadly alley of lead.

Kelly was hollering . . . something . . . Donegan could see his mouth moving but couldn't hear a thing but for the shouts of the warriors, the pounding of his own blood in his ears, and the snorting of the roan suddenly goaded into a gallop.

He prayed again in the space of the next heartbeat, thankful that Indian marksmanship was a sometime and indifferent matter. It was all that saved their lives that afternoon in the valley of the Tongue River.

The roan gelding stumbled, almost went down, then lunged forward another half-dozen steps before Seamus was sure of it. The paunch-water sounds, the wheezing, the bloody phlegm clinging at the nostrils . . . and that unmistakable fear in its widening eyes. The look of an animal not knowing what was happening to it—but sensing something feral and deadly all the same.

He came out of the saddle as the horse sank to its knees with a raspy grunt, stepping off and collapsing to his own knees beside the animal on the icy ground. Then heard that familiar smack of lead against flesh, like a wet hand slapping putty. The same sound he had listened to as the General had carried him those last few yards to a narrow sandbar in the middle of a nameless river seconds before Roman Nose's Cheyenne rode down on Major George Forsyth's fifty scouts.* The roan groaned a second time, raising its head and fighting to rise as voices cracked the cold, dry air all around him. Indian taunts as they lunged out of hiding. Kelly and the rest bellowing as they sought cover.

Seamus looked down at the valiant animal breathing its last in the cold and fought back the tears. After dragging the Winchester from its boot, he quickly patted the big, strong neck as the roan shuddered, that one eye rolling back to white.

* *The Stalkers*, vol. 3, The Plainsmen Series.

How cold it made Donegan feel at that moment—to lose a horse soldier's best friend.

As the Irishman hunkered down behind the big animal, twenty yards away he watched Leforge struggling beneath his own horse, one leg caught. With the other leg the squaw man had cocked against the animal's backbone, he shoved and pushed until he got his leg free. Wrenching his pistol out, Leforge held the muzzle down on the beast's forehead and without hesitation fired a shot. Whirling to snap off another at the closest of the yelling warriors, he clumsily spun on his heel and limped toward the cover of some buckbrush, his injured leg nearly giving way under him in the deep snow and uneven ground.

As bullets kicked up spouts of earth and snow about him, Leforge hobbled into a narrow hollow behind some cedar and plopped to his belly, pressing himself into the ground to make as small a target as he could.

At that very moment Luther Kelly was heeling his horse about in a tight circle, spraying snow in a high rooster tail from its hooves, his mouth shouting something at Leforge. One side to the other, Kelly searched frantically for the man. . . . Then suddenly he whipped his horse around in another tight circle among all the buckbrush, spotting Leforge's trail through the snow, making for scrub undergrowth. As much lead as the Sioux and Cheyenne had sailing across that broken ground, Seamus was nothing short of amazed that Kelly escaped from that deadly piece of open ground back to where the others were gathering in a copse of some cedar and oakbrush and a few old fallen cottonwood.

When Donegan glanced down, the roan was staring up at him, that one eye clear again, but bloodshot in terror. Seamus bent over the animal—suddenly remembering their march together from Laramie to Camp Robinson to surround Red Cloud's camp with Mackenzie's men; their cold trip north from Fetterman into the frozen wastes of the Crazy Woman Fork, and that charge into the Red Fork Valley with Lieutenant John A. McKinney's gallant men at the moment the ravine erupted with the fires of hell; and as he laid a hand along its powerful foreflank, Seamus recalled how this brave animal had tackled a hostile country alone with him as they had pushed over from the Little Powder and down to the Tongue, carrying dispatches for Nelson A. Miles.

The horse did not deserve to be left to die alone and in pain.

He drew his pistol with a trembling hand.

Such a magnificent creature.

Then dragged back the hammer with his thumb.

Like saying a painful farewell to another friend.

And placed the muzzle behind the ear as the horse struggled to rise.

So many friends . . . all those he had buried and left behind in this wilderness.

Squeezed back on the trigger.

Donegan was up and running in a crouch before he had to look again at the eye.

A horse soldier's dearest friend is usually the first to fall, he remembered an old master sergeant telling him before they'd ridden into the Shenandoah behind little Phil Sheridan. Don't ever get close to no man you ride with, the soldier had warned young Donegan. And never, no never—should you give a damn about no horse . . . cause they're always the first to die in battle.

Kelly was waving him in, standing there at the edge of that clump of cedar brush, down in a little hollow that reminded him of a buffalo wallow out on the Staked Plain. The rest were still up and on foot, yanking their horses over a rocky ledge some five to six feet high, dragging the reluctant animals down into the pocket. Lead smacked the sandstone rocks all around them, kicking up skiffs of snow, whining past but hitting nothing at all, or ricocheting with a zing that dusted them all with rock fragments.

"Damn, I thought you could run faster than that!" Kelly chided as Donegan planted one arm at the side of the hollow and cartwheeled his legs over the edge.

Collapsing to the ground, huffing to catch his breath, Seamus said, "Any race where I end up alive at the finish is a race I damn well figure I won!" He looked around—counting faces.

"We're all here," James Parker announced with great self-satisfaction. " 'Cept for the squaw man."

Wagging his head, Kelly said with amazement, "I can't

believe it myself, Irishman. Should have been more of us left out there, the way these redskins were throwing lead at us."

Seamus peered out at that open ground Kelly had just covered with the horse. "Didn't you see what become of Leforge?"

With a shrug the chief of scouts replied, "Truth be, I'm amazed any of us made it in here by the skin of our teeth at all."

"Don't never count your medicine before the sun goes down," John Johnston advised.

"They're moving in on us, Kelly!" George Johnson called out abruptly.

In the middistance they could make out a little movement behind the tall sage, a flurry here and there at the edges of the oakbrush.

"Sure as hell not giving us a damned thing to shoot at!" grumbled John Johnston as he rubbed the stock of his old Spencer with a horsehide mitten.

Suddenly the ground on their right opened up. A handful of warriors popped into sight, fired a ragged volley, then promptly disappeared. As the smoke from their guns drifted off on the harsh wind, a few warriors leaped up on the left, firing before they disappeared again among the sage and snowdrifts.

"You boys ever been pinned down afore?" Johnston asked, then spit a brown jet into the nearby snow. He dragged a sleeve down the yellowed gray of his chin whiskers where the tobacco had permanently stained his beard.

"I have, a time or two," Donegan admitted. "My first time north into this Injin country: with some soldiers on the Crazy Woman back to sixty-six.* Next time it happened, I was sitting with some good civilian marksmen in the middle of a corral at the hay field near Fort C. F. Smith.† Then I ate dead mule and waited for Roman Nose's bunch to ride down on us at Beecher Island—"#

"Injuns hunkered you down all them places?" James Parker interrupted.

---

* *Sioux Dawn*, vol. 1, The Plainsmen Series.
† *Red Cloud's Revenge*, vol. 2.
# *The Stalkers*, vol. 3.

Donegan looked quickly at the eyes gazing into his. "Ain't nothing to being pinned down—is there, Johnston?"

The old trapper nodded, smiling, a little tobacco juice dribbling down the deep crease wrinkling the corner of his mouth. "That's right, you gol-danged Irishman. Nothing to it. Why, the last time I was holed up by a bunch of Sioux, ain't none of us had a blasted chance of getting out with our hair. . . ."

When the old trapper paused a moment to pull out two more cartridges for his old Spencer carbine, an impatient George Johnson asked, "Yeah, so what happened, ol' man?"

"What happened?" Johnston replied, a grin creeping across his face before he winked. "Why—them gol-danged Sioux bastards charged on in an' they kill't us all!"

There was an uneasy rattle of laughter from those not as old and leathery as Johnston, men who could not quite yet laugh in the face of certain death.

Donegan looked around at them, face by face, as he squatted down in the snow behind a small shelf of sandstone and made himself a gun prop. These were trained riflemen—not a one of them a green youngster straight out of Jefferson Barracks, he thought. It cheered him some to think that as good as Kelly's bunch was with their guns, why—they were worth at least ten to one against those warriors who had them surrounded on the better part of three sides.

Ten-to-one odds, hell. From the looks of what horsemen were coming over the far ridge, more like twenty to one, or worse.

God-blame-it! Don't ever, ever talk about the odds, he scolded himself as he levered another cartridge through the Winchester.

The others saw them too, and more than one man in that hollow groaned in fear and resignation as those enemy horsemen bristled across the far ridgeline, pausing only a moment before riding down the slope into the cedar and sage, where they vaulted from their ponies and joined the rest in tightening the cordon around the white scouts.

"They flank us, we might as well be boot-heel soup," growled George Johnson.

"Just make sure they don't flank us, goddammit!" Parker snapped.

"Ain't a'gonna on my side, leastways," Johnson replied.

It appeared the warriors were intent on doing just that, creeping in here and there on the left and right flanks, inching into the horns of a great curved crescent.

Minutes later James Parker stuttered, "There's m-more of 'em than we c-can handle."

"You're right, son," grumbled the aging Johnston. "Got our peckers in a trap for sure now."

"They only have us on three sides," Kelly argued.

George Johnson said, "We can still make a run for it out the back door."

"If'n you think you can live through mounting up to make that ride," Johnston declared sourly.

"Why, lookee there, fellas!" Donegan declared to shush them all. "Our Injin friends set themselves up a little skirmish line back there."

The rest turned to look back in the direction of the soldier camp, finding that Buffalo Horn, along with the Jackson brothers and the pair of Crow scouts, had all just slid in behind some oakbrush taken root along the edge of a rocky outcrop better than two hundred yards to their rear.

"You think we can make it back to them in the saddle if they give us some cover?" George Johnson asked.

Donegan wagged his head, wheeling now to peer across the far ground as the enemy moved up on foot, dodging across the snow from bush to bush, narrowing the distance with every minute. "No. We'd never make it to 'em before most of us get dropped with a bullet in the back."

As more and more of the warriors appeared on top of the ridge, spurring their mounts right on down the slope into the bottom, where they had the small party of white men pinned down, the scouts concentrated on killing those who ventured too close. When a warrior would poke his head up to fire, the scouts readied themselves and tried to snap off their shots as quickly as they could when the warrior heads suddenly appeared. From time to time one of the six men would swear, cursing his bad luck to miss a shot, grumbling about his fate to be held down by more than a hundred warriors the way they were.

With more warriors on the way.

Still, in the midst of that tightening red noose, the men

began to cheer one another and themselves as they hit a target out there in the scrub oak and sage.

"Just hold 'em back a little longer," Donegan kept reminding them. "Them sojurs is sure to hear our racket soon enough."

Kelly agreed. "I'll bet the general's got an outfit on its way here already."

They all wheeled apprehensively at the sound of hoofbeats clattering up behind them, most ready to fire on the approaching horseman galloping in, looking about as calm and deliberate in his mission as he could be.

"I'll be God-bleeming-damned!" Seamus roared as he watched the Bannock scout rein to a halt, snow flitting from every hoof.

Out beyond them in the cedars the Sioux howled in dismay, wildly hurling bullets at the Indian scout as he dismounted in no seeming hurry, ground-hobbled his horse with the others, and then crouched near Kelly, where Buffalo Horn began adding his rifle to the fight.

Within minutes the uneasy feeling began to seep into the forefront of Donegan's thinking. Fewer and fewer warriors were popping up to take their shots at the scouts. In fact—the gunfire from the Sioux was tapering off altogether.

"Ain't this a strange thing to behold?" he asked the others.

"Yeah—what the hell you think they're up to now?" James Parker said.

"Think they're giving it up?" George Johnson asked.

"I think I smell a polecat," Johnston said, sniffing the air for emphasis.

"I'll lay odds they're working their way in on us," Parker declared.

"Yep," Kelly agreed. "Soon as they get some redskins worked into position, I figure the rest will open a real warm fire on us again, to hold us down while the others snake on up close enough to finish us off with one good rush."

Wringing his hands around his carbine, George Johnson cried, "Jesus! We can't just sit here till they come in to—"

"Shuddup!" John Johnston bellowed. "Your crying don't make a man's dying no easier!"

"Ain't none of us gonna die," Donegan snapped. "Now, sit there, Johnson—and keep up the work with your rifle."

"I figure they'll make their rush at us over that ledge," Kelly said a moment later, pointing with the long barrel of his carbine.

"It's your call, Kelly—but looks to me that you and the Bannock are the ones to flush 'em out," Donegan stated.

"Let's just hope it is a flush, Irishman," Kelly replied. "And not a full house."

Then Kelly bent close and whispered to Buffalo Horn before the two of them slid on their knees to the rocky bulwark of the sandstone ledge. There the white scout counted to three when they both rolled into view. As soon as they landed on their bellies, rifles ready, a trio of Sioux exploded from the rocks and sage, sprinting away. The moment Kelly and Buffalo Horn began firing, the three warriors dived onto their bellies and continued their escape by crawling, snaking their way through the sagebrush.

In that moment it seemed that half a hundred guns or more opened up on the two scouts, causing them both to flatten against the icy snow behind no more cover than some stunted oakbrush.

"Get your arses back in here and quick!" Donegan cried.

Bullets kicked up snow and bits of sandstone rock as the pair shoved their way into a retreat. Then Buffalo Horn stopped behind a low pile of rock and fired back at his tormentors.

"A flying exit of feathers, legs, and arms, boys!" Kelly called out when he started his slide back into the rocky hollow.

Bullets banged and zinged off the layers of nearby stone, splattering lead and sharp rock fragments as the Sioux continued to do their damndest to hold down the scouts until they could figure out how to flush their prey from its burrow.

"God-*damn!*" the old trapper muttered, turning slowly, putting some fingers to the side of his head.

"You're hit?" Parker asked, immediately crawling to Johnston's side.

Johnston pulled the fingers away from the side of his scalp above the ear and peered at them carefully. The smear of blood was already freezing. "Take a look at it for me," he ordered the younger man.

Parker pushed the fur cap up, parted some of the old man's long, greasy hair, and studied the wound. "Damn if you ain't lucky."

"It ain't luck saved this scalp all these gol-danged years," Johnston replied with a snort, tugging the side of his fur cap back down over the oozy wound. "I've had slim escapes afore . . . but that there was a close'un."

Suddenly Kelly hollered, "Buffalo Horn! Get in here!"

They all turned from Johnston, seeing that the Bannock had not retreated all the way back with Kelly. Instead, Buffalo Horn had slid into a narrow crevice where spring runoff had eroded away enough of the sandstone that he could lie down within the gap. There he could fire his rifle while remaining hidden from the Sioux until they were all but on top of him.

"Goddamn, if that Injun don't have some *huevos!*" James Parker said with no little admiration.

"Give 'em hell, Buffalo Horn!" cheered John Johnston. "Give them bastards bloody hell!"

They had been pinned down for the better part of two hours, Luther Kelly calculated, noticing the fall of the dim globe behind the thick clouds. For better than half of that time they could only hear what must have been a stiff fight of it taking place across the river, on the west bank of the Tongue.

From the looks of things, Miles had eventually ordered up some troops to rescue the white scouts. Captain James S. Casey had crossed the frozen river with his A Company and the Rodman gun that Casey's men had used with such success against Sitting Bull's village of Hunkpapa during the Battle of Cedar Creek back in October.*

In addition, through the bare skeletal cottonwoods, Kelly could make out what he believed was Lieutenant Charles E. Hargous's detachment of mounted infantry coming up to support Casey's men as dismounted skirmishers. They had been in the process of advancing toward a point opposite where the white scouts were pinned down on the east bank when Casey's relief was suddenly confronted with a bold show of force from

* *A Cold Day in Hell*, vol. 11, The Plainsmen Series.

more than 150 mounted warriors charging up the west bank
of the river.

Kelly watched as Casey ordered a halt. Then Hargous's
men rolled out of the saddle and deployed in a long skirmish
line among Casey's men as the captain's tried-and-tested gun
crew rolled the field piece into position and prepared to fire
rounds of deadly solid shot into the hard-charging horsemen.

The sun sank from the twilit sky by the time the first
round belched out of the muzzle of the Rodman, spewing jets
of fire and a thousand sparks that lit up the snow with an
eerie orange glow. The charge landed among the horsemen—scattering some, pushing most back in confusion.

Kelly, Donegan, and the rest immediately joined Casey's
men in a cheer as the gun crew reloaded and quickly adjusted
the altitude on the Rodman's carriage. A second charge whistled into the darkening mist forming off the frozen river. It too
exploded in a great burst of noise as earth and snow erupted
where it exploded in the midst of the enemy horsemen.

More ponies cried and warriors yelled, scattering in three
directions.

Again the skirmish line of soldiers cheered as Casey advanced them another twenty yards toward the enemy.

Back and forth the two sides skirmished for the better
part of another half hour: the stalwart warriors gathering
themselves up and charging in after each shell from the Rodman had exploded, taking advantage of the lull it took to
reload. Against each screaming flurry from the Sioux, Casey's
and Hargous's men valiantly held their line—firing back into
the teeth of each charge, giving the gun crew time to adjust the
limber, reposition the altitude, draw the windage, and ignite
each round of shot they sent whistling, whining, spewing fire
into the dusk of that coming night.

"Damn, if that ain't a fine sight!" James Parker observed
within that rocky hollow.

Kelly and the rest roared their approval each time Casey
inched his skirmishers forward another few yards.

Then suddenly the white scouts and Buffalo Horn turtled
their necks into their shoulders as a round whistled low right
over their heads and slammed into the open ground just beyond their position.

Warriors who had been creeping up through the shrinking light and oakbrush shrieked in surprise and pain as the icy snow and earth came showering down around them in hard clumps. Those not hurt began to gather up the wounded and the dead, pulling them away in retreat.

A second round whined low over the scouts' heads, exploding a little farther away from the rocky hollow, once again scattering the warriors and sending shards of sandstone and red earth into the deepening purple hues of twilight.

Now the Indians were moving back in full force on the east side of the river, yelling out to one another, carrying those who could not retreat on their own, some mounting horses but most trudging away from the battlefield on foot—retreating from the persistent and accurate shooting of the white scouts. As far away as possible from the soldiers' big gun that fired its shells from across the river.

On Casey and Hargous's skirmish line gunfire began to wither, tapering off until it grew quiet. Even deathly quiet, as night crept over the ridges to the east of the Tongue.

"I think we're done for the day, fellas," Kelly declared, warily getting to his knees and waving Buffalo Horn in from his crevice.

"They'll be back," John Johnston groaned. "And when they do, there'll be more of 'em than ticks on a strop hawg's back."

"Amen to that," Donegan said as he dusted the snow from the elbows of his canvas mackinaw and slapped the knees of his thick buffalo leggings. "Get what sleep you can tonight, boys. I figger tomorrow's fight's gonna start early . . . and last just as long as Miles can hold 'em off."

Chapter 28

8 January 1877

J ust how did a man sleep when he knew that dawn would bring him battle with Crazy Horse?

It was a restless camp that cold night beside the Tongue River as patches of stars appeared between the snow-laden clouds. Fires burned every few yards throughout the bivouac, sleepless soldiers huddled around the flames in their blankets, every man taking his turn at the double guard Miles had put out on the picket line. Because of the extreme cold, a soldier could stand no more than an hour of running guard duty out there in the darkness, where every clump of sage and oak-brush was sure to conceal a skulking warrior sneaking in for a scalp.

Certain that Tom Leforge lay dead somewhere on the battlefield, Kelly gave the order to fall back to the soldier camp when the Sioux and Cheyenne retreated at dusk. But try as he and the others did, they weren't able to convince Buffalo Horn to retreat with them. The Bannock wanted the chance to pick off a stray Sioux or two as the enemy turned its tail. One way or the other, Seamus figured, there was no man who could question the courage of that Indian.

About an hour after dark Leforge slipped in, shuddering from his hours of lying in the snow somewhere between the

Indians and the scouts on the battlefield. He hadn't dared to show himself, so close to the warriors was he. The squaw man gulped down his supper and coffee, then immediately rolled up in his blankets and fell fast asleep, back in the bosom of the soldiers.

Buffalo Horn himself finally showed up at the scouts' fire later that night, long after it had become fully dark.

"You shot two more?" Donegan said, asking in sign as well.

The Bannock nodded, then began to motion with his hands, speaking English words when he could remember how to put those words together in some understandable fashion.

"Cheyenne. Two," he explained, patting his belt where the two fresh scalps hung—their flesh frozen hard. "Two follow you to soldier village."

Kelly asked, "These two Cheyenne warriors—you say they were following us back here?"

"I wait by tree. Cheyenne no see Buffalo Horn," he explained, nodding. "I see Cheyenne. I shoot two."

"Some of them get away?" Donegan asked with his hands.

"One, maybeso," Buffalo Horn answered, and accepted the cup of coffee the Irishman picked up and handed him.

Seamus turned to pour himself another cup, finding the eyes of the old woman burning like coals into Buffalo Horn. He held up the pot for her, and she nodded. He poured her more coffee. She took a sip, then nudged the young girl closer to her side beneath the old blanket and stared into the fire to show that she no longer wished to acknowledge the white man standing at her elbow.

"You can hate him," Seamus said to her quietly in English. "But he is a warrior. Just like your husband and sons and nephews. They are warriors and they make war. They take scalps of their enemies who are brave. Those two scalps came from Cheyenne warriors brave enough to follow us back to camp."

Only once did her eyes flash up to his, just for a fraction of a second as she brought the tin cup to her lips and drank.

"You are warm enough?" he asked her in sign after setting the coffeepot down.

She would not look at him anymore. Instead she began speaking softly to the child under her arm. Seamus went back to the far side of the fire and squatted down in his blankets, propping himself against a large downed cottonwood trunk. He stared and stared at the flames until he drifted off.

Late that night he heard the woman's voice, then both of the other women calling out to the surrounding darkness. Rubbing his eyes, Seamus listened as Kelly and Buffalo Horn were aroused as well. Cheyenne voices drifted in from beyond the darkness.

"Bet they want to know if our captives are still alive," Kelly explained.

Seamus asked, "You figure that's what she's telling them?"

Back and forth the women yelled into the night, the dis-embodied male voices floating in from the darkness that ringed the scouts' fire there in Miles's soldier camp. Frank Baldwin showed up first, then Miles came over, rubbing a bare finger in his gritty eye before he stuffed his hand back into a mitten.

"What you make of it, Kelly?"

"All this talk—they're probably trying to figure out if there's a way they can free our captives—get them to slip away—"

A shot rang out, quickly followed by another, both coming from the direction of the warrior voices.

"The red-bellies are firing into camp!"

Sergeants bellowed orders into the darkness, and pickets hollered in reply. A couple more shots rattled the night as Miles put the entire camp on alert. The soldiers had themselves convinced that these opening salvos just might mean an attack was imminent.

But Donegan knew better. No attack was coming—not with the way the old woman and the others peered into the darkness without taking cover. Instead they remained huddled together around the fire, shouting into the night until they no longer received an answer.

It became clear that the Cheyenne warriors had pulled back from the picket lines, while the night grew all the colder, all the quieter still. Seamus watched the women, the children too—sensing that Miles was about to have himself his long-awaited fight with Crazy Horse. If the Cheyenne and Lakota had tried this hard to free some women and youngsters as night fell, what might the morning bring?

He sat there in the cold, snow falling on the thick wool blankets, flakes like huge curls of ash as they drifted down through the fire's light . . . thinking on Samantha and the boy. Remembering his own family. Knowing how cold must be the hearts of those Cheyenne who wanted nothing more than to rescue their kin. Knowing his own heart would hurt every bit as much if the tables were turned and this enemy had captured Sam and the babe from him.

How he would fight with the last fiber in his body, the last pump of his heart, to free them.

When, he asked himself, would the army ever realize that this whole war was about family, about how the brownskins were fighting to protect their families, their homes, the land where the bones of their ancestors had been buried?

Tomorrow the Bear Coat's soldiers would be fighting an enemy with everything in their culture to lose, an enemy who found itself backed into a corner. An enemy who suddenly had nothing left to lose.

A half mile away a tall volcano-shaped butte punched a black pyramid out of the starry sky to the south. Behind that ridge the enemy village was no more than twenty miles away, perhaps closer than that.

Dawn would damn well get here soon enough.

Morning Star had been ready to go back in to the White Rock Agency* before the soldiers attacked his village in the Red Fork Valley. But now he had seen again what the *ve-ho-e* soldiers did to the people they defeated. Perhaps it would be better to die out here as a free man than to live on a tiny piece of ground the white man gave him. To live where he could not move his lodge when he wanted, when the human waste and offal began to smell, when the seasons turned.

But he would not go back now.

"We must get our people back," Morning Star told the great council that was convened as the snowflakes grew fat and thick.

Fires leaped into the cold night sky all around them.

Crazy Horse came to stand beside Morning Star. "This Old-Man Chief my Lakota people call Dull Knife will not be

* Red Cloud Agency.

alone when he rides against the Bear Coat's soldiers come
morning. No more will he have a dull knife. He will have the
strength of the Lakota joining with his warriors. And that
makes for a very sharp weapon!"

The crowd roared with courage, warriors yelping like
wolves, some pawing the earth, snorting, and throwing their
heads about like buffalo bulls in the spring when heady juices
flow.

"We can wait no longer!" Little Wolf cried. "Let every
man among you prepare his family to leave this place. At first
light the lodges must come down, all your possessions should
be packed and loaded on travois. Ready to flee upriver."

"Our fighting men must say farewell to their families tonight," Morning Star reminded them, thinking of the sons he
had lost in the Red Fork Valley fight. "None of us knows for
sure who will return."

"*Mitakuye oyasin!* We are all related!" Crazy Horse declared to thunderous approval. "Because all families are my
own, I go to rescue the Shahiyela prisoners taken by the *wasicu*
soldiers. We are all relations this night! We will all be brothers
in arms come dawn when the soldiers awake to find us waiting!"

How loudly they cheered and stomped, that multitude of
men who would go fight, women and children who would stay
behind to wait the outcome of the battle. That night in the
cold and the snow no one said anything about how few rifles
and pistols the warriors had; no one spoke about how they
had but little ammunition. But the courage was strong in
those arms that held aloft the bows and quivers bristling with
iron-tipped arrows the likes of which had wiped out Long
Hair's soldiers beside the Little Sheep River.* Many shook war
clubs made of smooth riverbed stone or broken knife blades.
No one said anything about how few guns they would be
carrying into battle . . . because it did not matter.

They had strong hearts and the prayers of their people—the most powerful weapon a warrior would take with
him into the coming fight.

"We have courage!" Morning Star called out when the

* *Seize the Sky*, vol. 2, Son of the Plains Trilogy.

chiefs had decided to set off at once, move downriver into position, and be ready when the soldiers awakened at dawn.

Little Wolf cried, "And we have war chiefs among us who will never give up—leaders who commanded us at the Roseberry River,* men who led us at the Little Sheep River when Sitting Bull's vision of soldiers falling into camp came to be!"

Then Crazy Horse shouted to the war-fevered throng. "And we have what truly matters most: there are many among us who have been in battle with the soldiers many, many times—many warriors who are hardened like iron, those who are veterans of war against the *wasicu* . . . our hearts will not turn to water!"

They laid their plans quickly, deciding to draw the soldiers out at first light. Decoys would be sent north to lure the Bear Coat's men over the ridge and behind what the *Tse-Tsehese* called Belly Butte,† into the basin below it, where the main body of warriors would rush in from both sides, and as they had done at the Pine Woods Fort,# they would crush the soldiers in one swift, overwhelming attack.

Decoys were called for, and among all those who volunteered for the honor more than three-times-ten were selected to ride the strongest ponies. Some of the older warriors were chosen to stay behind with the women and children to guard the camp, to hurry the village south if for some reason the battle turned to disaster.

Then, as the anxious crowd grew expectantly quiet, Morning Star looked at Little Wolf, Crazy Horse, Little Big Man, and Hump. "It is time to go," he said.

Overhead somewhere the great northern star was spinning its path across the sky to mark the passage of the night. They had miles to ride before they would be in position for the coming attack, before the decoys could lead the soldiers into the trap.

"Yes," Crazy Horse agreed. "Young men and old, all warriors who will ride into the dark guided by the Great Mystery to protect our homes and our families . . . remember there

* Battle of the Rosebud, *Reap the Whirlwind.*
† Known as Battle Butte after 8 January 1877.
# Fort Phil Kearny, Fetterman Massacre, 21 December 1866, *Sioux Dawn,* vol. 1, The Plainsmen Series.

is no greater honor than to die defending what you hold most dear!"

As the men sprinted to their ponies, accompanied by the rattling clamor of shields, bows, lances, war clubs, and rifles—the noise of more than two thousand voices was deafening as men, women, and children all sang out the brave-heart songs. Although they had little, stripped of nearly everything by the soldiers, the *Ohmeseheso* had not given up. They had not given in. There was fight enough left in every one of the *Tse-Tsehese* to defend their people and their land.

He knew that in the great hoop of all things it mattered little how his people would fight when they were wealthy in ponies and weapons, when they were strong and numerous and well fed.

What mattered most was how the *Ohmeseheso* fought when they had so little that there was nothing left to lose.

It made Morning Star's tired, wounded heart brave enough to believe that this might well be his people's finest hour.

His sister was held prisoner by the Bear Coat's soldiers!

Crooked Nose Woman had gone on a simple journey with Old Wool Woman and the others to visit Tangle Hair's people, those Dog Soldier clans who stayed close to the Sacred Mountain of *Noaha-vose*.

And now the soldiers had captured her! Every warrior knew what *ve-ho-e* soldiers would do to a pretty girl if they caught her. There was no honor among the white man for a *Tse-Tsehese* rope chastity belt.

Wooden Leg knew he had to do everything in his power to free her and the others.

When the big-throated guns ended their afternoon fight with the soldiers, Wooden Leg did not return to the village with the rest of the warriors when darkness came. Instead, with a few others, he hung back among the brush and the cottonwood and the fog rising off the river as the snow fell harder and harder. Then he crept in across the dry snow—walking a few careful steps through the sagebrush, stopping to hold his breath and listen before proceeding, his eyes peering into the coal-cotton darkness. Far away now he could see the dancing specks of light: many soldier fires.

But between here and there would be many guards. They would be out in the dark. Wooden Leg and the rest could get only so close to the camp before they started to call out to their people.

"Crooked Nose Woman!"

A bullet whined somewhere to his right. A nervous soldier guard, no doubt.

"Crooked Nose—it is your brother!"

Another soldier bullet sang out, this time a little closer.

He slipped off to the right, away from the direction where he had seen the orange jet of flame spew from the soldier's gun.

Now he was growing desperate. He heard no answer. Were his people already dead?

"Crooked Nose woman—Wooden Leg calls to you!"

"Brother! There are too many!"

"*Wimeca yelo!* I am a man!" he shouted to her. "I can come rescue—"

"No, Wooden Leg!" came her answer. "Do not risk such a foolish errand. I know you to have the strongest heart. There is no need to prove your bravery to anyone!"

Oh, how his spirit leaped just to hear her voice! "Tell me you are safe!"

"We are safe."

"The soldiers—did they? Have they . . . harmed you in any way?"

"No. The soldiers gave us food, and we have a fire to warm the young ones."

"The children?"

"They have cold feet. Very cold. But there is a good white man looking after them."

"You are warm and have food?"

"Yes, and Old Wool Woman is here with all of us," came his sister's answer.

"I will think of some way to rescue you, Crooked Nose Woman!"

"I am afraid for the rest if the fighting starts, brother!"

"Be strong—and do not be afraid, Sister," he called out to her, even though his own voice cracked with emotion. "We will not leave this place without you!"

"But the village must flee! The soldiers . . . they will march and destroy our village again!"

"Do not fear that, Sister," he told her, trying to make his voice sound as brave as he could make it. "Crazy Horse will bring the others back here come morning. Then we will free you."

"Go with the wind, Brother!"

There was another shot fired from the soldier guards.

"Wooden Leg—are you all right?"

"They did not hit me," he answered, looking left and right, low along the ground to see if he could make out anything moving across the dimly lit snow. "I will be back for you tomorrow," he promised.

Her voice called out in a hopeful echo, "Tomorrow."

"Before the sun rises."

How very hard it was to tear himself away from the mere sound of her voice.

As soon as another warrior had informed him that his sister had been captured, Wooden Leg had leaped onto his pony and gone to the place where the soldier scouts had surrounded and seized the prisoners. He had followed along that trail, then left his horse behind and crawled as close as he could to the soldier camp. But try as he might, Wooden Leg was unable to see any of his people among all the white men, animals, and wagons. For a long time his heart was so heavy—certain his people had been killed by the *Ooetaneo-o** scouts working for the Bear Coat. Just the way the *Ho-nehe-taneo-o*† and the *Sosone-eo-o*# scouts had killed women and children in the valley of the Red Fork back in the Big Freezing Moon.

Then the skirmish with the *ve-ho-e* scouts had started nearby, which brought the soldiers out of their camp with one of their wagon guns. No better time was it for Wooden Leg to fight the white man. After all, his heart was hard and cold, just to think that the soldiers had killed his sister.

At dark the others had retreated back to their village. When the night had turned black, several of his friends had

---

* The Crow, or Absaraka, People.
† The Wolf People, or Pawnee.
# The Shoshone People.

said they would stay behind and join him when he crawled close to the soldier camp. They understood that Wooden Leg had to know for sure. Every warrior has relations. Every man has a family he will defend unto death.

What joy it brought his cold, small heart to hear his sister's voice call back to him from the night!

By the time Wooden Leg and his loyal friends were racing back toward the village, they heard the sounds of many hooves on the hard, winter-frozen ground. They stopped, listened, hearing the faint snort of many horses in the dark, hearing the muted murmur of many mouths. Then he and the others rode to a low hill to look down on the valley.

Coming along both the west bank and the east side of the river rode a great cavalcade: the strength of the *Ohmeseheso* people whom Three Stars Crook could not destroy when he attacked Old Bear's camp on the Powder, the people Three Fingers Kenzie could not destroy when he attacked Morning Star's camp in the Red Fork Valley. The finest warriors, old and young, rode knee to knee with those Lakota who had joined Crazy Horse in vowing never to give up to the white government men, never to go in to the agencies. How it made Wooden Leg's heart leap to see so many marching through the cold and the dark, like a throbbing of the land itself: men and horses going to battle across the blue-lit snow.

"*Nitaa-shema!* Let's go!" he urged those friends around him, so eager was he to start this fight. So much wrong done by the soldiers against the *Tse-Tsehese* was about to be made right.

How it made a young warrior's spirit sing! Come morning, it would be a good, good day to die protecting his People!

The Bear Coat and his soldiers must be taught a lesson this time, he thought as he urged his pony down the slope toward the great procession of warriors bundled in blankets and capotes and buffalo robes against the terrible cold. The *ve-ho-e* soldiers were like bothersome, nagging magpies swooping, diving, chattering after a sore-backed horse, landing now and then to poke their beaks into the skin ulcers and angry places where the horse's hide weeped and oozed. Usually a man could take some of the tarry oil he collected from the black springs to keep the nettlesome magpies off the horse long enough for the terrible sores to heal.

But this time there was no tarry oil. This time the village itself was the sore-backed horse: women and children, helpless. And the soldiers would continue diving and swooping and squawking until they were driven away, once and for all time.

There was no tarry oil to protect the village . . . but there were all these warriors, these men who would put their bodies between the soldiers and the lives of their loved ones.

For all that they held dear! For this land where the bones of their people were buried!

Hoka hey! Come dawn it would be a great day to die!

Chapter 29

8 January 1877

The gray, cheerless sky was just beginning to pale when the soldiers were ordered to roll out of their blankets. The sun was not yet up. As they greeted a temperature of fourteen degrees, most had to shake fresh snow off their bedrolls. Several new inches lay atop what had been in the valley the afternoon of the seventh. Off to the west the sky appeared all the more forbidding. Dark, snow-laden clouds obscured all but the foothills of the distant mountains.

Worse yet, it was still snowing in the valley of the Tongue.

In the predawn darkness men lumbered slowly among the cottonwood trees along that sweeping horseshoe of the river, going about their toilet while others built up the fires on the ground scraped clear of snow and started breakfast preparations: chopping at the frozen salt pork, cracking open wooden crates of hardtack crackers the men would soak in the spewing grease or dunk in their coffee until soft enough to chew.

Stepping away from the fire for a moment, Seamus looked over at the front flap of the surgeon's tent, finding the old woman seated there, right where she had been last night when he had closed his eyes. Her lined, cherrywood face gazed here and there impassively at all the activity among the soldiers. For a moment their eyes met—but in hers there shone no light of friendly recognition. He walked over, holding out a steaming cup, which she readily took from him and drank.

Once he had poured himself another cup, Donegan trudged to the nearby south side of camp. As the night reluctantly gave way to a snowy dawn, he peered beyond at the terrain surrounding them. To the north and east stood a series of low hills covered with cedar and stunted pine, which blended into red-tinged bluffs and ridges rising farther still.

More striking still, some four hundred yards southwest of him lay another long ridge, at the middle of which stood an abrupt, rounded knob covered with shale and talus. At the northern foot of that ridge ran a deep, snow-drifted coulee stretching all the way to the Tongue River itself.*

In the dim, graying light Donegan could make out what he thought might be the hint of movement along the top of the low knoll where last night Miles had ordered a detachment of his men to erect breastworks and hold that flat-topped piece of strategic ground. The wind was blowing hard enough, cruel enough, that Seamus could see how it tormented those soldiers who had to stand up there, exposed and out in the open on picket duty.

Some three hundred yards farther southeast from the knoll arose the most prominent feature of the entire landscape: the volcanic-shaped cone decked out in its stark red-earth and snow colors thrust up against the pale horizon.†

Beyond the butte the ridgeline meandered all the way into the eastern bluffs and hills, standing at least three hundred feet high, dotted with cedar and oakbrush and sage, the entire landscape buried in some eight to twelve inches of snow as dawn presumed to awaken this frozen land.

"Would you care to go with us, Mr. Donegan?"

Seamus turned, finding Miles and Kelly, along with a handful of the colonel's headquarters staff.

"Where are you off to?"

"There," and Miles pointed with a two-foot shaft of peeled cottonwood he had been carrying since arriving yesterday. "I want to be up there to those breastworks by the time it grows light enough to see."

* Present-day Battle Butte Creek.
† Soon to be shown on maps of the northern plains as Battle Butte.

"Yeah—I'll come along, General."

They trudged through the deep snow on foot, through the last of the bivouac tents and breakfast fires, on past a dozen or more mules pawing at the snow for their own morning meal, on up the long slope to the top of the flat-topped knoll. Stopping there, Miles stuffed the peeled staff under his armpit and put out his hand. Lieutenant Baird, his adjutant, pulled the field glasses from a scratched and weathered leather campaign case.

Along the gray horizon to the southeast a man could gaze into the distance, following the path of the Tongue as it flowed out of a stretch of broken country, around the far end of the Wolf Mountains from its birthplace in the Bighorns. At the eastern edge of the earth the snowy sky was quickly becoming all the brighter with the first hint of the sun's rising behind those low, ominous snow clouds. A cold, icy mist clung eerily to everything in the valley just below them. Most of the time the wind caused the flakes to swirl, collecting, then dispersing among the old cottonwood that lined the river.

"Great Jupiter!" Miles exclaimed quietly as he peered into the distance.

"What is it?" Frank Baldwin asked.

"They're coming this way," the colonel explained. "Here, Kelly—take a look for yourself."

Kelly stepped up and peered through the field glasses at the scene below them to the southwest. Then he handed the glasses to Donegan. "Have yourself a look."

From what he could estimate, Seamus figured there had to be more than six hundred horsemen quickly approaching from up the valley, advancing on both sides of the river toward the soldier bivouac. Quickly again he tried to calculate their numbers—just to goad himself with the odds. Then Donegan remembered. Only once before had he ever seen such a disciplined formation of Indian horsemen: when Roman Nose had led his Northern Cheyenne and Pawnee Killer's Sioux down on the twenty-eight men still able to fire their rifles from that nameless sandbar on the high plains of Colorado.*

* Beecher Island, *The Stalkers*, vol. 3, The Plainsmen Series.

As Donegan handed the glasses back to the colonel, Miles asked them both, "How many you make of it?"

Kelly shrugged. "Six hundred, maybe more."

"I'd say that's about right," Seamus agreed.

"And that's only the ones we can see," Miles reminded them. "No telling how many we can't count because of the fog behind them." The colonel waved his peeled wand in the air. "No telling how many are already somewhere in these hills."

"They easily have us two to one, General," Kelly said quietly. "Maybe worse than that."

For the next half hour the warriors pushed their ponies up from the river valley, on up the slopes of that ridgeline south of the soldier bivouac, emerging like black insects from the cottony, swirling fog that nestled among the trees and brush along the river. In addition to those horsemen gathering in clusters along the hills immediately across the river, the western end of the heights bristled with horsemen who gathered to look down at the soldiers on the flat-topped knob.

They began to call out to the soldiers in Lakota.

"You know any of that tongue?" Seamus asked Kelly.

Luther nodded, stepping out to the edge of the knoll with Miles and Donegan. "Listen."

They did listen for a few moments more; then Kelly turned to the others and said, "From what I can make of it—they're telling us that we're not going to eat any more fat meat."

"Fat meat?" Miles said, wagging his head in confusion. "I don't get it."

"Bacon," Donegan declared. "They mean bacon, General. Don't you see? What they're trying to tell us white men is that we've eaten our last breakfast."

Miles turned to Seamus, asking, "Eaten our last breakfast, have we?"

"That's their strongest call to battle, General," Kelly explained. "Those bucks are saying your men won't live to have another meal."

"You know their tongue," Donegan said to Kelly, "so why don't you go ahead and tell that bunch what we think of them as warriors?"

A smile crept across Kelly's mouth there in the early light

as the snow whipped around them in a whirling fury. "Not a thing to lose if I do."

Seamus watched the chief of scouts take a step away from them to unbutton the bottom of his heavy buffalo-hide coat. Then Kelly grabbed his crotch and gyrated his hips forward, calling out in Lakota.

"I will have many breakfasts, for I am strong," he hollered across the snowy heights. "But you will cower before me because you are women! None of you are men like me—for you are all women!"

They watched how that taunting challenge struck the warriors gathered on the heights to their left and across the river—angering the Sioux and Cheyenne beyond reason, working them into a fighting lather. It was just then seven A.M. as a few of the warriors began their first slow advance from the ridgeline down toward the open bowl where the soldier camp lay.

"I think you done just what you wanted to do," Seamus told Kelly. "Looks like they're ready to fight, General."

"Then let's be at them!" Miles roared enthusiastically, clapping his mittens together.

His first order sent back to camp directed First Lieutenant Mason Carter to take his K Company across the ice on the Tongue River and establish a defensive line at the base of the hills should the warriors threaten to make a daring sweep right into the army's bivouac. Next he ordered Captain Charles Dickey and First Lieutenant Cornelius Cusick to bring up companies E and F of the Twenty-second to form a skirmish line at the base of the low plateau just north of the knoll where Miles stood. Then the colonel had Second Lieutenant William Bowen bring up the supply train and station it at the edge of the timber skirting the base of the plateau where the wagons and animals might be better protected in the event Crazy Horse made a cavalry sweep from across the river, seeking to surround the soldier camp.

"Bring Pope up with the artillery!" the colonel ordered. "I want him to support Carter's company when those warriors charge his position."

Within minutes mules were hauling the two carriages into position at the base of the oblong plateau where the canvas tops were stripped back from the iron bows, scattering a flurry of accumulated snow over the gun crews working feverishly under Lieutenant James W. Pope's direction. First the twelve-pounder, under the command of Second Lieutenant Edward W. Casey, was rolled into position and its wheels chocked. Next came the men struggling with the Rodman gun, which would be under Pope's personal command. Both crews took elevation grades for the first time, charting distance and targets on those ridges and ravines across the frozen river where hundreds of warriors were beginning to gather in angry knots as K Company began its crossing of the ice.

Miles called out, "Major Casey!"

The captain hurried up and saluted. "General?"

"Station your company on either flank of our guns."

"Very good, sir!"

Arrayed on either side of Pope's and Casey's gun crews was Captain James Casey's A Company to act in support and defense of the artillery position. Then on the far left flank Miles called up Captain Ezra P. Ewers's E Company to position itself on the southwest side of the ridge, extending from the knoll below the artillery position, its own right flank suspended in the air.

Donegan stepped up into the midst of the frantic activity boiling around Nelson A. Miles. "They might cross below you, General."

"Yes, I've thought of that," Miles confided with a brooding squint of his eyes. "You were cavalry in the war, I take it?"

"The Second, sir."

"A good outfit, Donegan." Miles had a wry grin on his face as he continued. "So you would be the sort to think about horse troops sweeping around to take our rear, wouldn't you?"

"Damn right."

"Damn right indeed!" Miles agreed. "Mr. Baird, bring up Butler and McDonald. Place them down there, and there, flank to flank to protect against encirclement on our rear."

"Very good, General," and the adjutant hurried off toward the base of the knoll to convey his orders.

Within a matter of minutes the last of the troops in bivouac were trudging out through the snow already halfway to their knees, more falling around them. Captain Edmond Butler quickly arrayed his men, stretching C Company to the east as far as he dared so that its formation roughly paralleled the northern base of the plateau that Captain Casey, along with Lieutenants Pope and Casey, would be defending with the artillery. On Butler's right flank Lieutenant Robert McDonald attached the left flank of his D Company in another dangerously thin skirmish line. Both companies were told to watch the trees and riverbank to the northwest where the entire outfit had just abandoned its bivouac. It was there the enemy horsemen were expected to sweep across the frozen Tongue.

With McDonald riding beside him Captain Butler slowly urged his horse down that skirmish line of cold, shivering men as the snow continued to fall and the cruel north wind slashed straight into their faces. Butler would not want any of them to think about, much less realize, just how short a line a few score of soldiers made on that rugged, snowy landscape when it came to facing down the coming assault.

"Every man must be a hero today!" Butler told them with hints of his Irish homeland still evident in his peaty brogue. "For when this fight begins, there will be no reassuring touch of a comrade's elbow beside you! When the red bastards come for us, there will be no rear guard! This fight will be won or lost not by our regiment! Not even by our battalion—much less by a single company! No, men . . . today this fight will be won or lost by each and every man here, fighting alone!"

The cheer that Seamus heard erupt along that painfully thin line of infantry brought a mist of remembered camaraderie to his eyes, a tug at the sentimental strings of his heart—recalling how the officers of the Second Cavalry had worked up their horse soldiers before troop after troop would emerge slowly from the woods and halt, forming up company by company, knee to knee, stirrup to stirrup. Every man's heart in his throat, his saber clutched in a sweaty hand, knowing that in a few seconds the order would be given and they would spur their mounts with a deafening roar—racing toward row upon row of infantry and uncounted cannon that would be shredding their ranks, tearing man from horse, soldier from formation, limbs from body, while the grapeshot and canister slashed through them as if the gates of Hades itself had opened.

Still, those left in the saddle would ride on.

Looking at these shivering men now, Donegan hoped these soldiers would fight every bit as bravely this day as he knew Crazy Horse's cavalry was sure to—knowing that the Lakota and Cheyenne were once more protecting their homes, their families, their dying way of life.

"Mother of God, watch over each one of these boys . . . these men," he whispered, his words whisked away by the wind.

In those anxious moments for the soldiers and their officers, the Indians began to mill and circle across the river. But instead of making any charge on Carter's K Company, which took up a tight position on the west bank after stepping clear of the trees and willow, the horsemen slowly melted back into the ravines and the cedars, remaining out of sight for the most part and not making any show of force against Carter's lone company.

"By Jupiter!" Miles bellowed with his field glasses at his eyes. "Maybe we've got them cowed! Doesn't look like they'll try to cross and sweep us after all!"

"General, there's our real problem now," Donegan declared, pointing into the valley south of the long ridge.

Many, many more horsemen were appearing out of the cold fog, coming downstream on the east bank of the river behind the line of rugged bluffs.

"Just look at them," Miles marveled as hundreds of ponies carried warriors up the back slopes, where the Indians began dismounting in the snow, brandishing their weapons, shouting and yelling at the soldiers below.

Gunfire suddenly crackled west of the river. Those men gathered beside Miles atop the knoll spun on their heels to watch small knots of Indians down among the cedars and clumps of leafless willow open up a sporadic fire upon Carter's K Company. Within moments close to a hundred warriors burst out of hiding, all of them sprinting on foot, waving their weapons and screaming—headed straight for those fifty infantrymen.

Carter held them, held them in the face of that charge, ordering his first platoon to advance three paces, where they dropped to one knee to return fire, when the lieutenant coolly ordered up his second platoon to advance and fire three paces farther on. The Indians were no farther than fifty yards from the lone company, inching forward on both sides, threatening to sweep Carter's men on one flank or another. Still, K Company held their ground as Carter barked his orders, rallied his men, steadied them in their advance platoon by platoon, turning back every attempt the warriors made to sweep past him to the river.

No more than fifty scared soldiers, alone and by themselves, all but cut off across the frozen Tongue—as Carter moved among them on horseback: assuring them, shouting his orders, keeping them together, preventing them from having time to think of the danger, so busy did he keep them that they could think only of loading, firing, advancing. Loading, firing, advancing. Loading, firing, advancing—

"Mr. Pope!" the colonel hollered down to the gun position, "Put that Napoleon to work on those Indians across the river and take the pressure off Carter's outfit!"

"Very good, General!" the lieutenant replied, turning immediately to the officer assisting him with the mountain howitzer.

As Lieutenant Edward W. Casey barked his orders and elevation, the gun crew quickly snapped to, adjusted the caisson, rechocked the wheels, cranked the elevation, then stepped back in a flurry.

Young Casey cried, "Fire!"

The first twelve-pound shot was on its way across the foggy Tongue.

But Casey was already giving the order: "Reload! Be quick about it! Reload!"

Frantically his men shuffled in and out of position, first to jam the swab home down the howitzer's huge brass muzzle; then a second soldier jumped forward to ram home the pouch of coarse black powder. Then a third soldier hobbled forward with the ball clutched in both hands as another spiked the powder pouch through the touchhole, preparing the ignition of that second shot.

"Fire!" Casey yelled the instant his men jumped back from the muzzle.

Again the brass weapon rocked back on its carriage in the snow, belching even more gray-black smoke, which hung heavy on the cold air, its stench burning every man's nostrils downwind.

"Reload!" again cried the young lieutenant just three years out of the academy—even though his men were already leaping into position. This was no drill.

Across the river the second round collided with earth and snow, exploding among the brush at the mouth of a ravine where half a hundred warriors scattered as cascades of ice and red dirt came showering down from the sky above them.

In the disappearing echo of the cannon came the shrill, sudden call of Crazy Horse's warriors.

Behind Miles on the knoll floated those first shrieking whistles. The sort of sound that once a man hears it on the field of battle, he will never forget, if he lives to remember.

High-pitched, like the shriek of hawk or war eagle. First a handful, then a dozen . . . and finally more than a hundred of those whistles from the hundreds of warriors arrayed along the top of the ridge to the southeast of the soldiers.

Casey kept at his work: "Fire!"

That third round from the twelve-pounder crashed just beyond Carter's men, driving off the last of those warriors who might still threaten to ride over K Company and sweep across the river, flanking the entire outfit behind Butler's battalion.

"Whooeee! We've got that bunch on the run, General!" Pope cheered, turning immediately to pound Lieutenant Casey on the back.

"Yes," Miles answered approvingly, yet he did not celebrate long. Instead, the smile disappeared with the next gust of cold wind as the colonel turned back to the ridge to the southeast, where Donegan and the rest of the scouts were watching the enemy massing.

"General!" Hobart Bailey roared enthusiastically. "The artillery have broken their charge!"

But as the aide-de-camp's words were spilling from his lips, Bailey could already see that Miles was not listening, nor was he ready to celebrate.

Instead, the colonel's eyes narrowed, a deep furrow in his brow as he peered at all the warriors bristled above them along the snowy ridges like hair along the backbone of an angry dog. "Lieutenant, that bunch we just ran off over there across the river is the least of my worries now."

Chapter 30

Wiotehika 1877

Most often his people called this time the Moon of the Terrible Cold.

Crazy Horse shuddered—not so much because it had been an unending period of such terrible cold, but because his *Titunwan* Lakota people sometimes called this winter moon by another name.

Wiotehika. The Moon of Hard Times.

In the gray darkness of that morning-coming, Crazy Horse could smell the smoke from the many soldier fires. And every now and then gusts of that wind coming out of the north brought to his sensitive nostrils the smell of *wasicu* coffee boiling. There had been no coffee in the camp of his people for a long, long time. Perhaps as long ago as last summer, when they had destroyed the soldiers and took a little from the leather pouches on the big American horses. Maybe a little coffee stolen here and there from the crazed *wasicus* who scratched in the ground for the yellow rocks they found in the sacred *He Sapa*.

No, there hadn't been any coffee in the village for a long time now. There hadn't been much to truly celebrate either. With soldier armies roaming on either side of them, north and south, it had been only a matter of time before the white man would come to raid the hunting camps. As far back as he could remember, the buffalo had been chivied—stirred up, driven here and there, right on out of the traditional hunting grounds. No longer could his Hunkpatila count on finding the huge herds that used to blanket this country between the Shifting Sands River* and the Greasy Grass.†

What good days those had been! Hides and meat and happy times when men and women courted, babes were born, and the old ones took their last breath knowing their bones would bleach beneath the sun that blazed down upon their homeland as the endless hoop of the seasons turned.

All that celebration was gone now. Like ash from a long-dead fire, like the ash he had smeared on his face after his young daughter had died of the *wasicu's* dreaded spotted sickness. All the celebration gone now, gone like the dust of this land he would toss into the wind. The dust of this land—the very bones of his ancestors.

Spotted Tail, Red Cloud, and the others . . . they had sold the land that was the bones of his ancestors! How could one sell that to the white man?

But Crazy Horse knew the white man would take it anyhow.

The *wasicu* was just that way, he thought as he drank deep of the numbing cold wind and sent off another group of warriors to cross the ice and join those on the west side of the river. Eleven summers ago the white peace talkers were at the Laramie fort speaking the words of treaty with the Lakota peoples, asking that white man could use the thieves' road# north along the White Mountains.@ But at the same time that the peace talkers were trying to buy safety along that road, the white man's government was also sending soldiers to seize it by force.^

The *wasicu* always came to take what he wanted, no mat-

---

* The Powder River.
† The Little Bighorn River.
# The Bozeman Trail.
@ Bighorn Mountains.
^ Colonel Henry B. Carrington, marching north to build and garrison three forts along the Bozeman Trail: *Sioux Dawn*, vol. 1, The Plainsmen Series.

ter that the Indian did not want to sell . . . no matter that it was not the Indians' to sell.

Where was there left to run now? With Three Stars troubling the land north from the Holy Road, and now this angry Bear Coat punching his way south from the Elk River—there would be little peace for the Crazy Horse people. Too few buffalo left for meat to dry and hides to make their lodges. Too little time to savor the joy in life . . . what with having to pack up and flee, running all the time. Just tattered shreds and broken pieces of the old life left.

Was the Land of the Grandmother the only place to go now where the soldiers would not follow, fight, and kill his people? He wondered if the runner would find Sitting Bull, if the Hunkpapa chief would bring the rifles and bullets and his warriors south again to join the Crazy Horse people in taking another stand against the *wasicu*.

But maybe Sitting Bull was already gone—fleeing north instead of fighting. More and more Crazy Horse believed he was the last fighting Lakota left.

His wife, Black Shawl, had turned away from the great gathering around him last night in that moment Crazy Horse prepared to lead the others away from their camp to do battle with Bear Coat's soldiers. She had disappeared, pushing away through the crowd, dropping her wet eyes in sadness, going off to pack up their few belongings without saying a word to him before Crazy Horse led the warriors north. How heavy that had made his heart; how cold it was still. Black Shawl and so many other wives and mothers, sisters and daughters, all had turned away in resignation, knowing they must be about their packing, calling together the children and catching up the ponies, lashing the travois to the horses' backs, dismantling the smoke-blackened lodges and loading everything up so they would be ready to flee when the soldiers came.

No matter that the warriors were riding out to fight the Bear Coat's soldiers. The women knew that even if the warriors defeated the *wasicus* this time . . . more would come. There would be more packing and running and frightened dreams in the night.

"The soldiers are coming! The soldiers are coming!"

More running. More blood. More dead to mourn.

Just before dawn that morning the young, hot-blooded

decoys did exactly what the decoys had done that first winter morning at the Pine Woods Fort when they had become too anxious, too eager to count the first coup and lift the first scalps . . . and the trap did not work.

They should have stayed hidden longer from the Bear Coat's soldiers. Waited longer, tucked away and out of sight behind the ridge until the soldiers were lured south past Belly Butte into the narrowing throat of the canyon.

So the grand design of the war chiefs had turned to so much ash. All that was left now was to hold the soldiers back from the village while the camp of women and children fled upriver into the Panther Mountains.* Unless . . . by some blessing of the Great Mystery these warriors could stop the Bear Coat's soldiers and turn them back to their Elk River post with their tails tucked between their legs like whipped dogs.

For a moment his heart leaped with hope . . . then Crazy Horse once more remembered the admonishment of Sitting Bull. In his vision at the Deer Medicine Rocks last summer *Wakan Tanka* had told the Hunkpapa leader that the Lakota people were to take nothing from the soldier dead at the Greasy Grass. If they disobeyed, then the blessings of the Great Mystery would not surround the Lakota peoples for the rest of their days upon the earth.

Instead, in a fever of blood lust, the Hunkpapa, the Oglalla, the Sans Arc, the Miniconjou, and all the bands had joyously collected the spoils of that battle beside the Greasy Grass.

Now the *Titunwan* must all suffer for disobeying the Great Mystery.

At dawn the walk-a-heaps crossed the frozen river to confront the ten-times-ten horsemen Crazy Horse sent up the west bank along the foot of the buttes and ravines. Those men could have eventually swallowed up the soldiers on their own, but the Bear Coat fired both of his wagon guns as the cold fog rose off the river. Earth and snow and a dusting of frost blown from the grass every time a big shell exploded—the way a man would hold a handful of flour in his palm, then blow on it.

Warriors scattered, tried again to regather, only to hear

* Wolf Mountains.

the whistle of another shell from the wagon guns. Was there any way to silence the loud, booming roar of those weapons?

Finally he knew there was no heart in fighting those soldiers Bear Coat sent across the river, so Crazy Horse called his warriors back and they hurried to join the many others who were just then spreading out along on the hilltops looking down at the *wasicus* and their wagons and their tents.

For the moment there would be no thoughts of the reservation land, no thoughts of the agencies. For now there could be no thoughts of surrendering to the white man's ways.

Still, Crazy Horse wondered if Hump and Little Big Man, if White Bull and Two Moon, all felt these first real pangs of doubt the way he had suffered them this winter. Perhaps they, like he, had decided in their own hearts that the best path now was to protect the women and children . . . just as many of the chiefs were saying the wisest path might eventually be for them to take their women and children into the agencies.

Better that than to watch the faces of the women grow sunken and old before their time. Better that than to watch the eyes of the children grow hollow with despair, their bellies swollen from hunger, their fingers and toes blackened with winter's cold.

There were no buffalo left anyway.

This would be a good day to die.

For all the gunfire coming from the warriors gathered on the heights above the soldiers, there had been only two casualties so far—a couple of mules wounded by stray bullets fired from those Indians across the river from the supply train. The noisy animals brayed and bawled, kicking in their harness there among the wagons until some men came to calm them.

Seamus brooded there on the knoll over just how ineffective this sort of long-distance fighting truly was—for either side. Most of these soldiers weren't worth a tinker's dam at shooting their unfamiliar weapons—especially under battle conditions and in the horrid cold—and the majority of warriors simply never had enough ammunition to practice in order to become good shots themselves.

But the arrows were nettlesome.

From time to time some soldier would call out a shrill warning, and the rest would quickly look into the sky feathered with heavy gray storm clouds. There above them, falling out of the steady snow, would be half a hundred arrows given flight by the warriors dappling the crest of the flat-topped butte. Down, down, down in a deadly arc the shafts would hiss silently out of the low, cold clouds. Landing with a puff in the deep snow without much of a sound, sometimes clattering against the iron wheels of the wagon guns, or thwanging into the wood of the gun carriages, a noisy, bothersome clatter against steel and bronze and iron cannonball, nicking the flesh of those who hadn't taken shelter fast enough.

It was clear that Miles was growing exasperated at having to take refuge beneath the Napoleon gun's caisson.

"Get those prisoners up here!" he barked at his staff. "On the double!"

Frank Baldwin and Hobart Bailey sprinted away down the slope.

"More goddamned arrows coming, General!" some man railed.

A covey of the iron-tipped whispers wobbled down from the gray clouds—smacking, clattering, thunking . . . and then Seamus watched a detail of soldiers hurrying the women and children up the gentle slope of the low plateau, like flushing and herding a gaggle of geese across a snowy barnyard. Their sudden appearance among the wagon guns and the soldiers' position immediately angered the warriors arrayed on the north and east sides of the butte. Those fighting men close enough to recognize their own people cried out a warning to the women, and the prisoners shouted back to the hills just before the captives began to shrink behind the soldiers and their artillery.

The old woman ducked last of all, pulling down a young child with her, hunching over the girl like a protective hen as hail would slash out of the cruel clouds.

Seamus squinted into the sky beneath the edge of the wolf-hide cap, seeing the arrows just being released, climbing in a graceful arc. The old woman must have known. They must have told her it was coming.

Down below among the supply train this time he didn't hear the brassy bawl of the mules for the moment . . . instead he heard the frightened cries of the women around him on the knoll.

The instant the last of that wave of arrows had clattered to the ground, the captives sang out to the heights in shrill panic, perhaps telling the warriors that their arrows were not only falling in among the soldiers, but among their own people as well.

Instead of halting their aerial attack, the Sioux and Cheyenne shouted their warnings to the women, again and again.

With the next flight iron war-points clattered in among the white men, and a lone soldier called out, one of the arrows sinking into the back of his leg. Others leaped on him before the man could try yanking on the bloody shaft—a dangerous proposition with sinew-tied arrow points. An officer bawled for two men to take the soldier down the knoll, ordering them to have a surgeon see if the arrow had embedded itself in bone or not. Clumsily rising out of the snow and into the arms of his fellows, the wounded man limped between two comrades, heading for Dr. Tilton's improvised hospital there among the squared wagons of the supply train.

By now Lieutenant Carter's men were all back across the ice to the east side of the Tongue, moving up the slippery bank in single file, while some turned and stood watch to make sure no warriors darting back and forth on the west side of the river got close enough to take a shot. Minutes before, Miles had ordered K Company to rejoin the regiment on the east bank now that the warriors were concentrating along the bluffs to the south. The colonel stationed Carter's gallant men in the exposed position in the river bottom, where they would protect the west flank of the supply train.

"Major Casey?" Miles called out, using the captain's brevet rank.

The officer stepped forward and saluted. "Your orders, General?"

Miles pointed to the tallest point of the ridge with that short peeled shaft of cottonwood. "You see that cone, Major?"

"Yes, sir. High ground if ever I saw it."

"To take the top would be a tough climb for the men, wouldn't it?"

"Yes, it would be, General."

"Those slopes are crawling with Sioux," Miles explained, not taking his eyes off the butte.

Casey straightened his back like a ramrod. "General—if

it's to be done, I request the honor of leading A Company into the attack."

Miles turned now to look at the captain. "A Company it will be, Major. Push as far up the side as is humanly possible. It's up to you to take some of the pressure off our gun emplacements."

"Very good, General! With your compliments," Casey replied, moved back one step and saluted as he slapped his heels together.

Miles and the rest watched the captain hurry off to gather his officers, who then formed up their men at the top of the knoll and quickly told them of the task at hand. The sky was continuing to lower minute by minute as the clouds scudded out of the west, and the wind was coming up as Casey eagerly moved out at the head of A Company. Their neat formation quickly became a ragged square as the sixty-some men pushed around the base of the high knoll and onto the long, narrow neck of the plateau that gradually rose toward the cone.

Of a sudden Casey and his officers stopped, whirled about, and cried out in warning.

As a group the entire company dropped to their knees, hunched over as the arrows began to whisper down among them. Miraculously no man was seriously hurt as the officers carefully peered up from beneath their sealskin caps, rising immediately to order the men to their feet again. Every one of them yanked the arrows from a man next to him, the iron points barely penetrating the thick buffalo-hide coats and layers of wool. Some men had been grazed, scratched, or poked—but none complained of serious wounds as Casey bawled for them to strike out again.

In those long, thick, heavy buffalo-hide coats and leggings the men of A Company lumbered on across the uneven, broken ground and slick snow, that shifting square of soldiers crawling forward at an insect's pace like some dark many-legged creature inching over the clumps of sage and crusty snowdrifts.

Again the officers sang out as the arrows arched into the air, calling for the men to halt and hunker there at the base of the butte where the slope began to rise more sharply. Just above them more warriors clustered suddenly, yelling, taunting, shaking their weapons in the falling snow. A few knelt to take aim with their carbines.

Half sliding, half falling to one side as he struggled back to his feet, an angry Casey bellowed the order for his first ranks to fire a volley up the side.

A dozen men stepped forward by rank and closed file.

"Sergeant! Fire on those Indians! Push those red buggers back!"

"Clear that slope of the bastards!" an old noncom hollered as he waved the next rank up to fire their volley.

Waving his pistol over his head, Casey repeated, "Sweep that slope clean of the bloody demons!"

Slowly, three short paces at a time, the warriors fell back and A Company continued to move forward a foot at a time. Men stumbled, spilled, sprawled across the sharp slope, then pulled themselves out of the snow clumsily in their heavy winter gear. Throwing open the trapdoors on the Springfields the best they could with their bulky mittens, more often than not each soldier spilled at least one or sometimes two .45/70 cartridges into the deep snow before they got a fresh round chambered and the trapdoor locked down.

On the heights the racket of cries and shrieks and taunts grew in volume. For the first time that morning the warriors recognized that the Bear Coat was not just defending his position but was instead beginning to take the offensive. Shouts of derision and dismay were hurled down on the soldiers, no matter where they were on that battlefield.

"Lieutenant Bailey!" Miles cried out as soon as Casey moved his company away from the knoll and began their ascent.

"Sir!"

"My compliments to Captain Butler. Tell him he is to bring his company and McDonald's D up to this knoll."

"Yessir."

Miles lunged out with his arm, staying the young aide-de-camp. "Tell the captain that together they will be replacing Major Casey's A Company protecting these heights."

"Very good, General."

"Go!"

Seeing the young officer on his way, Miles turned, as in afterthought, staring to the northwest, gazing down into the

bivouac area they had abandoned not all that long ago at first
light. "Kelly, Donegan!"

Both of the scouts trudged over as the snow began to fall
a little thicker, and the wind cut a little crueler as it blustered
across that high ground.

"I've called up those two companies from down in the
bottom. Which means we're going to be short of a rear guard
if I don't do something, fellas," Miles said quietly when the
two civilians had reached his side.

"I'm afraid I don't understand," Kelly replied.

Miles looked into Donegan's face now. "Tell me what you
think, you old horse soldier. Wouldn't cavalry play havoc with
my rear?"

"Soft on the backside the way it's going to be—bleeming
right they would, General."

"Just what I was thinking," Miles grumbled, then slapped
the peeled branch across his other palm again and again as he
struggled with it. "All right, I'll dispatch a company over to
that high ground across the river, to the north—there."

Donegan followed where he was pointing, then nodded in
approval. "Very good, sir: no horsemen would dare charge
through that throat of land if you can put some riflemen on
the front part of that ridge."

"Exactly! I'll seal up my back door and protect my rear!"
Miles exclaimed with satisfaction as he turned quickly to
watch Adjutant Baird urging his mount back up the short
slope of the plateau. "No need to dismount, Lieutenant."

"Sir?"

"Another ride—this time to Lieutenant Cusick detailed
down with the wagons. Tell him I need his F Company to take
their entrenching tools from the supply train, ford the ice, and
dig themselves some rifle pits on the front slope of that ridge
over there."

Baird looked in the direction Miles pointed the stick.
"Across the river. Dig rifle pits on the front of that near slope.
Understood, sir."

He snagged hold of the adjutant's reins and stepped up to
the lieutenant's knee. "And tell Cusick that his men must burrow in and not let anything cross the river," Miles empha-
sized. "They are protecting . . . Tell the lieutenant that F
Company is all we have for a rear guard now."

Baird blinked, then saluted as his horse sidestepped nervously, jerking the reins away from Miles. Its ears stiffened, eyes wide with all the shrill whistling and the crackle of gunfire, sensing the tenseness of its rider. "Yes, General. Cusick's men are now our only rear guard."

"On the double, Lieutenant!"

"I'll tell him, sir. On the double!"

Donegan watched the young adjutant yank the reins to the side, wheeling his horse around to spur it away, down the side of the plateau, kicking up balls of snow and clods of red earth. Near the supply train Baird reined up and began relaying his orders to those soldiers of the Twenty-second Infantry. A few of them turned, glanced up the slope at the knoll where Miles stood, then wheeled again to dive into the supply wagons, where they pulled out the leather scabbards containing their eight-by-three-inch steel entrenchment tools. No shovels for the work at hand.

As he watched a moment more, Seamus said a little prayer for those foot soldiers who had their work cut out for them. Not only would they have to hack rifle pits out of some frozen, rocky, sandstone-encrusted soil . . . but they would have to cover their own backsides while they accomplished it.

Alone on the far side of the river, F Company would now be expected to protect a vulnerable rear flank.

Chapter 31

8 January 1877

When Casey's men hit the steepest of the snowy slopes right below the tall butte itself, it was immediately clear to everyone watching that those soldiers would never make it to the top of the cone.

Not in those bulky buffalo coats and leggings, they weren't. Not on that slippery ice. And not with the legions of warriors doing everything in their power to make as much trouble as they could for the soldiers below.

A bullet smashed into a wheel on the Napoleon gun carriage, sending splinters over the Irishman and the chief of scouts.

"Kelly!" Miles hollered. "You and Donegan—front and center!"

Loping to a stop before the colonel, Seamus could see that Miles's red face glowed from more than the bitter cold.

"Casey's going to get himself bogged down," the colonel growled, clearly impatient with his inability to drive the warriors back.

Donegan declared, "If he ain't already stopped dead in his tracks, General."

He glared right into the Irishman. "I hired you on to

guide for Kelly—and scouting is all I ever expected you to do, Mr. Donegan."

But just the way the colonel had said it made Donegan think there was a bit more on his mind. "If you've got something what itches you, better you scratch it here and now."

Miles cleared his throat. "You feel like taking a ride up to Major Casey?"

Seamus licked his cracked lips. "To tell him what?"

"Move him south along the base of the ridge."

Gazing across that six hundred yards or more, Donegan asked, "How far, General?"

For a moment Miles held the field glasses on the slopes of the jagged ridgeline that extended south by east from the knoll and ran all the way past that tall cone. He turned back to Donegan. "I want him to push along the side of those buttes until he gets himself past that high pointed one."

"There's no mistaking it, General," Kelly observed.

"Until he gets past that big one," Seamus repeated the order. "All right."

In the colonel's eyes shimmered deep appreciation. "You'll go?"

Seamus looked at the other civilian. "Unless Kelly wants to ride."

"Have at 'er, you ol' horse soldier," Kelly cheered.

"And one other thing, Donegan," Miles interrupted, suddenly snagging the Irishman's arm. "Tell him I'll have support coming his way."

"Who, General?"

"Major Butler's company."

Seamus nodded. "Butler—good."

"And McDonald too," Miles said with finality. "You tell Casey I'm sending him all that support so he'll have every chance to press his attack there where the enemy is gathering in their greatest numbers."

"A battalion ought to make the major happy," Donegan replied.

"Another hundred men ought to help him drive those red buggers off the heights, for good!" Miles roared.

In his clumsy buffalo-hide overshoes, Seamus had all he could do to keep his footing as he trotted along the shallow slope of the plateau toward the supply train where the stock was corralled when he suddenly became aware of just what he was setting off to do. More than that, it struck him what task Casey's men—along with those of Butler and McDonald—now had staring them in the eye.

Reaching the horses, he quickly snatched up the reins to Miles's own big animal, led it away from the rest, then stuffed his buffalo-hide-wrapped boot into the hooded stirrup with no room to spare. Rising quickly, Seamus settled uneasily upon the McClellan saddle, memories washing back over him of past days, past battles fought from a McClellan.

He grumbled a little under his breath as the horse side-stepped beneath a strange rider, trying to find a good place for his tailbone. Pushing back against the cantle, he shoved down on the stirrups as the horse twisted its head nervously, aware that this was not to be an ordinary ride.

"Easy, fella," Donegan cooed, leaning forward against the animal's ear.

At least the stirrups felt long enough for what short ride he figured to make of it. He didn't plan on having his butt banging that ungodly cavalry saddle seat for very long either. He'd ride flat out if the horse was up to it, through the snow and the bullets, taking the weight of it all in his knees, leaning out over the animal's withers.

"Hep, hep-a!" he urged, kicking the horse in the flanks, moving it out of the corral, where two companies of soldiers had forted up with the wagons.

Raising himself off the saddle, Seamus eased the animal into a lope, working up into a gallop with a little more urging. It seemed eager to run, perhaps eager to gallop if only to get away from the mules and the clatter around the supply train, to be unfettered.

That roar off to his right was the Rodman gun. Pope must be putting his gun crew back to work, perhaps this time to soften up the snowy heights before Casey and the rest went in afoot. Good thinking that was.

But far ahead, low on those slopes, he watched as the black smears became figures, and the figures became men struggling through the snow: slipping, falling down, struggling back up on their hands and knees, attempting to fire a round now and again every few yards they gained.

What if Miles's offensive did not work? What if Casey and

the rest got bogged down in the snow below those cliffs—trapped the way Captain Alex Moore's men had been trapped on the Powder River last winter*—caught there like sitting ducks, where the warriors would have a field day with them before Casey could withdraw, leading what men he had left still alive? What then?

To fort up with the wagons?

What chance did they stand doing that? Not with this outfit already short on rations . . . not here in the dead of winter with the thermometer reluctant to rise anywhere close to zero. If Casey's offensive failed, then that's exactly what they'd have to do: retreat and fort up. Every man waiting to freeze to death, to starve, or to be picked off by a tightening noose of Sioux and Cheyenne.

What ghost of a chance would any of these men have of making it back to the mouth of the Tongue River alive if this offensive of Casey's failed?

The heights still bristled with Indians, hundreds of them—all parading back and forth, yelling, blowing their whistles, hurling arrows down among the soldiers.

Every soldier had hoped the two guns would frighten and demoralize the warriors. In the past, artillery had always been successful in accomplishing that. It took the fighting steam right out of the warrior, confused him, and sometimes broke his spirit, his willingness to press on.

But today—that three-inch Rodman and the twelve-pounder simply weren't accomplishing much of anything beyond making a lot of noise and kicking up a lot of snow when the shells sailed on over the ridgetops. The Indians were still on the heights, and it seemed as if there were more of them than before.

Especially the closer to the base of the buttes he got with Miles's horse.

Into the back of Casey's A Company Seamus slowed, swinging out of the saddle even before the horse came to a complete stop. "Major Casey!"

"Here!"

"Donegan—company of scouts!"

The major was close enough now that he started to salute,

* *Blood Song*, vol. 8, The Plainsmen Series.

then instead held his hand out to the Irishman. He anxiously looked out on Donegan's backtrail across that gently rising, open ground as if expecting more than just one lone man.

Casey swallowed hard. "You've come to help?"

Seamus quickly looked left and right at the soldiers, old and young, as they peered at him expectantly. Their cheeks were rosy—a few already frostbitten, gone milky white. Most eyes bloodshot from lack of sleep. What eyes weren't filled with fear were filled with questions.

"I have come to help," Seamus answered, dragging a mitten under a runny nose. "The general sent me with word."

Casey grinned, his eyes coming alive as he cheered, "We're to pull back off this godforsaken slope?"

"I'm afraid not, Major."

Over the grumbling of the soldiers in the background, Donegan went on to explain what Miles wanted A Company to do in traversing the side of the slope.

"Back there," Seamus said, turning—finding the soldiers coming—pointing at them. "Take a look. That's Butler's company. And McDonald must be right behind him."

"Butler and McDonald?"

"Yes, Major. They're coming up to give you the strength it will take to hold the base of this ridge."

Casey wagged his head. "Don't you mean the strength I need to *take* the ridge and drive off the enemy?"

In that instant Seamus looked up at the top of the bluffs, saw the odds staring down at them . . . and suddenly realized that there was no better place to be than at the center of the action. If he failed here, it would be a quick death. Better than having to retreat, fort up, and die of starvation, or freeze to death.

There was but one choice now.

Donegan looped the reins over the front of the McClellan, then slapped the colonel's horse on the flank twice to send it on its way. He watched a moment more, the muffled hoofbeats carrying it down the long slope onto the gentle descent of land that stretched toward the river, the corral, and other animals. The big stallion knew where it was going.

He turned back to the officer.

"I'm with you, Major Casey—no matter what now. But I

gotta tell you: I don't think we're ever going to get your men up this ridge."

The soldier's eyes narrowed on Donegan, then peered over the scout's shoulder at those two oncoming companies who would bolster his command. "We're soldiers, Mr. Donegan. So we'll do what the general orders."

Seamus's eyes smarted as he said, "Very good, Major."

"You're the one I heard was a sergeant in the Second Cavalry during the Rebellion? Army of the Potomac?"

"Yes—but that was a long time ago."

"I've always figured a soldier once, a soldier you'll always be, Mr. Donegan." Casey tapped the Winchester, then gazed into the Irishman's eyes. "You any good with that repeater?"

"Fair enough."

"You feel like leading out this morning, Sergeant Donegan?"

Seamus took a deep breath, looking along the slope they would be traversing, sage and cedar puffing out of the deep snow, broken ground cut by a hundred erosion scars. "When it comes time to charge, there's no better place to be than at the point, Major."

"Very good. Sergeant! Form up the men and follow the scout. I'll wager he'll see us through this cakewalk if anyone can."

The young sergeant nodded. "Lead on, Mr. Donegan."

Starting away on foot, cutting sharply to the left, Seamus heard Casey barking orders to the men who were following him into hell. After ten yards the first snow kicked up in front of him as a bullet thudded into the frozen ground with a muffled thump. Donegan quickly glanced over his shoulder—finding the men with Butler and McDonald double-timing it now. Casey was waving them on as his own A Company trudged past the captain in the deep snow that had drifted to at least three feet in places with the incessant wind.

Overhead the sky continued lowering, clouds beginning to hover right over the heights where the warriors leaped back and forth, taunting the soldiers. Seamus was getting close enough to see that they had started several fires up there on the top of the ridge, black smudges of smoke slowly rising into the heavy air as the snow continued to come down all the harder. Several warriors hunkered around each fire, warming hands and feet, then rose to return to the firing line.

Behind him Seamus heard the soldiers grunting, laboring, struggling as much as he in the cold, dry air. One of his buffalo moccasins slipped. Donegan went down hard. His knee cried out in pain. Standing the repeater under him, he got back to his feet painfully and quickly rubbed the knee.

"You think we got us a chance at this?"

Turning, Seamus found an old corporal at his shoulder. "As much a chance as we can make of it."

The graybeard grinned a moment. "That's the spirit. Something these young sprouts don't have. You was cavalry, they say?"

"Yep." They set off again in front of the skirmish line.

"I was foot. I fit all the way from Manassas to Appomattox Wood. Always been foot." Then the old corporal turned aside to help one of the other men struggle back to his feet in the clumsy leggings and rubber-coated arctic boots. "Union man, I take it."

"Right again."

"I seen worse'n this, mister," the old soldier sighed. "Atlanta. Now, that was a seige."

"Atlanta," Seamus huffed, having heard all the stories. His chest was starting to burn as they struggled their way along the jagged face of the ridge.

"Right up under their goddamned gun walls," the soldier continued. "So close we could hear their gun crews talking that Johnny talk. Day after goddamned day, never knowing what day it would be my turn to get blown asshole from cockbag with their canister and grape. So we just huddled in there and some of the boys did a little praying too. Best thing to do until they ordered us to move out. A little praying."

"It help?" Seamus asked, hoping.

After a moment of raspy breathing the old soldier admitted, "No. Them what prayed got blowed to brains and bone just the same as the rest of us. It . . . it was like God wasn't on duty them days of war. Not for four goddamned long, bloody years . . . God wasn't listening to no man's prayers. So I give up praying. No one was listening anyhow."

Bullets slapped off the snowy tops of some loose sandstone shale nearby, ricocheting with a whine.

"Now might be a fine time for you to try again," Seamus suggested.

The old soldier grabbed his elbow suddenly, looked into Donegan's eyes, and quickly licked his tobacco-stained lower lip with a leathery-looking tongue. "I just might do that, stranger. Just might see if God's back on duty for us ol' soldiers . . . like you an' me."

Minutes ago Wooden Leg had spotted his sister among the rest of the captives as they'd been herded away from the soldiers' camp and brought to the base of the low plateau where the Bear Coat had uncovered his two wagon guns.

His heart leaped.

At least the *ve-ho-e* hadn't killed them the moment this fight had started. Such had been Wooden Leg's greatest fear.

But his second-greatest fear was that once the warriors had the soldiers completely surrounded and under siege, the white men would use the women and children to bargain with—perhaps even kill right before the warriors' eyes as the red hoop grew tighter and tighter around the Bear Coat's men.

"Wooden Leg!" Black Hawk yelled. "Come with us! We're following Big Crow to the top of the ridge to the east!"

He looked over Black Hawk's shoulder, in the direction where more and more warriors were flowing now as some gray, dull light seeped along the edges of that cold dawn sky. "I want to stay where I can watch Crooked Nose Woman."

Yellow Weasel loped up to say, "You can do nothing here!"

Wooden Leg felt frantic, watching the way the soldiers ducked the incoming flights of arrows, the way a stray bullet now and then sang off the iron of the wagon guns, splintered a wheel, how his sister huddled her body over that of a child with each new volley from the attacking warriors. How he wished that they could rush down and rescue the captives . . . wishing at least that he could stand before the hundreds of other warriors and convince them that their arrows and bullets might well kill the women and children.

He cried, "Do you see how we are endangering our own people? I must find a way to slip in there and—"

"The best that you can do to help your sister is to fight with us this day," Black Hawk replied with an edge to his words, sounding as one would correct a younger brother. "Crooked Nose Woman knows you are a warrior, that you will be fighting to free her and the others. There is nothing to be done here."

Yellow Weasel said, "Look, Wooden Leg! See how the soldiers are starting to walk along the bottom of the hill. Let's follow Big Crow and the rest to stop them from slipping around behind us!"

At that moment the *Tse-tsehese* war chief named Big Crow stopped and turned so suddenly that the long feathered trailer on his warbonnet slurred across the crusty snow like a sidewinder snake.

"*Ohmeseheso!*" he shouted. "Maybe we can even circle behind them!"

Beaver Claws cried out, "And sneak up behind those *ve-ho-e* in their silly buffalo coats and leggings!"

"I would like to kill some soldiers today!" Wooden Leg admitted with a roar. "They took my sister, and the little ones—and now they deserve to die!"

"Quick or slow, it does not matter to me!" boasted Wolf Tooth. "Just as long as we spill *ve-ho-e* blood!"

"Hurry, *Tse-tsehese!*" squalled Big Crow. "We must be over there on top of that ridge before the soldiers ever get close to the foot of Belly Butte!"

"Look!" warned Left-Handed Wolf. "Even more *ve-ho-e* are coming!"

Wooden Leg turned to peer down into the valley, his eyes narrowing with unmitigated hate. "Have faith, Uncle! No matter how many the Bear Coat sends against us—not one of the soldiers will reach the top of these hills alive!"

Chapter 32

8 January 1877

"Captain Butler!" James Casey called out as the men of C Company struggled up behind their commander. "Good to have you pitch in with us!"

Edmond Butler saluted. "Looks like we've been handed the yeoman's work of it today, Major."

"I'll say," Casey replied, turning back to watch the last company approaching. "C'mon, Mr. McDonald—bring your doughboys up here so mine won't get all the fun!"

"Your . . . orders . . . Major?" Robert McDonald huffed as he lumbered to a halt a good twenty yards ahead of his D Company.

Casey slapped a hand against McDonald's shoulder, sending up a small eruption of dry snow collected on the buffalo fur. "Lieutenant, deploy your men in light skirmish order on my right."

"Yes, sir," McDonald responded. "How far to the right do you need us to deploy, Major?"

For a moment Casey studied the tall volcanic butte. "Hang your right flank in the air opposite that highest point."

"The bastards are spreading out clean across the high ground," Butler grumbled thick as peat as they watched Mc-

Donald move off, waving and ordering his men to the right of the increasingly rugged slope.

Donegan's ears immediately perked at the sound of that voice clearly come from the Emerald Isle. He started to inch his way over toward the ground where the two officers stood—getting himself a good, close look at the forty-nine-year-old Butler.

"And that means they're spreading us too damned thin to boot," Casey replied, turning back to Butler. Then he spoke quietly, almost in confidence. "Look, Captain—I've saved the toughest job for you. I know what you're capable of doing in the field. You see, if those reds keep massing on our left, they could damn well roll right around us."

"You want me on the left flank, Major?"

Casey nodded.

Butler straightened, his lips grim with determination as he said, "They won't get around us, sir. Count on that."

Casey stepped back, saluted. "Good to have your men in this with me."

"Very good, Major," Butler replied. "We all want a piece of it today."

"I've waited long enough myself," Casey declared. "Deploy your company, then send word back to me should you find any in your outfit running low on ammunition."

Edmond Butler turned away to shout his orders, commands echoed down the line through the lieutenant, and finally to the old noncoms, who did their best to keep the trembling soldiers lined up as they started across the broken ground, old files struggling to keep every man's spirits up despite the cold, despite the bulky clothing that hampered a man's movements, despite the arrows that strayed far enough to land among them in the snow.

By the time McDonald was deployed on Casey's right, and Butler had spread his men left toward the base of a high timbered knoll south of the steep volcanic butte, the entire front line of battle now extended for more than a thousand yards, a thin blue wall running from the Tongue River on the north, down along snowy ridges to the steep hillsides above Butler, where it seemed more and more of the warriors were beginning to flock.

From these heights the Cheyenne and Sioux could easily

rush down and sweep around behind Casey's entire battalion—all three companies—therein threatening the gun positions, the supply-wagon corral, even Nelson A. Miles's escape route north . . . back to the Tongue River Cantonment.

You're a bleeming fool! Seamus thought to himself as he started forward, easing over toward Butler's company. Miles was far from even considering a retreat. No matter that the soldiers were facing odds better than three to one. No matter that they were all but out of rations. Why even worry that they were more than a hundred miles from their base?

Miles simply wasn't the sort of man to tuck tail and run.

No matter that he might very well lose half his men, hurling them against these steep, icy slopes.

Back and forth the warriors danced in and out of the thickening snow along the ridgetops. Gray smoke hung heavy, sleepy, refusing to rise from the many fires the Indians fed. At times as the soldiers stumbled and trudged across the slowly rising ground from the meadow, the warriors would huddle around their fires for a few minutes, then return to the edge of the bluffs in rotation. But as soon as three companies reached the sharp-sided coulee cutting the base of the bluffs, all the warriors suddenly bristled atop the slopes together.

"How deep is that snow down there?" someone growled behind Donegan as the first of them reached the lip of the ravine.*

"Can't be much deeper'n any of this," Seamus said as he started easing himself over the side.

The racket from the hilltops was growing, as if those heavy snow clouds rolling in amplified the shrieks and screeching from the warriors.

"There water down there?" one of the soldiers asked, down on his hands and knees at the lip of the ravine as Donegan slid, stumbled to the bottom.

"How deep is it?" Casey asked, suddenly appearing at the edge of the ravine.

Overhead more bullets whined. Once more Seamus was thankful that the Indians were shooting downhill—which caused most of their shots to sail harmlessly over the soldiers.

Hammering down one of his boots encased inside the

* Present-day Battle Butte Creek.

thick buffalo-hide outer moccasin, Donegan found the snow deep enough to spread out the long tails of his buffalo coat as he sank up to his crotch.

" 'Bout this deep, Major!"

"Any water?"

Wagging his head, Seamus answered, "None—it's all froze. Bring 'em on!"

In a heartbeat Casey had turned his horse at the lip of the ravine above the Irishman, signaling, calling out, moving his men up through the sagebrush and tall grass that tripped the men, snagged the long tails of their heavy coats. As Donegan began to wade through the snow, inching across the narrow ravine bottom, then started to clamber his way up the far side, the soldiers dropped over the north side by the dozens. Sliding, slipping, spilling into the deep snow, standing once more to dust ice from their Long Tom Springfields, holding their rifles overhead to push ahead the way a man would wade through water in a waist-deep stream.

Hurtling themselves against the far side, most slipped more times than not against the ice-slickened, snowy side. Then Donegan was at the top, turning, crouching low as he barked down at those right below him.

"Use your rifle butts, fellas!" he called out to them, first to one side, then the other, along the ravine wall. "Jab yourself a foothold," and he started to pantomime in the air with his own Winchester. "Jab yourself some handholds in the side."

By the dozens they cocked their rifles back over their shoulders, lunging forward violently against the frozen ground, the rifle butts sinking into the hard, unforgiving Montana soil. Foot by foot by foot they carved tiny niches into the side of the ravine for their hands, for their frozen toes encased within the clumsy arctics they wore. Leaning down to offer an empty hand, Seamus pulled the first man over the top.

Then as the warriors above them screamed louder, that soldier turned round, his back to the enemy on the ridge, crouching down as bullets whined past them. He too pulled up another soldier. Two became four, and those four grew to eight, hands going down, men grunting, scrambling, slipping and falling, rising to climb again in those tiny footholds on the side of that dry-bottomed ravine. Sixteen became thirty-two.

Hands rose, gripped by hands coming down . . . hauling, straining, cursing their way out.

Then Casey and Butler were down in the snow, McDonald heaving himself over the side, tripping and sliding on his back to the bottom like a child on a wooden toboggan. A pair of soldiers helped the lieutenant to his feet, and together they wobbled to the far side—the last of the battalion to close the file.

Ten or more at a time these clambered up the side, pulled over the lip by their comrades as the shrieks from the hilltops grew more strident. The snow was growing thick as Casey snapped a look left and right.

"Form up! Form up!"

Officers and noncoms barked commands as the three companies deployed themselves once more. Every now and then a bullet sang among them, causing the soldiers to flinch, some to duck aside. A stray arrow might hiss into the snow and sage in front of them.

It made Seamus shudder as the battalion started forward again. Those arrows landing in front of them now meant one thing: in a matter of moments, in no more than a few steps, these soldiers would be within range of the enemy's deadliest weapons. They had reached the foot of the slopes that would carry them right into the arms of the enemy.

To be hit with a bullet was one thing, Donegan brooded as he lunged and stumbled clumsily through the deep, drifted snow while the earth tilted slowly toward the sky. Quick and clean a bullet was—and if it hit a bone, that arm or leg was sure to come off. Although he did remember how Major Sandy Forsyth had refused amputation after nine long, hot days on a sandy scut of ground in a nameless fork of a high-plains river.

Oh, how the sawbones were kept busy in the Civil War, he remembered—for there was simply no repairing such a wound. Just take the goddamned arm or leg off and heave it aside, into the pile of arms and legs, feet and hands, outside the surgeons' tent. Bloody butchers leaving all those poor men crippled.

But an arrow—how silent, how clean as it sank inside a man's chest, his back, and all the worse yet: his soft gut. Blood and juices softening the sinew that held the long iron point to

the painted shaft the warrior had grooved so that the victim
bled internally. And once the sinew was soft enough, the shaft
was easily yanked free of the deep wound, leaving the deadly
chunk of iron deep inside. A man died slow, miserably, tor-
tured.

Not the clean death of a bullet wound.

By the time he had stumbled and fallen, and somehow
trudged another twenty yards toward a low clump of cedar,
Donegan could almost begin to make out the painted faces
above them. Close enough to see eyes, and the bright paints,
close enough to tell feathers from hair as the wind came up
and the thickening snow began to dance.

This suddenly had the makings of no ordinary snowfall.
Now the heady gusts were whipping the falling flakes sideways,
spinning devilishly every which way at a man, blinding him
for a moment as the wind slipped past the eyeholes he had cut
himself in a scrap of wool blanket. Snow crusted on his eyelashes, hardening with the frost of his breath suddenly freezing
in the supercold air.

All around him Butler's soldiers would kneel, aim, and
fire up the slope at the blurring figures cavorting along the
ridgetops. After a shot or two the soldiers reluctantly rose
from the deepening snow, reloading and lunging forward another five yards until they would halt again, take aim, and fire
at the enemy.

The bullets, the screeching curses, the arrows arcing down
in wave after wave, were all coming thicker now. Just like the
snow. Off to the far right McDonald was leading his men
against the first of the sharp slopes at the base of the tall cone
itself. That part of the hillside rose more than twenty feet, then
flattened out onto a narrow shelf where there wasn't a single
cedar or oakbrush to conceal them from the enemy once they
made it that far.

If any of them reached that shelf, Donegan thought, Mc-
Donald's men would be in the open, right below the warriors.

Hell, Seamus thought as he watched Butler's men huff
and lunge coming up behind him, angling off to the left. None
of them had any cover worth a shit anyway. And every last one
of them stood out against the snow like a black-backed dung
beetle scurrying away from an overturned buffalo chip.

Halting to blow like a winded packhorse, Donegan

dropped to one knee and drank in the cold, dry air, watching the last of Butler's men move off to the south in a scattered, ragged skirmish line as he yanked off his mitten and plunged his right hand through the slit in the side of his buffalo-hide coat. There, in the side pocket of his canvas mackinaw coat, he had stuffed the short brass cartridges. Bringing out a handful into the numbing cold, Seamus shook and shuddered as he fed the bullets one at a time into the cold receiver. . . .

. . . Remembering the seventeen-shot Henry rifles he and Sam Marr had purchased at Fort Laramie ten winters gone. One chambered and sixteen down the loading tube. A rifle he first used against the Sioux that boiling hot July day beside the Crazy Woman Crossing.

Right now July seemed as if it would take forever to reach these rugged mountains and high plains. Right now . . . it seemed as if forever itself might well separate him from Fort Laramie, from the boy and Samantha.

Stuffing his stiff, frozen hand back into his mitten, Donegan found the tiny slit he had cut for his trigger finger so he could fire the Winchester without taking off the mitten and gauntlet. He rolled onto his other knee, then went to his belly, flattening the snow as he peered up the slope at the enemy. Three dozen or more stood up there right in front of him. And out before them all pranced a tall one wearing a long war shirt, a bright-red blanket tied at his waist to keep his legs warm, and on his head a beautiful full headdress, its long tail slurring the snow behind his heels.

"He must be some big medicine," Seamus said under his breath. "Look at that bleeming bastard go to town—all that cock-struttin'."

On either side of the war chief were arrayed more than three dozen others, all of them shouting, screeching, some singing along with the one in the showy warbonnet. Didn't take much to figure out that was a war chief up there, doing his best to keep his men worked up into a fighting lather.

Nuzzling his left elbow down into the snow, Seamus slowly settled his chest onto the ground and spread his legs for a surer stance, bringing the Winchester into his shoulder.

Cocky son of a bitch, isn't he? Wailing and dancing, preening, prancing, and strutting . . . just daring one of us to knock him down.

Uphill . . . aiming up that slope—Seamus realized he would have to hold high. How much? He calculated and cocked the hammer back . . . drawing a sight picture on the warrior's head. If he had figured right, Donegan thought as he let half the air out of his lungs, then the .44-caliber bullet should smack the war chief right in the chest.

After all—he began to squeeze the trigger—someone had to get rid of that noisy bastard.

The wagon guns had been quiet for so long that the next belching roar from the knoll below Crazy Horse surprised him. The mouth of the big gun spewed a heavy cloud of smoke as it belched the big round ball into air with a hissing whistle.

Up, up, up into the air, over the first lines of warriors arrayed along the lower slopes.

It floated overhead long enough that the warriors assembled across the end of the ridge had time to scurry out of the way, scampering this way and that as the whistling, tumbling ball careened out of the sky in a lazy arc. When it finally crashed to earth in a spot where no warriors tarried, the ball exploded in a mighty gush of noise, snow, and splintered sandstone.

As the scattered puffs of dirty gray snow and red-rock shards and black clods of dirt began to rain down from the sky, the warriors immediately danced back into view of the *wasicu* soldiers—yelling at them once more, taunting the white men, laughing at the enemy because their noisy wagon gun had done harm to nothing but some rocks and crusty snow.

The sight caused Crazy Horse to recall the wagon gun Grattan's soldiers had pulled out to Conquering Bear's village the day after a visiting Miniconjou had killed that stray Mormon cow. The haughty soldier chief came demanding the warrior who had stolen and butchered that skinny old cow. It was a shame that so many soldiers had to die over one decrepit animal. A far greater shame that so many Lakota had to die on the Blue Water when soldier chief Harney had come marching on the revenge trail.

Crazy Horse had been just a youngster back then. Many, many winters long gone now. Summers of fighting, autumns of hunting, winters of waiting for spring when young men thought of little else but getting themselves nestled between the downy thighs of a pretty girl.

For Crazy Horse these noisy wagon guns aroused many memories of a lifetime spent fighting to hold the *wasicu* back. Was there a place where he could go for the winter without the soldiers following? Would there ever be again a hunting ground where he could ride after the buffalo, skin and butcher it, build his fire and eat his meal, sleep out the night in peace—without worrying when the soldiers would come?

Painfully he squeezed those hard thoughts out of his mind the way a man would chew the gristle loose from the good meat, swallowing the soft red loin and tossing the rest into the fire.

For a time it was amusing to watch the frantic activity around the wagon guns with those knots of soldiers looking very much like tiny black ants swarming around a prairie ant-hill—the creatures crawling over one another, then suddenly leaping back as one of the *wasicus* leaned in to fire the big gun.

It roared again.

The ball came whistling from the great throat in a belch of blackish smoke, sent ever higher, climbing into the snowy clouds, where it pierced the thick veils, disappearing for a moment as it reached the top of its arc to begin its fall back to earth.

Crazy Horse's warriors scattered, some of them pulling their ponies out of the way now, for this ball had managed to sail right on over the top of the ridge. Men stumbled against one another and fell in the snow, getting out of the ball's path, ponies rearing and whinnying.

The whistling was suddenly silenced as the black iron sphere splooshed into the crusty snow and all but disappeared against a drift trampled by many moccasins and hooves. For a moment every mouth was hushed—only the frightened ponies snorted and pranced, eyes still saucered with horror and fear. Men stared at the ball. Watching. Waiting. Expectant.

Then Spotted Blackbird slowly crawled to his knees, rose to his feet, and circled the fire where he had been warming his hands. Dusting off the knees of his blanket leggings, the young warrior took a few tentative steps toward the half-buried ball. He stopped, then took a few more steps. Closer he went to the white man's whistling weapon-ball as the rest watched in stunned silence.

When he was finally no more than an arm's length from it, Spotted Blackbird pulled his bow from the quiver strapped at his back. Gently he tapped the ball and leaped back as if stung by a rattlesnake.

Many of the others gathered around him at a safe distance gasped, leaping back too.

But nothing happened.

Spotted Blackbird stepped closer once more. Then tapped the black ball again—harder than ever—and immediately dropped into a protective crouch.

When no explosion shook the ground, the warrior walked right up to the object and smacked it solidly with the end of his elkhorn bow.

Then he began to strike it repeatedly, shouting in glee, dancing around and around it as he hammered the ball with blows. The other warriors came up to touch it too—counting coup on it as Spotted Blackbird had been the first to do.

It was great fun . . . until they heard the next whistle above their laughter, that warning cry of the black balls coming from the far side of the ridge. Warriors scattered, dashing to the top of the bluff, watching the ball sail up through the lowering clouds, in and out of the dancing white of the wind-driven snowstorm. Again every one of them scattered, yanking ponies and pushing one another out of the way. Only a fool would think that all the white man's exploding balls would land harmlessly in the snow like so much sandstone or a river boulder.

With a hissing rush the ball sailed down, down —exploding in a blinding profusion of meteoric light, splintering rock and scattering red earth over those huddling nearby behind sandstone breastworks. The clatter of falling earth ended, and the warriors leaped to their feet, dusting the snow and dirt and rock chips from their clothing, shouting again to the *wasicu*, holding their genitals, pulling aside their breechclouts to wag their rumps at the soldiers.

"Hit me here!" one of the Shahiyela yelled at the white men below, patting the crack in his ample rear end.

Back and forth it would go like this, Crazy Horse believed.

The warriors would not budge, and the big whistling balls would not drive them from this ridge.

But over to his right . . . now, that was a different matter.

Over there the soldiers were climbing out of the ravine that for a time had slowed their advance considerably. They wore too many clothes, he thought. The soldiers looked as if they had no legs as they struggled through the deep snow. Just the tops of their bodies, draped with those big buffalo-hide coats, the tails of which spread out like a whorl of prairie-flower petals come spring to this rolling country. Almost like tiny lodge men. Soldiers who looked like lodges. No legs had they, but still the *wasicu* pushed on.

After so many summers of fighting, after all those battles, Crazy Horse could tell the leaders, the soldier war chiefs, gesturing and waving and shouting to the others, urging them on—marching even into the face of the withering fire from the Shahiyela on that far end of the ridge.

Quickly he glanced at the knoll to the north to be sure. No, the Bear Coat was still there with the wagon guns. Then Crazy Horse looked back to the south where the soldier chiefs led their men lumbering to the bottom of the steep slope. It was there that Big Crow and his Shahiyela fired bullets and arrows down at the white men.

These were very, very stupid soldiers, Crazy Horse thought as the *wasicu* shot their rifles up the far slope at the Shahiyela warriors, then reloaded to advance another few steps before shooting again. Like the crawl of black ants up the steep side of a prairie anthill.

Yes, he thought: these are very, very stupid soldiers.

That . . . or very, very brave men.

Chapter 33

Hoop and Stick Moon 1877

"Grandfather!" Medicine Bear had cried out to the old man last night as the hundreds of warriors had begun to stream out of the village into the dark, kicking their ponies north through the snow and the cold in a huge cavalcade toward the Bear Coat's soldiers who had camped near Belly Butte.

Coal Bear turned slowly on his spindly legs there before the Sacred Hat lodge, finding Box Elder's young spiritual apprentice hurrying toward him. "Medicine Bear! You are not going with all the others to fight the *ve-ho-e* come the dawn?"

"Yes," he huffed, breathless with excitement. "I am going with the others, but I want to fight the white men the same way we fought them in the valley of the Red Fork."

The old man nodded, sighing. "You carried powerful magic that day, my son."

His heart swelled with pride. "Yes, Grandfather," he said, using the term of respect for the older man who was Keeper of the Sacred Medicine Hat. "But Box Elder is too weak to ride so far in this cold. So I go to ride and fight for him."

"*Hopo!* This is a good and mighty thing you do," Coal Bear replied.

"You can help me," Medicine Bear pleaded, his mouth

dry with apprehension as he stared intently into the old shaman's eyes. "I want to carry *Nimhoyoh* into the fight with
me."

"The Sacred Turner?"

Medicine Bear could see the extreme worry cross the old
man's face.

"I carried it before—"

Coal Bear interrupted. "I remember. In the battle against
Three Finger Kenzie.* Yes, the Red Fork Canyon . . . when
you carried *Nimhoyoh* above the rest of us all and thereby
turned away the soldier bullets so we could escape with the
Sacred Hat into the mountains."

The youngster hurried on with his plea. "When the battle
begins at dawn, I wish to protect the many warriors the way I
helped protect a few in that terrible battle."

Coal Bear stared dispassionately at the young man for a
few moments, then said, "Come inside." He pulled back the
hide flap and hobbled into the lodge.

A fire still glowed, warm and welcoming. Coal Bear's
woman had her back to them, turning to watch the two men
enter. She nodded in recognition, then returned to her work at
packing their few possessions into the second of only two
small rawhide parfleches. After losing everything to the
soldiers in the Red Fork Valley, all they now owned belonged
to *Esevone*—the Sacred Medicine Hat of the *Ohmeseheso*. The
last of their blankets had been folded and tied, everything
made ready for the time when the woman would yank the
pins from the lodge cover, when she and others would quickly
dismantle this lodge that was the new home their people provided for *Esevone.*

Though small—not near as grand as had been the previous lodge transported across the high plains for countless winters until it was destroyed by the *Ho-nehe-taneo-o,* the Wolf
People,† in that terrible fight—this was nonetheless the first
lodge the *Tse-Tsehese* women had collected hides for, sewn
together, and cut in the proper shape when they began their
slow rebuilding among the Crazy Horse people. From one
hunt, then another, they acquired the hides until they had

* The Dull Knife Battle, *A Cold Day in Hell,* vol. 11, The Plainsmen Series.
† The North brothers' battalion of Pawnee scouts.

enough to erect this small lodge. Once more the Sacred Medicine Hat had a proper resting place—there at the back, opposite the door, sitting against *Nimhoyoh*.

It was the Sacred Turner that Medicine Bear immediately
cast his eyes upon now as he entered Coal Bear's dwelling.
Nimhoyoh, what he had been called upon to carry that terribly
cold day of blood on the snow that was still so fresh in their
memories.

Coal Bear said, "I see you are wearing Box Elder's powerful shirt."

Young Medicine Bear ran his hands down the front of the
fire-smoked elk-hide shirt the great blind shaman of the
Ohmeseheso had given him to wear. The four long legs of
the elk hide swayed back and forth below his knees. "He told
me that if I wore it, you could not fail to give me the Turner."

Coal Bear finally grinned. "The old man is a smart one."
He turned to gaze down at the sacred objects as the noise
outside the lodge grew loud: men shouting farewells to families, women sobbing and children crying, dogs howling and
ponies snorting. "Like Box Elder, I think I can trust you to
protect the great power of *Nimhoyoh*. With your own eyes you
have seen how its magic turned the soldiers' bullets. There is
no other reason why all of us escaped from the village with
our lives when all around us the soldiers and their scouts
darted here and there."

That bitterly cold dawn in the Big Freezing Moon, with
the first gunshot and at the first shout of warning, Box Elder
had clambered to his feet. For many winters already his vision
had been clouded. As his apprentice, Medicine Bear was the
old man's eyes. Together they had scrambled to seize the most
important object in Box Elder's life before they had abandoned the shaman's lodge and plunged into the madness of
the retreating village. In that screaming, fleeing crowd they
had somehow managed to find Coal Bear, with *Esevone*
wrapped in its special bundle and tied upon his woman's
back.

In the midst of that confusion and panic Coal Bear himself had been holding the Sacred Turner, both hands clutching
the round cherrywood stick about the length of a man's arm.
Suspended from the stick was a crude rectangle of buffalo
rawhide, the edges of which had first been perforated, then

braided with a long strand of rawhide. From three sides of
Nimhoyoh hung many long buffalo tails, tied to the rawhide
shield much like scalp locks.

"Give the Turner to Medicine Bear!" Box Elder had ordered that morning when the greatness of their people had
turned to blood on the snow. "So that he might carry it above
him on his pony to turn away the soldier bullets!"

As instructed, the Medicine Hat Priest gave the heavy object to Box Elder's young apprentice so Medicine Bear could
ride behind them all on his skittish pony, holding aloft
Nimhoyoh, waving the thick hide of the Sacred Turner and its
long black buffalo tails back and forth to ward off the enemy's
bullets that kicked up snow and dirt from the ground at their
feet, knocking twigs and splinters from the trees all about
them until they reached the open valley.

Turning his sightless eyes to Medicine Bear, Box Elder had
said in a strong voice, "The powerful medicine of *Nimhoyoh*
you carry turns away all the bullets flying around us. Do not
be afraid!"

Nor would Medicine Bear be afraid now. He had seen for
himself the power of *Nimhoyoh*—how it turned the soldier
bullets to puffs of dust, nothing more than air.

Now this night Coal Bear turned and handed the long
cherrywood pole to the young apprentice and said, "Take this.
And with it protect our warriors."

Medicine Bear rubbed his hands around the cherrywood
handle, thinking quickly on the many generations who had
held this sacred object of such great and awesome power.
"Through its magic I will protect our warriors," he vowed.
"So that those warriors can protect all the *Ohmeseheso*."

Through the cold fog of dawn Medicine Bear rode, far
behind the first who had hurried from the village as the storm
clouds rolled in to cover the late rising of the moon. It was not
a hard thing to follow the trail of the others—the way was
wide and deep through the snow.

Just past the coming of day's gray light he heard the first
shots fired to the north. By the time Medicine Bear reached
the hills west of the river, he looked down to watch the
soldiers driving back the last of the warriors into the ravines
across the Tongue from the knoll where the *ve-ho-e* stood
around their wagon guns. With the warriors' retreat that band

of soldiers themselves withdrew across the river to rejoin the other white men.

But just when Medicine Bear had decided to cross the river himself to join those warriors flooding to the tops of the bluffs, many of the *Tse-Tsehese* fighting men came out of the coulees and brushy draws, drawn to the apprentice who held the Sacred Turner above his head.

"See!" Beaver Dam cried to the others, waving them on. "Do not run!"

"*Nimhoyoh!*" shouted Crow Necklace.

More and more painted faces appeared from the brush in the ravines. A large circle of warriors crowded around Medicine Bear's snorting pony.

"The Turner will protect us!"

"Attack the soldiers now!" Gypsum called.

"No," warned Brave Wolf, an older warrior. "What we must do is circle around behind the soldiers."

"Yes, go upriver," High Wolf agreed. "Then cross and come in behind the soldiers to free our people from them."

"Seize their wagons!"

"Steal their horses!"

"No bullets can harm us when we fight under the power of *Nimhoyoh!*"

By the time the warriors rounded up their ponies and set off through the deep snow, spreading out to follow Medicine Bear like the point of a great arrow, they emerged around the river bend to discover that soldiers already occupied the top of a low line of hills on the west bank of the river.

"What are they doing?" Spotted Blackbird shrieked in dismay.

Like the others, Medicine Bear stared into the distance, studying the actions of the white men.

"Are they digging?" someone asked.

"Like a fox at its burrow!" was the answer.

Indeed, it appeared that the soldiers were hurriedly digging rifle pits for themselves atop that bluff—entrenching all the faster once the warriors came into view.

An older man named Long Jaw placed a hand on Medicine Bear's forearm. "This is Box Elder's shirt."

"Yes," he answered. "My Grandfather gave it to me to wear into battle this day."

Long Jaw smiled at the apprentice. "It is good, Medicine Bear. You must lead us into this fight. Hold *Nimhoyoh* high over our heads so no bullets will touch us! So we can root these soldiers out like voles from their burrows!"

With a mighty yell from a hundred throats the *Ohmeseheso* charge began. In the van rode Medicine Bear, kicking his pony violently through the deep snowdrifts to keep it in front of the rest—mostly veteran warriors who carried many scars of countless battles against the *ve-ho-e* and other enemies.

Oh, how great was the honor of leading these men into battle!

He turned at the sudden shrill, high-pitched whistle, a foreign sound. Looking into the cloudy sky, Medicine Bear tried to find the cause of that strange noise. Then he saw it. A ball fired from the white man's wagon gun.

Sailing over the ranks of the warriors, the sphere crashed into that open ground between the horsemen and the soldiers entrenching among the red shale on the hilltop. Rocks and snow and shards of iron splintered into the cold morning air. Back tumbled the ponies and warriors, men crying out and horses whimpering in shock. Riderless horses bolted away. Men crawled on their knees, dragging themselves out of the snow. Everyone else milled aimlessly, some of them dazed.

Their charge was broken!

"Go! Go, Medicine Bear!" Long Jaw goaded, pointing to the slope of the nearby hill where the soldiers began to plop to their bellies, their rifles at ready. "Lead us now before the wagon gun shoots again!"

Swallowing down that first flush of fear, telling himself that no harm could come to him with the power of the Turner watching over them all, Medicine Bear did as he was instructed.

Wheeling the frightened pony in a circle, he yelped like a wolf, howling to give himself courage as he set off in front of the others. In that instant the others threw off the confusing mantle of shock and tore off again on horseback or on foot. A wide massed front of warriors followed the Turner onto that open ground that would lead them to the base of the soldiers' hill.

Right on over the shallow cannonball crater he leaped his

pony, paying it no heed as the soldier rifles opened up on them.

Back and forth he waved *Nimhoyoh,* giving its protection first to one side of the warrior formation, then to the other. Exactly as he had done in the battle against Three Finger Kenzie's pony soldiers. What he held in his hands at this moment was the sort of power that made the *Tse-Tsehese* a great people!

Power to turn soldier bullets away from the warriors who would sweep around behind the *ve-ho-e* camp, rescue the prisoners, then gallop over the last of the Bear Coat's soldiers.

Snarling wasps began to strike the ground all around him and the others at the front—soldier bullets. On through the middle of that hail charged the warriors who would protect the *Ohmeseheso!*

Suddenly Medicine Bear heard the smack of a bullet striking flesh and cracking bone. A warrior at his left hand pitched backward.

This could not be!

With his heart rising in his throat, Medicine Bear feared he had not done all he could to protect these fighting men. Back and forth more violently he waved the Turner.

Another horseman whirled off the back of his pony. And a third—barely hanging on, wavering atop his frightened animal.

All around him the once-mighty charge started to falter, men twisting to look at Medicine Bear, looking too at Long Jaw riding beside *Nimhoyoh.*

"Ride over them, Medicine Bear!" the older warrior shouted, his words without fear. "Ride right over the soldiers!"

"We have the power!" Brave Wolf hollered at his other elbow.

With renewed strength the warriors screamed their war cries. Those who had rifles, mostly soldier weapons captured at the Little Sheep River last summer, fired them. Those with bows had to wait to draw closer before they could shoot—close enough to see the fear on the faces of those soldiers hiding behind the chunks of red shale in their burrows.

But the closer they raced toward the *ve-ho-e,* the more bullets fell among the *Ohmeseheso.* Another man was struck.

He cried out. Faces once filled with confidence, eyes once filled with complete trust—now they turned to see if they had been abandoned by *Nimhoyoh*, if Medicine Bear had deserted them.

Worse than bullets, confusion and doubt struck them all. The Sacred Turner was still there above them, yet the soldier bullets were not turned to air. Ponies and men cried out each time one of them was struck with bullets that were supposed to become harmless.

Again the big wagon gun across the river belched its mighty roar. A whistle drew closer, and closer, and closer—and suddenly Medicine Bear knew it was coming for him.

Closer and closer! Falling right out of the sky . . .

He was turning his pony savagely to the right when the ball struck the animal on the left rear flank.

Pitched off as the pony careened to the side, Medicine Bear landed among the feet of other milling, frightened animals. Scrambling to his hands and knees, he crawled forward to snatch up *Nimhoyoh* again. Then turned, finding his pony struggling back onto its legs, by some miracle managing to shake off the great blow as a dog would shake water from its back.

Leaping to his feet among the confusion as the warriors turned back on themselves, Medicine Bear lunged for the single rawhide rein, caught it, and brought the animal close, cooing into its ear to calm it as bullets snarled past.

Only a few old veterans pressed on with the charge against the hillside now.

Another shot might come from the wagon gun at any moment. Better to withdraw—some were shouting—better to cross the river and join the others on the ridgetops.

Gently he ran his hand over the wound on the pony's flank: the hair rubbed cleanly off in a path as wide as his outstretched fingers and palm, from the top of the flank down the animal's thigh. The flesh had turned raw and angry, but as smooth as if Medicine Bear had shaved it with a sharp knife.

Closing his eyes, he tried hard to remember Coal Bear's prayer that freezing day in the Red Fork Valley. He must give thanks to the Powers because *Nimhoyoh* had just saved him and the pony. The powerful ball from the white man's wagon gun had not exploded.

Yet the warriors were retreating. They were not staying with Medicine Bear to defeat this band of soldiers, to sweep on across the river and around behind the Bear Coat's wagon camp.

Then Medicine Bear realized he had been spared. For some reason the Powers had spared his life. And he knew he must follow the rest of the warriors across the Tongue, carrying the power of *Nimhoyoh* into the fight on the far side of the river. And if need be—give his own life to protect the *Ohmeseheso*.

Closing his eyes, he suddenly remembered Coal Bear's prayer, uttered that freezing day in the Red Fork Valley as the greatness of the People went up in oily smoke.

Now it would become Medicine Bear's prayer. The life of one man mattered little when the life of the *Ohmeseheso* was at stake. Today was the day on which the People turned. If they failed in battle this day, then the *Ohmeseheso* were finished as a great people.

Crying aloud as the soldier bullets landed harmlessly all around him and the pony, Medicine Bear repeated Coal Bear's prayer: "Hear me, *Ma-heo-o!* Save my people! If you must take someone—take me, I pray you! But save my people!"

Chapter 34

8 January 1877

With every shot he took at the Indian, Donegan grew more certain that war chief up there led a most charmed life.

The way he danced and cavorted on the hilltop, what with all the bullets kicking up skiffs of snow, lead smacking off the rocky ledges behind him, sprays of dirt and sandstone puffing into the stiff breeze—and not one soldier able to drop the red son of a bitch.

He had seen bravery like this only a few times before in his decade in the far west—as recent as Mackenzie's fight with the Dull Knife Cheyenne. Twice warriors had come out of hiding, each dressed in their finest bonnets as they steered their ponies back and forth in front of the soldier lines: taunting, teasing, making the soldiers look the fools with their poor shooting. Nevertheless, on that cold day in hell some soldier or one of the scouts had done in the first daring warrior. And eventually the second toppled as well.

Still, for a time there back on that November day, Seamus had wondered if there truly was something to this thing of a warrior's magic. Exactly the way he was beginning to feel again down in the gnawing pit of his all but empty belly. What little hard biscuit and half-cooked bacon he had shoved down before the shooting began did him little good now after all the exertion and strain of slogging through knee-deep snow in heavy winter clothing.

Up and down the loose skirmish line formed by Butler's men the soldiers hollered to one another, exhorting their comrades to take their best shot at the prancing, preening, strutting cock-of-the-walk who leered at them from above, daring them all to shoot him.

But none of them could.

The first seconds and those first volleys were long-ago history now. It wasn't only that war chief in his big bonnet, but several others who jumped up and down on either side of him across the top of the same hill—showing themselves only long enough to take a shot at the soldiers advancing no faster than a snail's crawl. Then the riflemen in those rocks would duck back down behind their breastworks once more as the bullets smacked and zinged and whined around them. Up and down, up and down, up and down like the working of some steam piston on a locomotive. Never in the same place. Never the same warriors. No telling how many were up there the way they all dodged and zigged, twisted and zagged. There could be twenty. Or there could easily be as many as a hundred just right above the soldiers' heads.

Yet for all their gyrations, one thing was for sure. Unlike all the rest, that war chief in the big, showy bonnet wasn't ducking out of sight behind the breastworks the others had piled up in the snow. Instead, he stayed in full view, dancing one way a matter of ten yards, then prancing back a full twenty yards in the other direction as he sang and swiveled and waved his big rifle at the soldiers. Every now and then he would throw it against his shoulder and shoot down at the white men—then throw up the trapdoor, slipping another cartridge from the wide belt at his waist, and shove it into the breech.

A Springfield, Seamus thought to himself. Easy to recognize—what with the bands on that barrel. Carbine. Cavalry piece. Likely the son of a bitch got it at the Little Bighorn.

"Someone shoot that red bastard!" a man growled off to Donegan's right, behind his shoulder.

No more than a hundred yards separated the enemies now.

"We're trying, Sergeant!" a young soldier claimed with no little exasperation.

Then, as Seamus watched, the war chief on the ledge found himself out of cartridges. Hollering at those around him, he ducked out of sight.

"You think we got 'im, Sarge?"

"No," the noncom stated flatly. "Red snapper didn't fall. Just hidin'. So you ain't got 'im dead to rights."

"Went to reload," Donegan declared quietly to those nearby.

The men only nodded grimly before their eyes went back to the ledge above, concentrating as they rocked up onto their knees and hands, dragging their buffalo coats through the snow with a slur to claim a few more precious feet of the hillside. A foot at a time, if no more than inches. Hunker behind this clump of sage, fire if you spotted yourself a target—plan out your next crawl to the next sage bush for your next rest.

Maybe an hour later they were no farther than seventy yards from the warriors above them, each man scrambling, slipping, backsliding until he secured another grip in the icy, crusty, wind-whipped surface of the snow. Men who stared into that raw wind, most with nothing but their eyes exposed behind wool-blanket masks, small explosions of frosty breath puffing from the holes the soldiers had cut for their mouths. Lay and shoot, fight and survive, on this steep slope while the enemy rained down bullets and arrows . . . while the blizzard moved in, already obscuring the hills just across the Tongue behind a curtain of frothy white gauze. The wind howled, managing to find every loose crevice of a man's clothing, penetrating past the layers of buffalo hide, wool blanket, army wool, merino wool, and burlap sacking.

No matter how many layers—none of it could stop a man from shaking when it was no longer the cold that made him tremble so.

As the minutes dragged into another hour, as their desperate clawing advance up the steep hillside bogged down, it was becoming clear that this far southern end of Miles's line might not be going any farther. While the soldiers' big guns commanded the knoll on the north end of the valley, the greatest Indian strength held the tall hill on the east side of the valley at the opposite end of the ridge. Not only was it a position secured by military strength in sheer numbers, it was the one place on the battlefield where a lone warrior continued to rally his forces through the strength of his personal medicine.

Seamus wondered how long it would take before bullets won out over magic.

As Donegan lay there in the cold—some two feet of dry, flaky snow all around him as he repeatedly levered, aimed, and fired—his mind flitted back to dim, remembered glimpses of old Ireland: how the priests did all that they could to combat the pagan superstitions of the poor country people with superstitions of their own Mother Church. Centuries of druid legends were spurned, replaced with miraculous tales of water turned to wine, a loaf of bread become enough to feed a multitude . . . and a dead man commanded to come forth from his very own tomb, called out to walk again, his eyes able to see once more when they had been sightless for three days.

So just whose superstition was he to believe now?

"Damn, that was close," muttered a young soldier to Donegan's left. The man held up his arm so that it was plain to see the furrow and the hole made by the bullet's raking path.

"Keep your head down, sojur," Donegan advised with a wry grin. "Chances be they'll go and shoot over you. But always remember: when you're taking heights, keep your ever-living head flat on the ground."

At the sound of growing excitement among the enemy, Seamus peered up the slope, finding the war chief back again—this time gesturing to his kinsmen as he pranced along the ledge above, bullets landing all around him, smacking into the rocks. For a moment he stopped, shouting to the other warriors, appearing to goad them into joining him in making an assault on the white men.

One of the soldiers cried, "You think them sonsabitches gonna try charging us?"

"Not a charge," came the answer from off to Donegan's right.

Seamus looked, finally recognizing the speaker as Blackfoot half-breed William Jackson from nothing more than the scout's clothing.

Donegan shouted, "Jackson—you figger he's making bravery runs?"

The half-breed nodded behind the wolf-hide hat pulled down securely over the scrap of blanket protecting his face from the wind. "Four to do. He has made two."

Up piped a cocky soldier, "Which means the red-belly got him just two more runs back and forth to do!"

"Get 'im this time!" came the call, which was taken up by many voices.

More of the soldiers grunted onto their knees, scrambling for foot- and handholds on the icy slope. Some firing as others crawled inches closer to that most desired target. They were closing on fifty yards of the Indians above them. Close enough that either side could make their shots count, Donegan brooded. But—as always seemed the case—the anxious soldiers seemed to be frittering away their issue of ammunition without much effect on the enemy. At the same time, the warriors appeared to be growing even stingier with their cartridges. Firing less and less down into the soldier lines . . . perhaps waiting for a better shot, a certain target, a sure kill.

Donegan could hear the Jackson brothers hollering at each other now—unable to understand their Blackfoot tongue laced with an English curse word every now and then. If it hadn't been for that, the two would have been indistinguishable from the soldiers. Every man along this base of the ridge was masked in some way, a faceless battalion that struggled to hold on, more determined than ever as the minutes crawled past to knock down that strutting war chief above them.

With no more than fifty yards separating Butler's men from the brow of the hill where the warrior in the bonnet pranced in full view, the officers moved back and forth through the snow and sage on horseback just behind the soldiers—encouraging, assuring, rallying, reminding the men to husband their ammunition.

Seamus had no idea how many carbine cartridges he had left in his pocket for the Winchester—but something in his gut warned him that he shouldn't waste any more bullets on that war chief. Not the way the soldiers were throwing it away. Why, if they were ordered to push on to the top in one grand assault of the ridge, he would need every bullet he still had down in those pockets. Or if it came time that the warriors poured off the hill and Butler's men fell back, retreating all the way back to the wagon camp to fort up, then chances were Seamus would need every last bullet until he got his hands on his cartridge belts so heavy he had to carry them over his shoulders.

"I got 'im!" some man suddenly bellowed.

Donegan twisted to peer uphill, watching the war chief stagger back a yard, a hand slapping against his chest. The Indian hobbled to the side a few more steps, then clumsily spilled out of sight on the ledge directly above the Irishman.

Shrill cries erupted from the rocks around that high knoll. Warriors had watched their leader fall. They were angrier now—perhaps furious. Chances were good they might well work themselves into a suicidal frenzy and come spilling down from their breastworks.

But all that showed themselves were two warriors who leaped from behind the rocks, pitching to their hands and knees in the trampled snow, crawling from different directions toward the war chief's body. Then a third appeared, scurrying in a crouch toward the others as the soldiers shouted among themselves—boasting on who dropped the chief—then several soldiers had sense enough to remember to train their weapons on those who had come to rescue their daring leader.

Bullets sang against the rocks, but it was impossible to see where they were striking: both wind and snow had whipped themselves into an angry torrent that cut down a man's visibility to no more than the fifty yards between warriors and soldiers at that moment. Through the thick, flying snow Seamus saw the three Indians wheel about and hurry for cover. The soldier fire must have been enough to drive them away from the body.

Donegan laid his head on the crusty snow, closing his eyes a moment, of a sudden feeling the weary ache that pierced him to the marrow of every one of his bones, sensing the cold settling into the core of him despite the thick layers of clothing. Oh, how he only wanted to rest for a few minutes, maybe even to sleep—eyelids so heavy. Perhaps just a few winks . . .

Across the open ground the Napoleon gun boomed again. This time the whistle was a sodden, muffled one. It was snowing but good now, blowing at a man sideways. And if he lay there any longer, Donegan realized he might never get up. Fall asleep and freeze to death.

"Bastards!"

At some man's cry of frustration Seamus groggily raised his head, finding a young soldier crawling past. Behind them Butler and his noncoms were stirring the men, forcing them to move about in the ground swirl of snow whipped round and round like tiny tornado cones as the currents careened off the slopes. He peered again up the hill.

"They got 'im!" the soldier growled. "Bastards!" Then he looked at Donegan. "I wanted that scalp, you know."

"Ever you take a Injin's scalp?"

"Never—but I wanted that one's," the soldier admitted. "Brave one . . . wasn't he?"

Donegan could hear the ring of admiration in the man's voice. His own voice clotted with emotion as he replied, "Yes, sojur—that one was as brave as they come."

"Just leave me here," Big Crow pleaded with a voice sounding as hollow as cured horn. "I am going to die anyway. Go on home."

Wooden Leg watched Big Crow's eyes begin to mist with a terrible pain as he knelt over the wounded man. A Lakota man crawled up behind Wooden Leg to help.

With his soldier rifle and plenty of cartridges, the young *Tse-Tsehese* warrior had been fighting near the courageous and able war chief throughout the long, cold morning. And when it came time that Big Crow went out to taunt the soldiers by dancing in full view of the enemy, making his four courage runs—Wooden Leg knew better than to try to convince the man otherwise. When the war chief ran out of bullets and came back to the breastworks to ask others for some of their cartridges, no one spoke a word to try discouraging the brave man. After all, they knew Big Crow's was a powerful medicine.

Once he had his cartridge belt loaded again, the war chief gave a mighty shout and leaped over the breastworks again, singing and yelling at the enemy, dancing and shooting at the soldiers. While some among the *Ohmeseheso* might one day say that he was a shaman, a medicine man—Big Crow was in reality nothing more than a very brave warrior, as courageous a fighting man as Wooden Leg had ever known.

Big Crow was clearly moving his lips, but no words were coming out. Snow was gathering on his dark eyelashes, on the side of his face where the wind blew the flakes into a hardened crust. Then the pain glazing the dark eyes was gone for but a heartbeat, and they stared into Wooden Leg's face. For no more than a single, strong heartbeat—then the mist began to thicken over the eyes once more, and they half rolled back into his head.

"Come on!" the Lakota growled to another warrior approaching behind Wooden Leg.

Together the three of them huddled over the wounded man for a moment longer—as if none of them knew what to do—then Wooden Leg tore the blanket from his own back and laid it over Big Crow, tucking in the sides, down against the drifting snow and harsh wind. Not until that moment did Wooden Leg see the bullet holes that pocked his own blanket.

"Forget that!" one of the Lakota snorted. "We must pull him out of here!"

"Now the soldiers will charge up the hill!" agreed the other Lakota.

"Go if you wish!" Wooden Leg growled at them.

They looked at one another, shame showing on their faces. "No, we will help," one of them said.

Crabbing around on all fours, Wooden Leg stationed himself between Big Crow's feet. "Both of you—take his hands and pull him out!"

Without another word of protest the two Lakota warriors each snatched an arm and hauled the war chief off the ground. The three of them lumbered away with the wounded man's deadweight between them like a sack of wet flour.

Bullets were smacking the rocks, kicking up the ground all around them by then.

"See!" one of them shrieked in terror. "There—the soldiers are charging us!"

"No, the soldiers aren't coming!" Wooden Leg snapped at the two older men, shaking his head violently in despair as they began to settle Big Crow to the ground.

"But their bullets are coming!" the first one whimpered as he ducked away, belly-crawling into the rocks for safety.

The other turned and fled in a crouch without a word.

Wooden Leg collapsed alongside the war chief, breathing

hard. "I'll come back," he promised quickly, his lips brushing the wounded man's ear, words spoken in a whisper against the howl of the wind, the rattle of the guns, the shattering, slamming, singing racket of the ricochets of lead and red rock.

In that next instant Wooden Leg heaved himself up, diving headlong, flopping onto his belly, crawling to reach the breastworks where many of the *Ohmeseheso* warriors had gathered to fire down on the soldiers, joined by a good number of Lakota who had followed Crazy Horse to this far southern end of the long ridge.

With Big Crow's three rescuers no longer making targets of themselves, the rifle fire coming from the *ve-ho-e* slowed to a trickle.

"Listen to me!" Wooden Leg called out above the whine of the wind. "I do not ask that any of you come with me to bring Big Crow back to safety . . . but help me by drawing the soldiers' bullets away."

One of the frightened ones shook his head. "Big Crow had powerful medicine—so strong the *ve-ho-e* bullets should not harm him . . . but he is dead!"

"*Aiyeee!*" cried another one with desperation in his voice. "There is no hope if the soldiers can kill the most powerful among us!"

Wooden Leg pushed the two doubters aside. "Run! Run far away if you want—but Big Crow did not run! Big Crow did not believe we would lose this fight!"

"Yes!" Yellow Weasel shouted. "Big Crow was the bravest among us all! We must save him now!"

Another, Strange Owl, cried, "It is our turn to be as brave as Big Crow would want us to be!"

"Big Crow lost many relatives in the fight at the Red Fork Valley!" Wooden Leg explained. "And now, like me, one of his own relations is a captive of the Bear Coat's soldiers. He is loyal to his people! We must be as loyal to him!"

Of a sudden more than two-times-ten were on their feet, popping up and down, bursting into sight to draw the bullets, then falling behind the rocks once again. More leaped to their feet until half a hundred of them all along the top of the high knoll moved like the undulations of a prairie diamondback.

With immediate response the soldiers' guns began to boom again as the snow thickened into a white paste like the cattail gum Wooden Leg would smear on insect bites to draw the poison from the tiny wounds.

As he rose from his knees, Wooden Leg motioned to the two Lakota who huddled at his elbows. All three dashed faster than ever to the wounded Big Crow. Crouching between the war chief's knees, Wooden Leg looped his arms beneath the man's legs and lifted in concert with the others. Big Crow grunted from low in his belly as he was hoisted from the snow, his head slung back, wagging loosely in semiconsciousness.

Huffing in exertion, the trio fought the deep snow and uneven terrain, slipping a few times on rocks, dropping Big Crow once but picking him back up—until they had him behind the breastworks where Wooden Leg's brother suddenly appeared out of the blizzard.

"Yellow Hair!"

"Yes, Wooden Leg!" he called out, leading his horse up the slope. From its nostrils came great jets of steam.

"The fight here is over!" cried a Lakota voice behind them.

They both turned with the many others, surprised to find Crazy Horse shouting to his warriors, his arms outstretched in supplication to the skies.

"Shahiyela! We come to carry your brave man away," a Lakota fighting man called out, coming up to Wooden Leg and Yellow Hair with another, both of them holding on to a frightened pony between them.

"Help me, Yellow Hair," Wooden Leg ordered his brother. "We must put Big Crow on the back of their pony."

The younger man asked, "Is he dead?"

"No . . . but he will be soon." As Wooden Leg bent down to grab an arm and a leg, he paused a moment, looking at the war chief's blood on his own hands. When they lifted Big Crow and draped his body across the pony's backbone, the snow below the warrior was smeared with bright crimson. So very much blood. He stared and stared, and by the time Wooden Leg looked up again, the two Lakota warriors were moving down the slope with Big Crow's body.

He turned with the crush and clamor of ponies and fighting men, watching Crazy Horse leading his Lakota north along the brow of the ridge, a few of them beginning to catch up their ponies and disappear down the slope, slowly swallowed

by the blizzard. Yet most doggedly fanned out toward the big
cone, kneeling in the snow behind a clump of cedar, or finding
a rest for their rifles behind a pile of snow-covered stones.
They were preparing . . .

Turning to peer down the slope through the blizzard,
Wooden Leg could barely make out the blackened forms inching up the side of the hill toward them, figures without real
definition in the storm: blurry, fuzzy, out of focus.

In a blinding rush of fury Wooden Leg darted away, racing back to the place where Big Crow had been dancing,
taunting the soldiers. Sliding to a stop in the snow, he dared
not look down at the white men. If he saw them coming, his
courage might disappear on a strong gust of wind.

Instead he turned his back to the soldiers and went right
to work stuffing his bare hands into the icy snow, scrounging
with his fingertips, pulling up one piece of red shale after
another. Digging with all his might to pull more free, slab
after slab until he had the pile high enough.

Then he realized he was crying.

This memorial would last longer than a man's bones
bleaching on the prairie. It would always mark the spot where
a brave man fell. Where Big Crow gave his life for his people.

Then he sprinted back along the ridge.

"Come, Wooden Leg!" his brother shouted as he approached. Yellow Hair grabbed Wooden Leg's arm as he
dashed back to the pony's side. "We are going away from here
now!"

As Yellow Hair tugged on him, Wooden Leg stumbled
through the deepening snow—peering one last time at the
soldiers below as they continued their assault up the slope.
Out of the dancing mist he spotted a single horseman suddenly among the soldiers on foot, a box pitching from that
rider's grasp, splitting apart in the snow.

For a moment longer Wooden Leg stood there, watching
in amazement as the thick-coated furry figures lunged out of
the storm toward what the horseman had dropped, collapsing
to their knees in knots here and there to dig at the snow
around the broken box.

Farther down the ridge more *Tse-Tsehese* and Lakota warriors were still fighting as they slowly withdrew, dropping back
a few steps at a time—still firing their rifles, shooting their

silent arrows in the howl of the blizzard. For memory of Big
Crow's bravery, for his sister held captive by the soldiers . . .
for them Wooden Leg wanted to join that fight, the last of this
battle as the winter storm brought its heavy heel down upon
them all.

That, and he wanted to know what it was the lone horseman had brought that the soldiers went after like such crazed
madmen.

Chapter 35

8 January 1877

How these cold, frightened, hungry soldiers held their ground and did not turn and flee would one day be a wonder to all of those who would hear their tale of heroism.

Time and again Seamus himself had watched ordinary men stand against daunting odds, flinging their bodies against grapeshot and canister, or holding the line—waiting for the charge of cavalry's slashing sabers, men who withstood the cruel bombardment of artillery on little food and no sleep.

But never had Seamus Donegan witnessed such uncommon bravery as he did that day in the face of a Montana blizzard.

He was a man working for his wages—let no man ever accuse the Irishman of giving anything less than his steadfast best. What he had expected to be a terribly long and cold ride north to Tongue River Cantonment had instead turned out to be an even longer and much colder chase after Crazy Horse's village. There was little doubt he was earning his army pay, and every last dollar of that bonus George Crook had promised him.

But how these wretched five-year-hitch recruits held the line and gritted their teeth to keep them from chattering right out of their heads as they ducked Sioux bullets and arrows for no more than a paltry thirteen dollars a month . . . Seamus realized he would never know.

Without fail it always made his heart swell with pride to be fighting shoulder to shoulder among such brave men. Men as common as dirt—unlettered, ill-mannered in the presence of the gentler sex or their superior officers, more often than not unwashed, and most as lacking in the common graces as any of their species might be . . . but every last one of them made brave by circumstance and the events that caught them up and hurtled them along into history. Common, ordinary, everyday soldiers who many times back at their post didn't exhibit the good sense to pour piss out of a boot . . . soldiers who became something altogether different in the face of the enemy.

Ordinary men who showed their extraordinary courage in the face of extraordinary circumstances.

As soon as the war chief fell up there on that snowy ledge above them, two—then three—warriors darted out to attempt to retrieve his body. Now the soldiers had themselves a new target. But while the men fired one round after another without much thought, Seamus began once more to brood on just how much ammunition was being wasted.

"Captain Butler!"

At the call Donegan twisted about in his clumsy coat, finding the colonel's young aide-de-camp galloping up to the rear of the skirmish line C Company had dotted across the deep snow, perforated with Edmond Butler's fighting men.

"Over here!" the captain called.

"Sir! The general sends his compliments," Lieutenant Bailey gushed breathlessly.

"Yes? Yes, soldier?"

"The general respectfully wonders if you've bogged down, Captain. He asks me to communicate that he would like to see your line advance up the slope, sir."

His horse pawed at the snow anxiously. Butler glanced at the hillside with a knowing squint. "Up . . . up the slope?"

"Yes, Captain. The general extends his wishes that we don't get bogged down because the Indians are in control of the battle."

"Well, the goddamned Indians *are* in control of the heights!" Butler roared, exasperated.

Some of the men twittered behind him but shut up the instant Butler heeled around on them, fixing them all with his glare. He wheeled back on the orderly just as quickly.

"Captain—General Miles wishes to attack those heights—"

"Very well," Butler interrupted. "Give the general my compliments and tell him it will be our honor to charge the slopes that lay in my front."

With a salute Hobart Bailey started to rein aside, but Butler leaned over and snagged the soldier's bridle, stopping the horse with a jerk.

"Mr. Bailey, please convey to the general my immediate and crucial need for ammunition. My men are nearly out, and if we are to face the muzzles of those enemy guns . . . I'll need resupply."

"Ammunition, sir?"

"Yes"—and Butler pointed an arm right at the heights—"if the general asks us to do the impossible, at least give us more bullets."

"Ammunition—yessir!"

Butler freed the lieutenant's reins and slapped the mount at the same time, sending the young officer off toward the knoll where Miles would likely be standing among his gun crews, surveying the battlefield as a whole. Meanwhile, with the way the snow was beginning to come down in heavy, dancing sheets, Seamus realized Miles wouldn't have a bloody idea what was really going on this far to the south. If anything, Butler's men were no more than tiny, fuzzy specks of flotsam indistinct against the snowy hillside the general expected them to assault.

Calling his officers to the side of his mount, Butler told them in his thick brogue, "Gentlemen, you likely heard our orders."

"We're expected to take the summits," grumbled one of the sergeants.

"Prepare the men," Butler told them succinctly. "Get them up out of the snow and ready to move forward."

A soldier asked, "We aren't going to wait for the ammunition, sir?"

"We've been ordered to advance, Corporal," Butler snapped. "Now, pass the order along and see that your men are instructed to be conservative with their shots. Any more questions?"

When there were no further questions, the others turned away, moving quickly among the half a hundred, ordering the soldiers off their bellies and their rumps, to stand in the freezing wind, nervously awaiting the next command from the man who sat on horseback.

"Advance!" Butler cried, yanking back on the reins so his horse jerked to a halt.

Seamus found himself admiring this Edmond Butler—not just because they both were Irish born and therefore brother Patlanders. But Donegan couldn't help but admire the officer this Butler was turning out to be under fire. In this era of a clear class distinction between officers and their enlisted, Edmond Butler appeared to be one of the few who did not rub his company's nose in it.

Glad was he to find himself among the men of C Company for the dirty little task that lay before them this stormy morning.

He moved off with Butler's soldiers, turning once to look behind him at the disappearing form of that young rider on his way to the artillery knoll. The swirling snow swallowed Lieutenant Bailey in one gust, and he was gone.

Donegan prayed that Miles would send ammunition in time to save Butler's men from disaster. That, or C Company might well have to dig down through the snow and find rocks to throw at Crazy Horse's warriors arrayed shoulder to shoulder up there on the ridge. At least two hundred of them . . . waiting for Butler's fifty-some.

Four-to-one odds along with struggling through three feet of snow into the teeth of a high-plains blizzard. It just didn't get any more army than this.

Were they warm? he wondered. Was Samantha staying fed? And most of all—was she not worrying about him?

He had tried his best with that last letter almost a full month ago . . . to tell her she had nothing to worry about even though he was not coming home when he had promised. Coaxing her to stay warm and fed, and to be without worry—that again was his prayer as he stumbled over the sagebrush in a ragged forager's charge with the rest of Butler's men.

Now some of the soldiers on Casey's left were rising, beginning to move out with Butler's right flank, lunging through the snowdrifts like crippled cows in their bulky, wet winter clothing, some firing off a shot every five yards or so—and each time sternly reminded by their sergeants to conserve their ammunition.

Ahead of them on the slopes the warriors darted from side to side in that thick atmosphere of pasty snow falling down, flying sideways, in a fury all around at once. Every now and then a bullet struck near Donegan, ricocheting against a rock buried under the crusty snow with a sharp crack. Or a dull thud of a sound when they smacked into the frozen earth. A high-pitched whine when they just sailed on past his ear.

Damn this face mask, he cursed, tugging on it to be sure he could see through the eyeholes he himself had cut two days before they had marched south away from the Yellowstone.

Of a sudden those sounds coming from the high ridge changed. Blinking his frosted eyelashes, Seamus squinted, trying to focus on the distance ahead of them. The warriors had seen them coming—that much was for certain. Appeared the enemy was massing just about everything they had right in front of Butler's outfit now. Warriors streamed along the top of the ridge, the noise growing as the Sioux and Cheyenne yelled and yelped. Their numbers swelled again and again. Multiplied—disappeared in the snowstorm. Then reappeared larger than ever.

Cavalry were always taught not to let the number of enemy concern them—after all, cavalry had the benefit of horse and saber.

But this wasn't the War of Rebellion no more, Seamus brooded. And Butler's outfit wasn't mounted on no god-blessed horses. And, besides—the frontier cavalry didn't use its bleeming sabers anymore, anyhow.

So he counted and counted those forms on the ridge, and he walked and walked, slipped and fell, and rose to walk again, estimating that there were more than 450 warriors waiting for the soldiers on the top of the ridge. And more were coming.

Maybe as many as a third of the warriors on that entire battlefield were now clustered in front of Butler's outnumbered C Company.

But on and on the sixty-some of them marched, men

grunting and grumbling as they slipped and slid on the icy snow. Picking themselves back up and cursing as they lunged back into line. Remaining undaunted in the face of the daunting task: scale the heights, even into the very jaws of the enemy guns.

Just as it had been when he had watched Captain Guy V. Henry among his men during that deadly retreat at the Rosebud,* Seamus was proud to watch this Edmond Butler urge his weary, stumbling horse through a wide gap that opened in the lines to make a big, conspicuous target of himself out in front of them all—the animal lunging forward until Butler reined up and turned about, there before the oncoming ranks of his men, his pistol clutched in his woolen mitten, his other hand tugging the blanket scrap over his face to the side once more so the men could hear his voice, so his men could see his own resolve.

"C'mon, you doughboys!" he cried, his arm waving high in the air. "We can do it! C Company can do it!"

Up and down that scattered line now other voices called out, sergeants and corporals and even privates rallying their fellows with cheers, hoots, and hollers. Working themselves up for the impossible.

"I ain't got no more bullets, Cap'n!" a frantic soldier bawled somewhere to Donegan's right.

"Give the bloke a shell or two!" a sergeant ordered.

Another man shouted, "I need some shells too!"

"Share what you got with your bunkies, goddammit!" an old soldier snapped at them as he pushed aside the wool mask that hung from the front of his muskrat cap.

Butler loped the horse in front of a trio of soldiers now as they were exchanging cartridges. He shouted down to them, "Make them last till the general sends more—"

As if it happened in a slow, watery blur—the captain's horse began to spin round even before Donegan heard the smack of lead against solid flesh. A wet and sodden sound. The animal grunted as it came about, its hind legs going out from under it as surely as if it had been hamstrung by a pack of wolves. The sound of the horse's wheeze accompanied its

---

* *Reap the Whirlwind*, vol. 9, The Plainsmen Series.

fall to the ground as Butler flew off into the deep snow, landing in a heap.

A half-dozen men were there in a matter of moments, some going to their company commander, pulling him out of the snow, others kneeling protectively between him and the heights to block any more enemy bullets, while two went to the horse that struggled to rise.

Butler came up to his knees there in the snowdrift, shoving the soldiers aside, then jerked to a stop, fixed and motionless as he stared at the animal's fight to get its legs under it.

"Is . . . is there a chance?" the captain asked in a weak voice.

One of the soldiers kneeling at the animal's side took his mitten away from the horse's chest, holding it up, slick and glittering with blood. Huge ash-curl snowflakes instantly clung to the moist, dark blotch. "No, sir, Cap'n. Not a chance, this one."

"K-kill . . . it." Butler struggled to get the words out. "Kill it now!"

As the captain lunged to his feet, surged forward out of the snow, the half-dozen soldiers stepped aside to allow Butler through. He stood motionless as the lone infantryman stepped back, brought up his Springfield, then stalled.

Now Butler's voice was calm, suddenly devoid of emotion. "Shoot my horse, soldier."

Bringing the hammer back, the soldier started to shake as he brought the muzzle down behind the horse's ear and pulled the trigger all in one motion. Donegan turned away at that instant, pushing on into the snow. He'd seen more than his share of good, strong animals die on the ground with bullets in their brains.

Behind him he heard Butler call out to his men.

"Company C—get moving!"

Everywhere now the voices took up the call again.

Donegan heard the huffing behind him. He turned to find Captain Butler trudging forward on the double through the deep snow, leading his soldiers on foot, straining to stay out in front, having made a fine target of himself—good officer that he was.

"Bring up the left flank!" Butler's voice cried out.

A moment later the captain ordered, "Don't string out on the right!"

As they moved forward, that one man's voice rang above all the rest. "C'mon, men! C'mon and look 'em in the eye. This goddamned day is ours to win or lose!"

Right when they reached the sharp side of the slope, the men began to cheer; a few fired back at the hundreds of warriors on the top of the ridge above them, now no more than a hundred yards away. Many of these soldiers could do little more than cheer and march, stumble and follow along, as Butler led them against the enemy. Most had no ammunition left.

Seamus suddenly wondered if this was the place. If this hillside would be where it would all come to an end, fighting among men who were flat out of bullets, these men who were long on courage.

He wondered if a good Catholic should say a prayer at the very moment he stared death in the eye, wondered if he should say something silently to Samantha and the boy that God Himself might whisper to her heart the next time Sam prayed.

On all sides of him now the men were yelling, working up their courage as they flung themselves against the sheer face of the ridge, the Sioux and Cheyenne close enough that he could make out feathers and paint, the birds tied in the hair, the amulets hung around the necks—even in this Montana blizzard.

Seamus was among brave men once more. He was a warrior, making war on other warriors. Though they might not have many bullets left, Butler's C Company was not without its courage that cold winter day.

Marching into the face of enemy guns until they could get close enough to throw rocks, close enough to turn their Springfields around and use them for clubs.

Suddenly Butler called again, "Fix bayonets!"

Seamus had none, so he stuffed a hand inside his buffalo coat, down into the side pocket of his mackinaw. That pocket was empty. He did have the skinning knife. If it came down to that—

Up and down the line the soldiers yanked their bayonets

from the black-leather slings, jamming them over the muzzles of their Long Toms. Down, twist, and lock.

He quickly pulled the mitten from his left hand and stuck it into his other mackinaw pocket—searching. He sighed his prayer; then his fingertips touched them. All he had left was . . . a handful. Less than a full load for the tube nestled beneath the Winchester's barrel.

A voice steady and sure cried out, "Bayonets fixed, Major!"

"Come on, you doughboys!" Butler shouted against the screeching of the enemy, waving his pistol. "Show 'em the stuff you men are made of!"

"Permission to take Captain Butler his ammunition, General!" Frank Baldwin said enthusiastically as soon as Lieutenant Hobart Bailey came galloping up the plateau to report to Miles.

"How in the hell do you expect to—"

But Baldwin interrupted. "I'll take a case of it myself, sir."

"Those men need more than one case!" the colonel retorted. He started to turn aside, searching for Baird. "I'll order some men from the supply train to pack up some cases on the backs of our mules—"

"We don't have time, General."

Miles jerked around. That was the second time in as many seconds that the lieutenant had interrupted him. "We don't have time, Mr. Baldwin?"

"Begging pardon, General—I meant to say that Butler's men don't have time," Baldwin tried to explain. "You can order up the mules with more cases to come behind me. But—please allow me to go to their aid immediately."

The colonel began to shake his head, saying, "Perhaps it would be far too dangerous—"

"You've always depended upon me to do my duty, no matter how dangerous, General. In all those years you've known me."

For a long moment Miles considered the man standing before him. Then he pursed his lips in resignation and said, "Permission granted, Lieutenant."

Frank wasn't about to wait on Miles to change his mind. With a salute to the colonel Baldwin turned immediately and snatched the reins away from Bailey. "I'll leave your horse down at the wagon yard, Lieutenant!"

In one motion the lieutenant was stuffing an arctic boot into the stirrup, rising to the saddle, and wheeling away at a lope. As he came down on the McClellan, and stuffed the right boot in the hooded stirrup, Baldwin gave the animal a kick. It had worked hard all morning, racing back and forth across the open ground through the deep snow. Not only were the men on short rations, these animals were too.

He would leave the horse among the others, grabbing one already saddled if it was handy. At the same time he would get one of the supply sergeants to pull him a box of cartridges from the tailgate of a wagon, hoist it up to him, and then he would be on his way.

Swinging out of the saddle at the wagon corral, Baldwin was already yelling for Carter's soldiers into double time. "Get me the strongest horse you've got saddled, pronto!"

A handful of them stopped and turned on their heels immediately. The high-pitched wailing and keening of the women and children nearby raked a fingernail of dread down his spine. He watched a sergeant racing up.

Frank asked, "How long they been singing like this?"

"That?" the sergeant replied with his salute. "Ever since the fight started, sir."

As he landed in the snow and looped the reins to Bailey's horse around a wagon wheel, the lieutenant returned the sergeant's salute. "Grab me the first case of rifle ammo you can pull from the wagons, Sergeant."

"Yessir," he replied with enthusiasm, starting to turn.

"Sergeant," Baldwin said, reaching out to grab the man's arm, "I need more than that one case."

"Lieutenant?"

"As soon as you help me get that first case loaded up, I want you and your boys to pack up a couple of mules with two cases each and hurry them double time to the foot of the ridge."

Quickly glancing at the distant ridge where the action was clearly the hottest, the sergeant echoed, "The ridge, sir?"

"Follow me with the four cases just as quick as you can get them loaded up and yourself on a mule to ride."

"Yessir," the soldier answered this time without hesitation.

"Now, get me that case I'll be carrying."

In a matter of moments two soldiers reappeared with what appeared to be a strong piebald, saddled and ready to ride. Frank walked around the animal one time, flipped up the stirrup fender, and tugged on the cinch. He lifted a front hoof, then a rear hoof, and by that time the sergeant was leading another pair of soldiers back to the scene. They had between them a heavy wooden crate of Springfield ammunition, .45/70 caliber.

"All right, soldiers," Frank said as he took up the horse's reins and stuffed the bulky arctic boot into the stirrup, rising eagerly to the saddle, "pass that box up here to me."

The sergeant flinched, glancing at the two men who carried the crate. "Pass . . . pass it up to you, Lieutenant?"

Baldwin gestured impatiently for them to hand it over. "Here, c'mon. I've got to ride, and now."

"Sir, couldn't you wait and I'll get a pack animal for you to lead—"

"Give me the goddamned box of ammo, Sergeant!"

"Yes, sir!" the man replied, stepping aside and waving the pair forward.

The two soldiers clumsily manhandled the heavy weight of it up to the lieutenant, helping the officer center it on the front of the hornless McClellan saddle. Frank brought his legs up, feet still stuffed in the stirrups, so that his thighs could help balance the crate as much as a man could with one arm.

He only nodded, unable to salute the soldiers. "You've done well, men. Now, get those four cases coming behind me just as fast as you can! Lives depend upon it! Hep, hep-a!"

He got the reluctant horse started away, sideways at first, then cantering out of the wagon corral, rolling into an uneasy lope onto the open bottom-ground, heading due south along the gently rising slope toward the far left of the battlefield.

Despite the thickly falling flakes, ahead of him the snow lay trampled by the prints of many boots so that Baldwin was able to avoid the deep drifts for the most part. He eased the animal back to a fast walk as it struggled beneath the weight over its withers, about all he figured he should expect out of the horse, and certainly the fastest he wanted to travel with the wobbly, unwieldy, clumsy weight of the ammunition crate balanced precariously across the front of the saddle and his lap, one arm looped over it, locking it down in the only way he could secure it.

From time to time Frank glanced up to take a look at the soldiers pushing up the first rise of ground toward the Indian positions, but for most of the ride he concentrated solely on the few yards of icy terrain right in front of his horse's nose, especially as the creature began to show signs of weariness from fighting the deep snow and struggling beneath the shifting weight rocking back and forth across its withers.

Then he was close enough to the back of the skirmish line . . . and recognized the dark carcass in the snow.

An officer's horse.

The snow trampled all around it.

Frank passed by the carcass close enough to see the hole in the head, the glistening, frozen blood. A gust of wind laid a dusting of new snow in the open, glazed eyes as he moved around it. Frank shuddered and looked away.

Twenty yards away Butler's skirmish line stumbled forward ahead of him. They had their bayonets fixed, and they were yelling like demons. Just like banshees ripping out of the maw of hell as they lunged and fell, picked themselves back up, and kept crawling up that icy slope, scrambling for a foothold, something, anything.

He hammered his heels and calves against the mount's ribs. Then he realized his heart was in his throat. His teeth clenched all this time. How hard it was to open his mouth, to work his jaws, so tight was the unprotected skin from the cold wind and whipping snow without that blanket mask.

"Am . . . ammunition!" he cried into the wind, the word torn away from his lips the instant it was uttered.

At first they didn't hear him, so he called out again as the horse lunged within ten yards of their rear.

"Ammunition!" he got the word out at once, the sound of it again whipped off his tongue by the brutal slash of wind.

But, quite unexpectedly, one man turned, his wool mask dangling loosely, his breath puffing from beneath it in explosions of frost. The man stumbled back a step, surprised, then righted himself as he took a step forward—back toward Baldwin. Suddenly the soldier stopped, turned, shouting to the others.

"Ammunition! Ammunition!"

Another soldier turned so quickly, his legs got caught up in his long buffalo coat, spilling him into the deep snow. He leaped out of the drift as quickly as he had gone down. Now there were two of them yelling at the others close enough to hear over the howl of the wind, yelling over the crazed hollering they were all doing as they flung themselves against the ridgeline.

Bullets sang around them now. And the horse snorted, ears perked, frightened. Frank hadn't allowed himself the luxury of being frightened.

The third man recognized him. "It's Lieutenant Baldwin!"

Then a fourth soldier turned around, there beside the first as Frank urged the reluctant horse through the deep drifts. Right above them the small arms and carbines of the enemy crackled like a pine-pitch fire.

"He's got ammunition, boys!" another old soldier croaked in a broken voice as he jammed the butt of his Springfield down into the snow, weaving in the strong wind as he hung on to the muzzle of the weapon. "By God—Baldwin's got ammo!"

At that moment they all seemed to turn as a whole, more than half a hundred of them with their Long Toms at the ready, long, sharp, spearlike bayonets, or those with trowel bayonets fixed for their gallant charge. The first of them began to stumble Baldwin's way as his horse sidestepped away from the rush into a depression.

The animal stumbled, pitching to the side, then got its legs back under them both. But Baldwin could hold the crate no longer, his arm gone numb with the cold, more so with the cramping of the muscles as he lunged out with the rein hand. Frank felt it slip beneath his fingertips, felt the crate going, but there was nothing he could do except watch it tumble into the snow.

No matter now. They were around him in a dark circle of cheering, throbbing, swirling soldiers, each one diving in to rake up a box of cartridges, yelling at the others, bumping and falling and some of them even laughing.

"Crazy Horse is mine now!" one man called as he

scooped up a mitten filled with snow and glittery copper cartridges.

"Lemme at them red bastards!" another shouted.

Butler was suddenly there beside the horse, holding up his hand to Baldwin. His goddamned bare hand! "Lieutenant Baldwin?"

"Yessir, Captain!" Frank said, saluting, yanking off his horsehide gauntlet into the frighteningly cold windchill.

Butler's mouth moved wordlessly a moment as he shook Baldwin's hand. "T-thank you, Lieutenant."

"For the Fifth, Captain," Baldwin replied, feeling the tug of sentiment rise in his throat like a filmy knot.

Some of these men might well have followed Frank into Gray Beard's village on the Staked Plain to rescue those two little girls. Or they might have fought another high-plains blizzard to stay on Sitting Bull's trail if he had asked that of them. They were all Miles's men. The Fighting Fifth, by God!

Frank ripped his sealskin hat from his head, waving it aloft in a wide circle, shouting.

"The Fifth never gives in, Captain! The Fifth never gives up! Have at them, men! Follow me and have at them!"

Captain Butler turned away suddenly, dragging his bare hand under his dribbling nose, his eyes misting from the cold blast of air that scoured every face. Baldwin surged ahead suddenly on that weary horse—yanking on the reins, waving, urging them all to follow, rallying them from above on the back of that rearing animal as they shoved cartridges into their pockets, some stuffing them into their mouths.

They threw themselves against the heights. Against the rocks and snow and icy bluffs. Against Crazy Horse's finest.

"All right, you doughboys!" Butler cried as he waved his men onward, trudging ahead beside Baldwin's prancing horse. "By God, let's go finish this fight!"

Chapter 36

8 January 1877

I t wasn't just those rifle cartridges that gave Butler's men a boost when they were preparing to pitch into the Sioux and Cheyenne with little more than their bayonets.

Seamus realized it was the sudden appearance of Frank Baldwin himself. Perhaps the fact that the lieutenant's personal effort beyond the call of duty reminded them that they were not alone in charging this hillside. Reminded them that Miles and the gun crews and the rest of the corps were with them.

No matter that the ammo case split apart, landing on its corner in the snow and splitting open against the red sandstone shale that dotted the crumbling slope. There were enough cartridges there to rally an entire battalion.

In excited knots of frantic, lunging fever, the men dropped to their knees in the deep snow to retrieve the individual cartridge boxes, yanking off gloves and mittens with their teeth as they cried out, stuffing that bare flesh down into the snowdrift to retrieve two or three of the brass cartridges as if they were life itself.

Life itself for now.

In the midst of the scramble Butler turned and stepped away from Baldwin and his horse, shouting to rally the men.

The other officers and noncoms took up that call. "Let's go finish this fight!"

For a moment longer Seamus regarded the bearded soldier on the horse—recognizing him as one of Miles's staff for this Tongue River campaign—then turned slightly to see just what that horseman named Baldwin was studying to the north. Off in the middistance came four animals, long-eared, most likely mules. Two riders pulling the other two along, that pair with crates on their backs. They trotted as fast as they could through the ground snow being blown into ever-higher snowdrifts.

"Captain Butler!" Baldwin called to the man preparing his outfit to continue their climb. "Look, sir!"

Butler stopped short and turned. "What the devil are they?"

Baldwin shouted, "More ammunition, sir!"

The captain shook his head in relief. "Bring 'em on, by Jove! Now we will see this job through!"

"Permission to deliver ammunition to the other companies?"

Nodding to Baldwin, Edmond Butler said, "By all means, Lieutenant. By the great Jehovah, this is our day!"

In a matter of heartbeats the line had begun inching forward once more, this time rallied, resupplied, and stronger for it. But the terrain was still just as much an enemy as the Sioux and Cheyenne awaiting them on the top of the ridge. Snowdrifts, clumps of cedar and buckbrush, narrow slashes of erosion jagging down the side of the butte—all of it broke apart Butler's smooth skirmish line into little groups of no more than a handful of soldiers here, a half-dozen soldiers there.

But they were all heading in the same direction: up into the face of the enemy.

For the next twenty harrowing minutes the Indians massed on the heights—screaming in a rage more than ever, firing down at the soldiers who had now come closer than they ever had before to reaching the tops of those bluffs. Every now and then a man cried out as the gap between the enemies narrowed, as the two sides lunged close enough to see the eyes of their foe.

A warrior fell with a painful bellow, and immediately others dragged him back from the edge, another man stepping up to fill the hole.

Below, a soldier called out, going down noisily—begging for help from those nearby. Or another fell silently, not making a sound, nor uttering a word, as he sank slowly, slowly into the snow turned red and mushy with the soldier's warm life spilling out this winter day. A soldier here and there knelt by the fallen, to stay by the wounded until the day was won and the hospital stewards reached the battlefield.

On pushed the rest, up the rugged slopes, past the pitch and heave of this broken ridgeline, around the pine and cedar, over the sagebrush and shale, firing as they went, stopping to kneel, reloading now that they had a few more bullets to make a fight of it.

Now that the warriors began to step back. Back. Back some more from the edge as the soldiers crawled the last few yards to the top of the ridge—stumbling over the first of the breastworks abandoned by the Sioux and Cheyenne. Some fell, scrambling back to their feet as they continued to pursue the retreating red lines.

By now Baldwin had urged his horse to the right to join McDonald's men with more ammunition, rallying them against the last of the warrior holdouts refusing to leave their rocky fortress, an enemy reluctant to retreat.

In their eager enthusiasm at gaining the summit, most of McDonald's and Butler's men trampled right on past the fire rings where the enemy had warmed themselves.

Only a few soldiers looked down in their advance upon that trampled ground to notice the crimson smears, the pools of mushy red snow—realizing for the first time just how much damage they had inflicted on the enemy. So much damage that the enemy could no longer stand their ground.

Now that the soldiers had gained the heights—the day was decided.

Into the whirling ground blizzard the Sioux and Cheyenne disappeared down the far slope. They still screamed in fury at the soldiers as they caught up their ponies, loaded their wounded and dead, then slipped away into the thick veil of that frigid Montana snowstorm—perhaps daring the white men to follow their retreat.

Seamus prayed Miles would not.

These soldiers of his—at least the three companies making this courageous charge on the bluffs—they had had themselves more than enough fight for one day. They deserved to hunker around a fire and eat a warm meal, wrap themselves in a blanket or two. They deserved to savor the delicious reward of victory this day.

Just for the present, if only for today.

Because Donegan knew how fleeting a battlefield victory could be in this matter of war with Indians. For the most part the army had been winning each engagement with the hostiles across the last ten years—yet this war remained unwon.

When? he wondered as a few of the men began to raise a cheer on the heights, slapping one another on the back and dancing a jig there in the trampled snow atop the ridgeline. Some were waving arms and rifles and muskrat or sealskin caps to signal their victory to those comrades down on the plateau with Miles and his two field pieces.

When would these dirty little battles ever be over and this whole bleeming war a thing of the past? When would the Indians quit running away to lick their wounds, preparing to fight another day? When would it no longer be necessary for the army to poke, and prod, and probe into the wilderness to locate the roaming villages? When would he himself be forced to find another way to support his loved ones?

To find something else a simple man with big hands and ready courage could do to feed his family.

Seamus looked south beyond the far slope of that narrow ridgeline, seeing the last of the warriors disappear into the thickening veil of the blizzard—knowing they had families hidden away in some valley to the south, perhaps not all that far away. Families, wives and children, to protect.

And then he realized.

The battles would go on, the villages would continue to flee into the wilderness, the warriors would continue to fight until they could see nothing but misery for their families, nothing but pain for their women, and nothing but hunger for their little ones by continuing the fight. When there was no more buffalo, no more game to hunt . . . when there was no more peace for the camps no matter the season . . . when there was nothing but death and despair and hunger and constant harrying off the reservations—then the warriors would have no other choice but to protect their families the best way they could.

Only then would the warriors bring in their wives and children to the food and blankets and protection of the agencies.

Just past noon that Monday, after a five-hour engagement, the last shot rang out, muffled by the blizzard that had descended upon the valley of the Tongue River. Miles gave Pope the order to cease his bombardment of the Indian retreat.

"They're out of range now," the colonel said with a mix of satisfaction tinged with resignation. "Your job is done for the day, Pope."

But Miles turned to Dickey and Ewers, whose companies had spent the battle protecting the guns and the plateau. He ordered them in pursuit of the enemy.

"Take out their rear guard if possible," he commanded.

Ewers asked, "To their village if need be, General?"

With a wag of his head a weary-looking Miles said, "Follow them as long as the two of you deem it practical with this hellish weather closing down on us. We'll have camp ready below for your return."

Seamus watched more than a hundred men march out on the double, plunging into the ground blizzard, trudging on the trampled backtrail of retreat, grunting with exertion as the snow billowed around them, led after an undefeated enemy by a handful of officers on horseback. It did not take those two companies long to disappear into the storm.

The Irishman wagged his head at the futility of their mission: to chase on foot after Indians escaping on horseback.

"I hope they'll turn back before long."

Seamus turned to find the old soldier coming up to stop beside him. "The fight's over," Donegan replied. "Now all Miles has to do is stay alive until he gets back to the Yellowstone."

"Sounds like you ain't counting yourself in."

"I'm not," Donegan admitted. "Heading south."

The man's thick brows beetled up. "Follering them Sioux?"

Shaking his head, the Irishman replied, "Got a family

waiting for me down to Laramie. I ain't seen 'em in too damn long already."

The soldier asked with disbelief, "Going through Crazy Horse country?"

"I made it once already. I figure I can do it again."

"Man can do anything," the soldier agreed, "if he wants it bad enough and sets his mind squarely on it."

"My *heart's* set on it."

"C'mon, then," the old soldier said, turning Seamus away from the ridgetop. "If you're leaving come morning on such a fool's ride south, then let's feed you some proper victuals this last night you'll spend with the Fifth!"

Wooden Leg hung back for the last of the fighting, with those last warriors to abandon the ridge with Crazy Horse.

Some wanted to stay and fight the soldiers hand against hand . . . but once the *ve-ho-e* began to break over the lip and land on the top of the ridge in ones and twos, it was plain to see that their battle was lost.

The final few warriors gathered just south of the steep slope of Belly Butte and fired into those first soldiers to pursue them across the top of the bluff. With more and more of the white men pouring over the breastworks, firing their guns so hot and so fast that they just surely had to have all the ammunition in the world, Crazy Horse and Hump, Little Big Man and Little Wolf, began to shout for everyone to pull back.

"We will fight these soldiers another day!"

That cry burst from every throat.

"Another day!"

Down below on the southern slope where the young boys held on to the last of the war ponies, Wooden Leg found his horse. Sweeping the crusty snow off its back, he flung himself across its foreflanks. Turning once, he saw that the chiefs had fanned out on foot across the south slope—the last to retreat—assuring that all the wounded had been gathered up and carried from the ridge. Just since leaving the top of the butte, the clouds had tumbled in. Overhead, the storm had grown so thick that the cone of Belly Butte had disappeared in the blinding white swirl.

Sick at heart with another retreat, Wooden Leg sawed the rein and kicked the pony into motion. It snorted as it leaped away, perhaps in more of a hurry than Wooden Leg to be far from this terrible place.

His heart lay heavy and cold in his chest, remembering another winter battle, another winter retreat, another journey into the wilderness to escape the soldiers.*

With the next beat of that weary heart he heard the distant, muffled boom of the big wagon gun.

Hopo! The soldiers were still shooting, even though there were no more warriors on the ridge to shoot at.

But a moment later Wooden Leg understood. The incoming whistle rushing out of the blizzard clouds warned him.

No longer was that big-throated gun aiming for the ridge. Now the soldiers were shooting at the retreating Indians.

Off to the right near the riverbank where no horsemen rode, the shell exploded harmlessly, but with enough clatter and a shower of rocks to hurry on any of those who believed they could tarry behind for long. As the ridge disappeared behind him in the swirling fury of the storm, Wooden Leg listened to another boom of the wagon gun. He rode a little farther. And heard another boom, more distant. Finally the last of the gun's roars—muffled and sodden through the thickening storm.

Then there were no more. And the quiet that wrapped itself around the young warrior was deafening.

Quiet enough to hear the howling, wolfish wind and the groans of the wounded carried across the backs of ponies, cradled by horsemen if possible, any way the wounded could make this journey back toward the village that was sure to be on the move already.

Out of the dance of snow Wooden Leg suddenly recognized the two Lakota who had been with him to rescue Big Crow. He hurried his pony toward their horses. Between them walked another pony, Big Crow astride the animal, but bent over and tied against the horse's neck. The Lakota rode knee to knee with the wounded war chief, each of them holding on to Big Crow so he would not fall.

"He is dead?"

One of the Lakota shook his head. "I think he is alive."

* *Blood Song*, vol. 8, The Plainsmen Series.

"Big Crow!" Wooden Leg said with excitement from just behind the wounded man's pony.

Without raising himself up or twisting around, without so much as moving his head, the war chief mumbled, "Is that you, Wooden Leg? I cannot see."

"It is me," he answered. "I am here with you, Uncle."

"Good," he said with a fluid-filled cough. "Then you tell these *Ho-ohomo-eo-e** that they must let me go and leave me behind."

"Leave you behind?"

He gasped in pain. "You must leave me here, Wooden Leg. I am going to die anyway."

"This is what you truly want?"

"It is my last wish," Big Crow declared bravely. "Carry me no farther."

After explaining to the two Lakota that a warrior must not ignore a dying man's last wish, Wooden Leg led the others a little ways up the now-dry fork of a creek that in spring would flow down to the Tongue River. After no more than four arrow-flights in distance, Big Crow spoke again.

"Here. No farther. Find a place. Then leave me."

"Yes—the rocks are good here," Wooden Leg told the dying man.

When his pony came to a stop beneath him, Big Crow said quietly, "Go back to the rest of the warriors. Go on to the village. Tell my people that I have done my share to rescue the prisoners taken by the soldiers."

"I will tell them," Wooden Leg promised, his throat tasting sour with this parting from a great warrior. "For many generations to come, unto my grandchildren's grandchildren, the *Ohmeseheso* will know that an honorable man has died fighting for his people."

Not far ahead stood some large sandstone rocks on the north side of the ravine. Among them the three found a narrow crevice and therein made a place for the dying man.

Wooden Leg sighed with the heavy weight of a boulder on his chest. "You Lakota choose to bury a man on the open prairie," he explained to them as they cleared the last of the loose shale from the floor of that crack high in the tall rocks.

* Lakota.

"*Tse-Tsehese* warriors prefer to be buried among the rocks of this earth. The quicker to return our bodies to the dust of our Earth Mother."

Across the floor of that narrow crevice they spread a buffalo robe; then all three gently carried Big Crow up to that crack far up the side of the sandstone formation. With a valiant struggle Wooden Leg finished the task by himself, inching the war chief's body back into that crevice the width of his hand at a time.

"Big Crow, can you hear me?" Wooden Leg asked when he could move the man no farther.

For a long time there came no answer. He feared Big Crow had died while he'd been placing him in the death position. At long last the young warrior touched the war chief's face. It was cold. He sighed, ready to leave this hallowed place.

"I am no longer of this earth," Big Crow said in a hushed whisper that surprised the young warrior before him. "*Eshesso!* This be the way of all things! Go now, Wooden Leg—and protect our people . . . always."

For a few moments longer the young man sat there by the body he had folded back into the rocks, then covered with a blanket upon which he'd laid the beautiful warbonnet, all that time wondering if he really had seen Big Crow's lips move or not. The man's skin was cold and his eyes were closed as if in death.

Wooden Leg wasn't sure if he had heard those last words with his ears . . . or in his heart.

When he finally stood, the two Lakota warriors patiently waiting at his back, Wooden Leg whispered in reply.

"Like you—I will lay my body down and give my life to . . . to protect my people."

Chapter 37

8–10 January 1877

Damn, if it wasn't cold, despite all the fires these soldiers had blazing in their bivouac.

Maybe it was merely the howl of the wind, or the icy rip of each flake of snow as it slashed against a man's skin—but Luther Kelly couldn't remember when he had ever been colder.

After the last shot was fired from Pope's artillery, Miles could finally order Lieutenant Mason Carter's men of Company K, Fifth Cavalry, out of the snow and into the timber to begin building fires near the wagon camp. They were shortly joined by Lieutenant Cornelius Cusick's F Company of the Twenty-second, who trudged back across the ice on the Tongue River to shouts of victory.

During the five long hours of that morning's battle, the men of both outfits had hunkered down in their snowy rifle pits, shivering without stop as the fight raged on around them—unable to make themselves warm as the blizzard rolled in, not even allowed to move about to relieve themselves for fear of being picked off by troublesome Indian marksmen.

Then, once they had a few minutes around their fires and Miles had sent two other companies chasing after the retreating warriors, the colonel ordered Carter's and Cusick's weary troops back to the bottomland to dismantle what tents the wind hadn't toppled and hurtled away down the valley. What tents the soldiers brought back to the wagon camp at the foot of the plateau they struggled to raise where they could, in no special pattern, as the blizzard continued to build in strength throughout the afternoon.

Surgeons Tilton and Tesson had their stewards remove the nine wounded from the battlefield, making them as comfortable as possible in tents erected near fires down in among the cottonwood near the riverbank. Corporal Augustus Rothman of Casey's A Company was the lone fatality—dying instantly when a bullet smashed into his forehead during that gallant charge up the ridge against overwhelming odds. His fellow soldiers wrapped the body securely in a gray blanket and placed Rothman in one of the wagons until Miles would determine where ultimately to bury the corporal—on the battlefield or back at their Tongue River Cantonment.

Late that afternoon Ewers and Dickey brought their outfits limping back as twilight deepened the already gloomy weather. They reported in to the colonel their estimation that they had followed the retreating warriors for some three miles before turning around to fight their way back through ever-deepening snowdrifts piled up by the ground blizzard, to struggle against a wind that continued to chip away at their resolve.

At dusk the snow became an icy sleet, then gradually turned sodden. By dark the blizzard had wrung itself out and become a cold, driving rain. Men scurried here and there to secure dry wood where they could find it and prepared to spend a wet, miserable night around smoky fires.

Just past dark the first sniper fired into camp. A picket answered the shot. A few minutes later a second bullet tore through the bivouac, striking a cast-iron skillet with a loud clang and scattering the surprised soldiers. Luther Kelly momentarily looked up from his beans, then calmly scooped another spoonful into his mouth.

"Goddammit!" Miles roared, interrupted at his supper and leaping to his feet. *"Baldwin!"*

"Sir?" Frank Baldwin was there immediately.

"You and Bailey get moving to the company commanders," Miles growled. "Tell them to put out their fires for the rest of the night."

"P-put out their fires?" Bailey repeated.

"Yes—you tell them it's my order!" Miles snapped. "I don't want a single man killed by these damned snipers."

Kelly watched the two officers take off in different directions, waiting with Miles to hear the first loud protests drift back from the cold, drenched soldiers ordered to extinguish their fires for their own safety.

"Some Cheyenne snipers fired into our camp the night after Mackenzie drove them all into the hills," Donegan explained as he reluctantly kicked some more wet snow onto the hissing limbs at their feet.

The last of the yellow-and-blue flames went out with a sizzle, and the entire bivouac slowly pitched into darkness.

"Bringing up Mackenzie, eh?" Miles grumbled like a man nursing a wound that would not heal.

Donegan started to apologize. "Didn't mean nothing by it—"

"Well, gentlemen: I certainly feel we've accomplished every bit as much today as Crook did with Dull Knife's Cheyenne," Miles bristled defensively. "And we did it without any of Mackenzie's goddamned cavalry!"

Kelly flicked his eyes at the Irishman and gave a tiny shrug before he said, "A damn good job of it too, General. I think what you and your men can be most proud of is that you've bested the Lakota and Cheyenne on their own ground—where they chose to fight you."

"Bloody right," Miles said. "They picked this ground for their fight, didn't they, Kelly? And they damn well took the high ground, too—didn't they, Kelly? And—by the planets—we still drove them off! But, Mr. Kelly . . . I say Casey, Butler, and McDonald are due the lion's share of the praise!"

"Right, General," Kelly replied with genuine agreement. "You put the right officers at the right place on the field. Make no mistake about that, Seamus Donegan—the general here accomplished this whole campaign with no more than one officer to lead every company."

"True as sun there." Then Donegan cleared his throat. "I can't remember when I've seen soldiers any braver than the men of those three companies who took the ridge."

Miles nodded thoughtfully in the rainy darkness. "Yes, thank you, Mr. Donegan. These men . . . men of mine were stalwart today, weren't they? Despite the ground, the weather, and nearly running out of ammunition—they stayed in the scrap until the job was done, by damn!"

"Are we headed back to the Yellowstone?" Kelly asked.

"Perhaps in another day," the colonel answered with a sigh. "I've got an itch to find out what became of the hostiles' camp. So in the morning I mean to scratch that itch."

Near daylight on the ninth the rain had again become a wet, soggy snow as the men turned out, boiled coffee, and fried their ration of salt pork. Some chose to soak their hard-tack in their coffee, while others softened up the frozen, rock-like crackers in the bacon grease at the bottom of their mess kits. It was just about the most miserably cold, wet camp that Luther Kelly could remember ever awaking to.

After breakfast Miles selected six companies to join him in his search for the Crazy Horse village upriver. In addition, he brought along Lieutenant Hargous's mounted detachment, as well as his company of scouts. He left behind only Cusick's F Company of the Twenty-second to throw out pickets around the wagon camp as well as to post spotters atop those bluffs the Sioux and Cheyenne had defended the day before.

Behind the colonel and his staff, behind his scouts and mounted riflemen, the half-dozen companies were spread out in a wide skirmish formation that extended from the hills on the west side of the Tongue all the way across the river to the bluffs on the east bank. Miles led them out at a cautious pace, no man certain when they might encounter the enemy's rear guard or an ambush.

Instead, all they came across near midday that Tuesday was a campsite the enemy had abandoned sometime before the battle. Because of all the recent snow and rain, it proved impossible for the scouts to tell just how old the site truly was. For the better part of a quarter of an hour, the men all watched Miles silently move among the now-dead fire pits until he stopped, staring south for the longest time.

When he finally turned, the colonel told his staff, "Inform the company commanders that we are doing an about-face."

Baldwin argued with his characteristic enthusiasm, "But, General—they can't be that far ahead of us!"

Wagging his head with resignation, Miles replied, "That may well be, Lieutenant. But I don't think we're going to catch them again this time out. Not *this* outfit. We're already in trouble with our rations and grain for the stock."

"We'll march back to bivouac?" asked James Casey.

"Yes," and Miles nodded.

"Let me volunteer to pursue them with a battalion," Baldwin offered. "I can follow their trail and catch Crazy Horse unawares just like I caught Sitting—"

"No, Lieutenant," Miles interrupted as Baldwin was warming up to his appeal. "From the looks of things the hostiles are trying to make their way to the Bighorns."

"I can follow them even there," Baldwin pleaded. "You just give me the men and some animals—"

"And your men would eat what, Lieutenant?" Miles paused a moment to let that sink in for all of them gathered around him. "I don't have enough in the wagons for this outfit to have full rations on our march back to the Yellowstone, much less to supply a battalion that might be in the field for God knows how many days. And the weather, Mr. Baldwin . . . this goddamned weather! No man can say with any certainty just what the sky is going to do to us next in this country! No, Lieutenant—let's all just say we've done our damage, and that we're going home."

Kelly stepped up with his reins in hand. "As chief of scouts, I agree with the general," he told the officers. "The Crazy Horse people are done for. It's just a matter of time—no more than weeks at the most—before he has no choice but to take his people in to the reservation."

The colonel nodded with that support. "Yes, I think Crazy Horse is finished, Kelly. If he doesn't turn his village around and come in to surrender very soon, I'm certain a lot of his people are going to die from a cruel recipe of hunger and bitter cold."

In the icy bottomland of the Tongue River, Miles ordered his six companies to turn about and march north to their bivouac.

The weary, hungry foot soldiers reached their wagon camp near dusk.

• • • •

A crusty layer of new snow greeted the soldiers on the morning of the tenth as they rolled out to another day promising more subfreezing temperatures, in addition to a long march north and repeated crossings of the Tongue River.

In the last few predawn hours no groans were heard from the surgeons' tent. Seamus figured Dr. Tilton had finally put enough laudanum down Private Bernard McCann to put the poor soldier completely out. For the last two nights McCann had clearly been in tremendous pain from the bullet wound that had smashed through his upper right femur, the heaviest bone in the body.

Merciful God, if you plan on taking the man, make it quick, Seamus had asked through the long hours of the past two nights when he could not sleep for listening to the soldier's pain. Let him go in peace, I pray you.

"We're eating with the general this morning," Kelly announced as he came up out of the cold dawn to the sheltered place where Donegan had hunkered out of the wind between a couple of fallen cottonwood.

As Seamus finished wrapping his blankets inside the thick, waterproof canvas ducking of his bedroll, he asked, "What's on the menu?"

"Same as yesterday. Same as the day before," Kelly replied. "Same as we had the day before that."

Standing, Seamus rubbed his stomach with one hand in mock delight. "You sure know how to get a man's appetite up, don't you?"

Then the grin washed from Kelly's face. "You're still serious about this morning, are you? Still set on leaving us to ride south?"

With a nod Seamus said, "I'll light out after breakfast with Miles. Go see for myself how the country looks southeast from here."

"Injun sign?"

Donegan got to his feet and tossed the bedroll atop his saddle and blanket, lying there at the bottom of the tree where the two rifles stood ready. He wagged his head in resignation, then sighed, "This army's flushed 'em . . . again. No telling where they're scattering now."

Miles turned at the sound of their approach, along with most of those staff officers and a few of the scouts who had bedded down at a nearby fire. The colonel stepped away from his headquarters group, once again looking massive in his buffalo coat and dark, bushy beard.

"So, Kelly—have you convinced Mr. Donegan here to stay on with us?"

"I don't think there was ever a chance of that, General," Kelly replied, shrugging in apology.

"You could have a dangerous ride ahead of you," Miles said, holding his hand out to welcome Donegan to the fire.

Seamus shook the colonel's hand. "Not the first one of those I've had."

Miles let go of Donegan's hand and leaned back. "I get the feeling this won't be the last." Then the colonel turned to step between Kelly and Donegan, pounding a hand on each shoulder, nudging them toward the fire. "Bring these men some coffee, will you, Bailey? And let's get some meat cooking. Mr. Donegan is going to need something to stick to his ribs, something to last out this first day."

Donegan asked, "How will you fare on what you've got for rations, General?"

"We'll make it back," he answered stoically. "These men are made of the finest stuff. . . . There's no better soldiers on the plains."

Accepting a cup of coffee from Hobart Bailey, Seamus responded, "I've had the signal honor to fight alongside them, General."

"It's been an honor having you along for the march, Mr. Donegan. Perhaps you can join us again."

Blowing the steam off the coffee's surface, Seamus took a scalding sip, then said, "I'd like to tell you that hell itself would have to freeze over before I ever rode north to fight Injins with you in the winter . . . but twice now I've already seen how certain things can change my plans."

"I mean to go back to the cantonment, straightaway. And while the men and stock recoup their strength, I'm planning to attempt some diplomacy with the warrior bands," Miles explained as the slabs of pork were speared out of the blackened cast-iron skillets and flung onto the tiny oval tin halves of a soldier's mess kit. "By now I must surely have convinced the hostile chiefs that they must surrender—or I will dog them until their villages are totally destroyed, until their people are completely destitute."

"Diplomacy, General?" Kelly inquired around a mouthful of bacon. "You're going to send emissaries of peace out to those warrior villages?"

Miles nodded, chewing a piece of meat, his eyes flicking at the swarthy half-breed. "Bruguier here is the man I'll depend on to do it. With Sitting Bull roaming to the north of the Yellowstone, and Crazy Horse still at large here in the south, it stands to reason that I'm the one and only man who can bring either one—or maybe even both—to talk about surrendering and going into their agencies."

"Bruguier will no doubt have his hands full," Donegan said. Then he turned to the half-breed to ask, "You sure about this? Sure you can expect to find anything besides the end of a scalping knife waiting for you in those Lakota camps?"

"What are you asking him?" Miles demanded.

"Just that I'd be real surprised, General . . . surprised if Johnny Bruguier found himself welcome in those enemy villages after he came over to the army."

Johnny Bruguier looked at Miles impassively, as if he expected the colonel to do his talking for him.

Miles said, "I'll send one or two of the captives with Johnny when he goes, Mr. Donegan. They can tell their own people how my heart is right when I offer them good terms of surrender."

Shrugging, Bruguier added, "I gotta try, Donegan. Soon there's no more buffalo. And always the army keeps coming—until there will be no more warriors to feed the women and children anyway. I gotta try."

He held out his hand to the half-breed, a begrudging grin crossing his cold face. "All right, Bruguier. I wish you all the luck in the world." Then the Irishman turned back to the colonel. "I imagine if anyone can talk the Crazy Horse and Lone Wolf people in . . . I expect it will be one of their own people, General. You're smart to send some of them along with Johnny to talk surrender to the chiefs."

"I only pray my strategy works," Miles replied. "One way or the other—surrender or annihilation—this winter has been the beginning of the end for these people."

"And if your peace strategy doesn't work?" Kelly asked.

Miles turned to his chief of scouts. "Then the Fifth Infantry will be on the march again by spring."

That first night after the battle, Wooden Leg joined the small group of warriors who slipped back after nightfall and crept up through the snow to get close to the soldier camp. They did not need to stalk quietly through the snow flurries—the *ve-ho-e* had started big fires, and the white men were talking loud, laughing too, not at all worried about making noise.

Perhaps . . . one man or two might slip in among the shadows and the loud clamor, take out his knife, and cut the prisoners free.

But they found a tight ring of camp guards surrounding Bear Coat's men, so Crazy Horse's warriors could not get as close to the soldiers as they had planned, much less slip in to free the captives, as they had hoped. In utter frustration one of the Lakota fired his rifle at a tall shadow that crossed one of the roaring fires. That began a scary time of it for the warriors out beyond the last rings of dancing firelight. Soldiers fired back into the night. Warriors answered in kind as the big *ve-ho-e* fires were snuffed out one by one, frightened men kicking snow and dumping water onto the flames.

"Sister! Can you hear me?" Wooden Leg called out several times before she answered him.

In the midst of the yelling white men and the sporadic, infrequent gunfire, Crooked Nose Woman hollered back, "We are all right, Wooden Leg! Go back and tell our people we are all right. The soldiers are taking us to their home on the Elk River. We have food and are warm. Do not worry about us. We will be all right."

"Know that we will come for you there!"

"Do not throw your lives away on account of us," Crooked Nose Woman answered. "The soldiers have treated us kindly. Look to yourselves now. Protect those in the village."

"I will see you again soon!" Wooden Leg promised.

"That is my prayer too!" Crooked Nose Woman shouted. "Until I am back among my people. When this war is over and there is peace once again . . . be safe, Wooden Leg!"

Then he heard another *Tse-Tsehese* voice. It sounded old. Perhaps it was Old Wool Woman's. She was singing a news song—the way a camp crier would sing to tell others in the village of some important event.

> Young men, do not fight.
> Young men, the fighting is over.

> The *ve-ho-e* are not hurting us,
> Your people are not harmed.

> Young men, let the soldiers go.
> Young men, let the Bear Coat go
> in peace now.

One by one the *Ohmeseheso* warriors told the Lakota what Old Wool Woman was singing, and eventually the Indian guns fell silent. With a cracking voice she continued to sing her calming song as the warriors slipped back, back away from the outer ring of firelight.

> Young men, do not fight.
> Young men, the fighting is over.

> The *ve-ho-e* are taking us to the Elk River.
> Wait to see if the Bear Coat truly means
> his talk of peace.

> Let the soldiers go, young warriors.
> You cannot protect us any longer—
> Go back to our village
> And protect your families,
> Protect the *Tse-Tsehese* who are left
> With your bodies.

Wooden Leg lay there on the mushy snow in the dark, listening to the soldiers whisper in their camp, hearing the heavy, icy rain tumble through the skeletal branches of the aged cottonwoods over his head, thinking on Old Wool Woman's words.

How many of the People were left alive and free? After a winter, a spring, then a long summer and autumn, and now another winter of fighting the soldiers—how many? With very few lodges and ponies, very few weapons and sacred objects left them, the *Tse-Tsehese* truly had little. But now Wooden Leg was forced to consider just how few of them there were.

Once a rich people, the most powerful warriors on the

northern plains . . . now reduced to living in shabby rock-and-branch shelters, women and children running in fear of the soldiers because with so many battles, there were no longer enough warriors to protect them. No longer enough warriors to turn back all the soldiers.

They kept coming. And coming. And coming.

It seemed the *ve-ho-e* were like the stars. There were too many to count. Whenever Wooden Leg looked up at a summer sky, he was sure the stars covered everything from one edge of the earth to the other. From one distant point of the four winds to the other.

Although the clouds hid everything above this night, Wooden Leg began to weep with realization in that freezing drizzle of a rain.

Soon the white man would cover everything in the same way the stars covered the sky.

Chapter 38

Tioheynuka Wi 1877

BY TELEGRAPH

Raiding Redskins Again Rampant in Wyoming.

Terrible Snow-Storm all Over the West

WYOMING

Another Indian Skirmish

CHEYENNE, January 15.—The continued interruption in telegraph communications between Forts Laramie and Fetterman induced an escort of the Sixth cavalry, commanded by Sergeant Bessy, in returning from Hat creek to strike across the country, and come in on the Fetterman line last night. On the Elk Horn, thirty miles north of Fort Laramie, fresh traces of Indians were discovered, and to avoid a surprise in camp, the sergeant, with three men, made a reconnaissance, and about midnight collided with a party of fifteen Indians. In the fight which ensued, Bessy and Toggart were slightly wounded and Featherall badly wounded. They also lost three horses killed, when the Indians were forced to retire. A company of cavalry left Laramie to-day to endeavor to intercept the Indians.

CHICAGO

One to Three Feet of Snow.

CHICAGO, January 15.—Early this forenoon a heavy snow-storm, accompanied with a violent northeast wind, set in and has continued up to midnight to-night without abatement. . . . Advices from several states in the west show that the storm is very great and that from one to three feet of snow are on the ground.

*T*ioheynuka Wi. Moon of Frost in the Lodge.

They had barely survived the Moon of Hard Times. With no buffalo to be found and very little game, and with the way one winter storm followed on the heels of the last . . . the Crazy Horse village had been limping from one place to another after packing up and leaving the Buffalo Tongue River country in a hurry.

He Dog reined up his pony, turning to look down the slope into the valley where the long procession trudged through the snow and wind. Warriors dotted the hillsides along their route toward the White Mountains,* keeping a wary eye trained on the distance for any army columns prowling through this broken country. At each camp it seemed there were fewer lodges to come down and start away on that day's journey toward the foot of the mountains, where they hoped to find buffalo for meat and hides. And hope.

To find buffalo for hope.

So many had already given up all hope of living in the old way with the Hunkpatila of Crazy Horse. Most often they slipped away late at night, taking down their lodge if they had one, gathering their few belongings, leading their skinny po-

* Bighorn Mountains.

nies away from the camp circle in the dark and the rain or snow, sneaking off toward the agencies.

The village was not a grand cavalcade any longer.

The Shahiyela had buried their war chief, Big Crow, in the rocks. The Crazy Horse people had left behind two bodies upon the scaffolds they had erected high in the forks of the great old cottonwoods. He Dog knew one of them well—a friend named Runs-the-Bear. A brave Oglalla who had stayed to fight until the last. Both of the dead were very brave men who gave their lives in that fight at Belly Butte, their bones now resting high in the trees, resting for the ages—for the wild animals to pick apart, for the sun to bleach, for the winds to sigh over for all seasons to come.

And there were the wounded. Many wounded. How they must be suffering with the cold, with this journey the chiefs ordered. Then two more died. Two more high scaffolds. More women and children left without a man to protect them. Yet the others healed. For the rest of their days they would carry scars of their fight in the winter blizzard, but they had healed.

Like the pony belonging to the young Shahiyela named Medicine Bear. Struck by one of the big iron balls fired from one of the wagon guns, the hair along one flank had been completely scraped off in a long streak, right down to the bare hide. But now, as the raw abrasion healed, the track of the iron ball on its flank began to grow white hair. A white as brilliant as sun-struck snow.

The Great Mystery had protected both horse and rider during the battle and had gone on to mark that pony with a sign.

The warriors of the Hunkpatila and the Shahiyela could do no less than protect the shrinking village.

After watching from the hills He Dog hesitated returning to the camp at the end of each day's march. The children would be crying from empty bellies. Women would be wailing for their dead, their faces tracked with tears and ashes, their arms and legs gashed in mourning. There was little hope left in the people.

Even in the eyes of Crazy Horse.

This strange man, He Dog's good friend, no longer had the special light behind his eyes. No longer seemed to carry a fire in his belly. Crazy Horse surely heard the same sad crying, the same wails, He Dog thought—the same mourning all the rest of us hear.

Eight suns after the soldiers had started north with their prisoners, scouts for the village finally ran across a small herd of buffalo high up on the headwaters of the Buffalo Tongue River, near the foothills to the White Mountains draped in a thick winter white. Hunters killed all they could before the rest ran so far away, the tired ponies could not fight the deep snow to follow.

Wearily the women and children had stumbled through the icy drifts, doing their best to follow on foot in those paths beaten by the warriors' ponies to reach the fallen beasts. There were not many—but enough that the people ate well that night. There was more talk around the fires too, and even a little laughter. Laughter! For once in a long, long time the faces showed more than the shadows of death-approaching.

They all saw that the most seriously wounded warriors got the choice cuts, sucked at slivers of the heart dipped in gall to build their strength, thicken their blood. Next to be fed were the old ones and the children. And finally the strong women and warriors ate their fill. What was left they wrapped in the green hides and tied to the travois when the village moved on the next day.

Would they ever find a place where they could rest in peace? He Dog wondered. Or would they have to keep on moving, endlessly moving? Attempting to stay one step ahead, a half day ahead, of the soldiers?

Those people who had slipped away to sneak off to the agencies—he wondered how they were faring now. Was there ever enough pig meat, enough moldy flour, to fill all the bellies, ever enough of the paper-thin trader blankets to keep all the bodies warm against the cruel bite of the wolfish wind?

And for the first time He Dog truly hoped there was enough at the agencies to take care of his people who had given up and gone in. Because there wasn't enough buffalo left anymore. And what blankets the village had not been forced to abandon, what blankets the army had not captured and burned, surely those were not near enough to keep the little ones, the sick ones, the women warm as they trudged on through the winter snows beside the skinny ponies pulling the near-empty travois.

More and more he found himself praying there would be enough at the reservations for all who fled there.

Much of the rest of each day He Dog brooded about his friend. Was Crazy Horse like the rest of the *Titunwan* and *Tse-Tsehese* warriors? Was he finally tired of all the fleeing, the fighting, the running and the killing . . . enough to take his own family in to the agency?

Was Crazy Horse ready to surrender?

Would their battle with the Bear Coat at Belly Butte really be the last fight for Crazy Horse?

Was it to be the last fight of the once-mighty Lakota warrior bands?

The thought caused He Dog to shudder. How could any fighting man ever turn over his guns, give away his ponies, sit in the shade of agency buildings, and wait for the *wasicu* to hand out the rations?

He Dog hung his head as the people below went into camp along a little treeless creek. There would not be much shelter from the snarl of the wind this night.

He felt like a plum that had its juices squeezed from it: hollow, dry. Dying.

Oh, how he wanted to hope, wanted desperately to believe that Crazy Horse would never be anything less than a warrior.

BY TELEGRAPH

General Miles' Men Bull-Dozing Sitting Bull.

THE INDIANS

Sitting Bull Again Defeated

ST. PAUL, January 16.—*To Adjutant General of the Division of the Missouri:*—A dispatch received from Colonel Miles states that the 18th of December, three companies of the Fifth Infantry, under Lieutenant Baldwin, struck Sitting Bull's camp on Red Water and defeated him, with a loss of all the property in the camp and sixty mules and ponies. The Indians es-

caped with little besides what they had on their persons.

> (Signed,)
> ALFRED H. TERRY, Brigadier General

Luther Kelly and his scouts got the soldiers no more than
seven miles north along the Tongue River that tenth day of
January. After more than a day of rain the soggy ground began
to freeze in the afternoon, the sky clouded up, and it began to
snow all over again.

For the next two days it was much of the same: cold,
snow, half rations, slogging back and forth across the Tongue
time and again, the drenched soldiers shivering around smoky
fires each evening, complaining of frostbitten toes and fingers,
ears and noses.

Bernard McCann died quietly on the afternoon of the
twelfth as the regiment was going into camp. Surgeon Tilton
had never expected the young private to recover from his terrible leg wound but in the last four days had done all he could
to put McCann at peace. Like Corporal Rothman, the other
soldier killed at Battle Butte, McCann was wrapped securely in
a tent half, bound by rope, and laid among the cargo in a
wagon.

The following morning the Fifth Infantry marched on,
covering no more than fifteen miles on the thirteenth, making
their bivouac in one of their southbound camps. Once again
the mercury in Tilton's thermometer froze at forty degrees
below zero.

One day they were able to cross the Tongue River on the
ice, though the following would find the ice softening and
splintering, drenching soldiers, wagons, and mules—all hands
called out to throw ropes to those who floundered in the ice
floes, to pitch in and haul their fellows from the icy dangers.
Not a mile went by that at least a dozen soldiers didn't fall out,
some shuffling to one side of the trail and some to the other,
tearing off their boots and socks, rubbing cold snow on their
frostbitten toes or fingertips.

At one point Kelly spotted an old soldier scooping up a
handful of the crusty ice from the ground, massaging the end
of his nose with it.

"Goddamn it! Goddamn it!" the old file muttered.

"What's the matter?" Kelly inquired. "Nipped your nose?"

"Yeah—my nose and fingers and bloody well everything else—goddammit!"

Each night the men lumbered into bivouac with wet boots. The unlucky ones were ordered right on out to guard duty and did not get a chance to dry their footwear properly. But for all the complaints about the leaking overshoes and the frozen screws barely holding the boot soles in place, Tilton and Tesson did not have to amputate a single toe among that hardy regiment of foot soldiers.

A stalwart bunch they were, trudging toward home mile after mile, no man immune from the bouts of coughing that plagued them all day long, fevers and aches that kept many of the soldiers from getting any real rest at night. In the cold and the darkness the restless insomniacs huddled close to the fires, so close that many of the soldiers scorched their clothing—singeing the skirts of their long buffalo coats, leggings, and even their overshoes.

On Sunday the fourteenth the command reached the site where they had buried Private William Batty on their chase after the village. Although they hadn't seen any Indians since the ninth, Miles ordered pickets put out to guard against a surprise attack while relays began chipping away at the frozen earth until they recovered Batty's corpse. After the surgeons rewrapped the body, it was placed in the back of a wagon with the other two soldiers, and the march was resumed for the rest of the afternoon until they reached the site of their fifth southbound camp about the time a new blizzard swept down upon them.

Icy, frozen snow hurtled out of the north into their faces, accompanying their struggles for the next three days. So terrible had the weather become once more, so miserable were the men trudging half-bent at the waist into the gales, that Luther Kelly was reminded of Napoleon's army trudging through the snowy, wind-hewn steppes of Russia.

Just past two o'clock on Thursday, the eighteenth of January, the van of the column hoved into sight of the cantonment. In the near distance garrison guards cried out their news to others at the post. Men burst from the log cabins, pulling on coats and hats and mittens. As Miles and his weary winter warriors approached, the regimental band came loping out, formed a square, and began their rendition of "Marching Through Georgia."

"Just look at the men, will you, Kelly?" Miles suggested, having turned in the saddle to watch the faces of those trail-hardened soldiers behind them as they drew step by step ever closer to Tongue River Cantonment. "Grinning from ear to ear!"

"How could any of them be unhappy, General?" Luther asked. "They've marched more than two hundred miles through the roughest conditions, crossed the Tongue River more than a hundred fifty times going and coming—and now they see their barracks again at long last, where they can take shelter out of the winds and eat warm food after weeks of cold bacon and frozen hardtack—"

"Not to mention a good scrubbing!" Miles roared, giving himself a sniff. "Whew! I do believe I'm fit only to bunk in with my horse, Kelly!"

Without another word Luther reined his horse slowly to the side and let the colonel and his staff continue toward the cantonment's crude log buildings. Garrison soldiers waved their hats. Those returning warriors all raised their muskrat and sealskin caps, some pitched high in the raw air as cheers and huzzahs scared birds from the bare branches of surrounding trees. They were home, these men who had endured more over the last two months than most humans could ever imagine.

They were home.

Home.

And so that sentiment made Luther rein up there on the low rise, turning to gaze south . . . south by east . . . wondering, now that eight days had passed, just how much ground the Irishman had been able to cover—alone as he was in hostile country, plunging through the same icy sleet and driving blizzards.

Was he halfway there? Kelly wondered. Had he bumped into any hunting bands or war parties? Had he managed to stay out of sight and keep his hair?

Would he make it home to his family?

As the wind knifed cruelly across the side of his face,

Luther adjusted the wool muffler over his cheek, tugging it over his nose. And then he thought he knew.

A man like Seamus Donegan simply didn't know the meaning of the word "failure." No "can't." No "won't."

"Fare you well, friend," Kelly said in a whisper on that hilltop near Tongue River Cantonment, his words whipped from his lips and carried south on that brutal wind blustering out of the arctic regions. "Fare you well . . . until we meet again."

Chapter 39

10–16 January 1877

Telegraphic Briefs

Pay of Indian Agents

WASHINGTON, January 10.—The house committee on Indian affairs agreed this morning to report for passage the bill offered by Mr. Seelye at the last session, which authorizes the secretary of the interior, whichever in his discretion it seems wise, to add $100 yearly to the salary of each Indian agent, accruing after two years of continuous service. This increase to continue yearly, until the salary shall reach $2,000 a year, which shall be the agent's salary thereafter as long as he holds the place.

WYOMING

New Diggings Discovered

GREEN RIVER, January 10.—Eleven miners came into Camp Brown on the 6th instant for supplies from the head of Wood river, and bring coarse gold

with them. They report about thirty men now in the
diggings, working with rockers, making $10 per day
and upwards. One man found a nugget weighing $30.
The party report no snow on the route and very little
in camp. They return immediately.

That first morning alone again, Seamus climbed onto the
bluffs that bordered the eastern rim of the Tongue River
Valley, pausing for a moment to watch the soldiers at work
below. Some threw stacks of folded tents into the wagons,
others hitched the balky, braying mules into their traces, while
others kicked out their fires and began to fall into formation
for the drudgery of the day's march.

Somewhere in the midst of those four-hundred-some
men were those who had become friends in the space of less
than a month, along with those nameless soldiers he had
joined in climbing the icy slope, shoulder to shoulder. Faceless
men, all but their eyes hidden behind the crude wool masks.
Soldiers young, soldiers old—ordinary men called upon to
exercise extraordinary bravery: out of ammunition, when
many might have retreated, those three companies fixed bayonets and kept on moving beneath the galling fire of the enemy.

The wind smelled of snow up there—a sharp tang wafting
off that broken land to the north. Donegan pulled up the
collar to his heavy buffalo coat, then slowly put his fingers to
his brow in salute.

"To good sojurs," he said quietly. "For service beyond the
call of duty."

Turning the claybank aside, the Irishman put the Tongue
River at his back and continued his climb up the divide. Hours
later, at the crest, he looked back—finding the top half of the
Wolf Mountains obliterated by low slate clouds. More snow
before the night was done. He knew the Bighorns arose from
the plains somewhere to the southwest, but for now they were
hidden by distance, by storm clouds, by winter itself. He
prayed to see them off to his right one day real soon.

Down into the valley of Hanging Woman Creek they
dropped, that claybank mare and he, following the frozen
stream south by east until twilight. Wary and watchful all that
day, he had stayed down from the skyline, constantly watching

the horizon to the west for enemy horsemen. At the edge of a frozen stream piercing a small grove of cottonwood saplings, Seamus took shelter as the sun continued to drain its light from the west. He decided not to build a fire, no matter how small. Instead he took the horse to the creek, broke a hole in the thick slate of ice, and let the animal drink its fill from the narrow trickle as he loosened the cinch.

Then Seamus looped the reins around a wrist, settled back down against the brush, and closed his eyes.

It was well past slap dark and snowing when the horse tugged on the reins enough to wake him in its search for some fodder to eat. It hadn't been enough sleep to make him feel rested, but he hoped it would be enough that he could ride on through till morning. After tightening the cinch Donegan cut himself a thin sliver of tobacco and laid it inside his cheek. It always helped to give him a little stir, the better to keep himself awake for what he had to do.

He covered the fifty-some miles of that southeastern beeline to the Powder River in two and a half days, traveling at night in the most bitter conditions while temperatures once more dropped out of the bottom. At times he allowed himself a little fire, not really the sort for boiling coffee or frying his salt pork, just something small—the sort of fire that could cheer a man while a dull pewter sun came up in the east after a long night's ride, the sort of fire that could keep company with a lonely man as he stirred restlessly in his blankets throughout the day, dragging kindling together from time to time to keep that small fire going until it grew dark enough for them to move out again.

He watered them both twice a day—at morning and again at dusk. And never did he remove the saddle, choosing instead only to loosen the cinch while he dozed and the horse cropped at what grass it could find. There were times the animal nuzzled him during the day, awakening him from the light, fitful slumber Seamus allowed himself. Donegan stirred, stiff and cranky, untying the horse and moving it to another spot where it could dig and tear at more sustenance before he settled himself again. Much of the time the Irishman passed out in his blankets, sitting up with the Winchester across his lap and the Sharps laid out along his right leg. Other times he allowed himself the luxury of lying curled up on his side atop the dried mattress of some windblown grass at the base of a tree, or wrapped fetally atop some spongy sagebrush that kept him above most of the drifted snow.

When the light began to fade and he found himself too cold and stiff to sleep any longer, Seamus began to move again, slowly. Scrounging about for more kindling, anything dry enough for him to use one of his few remaining lucifers. Build himself a fire just big enough to rub his bare hands over, flames only high enough that he could yank off the army's buffalo overboots, then tug off the calf-high boots, just to hold his damp stockings and cold feet there by the flames for a few minutes while he wiggled his toes and the sky went to dark.

Each time he gazed at those first stars coming out to announce the coming of night, he remembered the way her eyes had glimmered by a fire's light on their honeymoon ride north from the Staked Plain of Texas, across the wilds to Colorado Territory, and on north to find a roost for her, eventually, at Fort Laramie. Many nights spent camping beneath the stars themselves as new bride and groom, rolled and twisted together, leg in leg, for warmth beneath the layers of canvas and wool blankets, staring up at a black dome not far different from this.

He wondered if she ever came out at night down to Laramie, to look up at the sky and think of his being somewhere beneath those same stars. He wondered if it helped the loneliness for her the way it helped his. Like a warming balm a man would knead into a sore muscle or open wound—this looking up at the same sky she was under at that same moment. It made Seamus feel that much closer to her, not near so far away, as he finally stood, kicked snow onto the tiny pile of burning sticks, then tightened the cinch and rode off under that endless black dome.

Surely she looked up at those same stars. He was all the closer to her because of it. Donegan was certain she must feel his presence, too, when she gazed at the sky that looked down upon them both. How it brought him comfort.

Upon striking the Powder after those first fifty-some miles, he figured he had his way home. Follow the river south. Past the mouth of the Crazy Woman Fork—where he had begun ten long years of fighting the Lakota and Cheyenne in this land, coming to know why they guarded this country so jealously. He had left childhood roots in Ireland to sail to Amerikay but found no home in Boston Towne, far less among the mobile, rootless, roaming camps of the Union cavalry. But once that terrible business was over back east, Donegan had wanted to be as far from all that had been as he could put himself.

Little had he expected that he would find a home in the west, to fall in love with the sheer immensity and rugged beauty of its towering mountains and endless prairies. Little had he expected he would ever find someone he so desperately wanted to share that home with.

"Stay warm, Samantha," he would whisper to himself each dawn as he closed his eyes and put himself to sleep thinking of the two of them waiting for him at Laramie. "Soon . . ."

How far would it be? he asked himself. How many miles down the Powder to Reno Cantonment from here? Fifty? No farther. He figured it had to be more than seventy, as much as eighty, miles from where he'd first struck the Powder. But what with the twists and loops of the river, it was hard for a man to tell just how many miles for sure.

At times he would pass a bare buffalo skull lying akimbo along his trail, a horn and skull plate half-in, half-out, of a dirty skiff of snow. When the shimmering winter moonlight shone bright enough on the landscape, Seamus recognized the tracks of an occasional coyote or deer or antelope crisscrossing the wind-sculpted snow as the two of them rose and fell, climbed and descended, the vaulting, heaving country. Day before yesterday a few prairie dogs poked their heads up from their dark holes, emerging into the bitter cold and strong wind to bark in protest before darting back out of sight as man and horse passed on by.

Then late one night he spotted the dim outlines of the buttes far away to the southeast, limned there against the skyline as a distant blood-tinged sunrise awoke a world far east of the Great Plains. That pale-orange strata of Pumpkin Buttes . . . oh, how the sight of them made his eyes strain to make out something to the south of him—where Reno Cantonment should lay.

Seamus dared push on past sunrise that morning, so eager was he to see another's face, so hungry to hear a voice other

than his own. After all, Reno Crossing meant that he had
returned to far more familiar country, perhaps even to a land
where a man might travel in far less danger than when he
plunged through the heart of Lakota hunting ground.

Early that afternoon, after more than 130 miles as a crow
would fly, Donegan came in sight of those mud-and-log huts
that Captain Edwin Pollock's Ninth U.S. Infantry had garrisoned in this northern country, an outpost at the precipice
of a deadly land—this last supply depot for Crook's last campaign. As he set the claybank mare into a lope, drawing closer
and closer, he saw that men were moving about, more coming
out of the sod-and-frame barracks as he became more than a
speck on the horizon. As he became a horseman. A man
emerging from a deadly, bloody ground. A lone plainsman.

"Just where in the hell did you come from?"

"The Belle Fourche," Donegan answered, his voice cracking a little from disuse, "by way of Tongue River Cantonment."

"T-tongue River?" stammered a middle-aged soldier.
"Miles's infantry?"

"Yes," he replied, eyeing a man who approached drinking
a steamy cup of coffee.

"You civilian? Ain't no deserter, are you?"

Donegan snorted. "Was I to desert, I'd be off to the
diggings in the Black Hills, or up to Last Chance in Montana
Territory. Last thing I'd want to do would be to put myself
around sojurs."

"See how stupid your god-blame-ed question was, Stacy?"
another one declared peevishly.

One of them peered up beneath a hand shading his eyes
and asked, "But you did come riding down from the Yaller-
stone?"

Seamus's eyes danced over the faces that came out to gaze
up at his in wonder and speculation, enjoying the music of the
voices, the feast for his eyes.

"I did, that. Marching more'n a hundred miles with the
Fifth Infantry," Seamus explained as he laid his wrists across
the saddle horn and let out a sigh. "Chasing Crazy Horse's
village."

"Crazy Horse!"

"He said the Fifth chased Crazy Horse!"

"Caught him too, we did," Donegan said. "Had us a good scrap of it till a blizzard blowed in."

The middle-aged soldier stepped forward. "My name's Pollock. Edwin Pollock. Commandant of this here fine post."

"I remember you, sir," Seamus replied, taking off a mitten and holding a hand down to the captain. "Name's Donegan, late of General Crook's Bighorn and Yellowstone Expedition."

"You're a mite late catching up with them, Donegan," Pollock said. "Crook's bunch passed through here before Christmas."

"I know," he said sadly, thinking back on that special holiday endured away from loved ones. "Crook himself sent me north to learn where Crazy Horse was."

One of the soldiers gleefully declared, "And from the sounds of it you sure as the devil found out where Crazy Horse was, by God!"

"Come on down from that horse," Pollock suggested. "We'll get some side meat frying for you, and I'm sure we can root out some beans and hard bread too."

"Always beans and hard bread wherever the army goes!" a soldier retorted.

Seamus drank three cups of coffee right off, swilling them down as soon as they were cool enough to drink while his first hot meal in a week was still cooking. Those men of the Ninth Infantry sat and stood around him as he wolfed down the beans and soaked his tacks in a new cup of coffee sweetened with heaping spoons of sugar. Seamus couldn't remember when army food had tasted so good.

Maybe it was only that he was almost halfway home. Maybe that's what made something so simple as a hot meal of pasty white beans, crusty hard bread, and a greasy slab of fatty pork such a king's feast late that afternoon among soldiers who asked him everything imaginable about the war going on to the north with Sitting Bull and Crazy Horse.

Why, they acted just the way schoolboys out to recess or old men gathered at the mercantile to whittle and gossip would act, wanting to hear every detail, every last facet of commonplace events like marching up the Tongue, crossing on the ice, burying soldiers, capturing Cheyenne prisoners, and storming an icy ridge when the whole damned outfit was down to its last few bullets. They fed him and coffee'd him and kept him talking until his throat was sore and it had been long dark for hours.

"We best let the man be now," Pollock finally said.

He turned to peer out at the night. "My horse?"

"We've watered and grained him," a soldier said. "Even rubbed some liniment on a sore on his right flank, just under the pad."

"I'm obliged," Seamus said thankfully. "Truly obliged to you men."

"You can bunk right in here," Pollock offered.

But the old soldier told Seamus, "Or spread your bedroll with the rest of us. When I cared for your horse, I brung your saddle and gear inside our humble barrack."

"Yes," Seamus decided suddenly, a tug at his heart deciding it. "I'll bunk in with you fellas if it won't put no one out."

Yes—to stay a while longer among these men who had cared for him and the horse . . . feeling so weary.

Captain Pollock said, "From the sounds of all your riding, bet you ain't had yourself a proper night's sleep in a month of Sundays."

Another man added, "I'll wager you could do with getting some shut-eye in out of the cold."

"I'll push on come morning," Seamus agreed as he stood, feeling the stiffness in near every muscle from being so long in sitting atop the half-log bench.

"After coffee and breakfast at reveille," Pollock said.

Using the officer's brevet rank, Donegan asked, "Could you have me up two hours before sunrise, Major?"

"I'll be sure one of the pickets on the last watch comes in to roust you," a sergeant offered.

He looked round at them again, slowly, some faces sinfully handsome and some downright mud ugly, the old and the young among them, sallow-eyed veteran and peach-cheeked shavetail too. Soldiers all . . . every bit like those soldiers he had ridden beside as they'd galloped into the face of Confederate cavalry and the pounding of Rebel artillery; like Captain Butler's brave men clambering for a foothold on the slopes of an icy hell. Soldiers paid so damned little by an unappreciative country that had scant idea of just what it asked of its fighting men.

Seamus rolled the wolf-hide hat in his hands nervously and told them, "Thank you fellas—for being here when I come riding in. For being here where likely no one else knows you're here. God bless each and every one of you . . . for leaving your families to come to this lonely place on the Powder River."

For a moment they all sat and stood there stunned into silence by his sudden words. One of them coughed self-consciously. Another turned aside and silently dragged a hand under his nose. And most of the rest found somewhere else for their eyes as they looked away, their own thoughts suddenly far, far from here. Away to loved ones.

Then he cursed himself inside, feeling sorry of that moment, having caused these soldiers to think of home, to think on others so far from this cold, winter wilderness.

"Most of all," Donegan concluded, his throat clotted, "I wanna thank you fellas for helping me on my way home to my family."

"W-where are they?" Pollock asked.

"Laramie."

"Laramie," a soldier repeated almost wistfully as he nodded, then looked away at the flames in the crude fireplace constructed along the outer wall of the hut.

"Y' ain't got far to go now," another declared.

A bearded corporal said, "Less'n two hundred miles by my reckoning."

The sergeant stood, laying his muskrat hat atop his head, tugging it down over his ears. "I've got a night watch to check on right now, Mr. Donegan . . . but I'll see you're up early for coffee and tacks afore lightin' out."

Epilogue

17–24 January 1877

Telegraphic Briefs

THE INDIANS

Raid on the Chugwater.

CHEYENNE, January 18.—Intelligence was received here to-day from Chugwater, fifty miles north of this city, that the Indians made a raid on the ranches near Chugwater station, last night, driving off about fifty horses. The Indians were followed by the ranchmen for several miles, but succeeded in getting away with the stock.

"You want me send a word or two on down the wire, so they can let your missus know you're coming?" the soldier at the key asked him.

"No," he said, having decided long ago that he would do just as he had promised, wanting her to keep her eye on the hills to the north of the post for sign of him. "Thank you anyway, sojur. But long ago I decided to make it a surprise."

There at the drafty key shack at Cottonwood Station, Seamus had shared a cup of coffee and a few stories of Miles's fight with Crazy Horse as three soldiers crowded in around that tiny Sibley stove. The wind gusted old snow outside beneath a lowering sky as his horse crunched on grain that filled the nose bag a kind soldier had draped over the claybank's ears. Then, with his own belly warmed, Seamus tugged the scrap of wool blanket back over his head, adjusted the eye-holes so he could see, then pulled the wolf-hide cap down over it.

"Welcome back . . . again," the key operator said as the three soldiers crowded one another there at the doorway, watching the civilian clumsily rise to the saddle in his heavy buffalo-hide coat and leggings.

Tapping his brow with his fingers, Seamus saluted. "Thank you for the coffee, fellas."

"You ain't got far now!" a soldier reminded.

For a moment Donegan gazed to the southeast down the Laramie-Fetterman Road. He had covered more than half the distance between the two posts already. "I got a boy to christen there. My son . . . to finally give my son a name."

Miles and hours later, after one more night spent beside a lonely fire, Seamus moved on that morning of the twenty-fourth, hurrying into the fourteenth day of his homeward journey. Snowless gusts of wind battered him and the mare all that day when they could not take shelter by riding down along the courses of the creeks. Then late that blustery afternoon, as he was staring across the changeless landscape, Donegan suddenly realized he was looking at the top of the gigantic flagstaff that stood in the middle of the Fort Laramie parade.

Like a beacon signaling homecoming sailors from the perilous depths and crushing waves . . . a little farther and he could see the whole of that flag—its stripes: the white like high-plains snow, the crimson blood of those who had laid down their lives to answer their nation's call. And the blue. Like her own starry eyes as they peered up into his.

Then, finally, he reined up the claybank on the brow of a brushy knoll just north of the post, feeling a tightness wrap his chest from the sweet anticipation as he gazed down at the bustling activity of tiny figures scurrying across the snow, trudging between the buildings, each one scuffing dark as beetles across the white expanse of the parade. A gust of wind kicked up swirls of ground snow around the figures from time to time.

Then Donegan put the weary mare into motion, urging her down the hill, heading for that patch of open ground right below him, between the long row of stables and cavalry barracks. Slowly, as the horse plodded through the snow, picking its way among the crusty drifts, the faraway figures began to loom closer, taking on human form at last despite their layers of heavy garments—every man and woman bundled against the frightening cold.

Closer still . . . when he realized that among all the soldiers stopping momentarily to give him a cursory look before continuing with their fatigue details, what with all the others who paid him no attention at all on this busiest of frontier forts—a single figure leaving one of the latrines stopped . . . turned and gazed to the north . . . then appeared to start directly for him.

Slowly, guardedly. Although tentative at first, the figure nonetheless stayed its course across the drifted snow as if on a compass heading that nothing would deter.

How he wanted to hope—

By then Seamus could make the figure out to be a woman from the way she moved beneath that long, heavy army wool coat, bundled as she was head to foot. Suddenly she burst into a lope, swinging one arm only, the other clutching some thick wrap—perhaps a muffler. Ungainly as she was in her heavy boots and long coat, the woman dashed his way resolutely.

Then of an instant he no longer had to hope.

Like a man sensing once more that magnetic pull of his one and only lodestone, Donegan gave the horse a tap with his heels, urging these last two hundred yards out of the animal that had carried him all the way home. Gasping for its breath, spears of frost shooting from its nostrils, a halo of white wreathed the horse's head—Seamus leaped from the saddle even before the claybank came to a halt.

On foot he stumbled those last five yards, tearing off the wolf-hide cap in one hand, the blanket face-mask with the other, hurling them both aside to enfold her and the bundled child in his arms instantly, sweeping them off her feet despite Samantha's bulky clothing, despite her giggling, weeping protests, the child clutched between them as he swung her round once, twice, then set her down in the snow. Both of them gasping for air, tears at their cheeks, planting kisses on those faces not seen for so long.

"It's your f-father, come home as he p-promised," Samantha squeaked, barely able to get any sound out past the clog in her throat.

Gently he pulled back the top layer of the crocheted blanket, finally able to peer down into the reddened face, the wide eyes that stared up at his. To see again those rosy cheeks, and that unruly curl of auburn hair spilling down the boy's forehead.

"Is this . . . ," he began to ask. "Sweet Mother of God—but he's growed in the time I've been gone."

She nodded, swiping a mitten across her cheek as she stared up at Seamus's ruddy, bearded face. "They have a way of doing that—so I'm told, Mr. Donegan."

Then she laid her cheek against his shoulder, closing her eyes and sighing. Despite the bulk of all her layers, he could still feel her trembling. For the longest time he stood there as soldiers and others passed by—content to clutch his family to his bosom, his chin resting atop Samantha's head. In the midst of that busy fort on the plains they were like a warm, quiet island of serenity for these stolen moments in the bitter cold.

After some time she pulled her red, wet cheek away to stare into his glistening gray eyes. "Happy New Year, Mr. Donegan."

He felt the tears spill again onto his wind-raw flesh. "Happy New Year to you, Mrs. Donegan."

She dragged her mitten under her nose, then pulled the blanket back from the boy's face once more. The babe's eyes came instantly alive as they focused on the man's face. Samantha said, "We've saved your Christmas for you—so to have one of our own. Together."

"It's not too late for Christmas?" he asked, his belly a'roil with so many feelings at once, he felt he might just explode like one of Pope's cannonballs.

She giggled behind one of her mittens a moment, saying, "It's never too late for Christmas, Seamus! Especially when a man can be as much a boy as you can!"

The tears were freezing on both their cheeks as he

snatched up the reins in one hand, then tugged Samantha around and positioned her beneath the other arm. Husband and wife walked slowly past the end of the cavalry barracks, on toward their tiny room, where they would celebrate their own family Christmas, where they would see in their own festive New Year.

"It will be a Christmas to remember," he whispered at the side of the wool shawl she had wrapped over her head. "I have me a good deal of money to pick up from post commander Evans for my recent services to the army."

"Back pay?"

"You might say that, Sam," he answered, so relieved that no soldier, officer, or chaplain had come to call on her, bearing the terrible news along with that princely ransom paid for carrying Crook's message all the way up to Nelson A. Miles, alone through the heart of Crazy Horse country.

She laid her head into the crook of his shoulder and closed her eyes, holding the boy tightly in the cradle of her left arm. "Oh, Seamus," she whispered in a puff of frost, "I've feared more in the last three months than I think I've ever feared in my whole life."

He looked down at her, love filling his heart all over again. "Feared what, Samantha? Feared that I would not return?"

She blinked, clearing her eyes as she smiled with those beautiful teeth of hers. "No, you silly goose—I feared most that if you did not come back to us, your son would go through life without a name of his own!"

"You wouldn't have named him on your own . . . if I hadn't come back to you both?"

"Yes," she admitted, finally. "I suppose I would have—eventually. When I could at last pull all the pieces of my shattered soul back together . . . I would have named this boy after his father."

"His . . . h-his father?"

Samantha stopped him, gazing up into her husband's face. "Yes, named our son after the bravest, most gentle and selfless father a child could ever have."

Afterword

Ah, the very stuff of history oft makes for some interesting speculation!

Crook and Miles did not enjoy a mutual respect during their years serving the Army of the West. Simmering animosities begun during this year of war on the northern plains would later boil to the surface during the final Apache campaigns in the southwest when Crook (who had experienced much success during the earlier Apache wars) was eventually "nudged" aside and Miles assigned to replace him.

At the time of this Great Sioux War there was clearly no affection shared between these two great military figures. If they communicated at all, they would have done so through normal military channels, which would have taken an excruciatingly long time. Today we realize just how little one column knew of the disposition of another column back then: their whereabouts, their contact with the roaming warrior bands, the status of their logistical lines of supply.

Back in 1876–77 great distances across the trackless and "wireless" wilderness dictated that Crook operate from the south not knowing what Miles was doing along the Yellowstone. And it meant that Miles continued to operate as he always had: wary of superiors Crook and Terry; seeking to better his own position with Sheridan and Sherman by accomplishing against the Sioux and Cheyenne what Crook had consistently failed to do; and in the end putting all his energies into earning his general's star.

From my reading of the two men, from giving so much thought to who they were down under their uniforms, and ultimately from trying to walk around in their boots as much as I can on the ground where these professional soldiers plied their deadly trade . . . if any overture had been attempted between the two armies, I'd put money on its having been Crook trying to get word to Miles.

Completely out of touch on the Belle Fourche in the Black Hills country, knowing that the Crazy Horse camps lay not all that far to the northwest, realizing that just beyond that dangerous country lay the Yellowstone and the mouth of the Tongue, where Miles might well be doing all he could to keep Sitting Bull from joining back up with Crazy Horse—it's simply not that great a leap of imagination to conceive of George Crook attempting to courier some dispatches to Colonel Miles.

After all, you have to consider what the alternative would have been: sending a rider south to Reno Cantonment, beyond to Fetterman; from there the message could be wired to Laramie, then along the Platte until the electronic impulses in that simple wire reached a point back east, where George Crook's questions could start north toward Chicago; from there they would travel across Phil Sheridan's desk, on to Minneapolis, where Alfred Terry would have his look at them prior to forwarding Crook's dispatches through a few more miles of telegraph to Fort Abraham Lincoln, and from there they would all rely on a network of overland, horse-mounted couriers because there was simply no paddle-wheel traffic on the upper rivers at that season!

Racing across the upper tier of territories just below the Canadian border, the army couriers might—and I emphasize *might*—reach Tongue River Cantonment with their leather envelope, barring attack by roving hostiles, a horse breaking a leg and putting a courier afoot, countless flooded or ice-bound rivers, or any of a dozen other reasons that would delay or prevent a rider from reaching the theater of operations against the Northern Sioux.

If any such attempt was made, I believe the smart money would have been on a rider making it from the Belle Fourche region across the Powder River country to the mouth of the Tongue. Look at your regional map in the front of the book. Trace a finger across the route I've just described. Then look at a map of the U.S. and trace another route from Minneapolis to Bismarck, on across Dakota Territory to Tongue River Cantonment. If Crook had wanted to find out what campaign Miles was pursuing in those weeks prior to Christmas when he was being forced to disband his own campaign due to supply problems, wouldn't Crook have gotten himself a volunteer?

Was Miles the sort who would have sent a courier off to communicate with Crook? I don't think so—not as jealous and thin-skinned as he was.

From the military record we know for a fact that Crook and Mackenzie sent out Lakota scouts (who had been invaluable during the Dull Knife campaign) from the Belle Fourche to the Little Powder, from there down to the Powder to look for any sign of the Crazy Horse village that continued to elude Crook in this most frustrating year of fight-and-chase-and-wait-for-resupply. From that point it wouldn't take a horseman much more than a week to complete the trip across that frozen winter wilderness. Just how much of a frozen wilderness it is in the winter . . . well, you'll have to come up here and see for yourself. That is, if you truly want to experience what these plainsmen, soldiers, and roaming villages endured that winter of record.

If I had to speculate, I'll say it happened just as I wrote it: Crook to Miles, Belle Fourche to the Yellowstone, a single rider traveling as fast as he dared across an icy landscape, suffering terribly from the cold and hunger and fear, but enduring not only because he had a job to do, but because he had others who were counting on him to provide for them.

Of course, as far as we know, Crook did not send a scout (civilian or otherwise) to Miles that winter, so we've taken a wee bit of license to get Seamus shipped off to this next battlefront of the Great Sioux War.

If you've found some fault with my line of reasoning, be sure to drop me a line. After all, one of my most important tasks in writing each of these twenty novels is to have everything plausible, probable, if not entirely possible. Much, much different from what I too often see on television, more different still from what Hollywood spends millions on to show us in the movie theaters.

Remember: you have my promise that I'll continue to do my best to make every one of Seamus Donegan's adventures so real that you will say, "If it didn't really happen that way, then—by God—Terry sure makes it seem like *it could have!*"

And while we're on the subject of speculation, can you imagine the lively debates, and what might have easily turned into fistfights, between the Democrats and Republicans counted among the officers of the Fifth Infantry as they argued over the controversy of just who would eventually be elected president back east? Those weeks dragging into months during that winter were very much akin to those weeks and months just before the Civil War broke out. In 1876 Reconstruction Republicans were aligned against the growing strength of the Democratic party in the defeated South. If, as President Grant was prepared to do to protect the Union, he had dispatched troops across the Mason-Dixon—many of those states threatened to secede a second time.

In such a scenario soldiers on the frontier again would have started to journey home to either north or south: saying farewell to friends and brothers in arms for perhaps the last time before they met on the field of battle . . . just as soldiers had done in 1861. History was indeed poised to repeat itself.

In this case, by the time the spring of 1877 arrived, Congress itself had reached a compromise that kept the nation from tearing itself apart. The Republicans would retain the White House, while the southern Democrats won the end of the much-hated Reconstruction.

Back on the northern plains Nelson A. Miles himself left little in the record for us to know fully what he promised the Sioux during his conferences with them in the autumn of 1876. It took the diligent research of author George E. Hyde *(Spotted Tail's Folk)* to unearth new material on Miles's offer of an agency in the Powder River country if the warrior bands would only surrender. In addition, Hyde located archival materials that testified to the fact that Crazy Horse bullied those families wanting to leave for the agencies during that autumn and winter of 1876–77.

It's unfortunate that Miles's faith and belief in those Sioux chiefs went unreciprocated for the most part. After his parleys with the leaders on Cedar Creek and a few days later on the Yellowstone *(A Cold Day in Hell)*, at the end of which the colonel took five chiefs prisoner as security against their people keeping their promises, very few of the Sioux ever went in to their reservations until the mass influx of the following summer. And those few who did drift back to the agencies that fall did not feel compelled to stay on their reservations for very long. They were soon lured out a second time to live in the old way . . . at least until Miles finally convinced them that there was no hope in wandering the old road.

Some of those Sioux chiefs and war leaders would eagerly sign up when Miles came asking for scouts during the Nez Perce War of 1877 . . . but that will be a two-part story I have yet to tell in the years ahead.

I hope that all of you had to pull on a sweater or at least toss another log onto the fire while reading of these two winter campaigns. If I've given you a shiver or two, then I've done my job to transport you back into that brutal time when men marched and slept, ate and fought, outdoors. And for those few of you who still need a little help in sensing the cold all the way to your marrow, gaze again at the three photographs we've reproduced from those days at the Tongue River Cantonment: look at the soldiers in their muskrat hats and buffalo coats; look at the gun crews around their artillery pieces; then carefully study the crude log barracks.

Believe me—those log huts were far preferable to taking the campaign trail when a man had little choice but to be out in the cold, day and night. For weeks on end the army surgeons' thermometers were unusable simply because the mercury froze in a tiny gray bulb at thirty-nine below zero. The following winter, when spirit thermometers were finally put into use by the army, at one point the temperature on those Montana plains registered sixty-six degrees below zero—and that was before the chill factor!

It was widely known that the country of the Powder and Tongue rivers was so inhospitable during the winter that it was "impossible for white men to winter there except in a well-prepared shelter." In fact, when Miles wrote General Terry of his intentions to pursue the warrior bands without pause,

Terry replied that it was "impossible to campaign in the winter, as the troops could not contend against the elements."

And for a time there it seemed everything was working against Nelson A. Miles getting his winter campaign under way. After his success at Cedar Creek, he wanted to follow and capture the "wounded and weakened" Sitting Bull. But first he had to prepare his troops against the elements. In those few days before they set off on the Fort Peck Expedition, the colonel learned just how desperate his situation was. There weren't enough horses and mules for the job at hand, and they didn't even have enough grain to feed what animals they did have. What's more, most of the regulation winter clothing he had ordered early in the fall still had not arrived from downriver, forcing his men to spend their skimpy salaries to purchase what they needed from the sutlers in the way of extra underwear, shirts and britches, caps and gloves. Most men wore layer upon layer, often pulling on at least five shirts and three pairs of trousers.

The fact that Crook had received the winter clothing *he* ordered for *his* campaign would continue to nettle Miles as he prepared to march north. In a letter to his wife Miles privately confided that an army investigation into the matter would likely ruin not only Crook himself, but the venal army quartermaster staff as well.

All the meteorological reports of the day state that the winter of 1876–77 was one of the most severe on record, especially across the Montana, Dakota, and Wyoming territories. Subzero cold and snow came early that year, and rarely did the snow disappear long enough to see bare ground before a new storm brought even more. Not only did the cold and the snow make waging war an even tougher proposition, the weather that winter killed off much of what game wasn't driven south. In the villages of the winter roamers, bellies went hungry because the buffalo and big-game animals simply were not available.

What those sunken cheeks and hollow eyes, those whimpers and cries from the Lakota and Cheyenne people, would surely have done to touch the hearts of their leaders—convincing them that little hope remained in following the old life. It seemed as if the weather itself had conspired to do all in its power to convince the winter roamers that they could no longer survive off their reservations.

For those troops Miles left behind to garrison the post while he was off on both campaigns, the daily fatigue work continued. More walls were raised and roof joists laid on. The insides of exterior walls were plastered to eliminate what they could of the howling Montana winds. One of the cabins that was entirely finished by the time the men returned from the Missouri River region was that used by the contract sutler. It was a place that would soon cause Miles some serious problems of morale and discipline.

As mentioned in the story, not only did the government sutler sell intoxicating spirits to the soldiers, but two or three other enterprising civilians showed up from downriver with some "high wines," brandies, and a potent whiskey. This liquor was sold to the soldiers without proper regulation in mid-December and the number of men locked up in the guardhouse multiplied until one officer observed, "the Guard House was always full to overflowing & Genl Miles said the whiskey caused him more trouble than the Indians."

After attempting several different solutions, the colonel finally closed down the sutler's saloon for good in the early spring of 1877. At that point the traders simply moved beyond the eastern border of the military reservation to set up shop. It infuriated Miles that one of the unscrupulous traders was selling a lethal moonshine concoction that left several of his soldiers dead. An unnamed band of angry soldiers soon took care of the problem themselves: either they ran the trader out of the country or they killed him, for the man was never seen in Montana Territory again, and nary a trace was found of the scalawag.

During the next year a civilian community slowly blossomed around the shantytown of whiskey traders' log cabins. First known as Milesburg, then called Milestown, and now known as Miles City, Montana—the place was never so notorious as it was back then. By 1879, however, the modest community could boast its own courthouse, a one-room school, several cafés to accompany its saloons, along with those shops where many industrious carpenters, painters, blacksmiths, and coopers plied their trades, totally dependent upon the post for their livelihood.

We are fortunate to have more than the military record when it comes to the Fort Peck Expedition and the wanderings of its three battalions in November–December of 1876. Three soldiers left us their observations of one another, the weather, and the day-to-day life on the campaign trail. Whereas the first is an account written by an unnamed soldier, which Jerry Greene found printed in the Leavenworth *Daily Times* (what must surely have been the soldier's hometown paper), the second-most valuable is that written by First Lieutenant George W. Baird (who served as regimental adjutant).

But by far the most enlightening is the daily field notes taken by Lieutenant Frank D. Baldwin himself. He faithfully recorded his observations in a pocket-sized notebook, which he later expanded into a ledger. It is this undated manuscript that rests in the William Carey Brown collection of the Western History Collections at the Norlin Library, University of Colorado, in Boulder.

Baldwin's minute remembrances add immensely to the historical record of the continued contact between the army and the Sitting Bull camps in the autumn and winter of 1876–77 as the army harried the Sioux and chased them about the country north of the Yellowstone. None of the Lakota participants in either the skirmish at Bark Creek or the fight at Ash Creek left any record with interpreters during the "reservation period," as they would leave accounts of other battles and conflicts with the soldiers. One wonders if it was merely too embarrassing for those veteran warriors to make mention of those two defeats, or if they simply determined it would be best to stay quiet, since those two encounters with the army only served further to prove Sitting Bull's admonition that to take spoils from the Little Bighorn dead would bring down the wrath of *Wakan Tanka* upon their people.

Late in the summer of 1920 Frank Baldwin journeyed to the high plains of Montana to accompany Joseph Culbertson to the site of their December 1876 attack on Sitting Bull. By then a general retired from the army, Baldwin and the young scout, who was barely eighteen winters old at the time of the expedition, wandered over the site, sharing reminiscences together. It wasn't long before a six-foot-high stone monument in the shape of a pyramid was erected on the site where Sitting Bull's people had abandoned their village that cold winter day when Baldwin's troops rumbled toward their camp in those noisy wagons.

Success at last against the leader of the "hostile" Sioux!

As Robert Utley describes in *The Lance and the Shield*, his master work about Sitting Bull:

> In the perception of the white citizenry, Sitting Bull was the man to get, the archdemon of the Sioux holdouts, the architect of Custer's defeat and death, the supreme monarch of all the savage legions arrayed against the forces of civilization. Newspapers vied with one another in profiling this all-powerful ruler, and no story was too silly for their readership.
>
> Equally silly was General Sheridan's effort to deflate Sitting Bull. He had no reason to believe, he declared, that such an individual as Sitting Bull even existed. "I have always understood 'Sitting-bull' to mean *the hostile Indians,* and not a great leader."
>
> . . . But precisely because he was a great leader, Sitting Bull had indeed come to mean, for Indians and whites alike, *the hostile Indians.*

If Phil Sheridan had trouble on this point—Nelson A. Miles sure knew Sitting Bull existed in the flesh. And make no mistake, so did Lieutenant Frank Baldwin.

This Ash Creek fight in Montana Territory is all but unknown, even among those who have a speaking acquaintance of the Great Sioux War. All too few understand just what a signal victory Baldwin and his small battalion accomplished by surprising the larger, stronger, confederated village and driving them into the wilderness with little more than what they had on their backs. They had no choice but to head south, hoping to find Crazy Horse, where they would be welcomed as they had welcomed him and the Cheyenne survivors the previous winter. Baldwin had turned the tables on the Lakota—and successfully shattered the myth of an all-powerful Hunkpapa-led coalition.

Considering the scale of this defeat at Ash Creek (and, once the Hunkpapa village reached the Crazy Horse camp, finding them so recently defeated by Miles at Battle Butte), it becomes all the more clear why it would take Sitting Bull and his chiefs only a matter of weeks to decide that their only course lay in fleeing across the line to Canada.

The army had the bands on the run, harried and harassed on the northern plains. So what do you think would have happened if the Lakota peace delegates from the Crazy Horse village had reached the cantonment to discuss terms of surrender with Miles?

So close—perhaps only a matter of several hundred yards—to have come on this journey with the blessings of Crazy Horse, Little Wolf, and Morning Star themselves . . . only to be set upon by the cowardly Crow auxiliaries Tom Leforge had recruited for Lieutenant Hargous.

Think of it: had not the Crow cold-bloodedly murdered those five brave men, within sight of a wavering Crazy Horse, such a surrender would have represented at least six hundred lodges—which meant more than some twelve hundred fighting men! Miles and the frontier army would have struck a powerful coup. Sitting Bull and his confederated chiefs would have been left completely isolated, alone, and vulnerable. Had not the Crow cowards committed those inexcusable murders against their ancient enemies, then escaped back to the safety of their reservation before they could be punished for their crimes . . . the Great Sioux War would have been over before Christmas!

Take a moment to consider it now: as things turned out, this cowardly act by Crow murderers caused the war to drag on at least another six months.

This half-day Battle of the Butte between Miles and Crazy Horse during a snowstorm in southeastern Montana is really not all that better known than Baldwin's Ash Creek fight. In fact, it was so little known among Indian Wars' historians that it was called the *Battle of Wolf Mountain.* Yet all one has to do is look at a good map of that part of Montana, and you will see that the Wolf Mountains are many miles from the site—the very same range crossed by Custer's Seventh Cavalry as they marched west from the Rosebud, past the Crow's Nest, on to the valley of the Little Bighorn. So what the academics might call the Battle of Wolf Mountain is better known in these parts as the Battle of the Butte.

Come up here and take one of my tours of the northern

plains when we travel to this site, and you will readily see just
how appropriate is that name.

One of the sources I relied upon before my very first trip
up the Tongue River to Battle Butte was a small self-published
book by the late Charles B. Erlanson. Having come to Montana in 1911 as a young wrangler, Erlanson went right to work
for the Flying V Ranch, and later cowboyed for the Three
Circle Ranch—both of which were on the Cheyenne Reservation. For better than fifty years Erlanson not only rode up and
down the Tongue River, back and forth across the ground
where this story took place, but also knew several of the old
Cheyenne storytellers who spoke of the fight, and of the toll
that terrible winter took upon the once-powerful Shahiyela
people.

One of Erlanson's closest informants was none other than
John Stands In Timber, the Cheyenne tribal historian who
collaborated with Margot Liberty on his book of Cheyenne
culture and stories. On one trip the two old horsemen made
to the battle site, Erlanson took a photograph of Stands in
Timber beside the low pile of red rocks Wooden Leg had
stacked up to mark the spot where Big Crow was shot. A stoic,
but bright-eyed, Cheyenne historian looks back at the camera,
pointing to that simple, but eloquent, marker with his wooden
cane.

As the howling blizzard closed down upon the valley of
the Tongue River, Miles ordered some of his unit to pursue the
fleeing enemy—in hopes of learning just how close was the
Crazy Horse camp. For many years a legend lived on that
stated the soldiers chased the warriors for miles up the valley,
passing through their hastily abandoned camp where they
fought the rear guard protecting the village, and where the
soldiers captured a huge store of dried meat.

Perhaps this historical error is what led no lesser an artist
than Frederic Remington to paint one of his most famous
works: *Miles Strikes the Village of Crazy Horse*. Although it
does give the viewer a clear conception of the blowing snow,
the bitter cold, the gusty wind, and the shoot-and-advance /
shoot-and-advance nature of such battles, along with the
drama of soldiers kneeling to fire in the foreground, with an
officer and an Indian scout behind them (who might clearly

be the Bannock called Buffalo Horn), Remington's painting is nonetheless nothing more than a work of the imagination.

The painting would be better ascribed to Mackenzie's attack on Morning Star's village: the on-foot, lodge-to-lodge fight of it made on 25 November 1876.

Truth is, the Sioux and Cheyenne village was at least seventeen miles south of Battle Butte. A man who knows firsthand the nature of not only that terrain but a half century of Montana snowstorms, Charlie Erlanson himself, said of this controversy, "The last part of the battle was fought in a blizzard of such intensity that it . . . would have been futile for Miles's foot soldiers to attempt to pursue the 'finest light cavalry in the world' through the deep snow."

Having myself visited the site on a clear winter day, with close to a foot of snow on the level, I have to concur not only with William Jackson (the half-breed Blackfoot scout with Miles), but with the current thinking of historians: that the pursuing soldiers did not chase the Indians to and through their village. Instead, the infantry would have been lucky to follow those fleeing horsemen a matter of two, perhaps three, miles at most, on foot before they were forced to turn back beneath the onslaught of a Montana blizzard.

By considering only the record of casualties, one might infer that this was an inconsequential affair brought to an indecisive conclusion only by the extremities of severe weather. But even the casualty counts are conflicting for some reason.

William Jackson states that three soldiers were killed (although his recollection may be clouded by time and by witnessing Batty's death earlier on their march upriver). He goes on to state that eight soldiers were wounded. Two other writers concur with these same figures, one of which was Captain Edmond Butler in his own brief account of the campaign.

So why, I ask myself, did Miles officially report one man killed and nine wounded during the battle? Because of the soldier who died on the northbound march, I think I can understand a discrepancy of one fatality—but this still does not account for the other death.

Perhaps it's nothing more than the fact that these eye witnesses are recalling Private Batty's death *before* the battle,

Corporal Rothman's death *during* the battle, and Private Mc-Cann's death *after* the battle.

As for the casualties on the Indian side of the fight, we first look at the "body count" given by the officers and enlisted men immediately after the fight. Lieutenant Baldwin wrote in his personal diary that the Indian loss "must have been considerable." Trumpeter Edwin M. Brown recorded in his journal that "the loss of the Indians was estimated at 15 killed and 25 wounded."

Another army source noted that ten Indians fell in front of the Casey-Butler-McDonald battalion, in addition to the war chief in the fancy warbonnet (Big Crow). In the subsequent reports submitted to Miles, the officers of the Fifth Infantry noted that as many as twenty-three Indians fell during the battle and were presumed dead. The colonel himself wrote that he believed the enemy's loss to be "about twelve or fifteen killed and twenty five or thirty wounded."

The belief of these officers that they had taken a great toll on the Crazy Horse warriors was strengthened the following day when they more carefully examined the Indian positions on the ridge, finding much blood on the snow as well as a great deal of blood trails along the escape route upriver.

Yet all of this appears to clash with what are consistent reports from the Indian participants themselves—those who, like Eagle Shield, eventually gave a rendition of the fight through interpreters. Wooden Leg states that Big Crow was the only Cheyenne casualty but goes on to say that two Sioux warriors were killed as well. Red Cloth, a Miniconjou, later testified that in addition to the two Sioux killed in the battle, three more Lakota had been wounded, and two of those had later died. Again and again the Indian reports consistently testify to a much, much smaller casualty count than Miles and his officers had represented.

Considering all the shooting from both sides, especially in light of all the bullets used up by Casey's, Butler's, and Mc-Donald's companies, it is surprising that there were not more Indian casualties. Still, this fact once more points up the true lack of marksmanship on the part of most frontier soldiers. The army supplied ammunition enough to waste in battle but would not provide ammunition to use for target practice at their posts.

In addition to the soldiers killed and wounded, the Indians did take a further toll with their marksmanship (or, some might argue, lack of it): three of the army's horses were killed, and one horse and two mules wounded.

Although we do not have a single written account of Sitting Bull's fight with Baldwin's battalion at Ash Creek in December, we are much more fortunate to have a record in the case of the Battle Butte fight. A handful of stories were made through interpreters in subsequent weeks, as the warrior bands began slipping back in to the agencies. But for the most part, more stories of the "Battle of Wolf Mountain" were related over the next ten years—not a long time at all, considering a culture with an oral tradition. These were people who passed along their history in a precise and unembellished manner. What is shown by the record from Cheyenne renderings to Sioux versions of the fight is that they all generally conform to the military record of the battle (while adding a detail here or there depending upon a particular warrior's individual exploits).

One of the most interesting facets of the warrior tales of the fight is that the warriors of Crazy Horse had again planned on using the tried-and-true decoy technique that had worked for them across the last ten years—ever since the Fetterman massacre in December 1866. Their statements record the fact that they planned to ambush the Bear Coat by using a small decoy party to draw the main body of the soldiers from their bivouac to a point some two miles upstream (between Battle Butte and the mouth of Wall Creek), where the mass of warriors lingered on ground the war chiefs considered favorable for the fight.

Again, as in most cases, the young, eager decoys advanced much too quickly, engaging the soldiers, revealing their positions, and thereby giving away the plan before they could lure the soldiers south. When the first shots were fired and the army engaged, the warriors waiting in ambush had no choice but to hurry north with their Henry and Winchester carbines, along with a few of the Springfields taken as spoils from the Custer dead.

This ruined ambush was but another indication to many of the war chiefs that their people had indeed failed to listen to the Great Mystery's warning not to take the spoils from the

Greasy Grass fight. Not only did their decoy plan not work, but they were forced by a potent winter storm to withdraw—two more acts by *Wakan Tanka* to show the Lakota people his great displeasure with them.

The village, with a population that ranged anywhere between twenty-five to thirty-five hundred people (of which at least a thousand were of "fighting age"), limped away to the south during the storm. While there was renewed talk of resistance, there was also a growing voice among those who recommended surrender at the reservations.

Wooden Leg himself would stay out until the Cheyenne went in after the spring. While the flowers bloomed along the Tongue River, he made the journey back to the rocks where he had carefully buried Big Crow. With the warmth of summer coming, Wooden Leg found the body, still wrapped in its buffalo robe, undisturbed by time and predators. Its location somewhere south of Battle Butte along the eastern rim of the Tongue River Valley remains a secret to this day—as it should. Big Crow continues to be a hero to his people.

The army selected some of their own for hero status following the battle. Private Philip Kennedy and Private Patton G. Whited, both from Captain Edmond Butler's C Company, were later awarded the Medal of Honor for their courage in being the first two men to reach the crest of the ridge in the face of heavy fire from the enemy. For his action in leading the charge, Butler himself was given a Medal of Honor and received a brevet rank of major.

In addition, Captain James Casey and Lieutenant Robert McDonald received Medals of Honor from the army for their heroism that day in the face of the enemy. Lieutenant Frank Baldwin went on to win universal acclaim for his singular act of bravery in bringing that case of ammunition to the battalion, then leading them against the snowy slope.

With so many who had distinguished themselves in the line of duty, it is sad and unfortunate to me that the officers of the Fifth Infantry soon split into rival camps when attempting to assess the results of the "Battle of Wolf Mountain."

A thin-skinned Butler attempted to minimize Baldwin's role in the charge against the heights—perhaps due to the fact that Baldwin's actions tended to diminish the yard-by-yard bravery exhibited by the Irish captain as well as Butler's readiness to continue pitching into the warriors despite being low on (or in some cases out of) ammunition for their Springfields.

In consequence, other officers far from the bluffs where the hottest fighting took place—men like Lieutenant James Pope and Adjutant George Baird—sought through the record to minimize Butler's gallant courage in the face of the enemy—leading his men in the assault as ordered by Miles.

Sad indeed that these personalities, all officers in one of the finest regiments involved in the Indian Wars, would descend to such petty backbiting and ego baiting. Even Baldwin—hero of McClellan Creek, the hero who held his men together at Bark Creek, and the hero who a few days later routed Sitting Bull at Ash Creek—yes, even Frank Baldwin would later snipe away at his fellow officers by saying:

> With the exception of Pope & Dickey there was not an officer on duty with companies who *seemed* to comprehend the character of the engagement beyond blindly defending the point they were assigned, or by chance might drift to.

Now, for those of you who haven't had yourselves enough of this crucial and pivotal month (or "Moon") in the Wolf Mountain country with our beloved gray-eyed Irishman, I have some suggested reading for you—titles I used in compiling my story of the beginning of the end for the warrior bands that terrible winter.

Battle of the Butte—General Miles' Fight with the Indians on Tongue River, January 8, 1877, by Charles B. Erlanson

Battles and Skirmishes of the Great Sioux War, 1876–1877—the Military View, edited by Jerome A. Greene

"The Battle of Wolf Mountain," by Don Rickey, Jr., *Montana, The Magazine of Western History,* vol. 13 (Spring, 1963)

Bury My Heart at Wounded Knee, by Dee Brown

Cheyenne Memories, by John Stands In Timber and Margot Liberty

Crazy Horse—The Strange Man of the Oglalas, by Mari Sandoz

Crazy Horse Called Them Walk-A-Heaps, by Neil Baird Thompson

Crazy Horse and Custer—The Parallel Lives of Two American Warriors, by Stephen E. Ambrose

Death on the Prairie—The Thirty Years' Struggle for the Western Plains, by Paul I. Wellman

A Dose of Soldiering—The Memoirs of Corporal E. A. Bode, Frontier Regular Infantry, 1877–1882, edited by Thomas T. Smith

Faintly Sounds the War-Cry—The Story of the Fight at Battle Butte, by Fred H. Werner

The Fighting Cheyennes, by George Bird Grinnell

Frontier Regulars—The United States Army and the Indian, 1866–1891, by Robert M. Utley

General George Crook, His Autobiography, edited by Martin F. Schmitt

"Historical Address of Brigadier General W. C. Brown," *Winners of the West,* August 30, 1932

Indian-Fighting Army, by Fairfax Downey

Indian Fights and Fighters, by Cyrus Townsend Brady

Lakota and Cheyenne—Indian Views of the Great Sioux War, 1876–1877, by Jerome A. Greene

The Lance and the Shield—The Life and Times of Sitting Bull, by Robert M. Utley

Memoirs of a White Crow Indian (Thomas H. LeForge), as told by Thomas B. Marquis

Nelson A. Miles—A Documentary Biography of his Military Career, 1861–1903, edited by Brian C. Pohanka

Nelson A. Miles and the Twilight of the Frontier Army, by Robert Wooster

People of the Sacred Mountain: A History of the Northern Cheyenne Chiefs and Warrior Societies, 1830–1879, by Peter J. Powell, S.J.

Personal Recollections and Observations of General Nelson A. Miles, introduction by Robert Wooster

The Plainsmen of the Yellowstone, by Mark H. Brown

Red Cloud and the Sioux Problem, by James C. Olson

Soldiers West—Biographies from the Military Frontier, edited by Paul Andrew Hutton

Spotted Tail's Folk—A History of the Brule Sioux, by George E. Hyde

Stone Song—A Novel of the Life of Crazy Horse, by Winfred Blevins

Sweet Medicine: The Continuing Role of the Sacred Arrows, the Sun Dance, and the Sacred Buffalo Hat in Northern Cheyenne History, by Peter J. Powell, S.J.

The U.S. Army in the West, 1870–1880—Uniforms, Weapons, and Equipment, by Douglas C. McChristian

War Cries on Horseback—The Story of the Indian Wars of the Great Plains, by Stephen Longstreet

War in the West—The Indian Campaigns, by Don Rickey

Warpath and Council Fire—The Plains Indians' Struggle for Survival in War and in Diplomacy, by Stanley Vestal

William Jackson, Indian Scout, as told by James Willard Schultz

Wolves for the Blue Soldiers—Indian Scouts and Auxiliaries with the United States Army, 1860–1890, by Thomas W. Dunlay

Wooden Leg—A Warrior Who Fought Custer, interpreted by Thomas B. Marquis

Yellowstone Command—Colonel Nelson A. Miles and the Great Sioux War, 1876–1877, by Jerome A. Greene

"Yellowstone Kelly"—the Memoirs of Luther S. Kelly, edited by Milo Milton Quaife

To the small-minded it seems that great battles must surely have horrendous death tolls. Such niggardly people point to the Alamo, the Fetterman fight, and the Custer battle—none of which had any immediate or lasting effect on the war of which it was a part.

On the other hand, the Battle of the Butte, this "Battle of Wolf Mountain," was to seal the fate of the winter roamers, those warrior bands who for the better part of a year had stymied, defeated to fight another day, or completely crushed the finest outfits in the frontier army.

After 8 January 1877 the Cheyenne were done. What Mackenzie had begun at the Battle of the Red Fork in November was finished at Battle Butte by the Fifth Infantry. The richest tribe on the northern plains had suffered all they could. They would surrender to Miles or trudge into their agencies that spring . . . to begin a last and even more tragic chapter in their history at Fort Robinson (a story we will tell in a forthcoming volume).

With so little buffalo and game to feed the camps, with such extreme cold and the constant harrying by soldiers from both the north and the south, the Sioux bands splintered, fractured, never to coalesce again as they had in the spring and summer of 1876—the zenith of their greatness. As the camps fractured into bands, the bands split into clans, and the clans broke apart into family units, there seemed no longer to be any use in trying to stay together in the great camp circles that had greeted Reno's charge that hot June day, the great confederation that had encircled and utterly crushed Custer's five companies.

This terrible winter a man had to worry about his family—feeding them, keeping them warm, keeping them safe from the wolfish armies prowling their traditional hunting grounds.

After a while this matter of the unceded hunting grounds did not matter. There weren't any buffalo left anyway. If a man could not be a hunter and provide for his family—of what use was he to his people?

The stormy fight at Battle Butte pierced these two great nations to the very heart of what they were as a culture. The bleeding had begun, drop by drop, that winter and continued into a cold, rainy spring. There would be no way to stop that bleeding.

The hoop was unraveling.

What once was would never be again.

Saddest of all—it was to be Crazy Horse's last fight.

At Battle Butte he chose the ground where he would engage his antagonist, Nelson A. Miles. This was the fight that proved the Bear Coat good at his word. At the Cedar Creek parleys* he had promised the Sioux he would not give them any rest that winter. Miles kept his vow. The winter roamers learned that the army could and would hunt them down, despite the most severe weather.

Day by day, moon by moon, it was becoming more and more clear that there would be no peace until they went in to their agencies.

This last battle for Crazy Horse was a fight that stripped the Northern Cheyenne of what little they still had left after close to a year of constant war.

This was a winter that proved to Crazy Horse that his people could not go on any longer.

After 8 January 1877, the choices were as clear as a high-country stream: follow Sitting Bull in fleeing to Canada . . . or limp into one of the agencies and hope for the mercy of those who have labored long and hard to defeat you.

For Crazy Horse, the greatest warrior of the *Titunwan* Lakota nation, the hardest thing for him to do was to consider giving up his war pony, handing over his weapons, and abandoning the path being a defender of his people. Harder still to leave the land that rested in his bones and ran in his blood.

* *A Cold Day in Hell,* vol. 11, The Plainsmen Series.

If the Battle of the Butte accomplished nothing more, it convinced Crazy Horse that the war was over.

The fight was done.

No longer was there any home on the face of his beloved land for a warrior.

Many winters before, his feet had been planted on the road that would hurtle him toward his youthful vision of a man he called Horse Rider—a vision in which Horse Rider could not be killed by the white man. Instead, Crazy Horse knew Horse Rider was to die at the hands of his own people . . . the way they clawed at him, tugged at him, trying to hold him back.

With his fight against the white man done, Crazy Horse knew he had those last terrible steps to take along the trail that would lead him to his fate.

And to the spiritual death of his people.

The Battle of the Butte was his last fight.

So what did death matter when his people no longer had need of a warrior, no longer had need of a Shirt Wearer . . . no longer had need of this Strange Man of the Oglalla?

            —Terry C. Johnston
             Battle of the Butte
             Quarter Circle U Ranch, Montana
             8 January 1996

ABOUT THE AUTHOR

TERRY C. JOHNSTON was born in 1947 on the plains of Kansas, and has lived all his life in the American West. His first novel, *Carry the Wind,* won the Medicine Pipe Bearer's Award from the Western Writers of America, and his subsequent books have appeared on bestseller lists throughout the country. He lives and writes in Big Sky country near Billings, Montana. For a week every July, the author takes readers on his very own "Terry C. Johnston's West: A Novelist's Journey into the Indian Wars"—a HistoryAmerica tour to the famous battlesites and landmarks of the historical West. All those desiring information on taking part in the author's summer tours can write to him at:

TERRY C. JOHNSTON
P. O. Box 50594
Billings, MT 59105

SON OF THE PLAINS

TERRY C. JOHNSTON

Few names of the American frontier resonate like that of George Armstrong Custer, whose fiery temperament and grand vision led him to triumph and tragedy. Now bestselling chronicler Terry C. Johnston brings to life the Custer legacy as never before in this masterful trilogy.

Long Winter Gone
___28621-8 $6.50/$8.99 in Canada

In 1868, George Custer captured a raven-haired firebrand of only seventeen. He risked his reputation and career for her—for in love, as on any other battlefield, Custer would never know retreat.

Seize the Sky
___28910-1 $6.50/$8.99 in Canada

What should have been Custer's greatest triumph, a march on the Sioux in June 1876, became an utterly devastating defeat that would ring through the ages.

Whisper of the Wolf
___29179-3 $6.50/$8.99 in Canada

Yellow Bird, George Custer's son, grew to manhood with the Cheyennes, bound to his father by their warrior's spirit, preparing to fight for his home, his life, and his own son.

___29974-3	**Reap the Whirlwind**	$6.50/$8.50 in Canada
___56240-1	**Cry of the Hawk**	$6.50/$8.99 in Canada
___56770-5	**Winter Rain**	$6.50/$8.99 in Canada
___57257-1	**Dream Catcher**	$6.50/$8.99 in Canada
___29975-1	**Trumpet on the Land**	$6.50/$8.50 in Canada
___57281-4	**Dance on the Wind**	$6.50/$8.99 in Canada
___29976-X	**A Cold Day in Hell**	$6.50/$8.99 in Canada
___29977-8	**Wolf Mountain Moon**	$6.50/$8.99 in Canada

Ask for these books at your local bookstore or use this page to order.

Please send me the books I have checked above. I am enclosing $____(add $2.50 to cover postage and handling). Send check or money order, no cash or C.O.D.'s, please.

Name _____

Address _____

City/State/Zip _____

Send order to: Bantam Books, Dept. TJ, 2451 S. Wolf Rd., Des Plaines, IL 60018
Allow four to six weeks for delivery.
Prices and availability subject to change without notice.   TJ 2/97